OF SHADOW AND LIGHT

EBONY OLSON

EBANDMUSE
PUBLICATIONS

Published 2019

Published by

EbandMuse Publications

Sydney, Australia

ISBN: 978-0-6485000-3-2

http://ebonyolson.com/

❀ Created with Vellum

She will be the one to take his coldness,
She will unveil the Unseelie darkness and show them light.
She will unite what should never have broken.
The daughter of the moon will teach him love and the radiance of the sun.
Her inner light will purify the tainted ones,
And she will guide the Fae by wisp-light.

'Prophecy of the Dark Prince'

ALSO BY EBONY OLSON

Hotel Series

Henderson

Cassidy

Holmes

Best Man

Black Mark Series

Black Mark's Resistance

Black Mark's Secret

Black Mark's Heart

Angelis Series

Spectra

Hierarch Series

Succumb

Numinous

Masked

1
———

SINK

"Stop chewing on that," Lisa snapped yanking my finger out of my mouth.

"I can't help it. I'm freezing and starving," I murmured trying to keep the shiver out of my voice. Stepping to the side, I looked at the line to get into the club. It was too long tonight; there was no way we were getting inside.

Lisa went back to fidgeting with her blond curls. "Would you relax. Tirades will open soon. Half of those inside will leave, and we'll get in. Just chill. You will never survive the streets if you whine all the time."

"Chilling isn't a problem." Since the music was audible outside, I started dancing on the spot to keep warm.

Lisa had been on the streets for six months now. When we met a few weeks ago, she made it sound so much more appealing than my home situation, so I'd packed the measly belongings I owned and joined her. We spent the nights clubbing so we were inside and warm, and the days at the university, sleeping in the library or stealing people's scraps in the cafeteria between classes - Easier done than you would think. You just carried a dishcloth, wiped a table as you collected a tray, and walked off.

Lisa's big brown eyes latched onto my hand as I lifted it to my mouth again. With a huff, she started playing with my dark hair. "We'll be fine, Mess. Stop fretting, okay?" Nodding, I forced myself to relax.

"Ladies." A man materialized out of the darkness next to us. Truthfully, he'd probably been leaning on the lamp post there, and I just hadn't paid attention to him until he spoke to us. Lisa's eyes widened, her shoulders rolled back so that her small breasts were the focal point in their push up bra. Knowing that move already, I lifted my eyes to see just how good looking this man was.

If I were to describe him, it would be in one word. Shadowed. The man was good looking, but to me, he seemed to surrounded by shadows which made him blurry and stopped me from really describing his features in detail. Dark hair, but no specific color, dark eyes that I wouldn't say were brown, and an average complexion. The man wore all black, so in the pale streetlight, the only color on him was his mouth. Red, as if he'd just finished eating pomegranates.

"You look like girls out for a night of fun. I'm heading to an underground nightclub that stays open till dawn. I wouldn't mind a beautiful entourage."

"What's the entry cost?" Lisa flirted while she sussed it out.

"Free," he advised, typing something into his phone. "There's food too. In fact, it's the owners birthday tonight, so he's catering."

He had Lisa's interest now. "Where's this club?"

"Just outside of town. I'm heading there now if you want to join me?"

Lifting her pale brow in challenge, Lisa scoffed. "Cause I'm stupid enough to go off with a strange man."

The man smirked. "There's a bus. It picks up other patrons, so no one drinks and drives. The owner is very big on the safety of his patrons." He pointed up the street where a bus was approaching. It was painted black with purple neon lights along the sides. "I'm Gus, by the way." Stepping to the curb, Gus waved down the bus.

"Come on." Lisa took my hand.

"Are you sure?" Didn't she just mention not being stupid and going off with a strange man? The bus pulled up where a girl and three guys who were already waiting stepped inside. Laughter and music blasting out into the cold night from inside, offering warmth and safety. Gus put his foot on the first step and raised an eyebrow at us.

"I'm sure." Squeezing my hand, Lisa strode towards the bus.

Gus's smile was closed lipped, his eyes reflecting the neon purple side lights as he led the way on board. Lisa followed dragging me after her. As I reached the top of the steps, the heavily tinted doors slammed behind us. For a moment, my pulse thrummed in the side of my neck, making it feel like someone was tapping my carotid artery.

The scene before me was a busload of relatively young people having a great time on a party bus. My lungs exhaled with relief as skimpily clad girls danced, some trying to use the poles, guys cheered and laughed as they drank their beer, the atmosphere relaxed and not unlike any bar on campus.

Releasing a squeal of joy, Lisa shrugged out of her jacket as she headed for the seat Gus was saving for us. Taking a deep breath, my head spun under the onslaught of men's cologne and women's perfume filling the bus. Blinking rapidly, I shook my head till it cleared, dark shadows racing across my vision as I followed Lisa. My hand still captive with hers until we took our seats.

"Do you want a drink?" Signaling the man behind the bar, Gus noted Lisa's hesitation. "My shout."

"I'll have a beer. Thanks."

Nodding, Gus looked at me. "I'm fine for now, thanks. Drinking and moving isn't a good combination for me."

"Motion sickness?" When I nodded, Gus patted my leg in reassurance as he stood to go to the bar. His touch left a chill on the bare skin of my thigh causing me to rub it to warm it up.

Watching me, Lisa put her mouth to my ear. "Are you still cold?"

The bus was fairly warm by the layers all the other occupants were removed, but I always took forever to warm up. Poor circulation or some such. "What are you doing?"

"One drink won't hurt."

"We're underage. I don't want to get thrown out for drinking alcohol as a minor. We're just here for warmth and food, remember?"

"Shh! Like anyone could tell that looking at us." At only nineteen, Lisa was hot and could easily pass for twenty-one. When she graduated high school last year, her step-father kicked her out because she refused to earn her keep by letting him charge his associates to screw her. Lisa's attitude was if men were paying to have sex with her, she'd be the one making money, not her scum-sucking step-father. I admired her for that.

Everyone was partying and having a great time as the bus moved to the next stop and picked up more people. Busy watching Lisa flirt with Gus, it took me a while to notice we hadn't stopped in some time. Peering out the heavily tinted windows, I cupped my hands around my face to block the inside light from my vision. Trees.

"Something wrong?" A woman asked sitting down next to me. Jumping back from the window at her sudden appearance, I looked her over. She was beautiful, but like Gus, she had that shadowed sensation which stopped me making out any exact details. In fact, the harder I looked, the less detail I could see. Her eyes appraised me hungrily, lingering on my jugular.

Licking my lips, I created a little more distance between us. "We're not in the city anymore." The woman raised an eyebrow, eyes jumping to mine, narrow in focus. "Gus said the club was just outside the city, but I can't see anything but trees."

The woman smiled, her shoulders easing back a little. "It is. There are a lot of people arriving for the banquet, so they've asked the bus to drive around an extra thirty minutes, so they can stagger the entry and avoid a large queue."

"Oh." As inexperienced in clubbing or these sort of underground clubs as I was, I decided to accept the excuse. However, the nagging sensation everything wasn't as it seems kept grating at my nerves.

The woman exchanged a judgemental look with Gus. "This one has eyes of light."

"I realized that after she was on the bus."

Standing up, the woman shook her head as she moved away. "Watch her hands when the fun starts."

Tilting her head "What language are you speaking? It sounds cool when you speak it."

"How many bears have you had?"

Shrugging me off, Lisa ignored my whispered question and returned to batting her eyelids at the handsome enabler beside her.

"Eirnish." Looking past Lisa, Gus noticed my frown at his answer. Smiling at me, he reached out to tug at my jacket collar. "Are you cold?"

Unhappy to have lost Gus's attention, Lisa turned her shoulder to try and block me out. "Mess takes a while to warm up."

Tall enough to lean forward a little more and maintain eye contact, Gus waited out my answer. "Poor circulation."

Tilting his head in interest, Gus appraised me again. "Huh, me too."

The bus hit a bump the same time a loud mechanical noise started outside. Gus smiled as the bus came to a halt. "We're here!"

We let the others go first, then Gus put an arm around Lisa and me, and walked us off the bus last. We alighted into an underground car park filled with expensive sports cars. My eyes went wide. Whoever came to this club had money.

Turning my head towards the mechanical noise, I watched as the carpark gate closed and locked. Instantly, I started searching for an emergency exit, but other than the door we were walking towards, I couldn't see another way out.

Holding my tongue, I shivered in fear with a very uneasy feeling crawling up my spine like a venomous spider. The same feeling I had when my adoptive mother married Chris when I was six. She met him, married him, then died, all in twelve months. The turnaround left me with a stepfather who felt burdened with me, and a year later, a stepmother who detested me.

"Still cold?"

Shaking my head at Gus, I kept my mouth shut. The truth was, I was too anxious to feel the cold now. We stopped in line at the door where a big man was stamping everyone's wrist and scanning every-one's license. He physically placed everyone's license on a scanner and copied them. They were keeping an electronic database of everyone who attended the club.

Waiting patiently, Gus grinned at us. "When he asks, you want a red stamp." Giving him a lascivious smile Lisa batted her eyelashes.

Listening as the bouncer asked the drunk guys in front of us if they wanted red or blue, I frowned at the lack of explanation. "What's the difference?"

Gus, yet again, studied me. "You know, no one has ever asked that question." Still failing to answer it, Gus stepped us forward letting Lisa hand over her license.

"Red," Lisa purred when asked. The bouncer winked at Gus and stamped a big red bat on Lisa's delicate wrist.

"Red or Blue?" The bouncer asked taking my license to scan.

"What if I don't like either color?"

The bouncer raised a brow at me. He, like Gus, tilted his head to study me. "She's different."

Side-eying me, Gus nodded. "I've noticed."

"Hmmm." The bouncer considered me. He took my wrist in his hand and turned up the delicate side to look at it. Brushing his thumb over my birthmark, his brow furrowed as he peered at my pale flesh and the purple mark that looked like intertwined hearts. "Looks like purple is your color." With another glance at my face, the bouncer opened a drawer and took out a different ink pad and stamp.

"A present for the birthday boy then." With a smirk, he stamped a black cursive **W** on my wrist while Gus chuckled.

"I'm sorry, what?" Glaring at them, I snatched my wrist back.

Both Gus and the bouncer stared at me. "You understood that?" Gus asked.

"Of course I did. I'm not stupid!"

"Mess?" Lisa looked confused. "When did you learn another language?"

Frowning at all of them, my eyes went back to Lisa. "You only had the one beer, right?"

Gus laughed, but it was a nervous laugh as he rounded us both up and headed inside. Exchanging a nervous look with the bouncer, Gus sobered as the bouncer picked up his phone while we walked inside. The heavy door slammed shut behind us, the noise reverberating through my body as if I was hollow and the sound of doom echoed inside me. It took everything in me not to turn around and run back out into the carpark looking for an exit.

Passing down a small dark passageway, we entered a large cavernous space. The roof was three stories high and consisted of gothic style arches that seemed carved into a natural rock ceiling. There were open areas for balconies on the upper levels, arching around the walls like the viewing booths at the old style theatres. All of them with their black curtains closed tonight.

Ignoring the music playing, I stood in awe of the room itself. It wasn't massive, possibly the size of my school gymnasium for floor space. One half of the room contained the dance floor and DJ. The other half held the bar, the long table of food, and some lounges and armchairs, on which, people were already getting tongue tied to each other.

Stopping at the edge of the dance floor, Gus smiled at us both. "Shall we dance?"

"You two go ahead. I'll get some food." Indicating the table, I stepped out of Gus's arm. Lisa mouthed thank you as Gus led her into the grinding throng of bodies. Slowly meandering my way to the food table, I took the path closest to the wall to avoid the crowds. Reaching out, I touched the stone look walls only to find they were stone. No one would bother duplicating the grit of touching earth for decoration, nor would you want to.

Above touch was the sense of earth. Taking a breath to stabilize as a pulse of balance flowed into my fingertips. With that one touch, I knew we were underground. Interestingly, the stone work soothed me a little. This was a place that had stood for a long time, that was used regularly, and that they intended to keep using. It's not the sort of work you do just to burn the place down to hide the mass genocide that took place inside like maybe a shed.

A sheer curtain hung behind the buffet table creating a semi-covered hallway between the table and the wall. A slight breeze stirred the curtains as a door opened behind them, a short woman emerging into the veiled corridor carrying a large platter of fruit. It was much too big for the small woman, and she nearly stumbled with it.

Catching the tray with one arm and her with the other, I helped her stand before I placed the fruit on the table. The woman looked at me with large black eyes, much too big for her face.

"Are you okay?"

She looked old enough to be my mother but only came up to my chest. Gazing around the room hesitantly, she then back to me. "Only the fruit is safe," she hissed, then dashed back through the door.

Frowning, I tucked my dark hair back behind my ear. "Okay...." Talk about weird encounters.

Looking over the table, I browsed the selections of cupcakes, various cheesecakes, fresh fruit, and cream at one end. At the other was steaming hot food that looked direct from a Yum Cha restaurant. Various dumplings, pork buns, and other steamed foods. It smelled and looked delicious. Watching others walk up to grab food, I eagerly waited for them to make a selection. Starving, my stomach vocalized how much it needed sustenance. Licking my lips, I was already making my selection in my mind, watching the others step to the side with their plates full. Finally my turn, I placed a pork bun on my plate.

"Yum, this is so good," murmured the guy who had gone before me. Looking his way, I froze. He was smiling and happy, but as he ate, the food in his hand changed to look rotten. Maggots squirmed over the meat inside, blood dripped down his wrist, and the smell was rotten eggs. Peering at the man's face, I realized I was wrong, he was a boy. He looked to be a year younger than my eighteen, and by the looks of his unwashed jeans and shirt, also homeless. Blood dribbled down his chin as meat juices would, and I watched a maggot squirm free of his lips on the blood.

Vomiting in my mouth, I dropped my plate on the table and ran to the bathroom just past the buffet table. Just making it into a stall, I puked bile. I hadn't eaten in twenty-four hours, so there was no food to vomit, but my body was going to try.

"Are you okay?"

Peering over my shoulder, I saw a stunning woman, shadows swirling around her. "Yeah, just reacted to a bad smell." I was going nuts, surely.

With a smug smile growing on her face, the woman walked forward grabbing my wrist. "Red or blue?"

"Black!" Snatching my wrist back, the woman frowned, her shadows howled around her, and for a moment, the beauty faded to expose gaunt, red-eyed paleness, like she was covered in talc with purple markings like tribal tattoos up her arms.

'Glamor is free.'

When I blinked, she was beautiful again. Examing the mark on my wrist, the woman snarled and stormed away from me. Flopping over the toilet bowl momentarily, I waited for the energy to hoist myself up. The needed to get out of here got me to my feet. Washing my face at the basin, I stared back at my turquoise eyes. My step-mother used to call them unholy demonic eyes, but then again, she considered me a slut's offspring or a fatherless bitch.

Stripping off my jacket, I looked myself over. Unable to ever get a tan, my skin was too pale. With how easily you could see my veins, I was basically translucent. My breasts were a bit more than a handful, then again, I had small hands, so maybe they were the average person's handful. My legs were long and gangly. The short dress I was wearing made them look even longer. The dress was Lisa's, I only owned two pairs of jeans, a couple of shirts, and a jumper.

My step-mother didn't believe in spending money on me for anything but the necesseties. Hell, she'd only bought me a bra because the school I'd been at complained that it was improper for a girl of fourteen not to own one. So I got one and had to wash it by hand every night. The underwear I was currently wearing was a five finger discount, the heels were left behind after a university party. At least my childhood prepared me for living in the university boiler room.

There were rich men here tonight. Lisa planned to try and get herself a sugar daddy, that was always her plan to get her life back on track. Maybe I should consider it. Assessing my reflection, I shook my head. "Not a chance. You're a mess, and no one wants you."

Nothing about me was going to score me a sugar daddy, not when there were natural beauties like Lisa out there. Scowling at myself for even considering it, I grabbed my jacket and went back out to the nightclub. Still hungry, I remembered the lady saying only the fruit was safe, so I decided to give it a try. If it sprouted maggots and blood, I was out of here.

Grabbing a clean plate from the Buffett, I went for the fruit that everyone was avoiding. After piling my plate high, I retreated behind the sheer curtain and held up the wall while I ate. Nothing gross happened with the fruit, though, I deliberately avoided watching other people eat, focusing entirely on the food I was holding. When my plate was empty and my stomach satisfied, I focused on the dance floor.

Lisa and Gus were dancing like they were in the bedroom. Their hands and mouths all over each other. If it weren't for the clothes, it would be porn. Sighing, I hoped she found her sugar daddy. She'd been through worse than me and had more strength then I could ever possess. She deserved happiness.

"Happy Birthday, Ty!"

My focus shifted back to the buffet table to a group nearby. My breath caught in my throat. The man called Ty that everyone was congratulating was gorgeous. Truly gorgeous. No shadows were swirling around him to stop me seeing the detail. This man with his pale skin, tall, slender build and his sharp bone structure, was appealing in a way no other man had been for me before.

Appearing to be late-twenties, he was dressed all in black. Black shiny slacks, black shiny collard shirt, a black jacquard jacket and matching tie. He walked with a black walking cane, though, he didn't use it for support, and he walked like he owned the place.

"Nice party you've thrown," the man he'd just murmured something too praised. The owner. That's what Gus had said. It was the owner's birthday. This man, Ty, was the owner.

My wrist itched. Looking down, a small purple glow was emitting from the black ink stamped on my wrist. Confused, I looked up to watch Ty prowl the buffet, but not even considering the food. He was focused on the faces of the females filling their plates and stomachs. By the looks of them, they were homeless too.

My wrist burned as Ty came parallel with me, only the curtain and buffet separating us. Ty glanced at me. His deep-set dark eyes made darker by the shadow of his brow. The overhead light threw a shadow on his high cheekbones, making him look positively gorgeous and dangerous all at once.

He observed me between one step and the next. My wrist pulsed with the purple light from the ink burning into my flesh. Grimacing from the pain, I closed my eyes and bit my lip to stop from crying out. Suddenly, the pain was gone. Looking up, so was the owner.

'A present for the birthday boy then.'

Fear pounded in my heart. The cursive **W** was no longer a stamp on my wrist, but a black and purple tattoo, etched permanently into my flesh.

2

———

LOST

Aloud gong reverberated through the room, vibrating every molecule in my body, sounding until the music stopped, until everything stopped. Spotlights focused on the first level arch above the DJ booth. Ty, the owner, stood there waiting. Applause broke out, the shadowed creatures enthusiastic, the others going along with everyone else.

"There is a door," a small voice hissed next to me, "at the end of this wall." Looking down, I saw the woman I'd saved from falling earlier. Her large eyes blinked up into mine. "If you can get to it when it starts, you might survive the night."

"What do you mean?"

"Provided you didn't eat the food. If you ate or drank the food, you will moan while they devour you." My eyes widened. Before I could speak, she placed a long bony finger to my lips. Cold. "You helped Margo; I'll help you this once." Her heavy lisp made her sound like a snake. "When the gong strikes three times. Run." With that, she vanished. As the applause closed out, I stood wide-eyed.

"Thank you, everyone, for coming tonight. Those who are friends, those who are guests," Ty started his speech.

Without thinking, my feet had me moving, slowly, one step at a time, along the length of the wall, towards the hidden door the woman had revealed to me.

"In a moment, the clock will toll three o'clock, and it will officially be my birthday." Indicating the clock on the wall opposite where he stood, the crowd turned look at the clock, but my feet kept moving away from the buffet, towards the door.

"Two hundred and twenty-five years can go in a flash." The guests laughed, the shadowed figures did not. "I can't believe I'm celebrating another birthday again. Can you believe it's been twelve months since I opened this nightclub, changing the way we hunted?" Cheers went up. "Yes, change is good my friends. Adapting to the outside world has brought our numbers back up, has seen us at our healthiest and the most powerful we've been in centuries."

Another roar of support, but now only from the shadow creatures. Tiptoeing further towards the hidden door. I was trembling. When Ty's eyes landed on me, flashing silver in the light, I froze. He lifted a brow. "Tonight, we will celebrate in the traditional ways. All will partake in pleasure, feast on flesh, and drown in blood." Covering my mouth to hold in a scream, I couldn't prevent the fear that leaked from my eyes and down my cheeks as the shadowed roared their agreement. Ty chuckled before turning his eyes to the clock. The other guests stood enthralled, smiling at Ty's words, entirely oblivious to the meaning.

Searching the crowd, I spotted Lisa looking around excitedly. Gus wrapped his arms around her and pulled her close, whispering to her. Her smile grew. Gus's grip tightening, his eyes looking over her head to meet mine. The shadows swirled around him and slipped away. Talc white skin, flame-red eyes, sharp glistening white teeth flashed at me before he blew me a kiss.

"Esha will start the banquet, then, as the clock strikes three, my friends, Feast and be merry."

A curtain below where Ty was standing drew back to reveal a raised dais. One of the white-skinned monsters stood there kissing a human girl passionately. The shadows were falling throughout the room, exposing many of the talc skinned creatures, and many others that the words ogres, trolls, and goblins seemed suited too. None of the humans seemed to notice the shadow curtain come down, or recognize the difference in those standing close to them, rapt as they were in the show.

The man on stage was shirtless, displaying a hard muscled, lean body covered in purple tribal markings. While everyone watched, he pushed the woman's dress from her shoulders and ripped the front of it open. The girl jolted from the force of it, but moaned for him. As he discarded her clothing, her eyes seemed vacant of the awareness that they weren't alone. Sickness crept beneath my skin as I recognized that spaced out expression all too well.

For a moment, sorrow filled my heart, drowning out the fear. This girl had no idea what was happening to her, yet, her movements were unhindered by intoxication, nor were her eyes glazed with the high of pharmaceuticals. She was sober and willing, but unaware of the space around her, or that time was ticking by her. Too many times I had vanished into a similar state. It's what drove me out to the streets.

Like a slap in the face, I realized I'd stopped moving. As the man on stage discarded his pants, a subtle rattle filling the silence, my feet found their momentum again. My eyes sort the darkness of the wall, the escape of the hidden door. While everyone else stood enchanted, I searched for the way out. The woman's loud gasp and moan drew my attention back to the stage. Looking over my shoulder, I watched the man impale her, driving into her, their lust spilling out from the stage like a wave the flowed over the audience.

The slight rattle grew, many more joined with the first, as if the audience held maracas, shaking them in their support and encouragement. The noise was curious, and as it filled my ears, vibrating through water molecules of my body, I found myself stimulated, aroused, and drawn to the stage. My feet hesitated, turning me to fully appreciate the beauty of the mating taking place on stage.

The passion was undeniable, his powerful thrusts, the way she touched him, his caresses, her kisses. The entire scene called to a part of me, my left hand tingled, a need filling me. Just as I took my first step back towards the gathering, the man dropped his mouth to the woman's throat and bit her. She cried out in pleasure, a little pain in the mix.

The clock struck once. The man on stage lifted his face to look at the clock, his mouth covered in blood, the wound on the woman's neck exposed for all to see. My stomach hollowed, the spell of the moment broken for me. Stepping back, I searched the crowd to see if anyone else was terrified by what was happening. All eyes remained on the couple on the stage, unaffected as the man returned to devouring her blood, while he mated with her.

A pair of fire-red eyes found mine in the crowd. Gus grinned as he met my gaze, his eyes narrowing in evil delight. He pressed his mouth to Lisa's, kissing her like the man on stage had kissed the woman he now drained. While I watched on horrified, it happen all over the room. The talc white monsters kissed the humans in their hold; the larger, scarier creatures started to remove the clothes of their human companions.

My feet were moving without hesitation now, drawing closer to the door, my eyes wide as the clock struck the second time. Moans were echoing throughout the room. Bodies falling to the floor in a lust filled orgy. Naked limbs were spreading, welcoming the creatures to take what they will from the flesh. No one objected; everyone gave willingly.

A sensation of understanding filled my mind. *You give to receive.* The free food, free drinks, offered to the homeless. They fed us, rehydrated us, sated our need. Now, it was time to return the favor. My eyes returned to the balcony. Ty stood above it all, watching the scene unfold. I expected to see the same evil grin that Gus had given me before he took Lisa to the floor and I lost her in the tangle of naked limbs. Instead, the birthday boy watched, not with interest or joy, but with boredom. Nothing happening in this room excited him.

Then his eyes lifted and found me, a beacon standing beyond the sea of depravity. Ty's shoulders shifted back, he stood straighter, his head tilted, and the side of his mouth lifted. I was wrong. There was something in this room that excited him.

My back hit the wall as the clock struck for the third time. Lustful moans filled the room. Masculine grunts of exertion, heavy breathing, female moans, and giggles joined with the multitude of maracas to provide an erotic soundtrack to the orgy taking place.

As the third chime rang out, the feasting began. Teeth sank into hot human flesh and ripped it open. All around the room, blood was flowing. Those that had elected to have the red bat stamp provided sustenance to the talc skinned, tattooed monsters with red eyes. I'd found the show on stage hard enough to stomach, but it didn't impact me. Nothing did after the life I'd already lived.

Over the last year, I thought I was numb to the atrocities of life, yet when those with the blue beast stamps started to repay this clubs generosity, a part of me I never knew still lived, died.

They gave their flesh to the large troll-like beings and the little humanoid-looking goblins. The creatures sank their teeth into their victims, ripping and tearing at their bodies as they devoured flesh straight from the bones of the living. I watched horrified as skin and muscles were viciously shredded, blood spurting into the air like fountains as veins were torn open.

Unlike the talc-skinned creatures who took a human each, the small nasty goblins moved like a swarm of piranhas. As one of the larger predators finished with their prey, the tiny, sharp-toothed creatures crowded over the corpse, taking huge chunks of flesh into their mouths, chewing open-lipped, blood dripping down their chins. The entire scene was chaotic, heartwrenching, fear-provoking, and yet unsettling in another way. There should have been shrieking, and the lack of it made it all surreal. Everyone moaned as if the teeth ripping them apart were the sensual caress of a lover.

My watering eyes dropped to the fresh tattoo on my wrist. My fingers were trembling as I touched the purple and black scarring in my flesh. I didn't want to find out what happened to those branded with a black **W**.

I need a door!

Startling, I found a handle digging into my back. Yanking the door open, I ran from the erotic massacre into an endless hall. The sound of bones crunching chased me from the room, the noise crippling me. Unable to bear any more, I dropped to my knees and hurled my stomach contents to the floor. The door swung closed behind me. A solid slam reverberated down the stone corridor, shutting me out of the morbid banquet. After the aural overstimulation of the nightclub, the silence was resounding and deafening. Peering over my shoulder, a stone wall stood where seconds ago I escaped through a door.

Confused, I forced myself to stand and walk back over to the wall. My hands felt over the smooth stone to discover there was no handle, no cracks, nothing to indicate a door. Cautiously, I considered the corridor, trying to work out which way I should go. I held in a scream at the emptiness of it, unsure where it led. My head was telling me I was dead no matter what. Apparently, by the length of this one hall, the place was massive. Reminiscent of the movie Labirynth I'd enjoyed watching as a child, the chances of finding my way out without someone discovering me were slim.

I want to go home, I thought to myself. But, where was home? I hadn't had a home since I was five, and I couldn't remember where that was even then. Sobbing, I tried to steady my breathing. If I couldn't find my right home, what did I need most right now? *I need a safe place and a way to escape.*

A flash of color caught my eye. As I watched, a beautiful blue butterfly flittered its way up the corridor towards me. In awe of this moment of beauty, I stood still and observed its peace as it fluttered past me. Still watching it when it was ten meters away, the butterfly turned towards the wall, then went through it. Startled, I quickly moved down the hall and discovered an opening into another corridor. The butterfly was making its way along it swiftly as if it sensed the predators lurking just behind the wall here.

Taking a deep breath, I stepped out of my thrift store heels and chased after the butterfly. I'd run track at school and found running was one of the few things I could do well. Tonight, I beat my personal best.

3

THE FOREST

❖

The butterfly flew from corridor to corridor, and I followed. If I could find my way back to the car park, I could hide in a car, or on the bus, and hopefully, I'd be able to get back to town. That was what I planned as I chased the butterfly down those empty corridors. There were many doors, but no indicator of what rooms they led to, and they were all frustratingly the same.

At the end of another corridor, I lost sight of the butterfly. The only way to go was left, so I went left, my bare feet slapping on the sandstone floors till I reached a dead end. With a scowl, I stopped. "Shit! I need a safe place to hide." Slamming my hands against the stone in my way, a solid thump met my impact, and I lifted my head to examine the timber doors before me.

Stepping back, I observed a forest of trees engraved upon the large doors. My mouth fell open. Only a stone wall was here a moment ago. Moving forward tentatively, I pushed on the door. It creaked open. The sounds of a tranquil forest reached me, the smells of earth and fresh air hit me.

Hurrying through the doors, I closed them behind me. Sprawling before me was a beautiful night forest. For a moment, I thought I was outside, but then the little details started to filter through the tired haze in my brain. There was light as if a moon shone into the garden, but all that stood above me was darkness.

A path lit by the not-there moonlight appeared before me. Understanding that safety lay ahead of me, not back through the doors, I followed the light into the forest. Soft grass cushioned the impact of my feet, and magnificent trees rose high above me into the darkness. Perhaps, I was outside, and the reason there was no stars or moon was the canopy of the trees blocked it out?

Studying the path ahead, the eerie light that seemed to light only the one direction, I knew that wasn't the case. The moonlight was guiding me, but I trusted whatever led me this way. The further I traveled into the forest, the more at ease I became. The fear from my earlier encounter seeped from my body with every step I took as if the ground beneath me absorbed it, and soothed me as I walked further into the garden.

The path led me to natural steps formed from the roots of trees rising from the ground, the light guided me to the base of the tree and stopped. Searching around me, I found myself surrounded by darkness. Even the path I followed to get here vanished from sight, yet, I didn't feel as if my journey was over. Unable to find anything around me on the ground, I looked up.

A smile spread across my face as I caught sight of a hammock high in the branches. Jumping up to grab the tree limb above me, I lifted myself up and climbed quickly. Checking to make sure it was secure, I fell into the hanging bed. It rocked as I snuggled down into it. I felt safe. "Thank you." My eyes growing heavy.

A gentle breeze blew through the trees, a whisper almost too quiet to hear. *'Sleep, we'll protect you.'*

⁓

SHE CAME WITH THE SUNRISE. Not that the sun was visible, but the forest filled with light. Beautiful emerald greens, fields of flowers, crystal clear brooks, all became visible from where I hung high in the tree. "Messina, come down," the woman called to me, her voice enchanting, and just like I remembered it.

She looked like me, but her hair was a rope of golden silk, and her skin was the color of honey. We had the same turquoise eyes and heart-shaped face. When she smiled, it felt like the sun was shining upon me. "I've waited so long to see you grown." Her long fingers combed through my hair. "I'm sorry I sent you away, that I couldn't escape to find you."

"You've found me now." I smiled brightly as she braided my hair for me.

Her smile faded. "What happened to you? How did you come back here and find my tree?"

"I don't remember what happened. I was told the police found me wandering along a road, but when I couldn't tell them where my home was, they gave me a new one. Eventually, not having a home was a better choice than the one on offer. My friend Lisa and I came here looking for warmth and food. They killed her. They stamped her red and drank her blood." Lifting my wrist, I showed her my mark. "They gave me to the owner, but I ran. This is the first time I've felt safe since you sent me away. Please, let me stay."

The woman swiped the crystal tears caressing her cheek. "You are born of their world as much as mine. I should have known it would draw you home. My garden will protect you now. The faerie mound recognized your blood and heard what you desired most. It led you to me, but you cannot stay here indefinitely."

"How do I escape?"

The woman took my wrist and caressed the black and purple mark there. Her thumb rubbed over the birthmark just below the fresh tattoo. "You don't. Not yet. He'll be looking for you. We need to wait till he realizes you escaped him again. I would send you to my home, but I realized too late, you were safer with your father."

"Did I know my father?"

"Yes."

"Was he angry when you sent me away?"

"He was never that sort of father."

A burn of disappointment passed through me. I'd always hoped my real father loved me, looked for me, wanted me. "What's your name?" I'd dreamt of her many times, but it was the memories of her that had lingered, even when all my other memories had escaped me. This wasn't a dream, though. It felt different. This encounter felt real.

"Nora." She caressed my cheek gently as she finished styling my hair. "You are going to need food and supplies, so you'll need a dress, something that allows you to blend."

"Blend? They are monsters; I'll stand out like a sore thumb."

"Nonsense, there are plenty of the fallen Sidhe amongst the Sluagh and goblins. They'll think nothing of a new face wandering the halls."

I wasn't so convinced, but Nora had me stand and walk for her. Shaking her head, she stood with me. "No, you belong, you need to look like you do. This is how you must walk." She walked a line, her shoulders back, confident of herself. "Do not make eye contact with the Sluagh, ensure you make eye contact with goblins, and if you see a troll or red cap, just get out of there before they get close to you."

"What do the trolls and Red caps look like?"

Hesitating, Nora waved her hand, a cloud of golden dust floated before me, forming an image of a giant man with a red cap on his head, dipping it in the blood of a flayed man.

"They are the best warriors of the Unseelie, second to the Sluagh. Red Caps are the most vicious, and the noblest of all the Unseelie. They are one of the few who still place duty higher than self."

The image faded and another took its place. This one had a large man, his stomach large and protruding over his kilt. He carried a mallet and scimitar both dirty as if rusted and covered in dried blood. Spit filled my mouth; I swallowed it in a lump of fear. "Yes, I saw a few of those at the feast."

Waving her hand the image turned into golden dust as it fell to the ground. "Trolls. They have no empathy and live only to fulfill their own needs. If you have nothing to offer them, you are food only."

My wrist pulsed, a sudden jerk of pain that eased quickly. The tattoo was glowing faintly. "What does this mean?"

"It is his mark." Nora shook her head in despair. "You were marked to serve him. When he accepted you as his servant, he branded you. He can find you by your mark. As he gets closer, it will glow brighter. It also allows you to know when you are close to him so you will be able to avoid him, hopefully."

"Serve him how?"

"However he wishes, Messina. You belong to him now. He can do whatever he likes with you, and none will stop him. It will protect you from the others. If they tried to harm you and you flashed that mark, they would leave you be. However, if you show that mark, they will undoubtedly take you to him now, since they would all know he is looking for you."

Tears ran down my cheeks. "Can the mark ever be removed?"

Turning her face away, as if the answer was hard for her to say, Noras wouldn't meet my eyes. "Only if he chooses it. To think, I sent you away to protect you from him, only for him to find you again. This must be her doing." Nora forced herself to meet my eyes, seriousness conveyed in the intensity of my mirror. "Messina, you must know, if he ever removed the mark, he would give you to his people to devour. At that point, you would need to reveal the name of your parents. It would be the only thing to save you. But, you would never do that unless your life was in absolute peril."

"Why?"

"To reveal the name of your parents would curse you to a much worse fate then enslavement to the dark prince."

"What could be worse than enslavement to such an evil being?" Feeling my resolve slowly crumble with the fear I recognized in her eyes, I huddled in on myself.

"Being eternally bound to a Seelie lord that will use you for the title your true name will give him. They've all been looking for you, Messina. Many will want to use you; many more will want you dead. It's why I sent you away, but fate will not be duped twice." Standing, she caressed my head and faded with the light into the creeping darkness of night.

4
____

BLENDING

❖

Over the next few weeks, I took the time to explore the garden. It wasn't as big as it seemed that first night. Day and night both existed in the enclosed forest, just as it did in the outside world. There was no actual sun, but daylight filled the illusion of an endless sky above me, enabling investigation of my sanctuary.

Living in the garden was not unlike what I imagined a hippie commune to be like, or maybe, considering I was the only living person there, the garden of Eden. For the most part, I was content to stay here, then my wrist would itch and glow, and the memory of what brought me to this garden made my heart ache.

In the first few days, the purple and black tattoo would start glowing just after sundown and grow brighter over the next hour. Ty was searching for me. Every time it grew bright enough to light the darkness around me, I feared he'd tracked me to the hidden door of the forest. My imagination saw him searching that dead-end corridor, but he couldn't find the high timber doors to access Nora's garden.

The timing also gave me a hint to when Ty was about in the castle. Nora told me the creatures were nocturnal, that the ones I could blend with usually held high profile jobs in the human world.

For this reason, an hour before sunset was the best time to seek food from the kitchens. To the goblins, all Sidhe looked alike, but they would question my being there if it fell within the usual work time hours.

Giving me directions to the kitchens, Nora ensured I could repeat them back to her by rote. The risk of walking through the wrong door and getting caught was high, but if I knew the way, and held my head high as if I belonged, I should survive the excursion.

We roleplayed how to deal with the goblins if I saw them, ensuring I knew how to behave towards the creatures considered the lesser ranked of the Unseelie. Mostly, Nora sang me a lullaby to help me sleep each night.

It took over two weeks to build up the courage to leave the garden. Actually, it took desperation. The garden provided me with fruits, vegetables, and fresh water, but I craved protein. So, four days after my brand stopped glowing, I made my way to the garden door and exited into the corridor. The stone hall was empty, as expected, and I made my way quickly through the maze of corridors to find the kitchen.

Wearing a dark purple velvet and black lace, backless dress that Nora had given me, I was assured I would look just like every other Sidhe female in the castle. It was low cut across the bust but had long sleeves and a long skirt, so I felt more comfortable than I had in Lisa's barely-there mini-dress.

There was no point wearing underwear. The dress didn't allow for a bra, and while I was okay to wash my body in the stream through the garden, I'd given up washing my knickers daily a week ago. There were other priorities. Like memorizing my way through the maze that was the Unseelie court.

No, I didn't know what that meant. All Nora explained is that the Sidhe were a race of people. The good Sidhe lived in the Seelie court; the evil Sidhe lived with the monsters of the Fae world in the Unseelie court.

To me, that seemed a very black and white description. Nothing in my life had ever been black and white, so my nature was to distrust such a generalization. "Surely, they are not all evil?"

"You saw what they did with your own eyes, Messina. Do you doubt what I tell you?"

While I couldn't argue with her because her answer made me think of Lisa, I couldn't help but remember that not one person in that room screamed in pain while they died. Having screamed my throat raw growing up in my guardian's care, my mind filled with shades of grey over the exact definition of the word evil. Still, I didn't voice my challenge. Bowing my head in acceptance, I appeased her.

After fifteen minutes of walking, and only one wrong turn, I reached the kitchen. There was no one in the corridors, and I was grateful to find the kitchen empty.

Opening the fridge, I smiled spotting the milk and cheese. Taking a deep breath and thinking things through, I searched the draws and shelves on view. From the cupboard, I removed a flask and filled it with milk. Cutting the block of cheese in half, I wrapped a portion to take with me, while nibbling on another piece.

Closing the fridge, ready to raid the pantry, I froze when I discovered I was no longer alone. The woman who aided my escape, Margo, stood appraising me. "He's been looking for you," she lisped. "He knows you are still here and has been waiting for you to emerge for food."

Moving to my scavenge pile; Margo gathered them into a hessian bag while adding some crackers, a knife, and some dip. "He has started to think you starved yourself to death, but we are all ordered to report the presence of a human immediately."

"Are you going to report me?" Perhaps she already had and was delaying until he arrived.

Margo looked me up and down. "I see no human here."

My lips twisted, tempted to smile, but still untrusting. "Why are you helping me?" No one had ever helped me before. Not when they saw the bruises, or when my regular visits to the hospital should have alerted someone to my suffering. Never. So why would this woman who lived with monsters be the first to do so?

"You are not the only half-bred here," Margo snarled as she handed me the bag. "Goblins are loyal to no one but themselves. It suits me to help you. One day, I might want your help again, and would need your good graces." Sharp demonic teeth gleamed at me when Margo smiled. "You will teach me about humans, and I will teach you about the people here."

Holding up my wrist, I flashed the tattoo. "Won't he be angry if you help me?"

"Margo sees no human here. Just another Sidhe." Grabbing a notepad and pencil, she shoved them in the bag. "Talking will not always be safe. Write about your people on this." Margo turned towards the pantry. "Daily is not safe. That supply should see you through a few days. Never come here on weekends."

"What day is it?"

"Friday," Margo called over her shoulder as she stepped inside the large pantry. It was twice as big as the kitchen area, which seemed designed for multiple people to utilize it simultaneously.

"Thank you, Margo." Hefting the shopping bag on my shoulder, I started for the door.

Margo shut the pantry door behind her ending our conversation. Smiling, I made my way back down the corridor. Several corridors away from the kitchen, I passed a goblin. I made eye contact with the tiny creature like Nora taught me. He continued down the hall without anything but a snarl towards me. At least I think it was a he. There was a very asexual appearance about the goblins.

The realization that Margo was half goblin distracted me from trying to discern sex. Margo was shortish and had the same large black eyes. Her skin was softer than the goblin's I'd passed, and she could pass for a petite human if she wore sunglasses, leaving me sure her other half was human. Caught up in thoughts of how a human came to spend enough time with a goblin to mate with it, I made my way back to the safety of Nora's garden.

That night, I set out my picnic and rationed out my portions to see me through the weekend. I was beginning to love my home in the garden. Over the next three weeks, coming and going to the kitchen without issue, I grew comfortable with my life here. For the first time since I was five, I was happy. My lodgings were warm and dry; good healthy food was abundant; the hammock was the most comfortable place I'd ever had to sleep; and, I loved the dress the faerie mound left for me.

Only the regular itch and glowing of my wrist tattoo ruined my happiness here. But, as the weeks went by, and the itching happened less regularly, I realized eventually, that danger would pass too. With patience, this could become my new life.

Margo started giving me books to read. They were books about the Sidhe and the different creatures in the Unseelie court. She was teaching me about my new home. In exchange, she wrote questions on the pad asking about the human world every Monday, Wednesday, and Friday that I went to the kitchen.

The books gave me the knowledge about the Sluagh, the eaters of human souls. The first afternoon I encountered them, I could recognize them by the tribal style tattoo birthmarks over their entire torso and arms. They looked like the Sidhe in height and physical build, but their cheeks were gaunt as if they were anorexic. The chalk white skin of the Sluagh almost seemed to be made of talc or that they were painted with a powdery substance.

Both the male and female I passed wore black leather. The man wore black leather pants, leaving his muscular chest bare to show his markings. The woman wore a short skirt and a matching, intricate bra, revealing as much of her flesh as possible. Unlike the goblins, there was no confusion over the sex of the Sluagh. The men I encountered over the coming weeks were striking and masculine. The females were lithe and feminine.

Today, again, I encountered two Sluagh after leaving the kitchen. Stopping to ensure I didn't run into them, I kept my eyes low as Nora instructed, making sure not to make eye contact. "That's a pretty mouth. Can I kiss it?" My eyes widened at the females tease, and my heart picked up the pace a little. The man with her laughed and whispered something in her ear about the young sidhe being inexperienced, and then they continued in front of me.

From what I'd read, the Sluagh were the scariest of all the Unseelie creatures. They were the most powerful in majicks, they could fly, and they were vicious, feeding off the blood and souls of their victims. They couldn't breed, so they enslaved select humans to swell their ranks. The dark prince was their commander, despite being a half-breed Sidhe himself. He catered to all the Unseelie creatures, but mainly to his kin, the Sluagh.

Shortly after the Sluagh passed, a large Sidhe entered the corridor. He held considerable stature and muscle bulk, taking up a good portion of the hall as he moved towards me. On top of this, his presence made him seem giant sized and swept through the corridor well ahead of him. It was for this reason that I looked up in time to see the Sluagh go to a knee as the man passed. Not having any idea who this man was, I curtsied as he reached me.

The Sidhe stopped to assess me. "Do we know each other?" His voice humored, but friendly. "Look at me!"

With fear pounding in my chest, making breathing difficult, I lifted my eyes, my body staying in the curtsy. The Sidhe considered me. His face was ageless, yet his eyes seemed old. There was something familiar about him that I couldn't connect in my brain, distracting me from the danger as I tried to place why I felt like I knew this man. He reached out and touched my cheek, staring into my eyes with adulterated interest. "Your age?"

"Eighteen."

"Is that so?" He considered me some more, eyes glancing at my bust, appraising me, his golden green eyes full of interest. "We should get to know each other. A king should know all his subjects, especially the beautiful ones."

Palpitations racked my chest with the anxiety of who the Sidhe was standing before me. The king of the Unseelie, and he was hitting on me. Horrified and curious all at once, we stared into each other's eyes. His brows furrowed after a moment, and he snapped his hand back, eyes now keenly focused on my features. "Eighteen. Are you sure?"

"No. I lost my mother young, and those that took me in guessed my age." Touching my cheek absently, I wondered why his touch wasn't as cold as most people I met. It wasn't warm either.

The king watched me, his eyes flicking to my hand, pupils pinpoint focused before dilating. I was too lost in his presence to consider what he was thinking. The King's eyebrows lifted as a mischievous smile lifted the sides of his mouth. Without another word, he turned and continued down the corridor.

He was gone before the whirling thoughts in my head slowed enough for me to realize I was standing out in the open. Confused by what occurred, I hurried back to the forest. It was a Friday, and after that encounter, I was happy to have two days of isolation with the weekend ahead.

5

———

TYNAN

❖

"She must be dead by now," Esha huffed, sick of walking the corridors in search of the missing Seelie half-breed.

"I can still feel her through the mark. She's here some-where." Tynan stared at the blank wall before him. The stone wall of the dead end in the old, disused human servant wing of the castle; a relic of an era when the Fae ruled as gods over the mange that infested the earth. "Show me what is beyond this wall," Tynan ordered the faerie mound. Like every other time for the last five weeks, the living castle of the Unseelie Fae ignored his order. He'd even tried saying please when Esha wasn't with him once.

"Perhaps the faerie mound took her to the Seelie court." Esha was bored and wanted to forget about the Seelie half-breed.

"Why on earth would the mound grant passage to a half-breed Seelie baring my mark?" The idea frustrated Tynan; his patience was barely held by a tether. "She should never have even escaped the banquet."

"But she did. So why is it so hard to believe that a Seelie half-breed who could resist the spell on the food and escape the confines of the room, could escape the mound and you?" Taking a deep breath, Tynan turned his black eyes to meet Esha's ruby orbs. Esha backed up a step when a silver light flashed in the darkness. "Look, wherever she is, it's been five weeks. I doubt she's going to show up tonight. Can we please get over to the club already?"

Glaring at the stone wall one last time, Tynan turned to consider the corridor. "Tomorrow morning, I want all the rooms in the human wing searched. Perhaps one of them created a hide, and my present found it." He didn't wait for a response. Turning on his heel, Tynan strode the corridor, his anger marching ahead of him. When they turned into the central passage, those making their way to the night-club felt the dark prince's annoyance and quickly moved out of his way.

"What's up his arse tonight?" Brie's voice murmured behind Tynan's right shoulder.

"The missing half-breed," Esha hissed.

"Still can't locate her?" The answer wasn't audible, but his connection to Esha allowed Tynan to perceive the shake of his friend's head.

When the Sidhe war brought the Unseelie into the bloody battle-fields over two centuries ago, Esha and Tynan bonded as brothers, pledging to protect each other before they waded into the last battle. As the sun rose, Tynan stood victorious over the Sun King, but he'd never have made it without Esha beside him. Their bond formed, and their loyalty to one another had never wavered.

"My prince," Brie called. "You can't walk into that club with your current mood. All the humans would run from you without knowing why, and then my fun for the night would be taken. You know how I get when I have to go without."

Tynan's feet stopped, eyes narrowing on the door ahead. Slowly, he turned to aim his anger at the beautiful Unseelie before him. Like most of the Sluagh, Brie wore Steampunk fashion, but Brie was their queen of style.

Tonight, she wore a top hat; her brown hair wrapped up in an intricate form beneath. An eye patch covered one of her beautiful lava eyes. A short gold velvet skirt with pale gold silk frill trims hung from her hips, the decorated suspender stockings she wore exposed where they clipped at mid-thigh. Her brown leather double-breasted mid-drift coat adorned with brass buttons and chains. The neckline of her outfit guiding the eyes to the tribal design adorning her bare white chest, the mounds of her breasts barely encased in the brown leather.

Brie flinched as the prince's silver gaze scanned her body. "I'd be more than happy to provide you with a night's worth of fun, Brie." Tynan stepped towards her. Brie bit her lip, a tiny tip of fang showing. When he stepped into her, Brie backed into the wall behind her. "You should feel honored to have your prince's interest. Does your loyalty not extend to providing me with what I need?"

Cringing at the thought, Brie turned her face away in shame. "My body was not made to service the goddess's chosen one. I will serve in every other way my prince desires."

"Except in serving my desires?"

"No, Prince Tynan. I cannot."

Tynan's height and strength loomed over her, his body keeping her pinned to the wall without touching her, while he watched as she avoided meeting his eyes. She was beautiful in a Sluagh way. Tynan wanted to rip her jacket open and grab her bare breasts, biting her nipples till she begged him to lift her skirt and drive into her. He wanted to punish her for not wanting him.

Watching her eyes take in his body against hers, Tynan caught the scent of her excitement. Brie was turned on, she wanted him, but she wasn't willing to find out if the rumors of his curse were true. It angered Tynan anew, and her fear thrilled him.

Lowering his mouth to her ear, the sound of his arousal filled the air around them. Her eyes widened at the faint rattle, the vibrations of Tynan's desire pressing against her thigh. "Tell me again how my mood affects your pleasure, Brie, and I'll use this mood to take my pleasure from your flesh, blood, and screams."

"Yes, Prince Tynan. I apologize," Brie muttered to her shoulder.

Stepping back, Tynan strode purposefully for the club doors. Now he was hungry, and while one of his kind would be preferred to sate his desire, the prince would never force a woman to service him like that.

Occasionally, over the years, a new Sluagh would brave the rumors and take Tynan to her bed. The experience was always enough to reinforce the stories of his curse for another decade or more. For that reason, like his kin who used humans for food and pleasure, Tynan sort human flesh to satisfy his physical needs, because no woman of the Unseelie would sacrifice their fun in favor of anyone else, even their prince. In the Unseelie, pleasure came before duty.

At the door to the club, Tynan stopped, took a deep breath and yanked the door open. The truth was, over the last five weeks, it didn't matter who he picked up to use for his needs. When Tynan came close to release, he would close his eyes and imagine turquoise eyes in a pale face surrounded by dark hair. The Seelie eyes of Messina Doe haunted Tynan's dreams and called his lust to burn hotter than it ever had before. He needed to find her, have her, see those eyes and pale skin beneath him. Once he'd had her, Tynan could get back to how things were before he saw her five weeks ago. Once he'd felt her coldness, heard her screams, and seen the fear in her eyes of his curse, she'd stop haunting him.

"Prince Tynan," Amp greeted as he slipped into the booth Tynan occupied. Peering at the Unseelie Sidhe as he slid into the seat opposite him, Tynan wondered quietly to himself why the captain of the Lunar guard would seek him out purposely.

"Amp," Tynan acknowledged and returned his eyes to his prey for the evening. She was dancing and flirting excessively, her dress barely covering her long pale legs.

"My king asked me to give you a message, but he wants me to extract a promise and a debt from you before he gives you this gift."

Lifting a brow, Tynan signaled Esha and pointed to the girl. Once his friend was standing talking to her, Tynan gave Amp his full attention. Esha would keep the others from stealing his prey until he was ready to dine. "And what would the king know that he feels valuable enough to compel me to give him a promise?"

Amp held the typical Unseelie Sidhe coloring. Dark hair, pale skin, dark blue eyes. He was fit, and one of the best fighters amongst the Sidhe. Tynan admired him as a man and captain, but he was still Sidhe first and foremost. Dark or light, they'd cost the Sluagh their future when the Sidhe dragged them into their war with the sun god. King Mabon still hadn't paid his debt to Tynan for saving his crown.

"The King knows where to find your missing birthday present." Amp's lips twitched when Tynan sat a little straighter. "Before I can tell you where to find her, you must give me your word the girl will not suffer permanent harm. Anything you do to her for fun or punishment must be mendable and leave no physical scar of impairment. In return, the king will only charge you two decades of debt for the information."

Leaning back a little, Tynan studied Amp. "Is this a joke?"

"I assure you; the offer is real." Amp picked up his drink and took a mouthful, wrinkling his nose in distaste.

Tynan considered him. The drink was one he'd ingested many times without issue. Amp was calm, doing his job. He hated it. There was something about this deal he found unpalatable. "Why would the king demand the safety of a human half-breed sun child and still hand her over?" Mabon liked to keep a Seelie beauty for his pleasure. His last had been Nora Bayne. Her death had angered Tynan into a decade of rage.

"You have your mark on her. She is yours, but to claim the missing girl, the king wants two decades of his five-hundred-year debt erased, and a promise of safety and protection for the girl." Amp took another unhappy drink. "A bodyguard will be provided to ensure you don't lose control and harm her accidentally."

Taking a mouthful of his drink, Tynan relayed the deal Mabon was offering to Esha to get his take on this. He had a good interaction with the Lunar guard. *I have no idea, Ty. This sort of request is not something I've ever experienced in my centuries of life. This girl must have something the king wants if he wants her safe.'* Esha's thoughts were similar to the Prince's.

"Tell me, Amp. How does your King know where to find my present?"

"He saw her, and observed the mark on her wrist," Amp gritted his teeth. He sat forward. "I'm not going to lie. I don't agree with her being handed over to you, Prince Tynan. She is one of our kind. Half-breed or not, it is Sidhe blood in her veins and Sidhe are not the play-things for the Sluagh."

His no-nonsense attitude is why Tynan liked Amp. The captain was honest and cared for his people as the prince cared for the Sluagh. Amp would make a good king when Mabon finally died. Of course, Tynan planned to kill him the moment that happened and seize the king's crown for his head. Still, he was never one to deny admiration for his foes. Tynan yawned as if bored. "It is Seelie blood in her veins. She's barely worth protecting unless that Seelie blood can buy favors from the sun court?"

Amp's jaw clicked shut. Tynan sat back again. So, the king wanted this girl for leverage. That meant he knew who her sire was and he determined it from a short encounter with her. Her kin must be high in the Seelie court, perhaps the Solaris guard captain, or one of the lords. Now Tynan needed the girl to determine her heritage and use that card before Mabon could. Drawing the conversation out, Tynan took another mouthful of his drink. When he finished, Tynan slid the glass away and stood buttoning his jacket.

"I accept the terms of trade; on the condition, the bodyguard is one of my choosing." Having a Lunar guard at his residence wasn't going to happen. There were others who the king would entrust to care for a valuable piece of treasure.

"We won't trust a Sluagh."

It made Tynan smirk. "A red cap. The proudest of all the Unseelie. Pride is a good candidate."

Amp inhaled, his eyes studying the swirling amber liquid in his glass. "Pride is a good soldier and a loyal man. I agree, he is a good choice. I will agree on behalf of Mabon."

"Then I agree to the terms. Where is my present?" It took everything Tynan had to hold in his anticipation. He could feel his fingers itching to touch her pale flesh.

Amp swallowed the rest of his drink in one hit. "The king found her leaving the kitchen on Friday afternoon. She is dressed as a Sidhe woman and can pass as one. The king thought her one of ours and planned to take her back to his room for a taste, till he saw her eyes. When he saw your mark, he let her be."

"So, she still wanders free?"

"She walks the mound as if she was born here," Amp confirmed. "If you watch the kitchen, you'll find the present you seek." Standing, Amp met the Prince's black eyes evenly. "No permanent harm, and try not to drive her insane. Mabon has plans for her when you finish playing with her."

"Pride will ensure her safety," Tynan assured, skipping around a direct promise of not hurting the girl. She'd made him wait a month to open his present. Tynan was going to make her scream for him. First, since he would need to hunt her down still, he'd take the pretty pale human girl in her place for tonight. Turning away from Amp, Tynan moved towards his prey. *'Esha, my present likes to visit the kitchen in disguise as an Unseelie Sidhe. Disguise yourself and follow her to her hiding place. Then, bring her to me.'*

6

CARELESS

❖

Wednesday I grabbed up the hessian bag, as usual, shoving the empty wrappings and flask back inside, along with the notepad answering Margo's question from Monday.

Opening the garden door quietly, I checked the coast was clear, then stepped out and swung the door shut. I was halfway down this stretch of the corridor before my wrist itched. Looking down to see it glowing softly.

Wide-eyed, I turned to race back to the safety of Nora's garden, only to find a male Sluagh stood in the way, his ruby red eyes smiling down at me. "Messina Doe," he purred. "We've been looking for you." Grabbing my shoulder, he spun me and threw me face first against the stone wall before I could fathom how this happened. I tried to run, but he took my arm and bent it up behind me, pinning me against the wall. "No!"

"Yes. A silly little girl. Did you think you could hide from us forever?" Yanking my arm harder, his spare hand caressing my itching brand. "The King saw your mark last week and let the prince know you were dressed as the Sidhe, accessing the kitchen. I waited three days in the kitchen and followed you back here. I intended to take you from your hiding spot, but I can't seem to find the door. So, I waited right here for you to come back out."

From where my cheek pressed against the cold stone wall, I watched a figure clad in black appear around the corner at the end of the corridor, and stride towards us with purpose. My eyes were too watery to focus, but I knew who was coming, could feel his approach in the tattoo on my wrist. If he got to me, I knew I would suffer worse than Lisa did. I needed to escape, or die trying.

With every ounce of my strength, I pushed back against the Sluagh holding me, using his hold on me, forcing him to take my weight. "What are you doing?" he laughed. "You realize I will dislocate your shoulder? Do you know how much pain you will be in?"

"Go ahead, make my day." The Dirty Harry reference lost on this creature. Jumping my feet to the wall, I balled myself into a tight tuck and shoved back as hard as I could. We crashed into the wall on the other side of the corridor with a loud thump. The Sluagh grunted and released me, but not before I heard a loud pop and I screamed in agony.

I didn't allow myself to flop to the ground as I wanted. Pushing myself up, I bolted for the garden door. Struggling to find my natural gait with my shoulder out of place. A meter away, I was reaching for the handle when I was crash-tackled to the stone floor. Another loud pop as my shoulder was forced back into its socket, tore another scream from my lungs, this one coupled with the anguish of being caught. Fear was pounding in my chest, pessimism leaching through my body, whispering my doom.

The Sluagh growled as he rolled me beneath him and pinned me down with his body. "You're a wild little thing. Maybe I should put my seed inside you and grow another half-blood prince."

"Really? You're quoting Harry Potter at me.

The Sluagh looked confused by the reference. Lifting my knee to his groin, I prayed to all that's sacred that his anatomy felt the same pain as a human male. With a loud grunt, he rolled to the side, releasing me.

"Thank the gods for sticking with an original design. Getting onto my hands and knees, I intended to try for the door again. Instead, I was looking down on black polished shoes and the tip of a sword pointing to my heart.

"I think that's enough flirting between you two, don't you think, Esha?" Recognizing the voice of my nightmares, I trembled. Slowly, I lifted my head to look up at the smiling man. He was gorgeous, broad shoulders, but lean, and his face was angular and symmetrical in a way that enchanted me.

"I'm sorry, Prince Tynan, she's quite determined not to be caught." Esha, the Sluagh grumbled as he got to his feet.

"I would say so. She obviously has a healthy sense of self-preservation." Tynan tilted his head, onyx eyes assessing me. "She's quite the clever little thing, Esha, or she wouldn't have been able to hide from me for over a month." He flicked his eyes to the Sluagh. "Get her up."

Rough hands grabbed my upper arms from behind and lifted me without effort, placing me on my feet in front of his prince. My bruised shoulder protested the movement, and I gritted my teeth on another scream. Tynan slid his sword back into its cane casing and collected my bag from the ground. He rifled through it, pulling out the notepad and reading it.

"What do humans hunt? We don't hunt, we work for money and use the money to buy our food and anything else we need. We breed the animals we eat and people who work as farmers care for them. The animals then go to the abattoir to be slaughtered for consumption," Tynan read out loud. He frowned. "Someone has been helping you in exchange for information on humans?" I didn't answer him. "Someone defied me."

"The Unseelie is not loyal to anyone but themselves," I sneered.

Tynan lifted a brow. "So, you know. Did you know coming in?" I pressed my lips together. "Gus told me you were living on the streets, cold and hungry. It was the food that lured you in, wasn't it?" He put everything back in the bag. "Why didn't you eat if you were so hungry?" When I glared at him, he stepped forward, gripping my chin hard. "Messina, tsk tsk. The brand doesn't only allow me to find you."

Pain erupted in my wrist like a saw slowly cutting through my arm, the teeth of the serrated blade grating against my wrist bones. Gritting my teeth, I mewled in agony, trying to curl over myself, but Esha held me so I couldn't. Tears fell down my face, but I glared at Tynan just the same.

The prince watched fascinated. "You have a high pain threshold. You're going to need it if you keep defying me."

"Get raised by humans who think you are demon spawn. It's amazing the things to which you become accustomed."

Tynan's eyes glowed silver with his sudden anger. A kaleidoscope of silver tones dragged me into hell. My body was on fire, blood boiling in my veins, nerve sheaths burning away, muscles ripping and tearing beneath my skin. My head was yanked back by my hair so he could look down on me with those angry glowing silver eyes. "Who helped you!"

"I'm not Unseelie. I know loyalty."

Roaring, Tynan threw me forward. Pain erupted in my skull, jarring down my neck like a jackhammer when my head slammed into the stone. My world faded to black as I fell limp to the stone floor.

7

DARK PRINCE

❖

It was the yelling that woke me, at least I thought it was. It actually could have been screaming. "...must know who it is!" A familiar voice yelled.

"I swear, Master Esha, I don't kno..." The frightened voice cut off as it morphed into a horrific scream.

The memory of the Sluagh who'd caught me fast-forwarded through my mind, catching me up on what I'd happily forgotten while unconscious. The playback ended on prince Tynan. Was it wrong that I moaned on that image?

"I don't believe you."

Another torturous scream answered.

"You know every goblin in the court. You would know who would seek this information."

More screaming. Actually, I don't think it had stopped; the sound did nothing for my headache.

Drawing my awareness back to self, I found my head was pounding, and my body was aching like I'd crossed paths with a freight train. Opening my eyes, I cursed when I saw a reflection of myself looking back at me.

The canopy of the bed I was on had a reflective surface. I would never want to wake up looking at myself in the morning. When there is a considerable bruise above your right eye, and you fell unconscious crying with your hair being ripped out, you certainly don't want to see yourself first thing on opening your eyes.

Groaning in pain, I sat up and looked around. I wasn't worried about anyone detecting me. I could sing into a deodorant can, and dance around the room and no one was going to hear me over that screaming.

The room was large, opulent, and way overdone on the decor, but at least the purple tones in the room were agreeable. Sliding off the bed, I cringed at the pain in my legs. Lifting the skirt, I sighed at the grazed and bruised skin of my knees. "Next time fight on a carpeted surface, Mess," I scolded myself. Standing up straight caused me to cringe. "A soft surface at that."

Opening the door, I stepped out of the room. There was a walkway that overlooked a sizeable living area. Just to the left, leaning on the railing, was a big man wearing a red fez hat and what appeared to be a tuxedo, watching the proceedings downstairs. I audibly shivered to recognize the red cap and the type of creature he was.

"I won't harm you. I'm here to protect you."

"Any chance you'll help me escape?"

He turned his face to me. Strangely, he wasn't unappealing. He wasn't appealing either, but it wasn't the face of nightmares. "No."

"Can you direct me to the bathroom in that case?" When I shrugged, I winced at the pain in my shoulder. He pointed behind him. "Thanks."

Moving a step closer, I looked down on the scene below. Esha was standing over a dark-skinned goblin, or maybe that was all the blood covering his tiny body. The creature knelt in the middle of what would typically be an elegant lounge room. Tynan stood by the fireplace. He looked like he was chilling watching an episode of Myth-Busters, the way he casually drank from a chalice without any indication there was torture taking place. The floors were timber, stained cherry wine color. The opposite wall was all glass. Double height windows with light shining through, glinting off the cherry wood floors to indicate it was real sunlight. We were above ground.

Cringing when Esha slashed across the goblins naked chest with the poker he held, eliciting more screaming, I turned my back on the scene and went into the bathroom and washed myself up. Just washing the snot from my face and quickly rebraiding my hair to be presentable.

Moving the shoulder of my dress to the side, I frowned at the bruising. I'd had worse. My stepparents first dislocated that shoulder when I was ten. Now, it quite quickly came in and out. The number of times my stepmother reefed it out before I was fourteen had already used up both hands to count.

Opening the cupboard, I wasn't surprised to find no antiseptic cream, so I just wet the hand towel and gently patted clean my forehead and knees of dried blood.

When I finally walked back out on the balcony, the screaming had finally stopped. "Dead or unconscious?"

The red cap's head was nearly as large as my chest, and I was pretty sure he could make a giant grizzly bear feel small. The blood flowing over and circling the rim of his hat like red fondue did not help him look gentle.

He graced me with a smirk, making his copper eyes look slightly less creepy. "Unconscious."

Nodding, I leaned onto the railing with him. All the furnishings were black, and with the amount of blood splashed around the place, I'm guessing that was for a reason. "Is the timber that actual color, or is it badly stained with blood?"

The red cap chuckled. "It is wine wood. It's stain resistant."

I observed the blood pooling around the goblin. "Probably a good thing if this is general practice."

Tynan moved away from the fireplace, making a gesture as he took a seat on the black leather modular lounge. Two Sluagh came forward from underneath us and collected the goblin body, carrying it away. Another goblin materialized and started cleaning up.

Esha put the poker back by the fireplace and looked at Tynan.

Nothing was said, but the look they exchanged told me they were communicating. Esha glanced up at me then bowed to Tynan before walking out.

"Bring her down, Pride," Tynan directed without even looking away from the fire.

The red cap stood straight. Pride was more than twice my height. No wonder they needed such high ceilings here. "You're up," he muttered, then walked to the end of the balcony waiting by a flight of stairs.

Tynan smirked when I stayed standing still. "Are you so keen to be alone with me in your bedroom, Messina?" Jolting a little as Tynan turned his dark gaze to me, his eyes flaring silver. "Don't make me come up there."

"I'm not trying to be disobedient. I'm just struggling to walk." My feet felt glued to the floor. I couldn't move if I wanted to.

"Pride, help my gift downstairs, please. Gently. She only thinks she's invincible."

Pride collected me in a bride hold and carried me down the stairs before I could register the hidden compliment. He deposited me directly in front of Tynan, bowed his head and stepped over to the side, under the balcony, where the Sluagh had been earlier. "Leave us."

"The King ordered-"

"I will not harm her, Pride. You have my word," Tynan rebutted annoyed. Pride grunted. Tynan smirked. "Well, no more than usual."

"Snigger all you like, Prince, it is my head the King will take if she is permanently damaged," Pride argued unhappily.

Tynan waved it away. "I have waited long enough to open my birthday present, Pride. I'm annoyed, so get out while you still have legs to do so."

Pride turned his copper eyes to me, bowed his head once, pivoted with more grace than a man that large should possess, and disappeared up the hall. Returning my gaze to Tynan, I found it difficult to swallow.

"Strip."

"No."

"You are my servant; you will do as I order," Tynan returned without a hint of malice, just explaining the rules to the newbie.

"I have never willingly given up my freedom. I will not bow to your will."

Tynan huffed. He placed the chalice on the coffee table and stood casually. "Look at me." I lifted my eyes as directed. "This is my world you are in now, Messina. There are no laws to protect you here. You live and breathe by my will. You don't want to serve me, I can remove my mark, remove my protection, and I'll feed you to the goblins as an apology for inconveniencing their archivist." He circled me like a shark, growing closer with each circle. "Unlike my birthday guests, you won't find them eating you alive pleasurable. You would feel every bite, nibble, rip."

Shivering on the memory of the banquet scene, I managed to hold in a sob that rose in my chest as I remembered Lisa's smile.

"So, what will it be, Messina?" Tynan asked as he retook his seat.

Closing my eyes, tears running free as I did, I gathered my skirts and lifted the dress over my head, dropping it to the floor by my feet, my body quaking with fear. Sitting there watching me, Tynan analyzed every inch of my body quietly, for several minutes. "You've never been naked in front of anybody before have you?" He finally asked.

"Not like this."

"Are you a virgin?"

I cringed. "No."

"Good. Breaking you in would be time-consuming." Moving towards me, Tynan ran a finger over my bruised shoulder. Warmth trailed his touch. I bit my lip with a sigh, my eyes going wide at the sensation. "Are you in pain?"

"Yes."

"Good, lie down." Tynan gestured to the lounge. When I just stood there looking at him, he raised a brow in challenge. Inhaling deeply, I laid down on the sofa and made myself as comfortable as I could.

Tynan slipped from his suit jacket, throwing it on the back of the lounge before he started removing the rest of his clothing. Closing my eyes on the building tears, I tried my best not to make a sound.

When I heard a buzzing sound, I startled, eyes springing open, the sight making me gasp in awe. Tynan stood above me, pants still in place, his hands held out above me, his tribal markings glowing purple on his skin.

Suddenly, bright white light shined down on me like I was in a hospital theatre. My body convulsed, back arching, arms, and legs tensing like they'd been pulled tightly in opposite directions. The tension snapped. My body dropped to the lounge and warmth trickled through my limbs, warming me from within as it crept like a slow leak throughout every cell in my body.

Dropping his hands to his sides with a sigh, Tynan walked to the table holding his chalice. Feeling fantastic, I lay there panting, out of breath, but the best I'd felt in years.

"Your stepparents hurt you a lot. A child shouldn't be harmed like that. Even the Unseelie aren't that cruel."

Forcing my throat to deal with the excess saliva in my mouth, I gasped for breath between, and force swallowed again trying to control my breathing. I wanted to purr for how wonderful my body felt.

Placing the cup down, Tynan returned to me. Planting one knee on the lounge, he leaned over me. He ensured our eyes met before he continued. "Not everything I do to you will be to harm you, Messina. Serve me well, serve me loyally, and your pain should be very minimal." Tynan scanned his eyes over me. "I'm only half Sluagh. I can be gentle if it's warranted."

Finally, I managed to bring my breathing under control, allowing me to relax completely. Emotions I'd buried deep down rose to the surface as Tynan smiled while wiping tears from my face tenderly. Chasing the warmth of his touch, I couldn't remember anyone ever feeling warm to me except Nora.

"Who helped you hide from me, Messina?" Tynan's eyes were expectant, so warm and welcoming, offering reward and affection for my cooperation. Closing my eyes, I choked on a sob, because I knew it was a lie. Opening my eyes again, I shook my head.

Silver fire lit deep in his pupils, the only warning I received before he struck out quickly. The crack was audible, preceding my brains acknowledgment of the impact of his fist on my ribs.

Screaming, I curled to the opposite side, coughing when the scream died down. "You lied," I wheezed in pain. "You promised Pride you wouldn't harm me."

"I promised him no more than usual." Tynan didn't smile as I expected. He put one hand on the lounge next to my head, sweeping some escaped strands off my face.

"And as you just experienced, I can break you and repair you at my will. That's what you are failing to understand here, Messina. Everything that happens to you from this point onwards is my will. Good or bad, everything you experience will be at my mercy. I can take you to the brink of death and still bring you back."

Taking my left hand, Tynan caressed his brand. "You belong to me. Every pleasure your body feels will be my gift to you. Every torturous pain...." Placing my hand over the fractured ribs, Tynan pressed it down. I screamed as he used my hand to push the break out of place and caused it to slice into my lung.

The agony of having my bones forced out of place, of the sharp shard stabbing into the tissue of my lung burned through my entire body. All my air was escaping through the wound while my head drowned in a bucket of temperate water.

Removing the pressure of his weight from my hand, Tynan lifted my wrist to his mouth and kissed his branding while I coughed up the blood now pouring into my chest cavity. "You are mine, Messina. Utterly, and entirely, mine," he whispered in my ear before taking my earlobe in his mouth.

"The mound," I yelled when he bit down hard. Gasping for air to talk, struggling while I drowned in my blood. "The faerie mound helped me." Tynan pulled back with a frown. "I asked for a way out. The door appeared. I asked for a safe place..." I couldn't talk anymore.

There was the weight of an elephant pushing down on my chest preventing me from breathing.

Touching my face gently, Tynan wiped the blood from my lip. "That would mean you have Unseelie blood in you." Tynan tilted his head considering me. "I knew you were a half-breed Sidhe, Messina. The moment I saw your eyes at my birthday party. I just expected your dark half to be human, not Unseelie."

He put his mouth to my ear as my body heaved for what felt like my final breaths. "Remember this feeling, Messina. Every time you consider lying to me. Remember. This. Feeling."

He lifted his hands above my broken ribs. White light flashed. Bright, pure, and hot, like lightning, blinding me, chasing me into the darkness. I don't think I was unconscious, but I was spaced out and not present for a few moments. Blind and deaf to the world, free from the restraints of my body.

Slowly, my vision crept back in from the outside. Reality chased the white light to the center of my pupil and then ate it whole. The sound faded back in like an audio track. Tynan stood near me, dressed again and talking to a female Sluagh.

"...the records from nineteen years ago. See if any match up to these details." Tynan handed her a printout of my driver's license.

"You're keeping her?" The female scowled. Tynan lifted a brow as he flipped through a pile of paperwork. "You've enjoyed her flesh, let us enjoy it too," the female pressed.

"She was a gift, Trell. I would not be so rude as to dispose of such a wonderful gift so soon and barely used."

The girl growled. "She was gifted as a joke!"

Moving quickly, Tynan caught her neck in his hand, squeezing it. "Braque thought she was human and part Seelie Sidhe. What he gifted me is worth more than he could have ever guessed if she is what I think she is. You, nor any other in this court will lay a finger on her, or you will bear my wrath."

He threw her across the room, the thud of her body slamming into the post for the balcony followed by the grunt when she dropped to the ground. "You know the rules, Trell. She bears my mark. No one can touch her without my permission," Tynan reminded like a school teacher would the previous lesson.

"I'm sorry, Prince Tynan," Trell sniveled before racing out of the room.

Tynan's eyes dropped to me on the couch. My fingers curled into the blanket that covered me.

"I'm going out. For your safety, don't leave my suite." Picking up the pile of paperwork, he left.

Pride strolled over a moment later and looked down at me, concern evident in his eyes. "Was it bad?"

"I've suffered worse."

Pride picked my dress up off the floor and laid it beside me on the sofa. "How very sad. Come, your king wishes a word."

8

THE KING

❖

The king's residence was at the far end of the building, and several levels up from Tynan's. Pride escorted me. Everyone we encountered on the way moved quickly aside and barely looked at us. I put my arm through Pride's so we were walking arm in arm, albeit his arm was the breadth of my body. He looked down at me wide-eyed. "I think I just fell in love with you, Pride."

Pride blinked. "Why?"

"Because you seem to be the big bad. That makes me want to be best friends with you."

Pride chuckled. A tremendous sound that echoed through the halls of the castle, wrapping around my body like the softest silk, and left me wanting to roll around the ground purring like a cat with catnip.

Big double doors stood guarded by Unseelie Sidhe at the end of the corridor. There were two either side of the door and a third, more deadly looking turned to appraise us as we approached. "Messina Doe to see the King as requested, Amp."

"Thank you, Pride. I'll take her from here," the dangerous looking one, Amp, replied. One of the guards stepped away from his post and opened the door.

When I looked at Pride unsure, Pride nodded his head sternly, encouraging me forward. Taking a brave breath, I walked through the doors into the entry foyer with Amp. The door guard shut the door behind us.

"I am Amp Ó Macha-Mór, Captain of the Lunar guard," he introduced himself with a slight bow of his head. "King Mabon has searched for you a long time, Messina. He is happy you have returned home but unhappy about the circumstances of your return." Taking my left hand, Amp assessed Tynan's tattoo. "There are rules we must observe. To break them would cause a war with an uneasy ally. Know, that I will help you where I can, but in the end, it is King Mabon who must negotiate with the Prince about your care." With that said, Amp opened the next set of doors.

The layout was much the same as Tynan's suite. The entry foyer led to a hallway with many doors on either side, before opening onto a sumptuous entertaining area. Double height glass windows, and an upstairs area that overlooked the living space. The difference was the color scheme. While Tynan's suites were dark and decadent, the King's were light and clinical. White furnishings, gold decorations, polished stone floor. It was almost sterile. I found myself preferring the warmth of Tynan's suite.

The King sat on the lounge wrapped in a robe, two naked Sidhe females giggling as they flirted with him. "Ah, finally," the king interrupted their banter when he saw me. "Ladies, leave."

The women pouted, then glared at me with their golden eyes. "Who is she?" The woman with long black hair and a black cobweb inked down one side of her face and body inquired as she stood.

"Don't be jealous, Arachne. This lovely young lady is Tynan's new pet." The king waved his hand at me. "Show my lovers your wrist, Messina." I held out my left wrist to show Tynan's mark.

Arachne chortled. "You can't touch her, Mabon."

The King smirked. "No, I can't. So, bury your petty jealousies and run along."

The dark-haired women rose and sauntered past me. "Hope you

like the cold, Messina. That's all the prince can offer you," Arachne sneered as she passed by me.

"Thank you, Amp," Mabon dismissed the captain. He waited till he heard the door shut and we were alone, then rose. "So, you are Nora's daughter?" He frowned looking me over when I froze. "You know that name?" The King observed my reaction. "You remember her?"

"Yes, but I haven't seen her since I was five."

"You have her eyes and face." Mabon studied me. "I recognized who you were when I saw Nora looking back at me. When I saw the Prince's brand on your wrist, I knew you were the half-cast Seelie the castle had been torn apart looking for." He stopped, face pensive as he stared through me. "I have a hard decision to make. I'm not one to make it lightly, and I prefer to make well-informed choices." Mabon gestured I should take a seat. He poured me some tea, and I accepted it politely. "How did you survive the birthday celebrations?"

"Several random events. Luck, maybe fate."

The King stirred his tea as he sat back down. "How did you come to be here?"

I told the king how Gus found Lisa and me, the questioning of the stamps, seeing the bugs in the food, staying hidden during the party and how I'd found the door. In other words, I told him everything but Margo. I even revealed how I found the garden and hid there, but I didn't mention dreaming of my mother.

"Hmmm." The King placed his empty teacup aside. "So, you can see through glamor? That's a rare gift, not many here can see through a Sluagh's disguise. The mound recognizes you and hears you also. Does Tynan know?"

"The mound yes, the glamor no."

"He will know you were born here then, that you are full-blooded Sidhe." Mabon stood and went to the windows. "What to do, what to do? It's only a matter of time for him to discover the truth of you. How will he react or respond? Do I leave you in his care now? Do I break the bond and take you from him before he can do lasting damage?"

"I..." I tried to voice my opinion, but the King was too busy talking to himself.

"They will want you back. The Seelie have already lost you once, have probably been searching for you all these years. I could ransom you, force them to give you a good match. Should I breed you here first and leave a legitimate heir? Or loan you to them for the same purpose?" Mabon turned to face me. "Do I leave you in his care? That is the immediate question. Yes allows me time. No requires immediate action on the others." He walked towards me. "Did he harm you?"

"Not permanently," I answered diplomatically, unsure if I trusted the King after half of what he just said.

The King sighed, understanding the answer. "I need time."

The decision was made to leave me as Tynan's pet. "Could you..." I hesitated over the wording, "place restrictions on my time in his care?"

The King tilted his head. Taking a deep breath, he shook his head. "I have interfered already, something Tynan noted keenly. I believe his people are already searching the archives for your birth records. When I told him where to find you, I insisted he does not harm you. Tynan very diplomatically reminded my representative what that mark means." He pointed to my left wrist.

"So, you negotiated no permanent harm?"

"Yes. I also appointed Pride as your guard, but even that is limited when you are in Tynan's suites." Mabon took a deep breath, his eyes hardening with determination. "I need time. You remain the property of Prince Tynan to do with as he pleases, as long as it causes you no permanent injury, and Pride will protect you from the jealous Sluagh."

I frowned. "But not the jealous Sidhe?"

Mabon laughed. "The Sidhe do not deal in half-breeds, Messina. They do not want Tynan who is half-Sluagh, and they will not want you while they think you are part human." The way he rolled the word human in his mouth like it was a sour grape, indicated to me human was far worse than being half-Sluagh.

"The Sluagh, however, adore their prince. The females swoon for him, and the men envy him. Despite our laws, they will take a bite of fruit as sweet as you if they think they can get away with it."

The King considered me. "You will, however, need to be trained. You have natural abilities that you've probably never learned to control, and you need to know how to fight. I will organize it to happen."

Standing, I turned to leave, recognizing a dismissal when I heard one.

"Messina." I twisted back to meet his eyes. "I'm sorry your mother's action in sending you from here led to a life of misery. I apologize in advance that your return will not improve your circumstances."

Meeting his eyes, I bowed my head slightly, then turned and walked toward the door. I hadn't given up the idea of escape yet, but I needed advice. I needed to get back to the garden, sleep, and speak with Nora. I needed to escape the Unseelie court. I needed to...

"Pay attention to your surroundings," Pride's voice boomed, bringing me back to the present. Pride stood in front of me, hunched over and peering into my eyes. "Ah, there you are. I thought perhaps a Sluagh got to you while you were in there and stole your soul."

"Sorry, just trying to understand things," I dismissed my absent mind.

"Planning your escape?" Pride snickered.

"Of course." I smiled back as I threaded my arm through his. "My dear Pride, would you take me back to the room where I hid? I want to get the rest of my stuff. I can't escape from there. If I could, I would have done it weeks ago. I promise there is one way in and one way out."

"One way in, which only you can access if I understood Esha's rant correctly?"

"I will take you in with me," I offered cautiously. My knowledge of the faerie mound was limited, and I couldn't be sure the door would be there for me if one of the Unseelie were with me.

Pride stopped walking, captured my shoulders in his large hands and looked into my eyes. "You will do nothing more to cause the prince to harm you."

"And by that you mean...?"

"Give in to his will. Whatever he wants, give it to him." Angry, I turned my face away. Pride stood straight. "If you live by his will for a month, I'll take you to your hide for your stuff. I swear it."

"You suppose I will live for another month under the Prince's care?"

"He gave me his word. In nearly three centuries, the prince has never broken his word willingly."

"But he has broken it?"

Pride sucked in air through his nostrils, strands of my hair lifted in the updraft. "There are always external forces at play. The prince gave his word to ensure a princess's safety once, and he did. He failed to see the threat to her wellbeing by those aligned with her, and she died. That didn't break his word. The prince honored his word within his power to do so."

Pride started walking, the conversation over. Staying alongside Pride, I remained silent. I could either submit to the prince or I couldn't. Free will had always been important to me.

When we entered Tynan's suites, I felt my shoulders relax. There was a safety in his apartment that I didn't feel anywhere else. The strangeness of that reaction confused me. Exhausted, I collapsed onto the lounge, pulled the blanket up, and hugged it tight around me. "It's boring here."

"For one with no duty to perform, it would be," Pride commented, standing by the window. "That will change. The prince will give you duty. However, you should remember the Unseelie code."

Tilting my head, I tried to remember reading something about a code of conduct.

Pride beamed at me, rolling his shoulders back and puffing out his chest proudly as he educated me. "Change is good; glamor is free; honor is a lie; and passion before duty."

"Are you subtlety telling me the loophole? That if I can find something I'm passionate about, I don't have to bow to his will?"

"I am reminding you, that passion is considered the truest state of being. The Unseelie act on pure instinct and passion, without thought to consequence. I believe it's always made an excellent defense for one's actions."

I met Pride's smile with my own. "In that case, I'm going to need a few things."

I WAS HOPING to have my supplies before Tynan arrived home that evening; however, the Sluagh didn't survive this long for being stupid. When Tynan came into the lounge room that night, Trell and Esha were with him, arms laden with bags.

"Is that my art supplies?" I asked excitedly.

When Tynan raised a brow at my enthusiasm, my smile dropped. I could almost feel the collar cinching around my throat. Why did I expect he would be any different to every other man in my life? They always wanted something from me.

"Yes..." Tynan dragged the confirmation out. "Everything you requested. The art supplies, the books, the laptop with restricted internet access."

"But?" You could see it coming a mile away.

When Tynan made a gesture to Esha and Trell, I watched my passions get walked back down the corridor and into a room. I was a puppy losing a juicy bone.

"But you'll have to earn your rewards." Placing his bag on the floor, Tynan sauntered towards me. "Nothing is freely given in the Unseelie court, Messina."

The back of my eyes itched as hope died a horrible death in my soul. "Just like the human world. I'm starting to see a lot of similarities."

Tynan didn't look happy at my comparison. "I am not an ogre, Messina. Kiss me and earn your first reward."

"What?" My eyes went wide at the request.

Tynan lowered his voice. "Welcome me home like a loving wife would welcome her husband, and I will grant you one sketch pad and a pencil."

Staring into his eyes, sure this was a trap, but only curiosity shined back at me. Clearing my throat, I stepped forward, placed my hands on his shoulders, and rose on tiptoe as I went to kiss his cheek. "Welcome home, darling."

Pulling back enough to stop me kissing his cheek, Tynan cupped my face in his hand and looked deep into my eyes. "Make me believe it, Messina."

His mouth pressed against mine, his lips unusually warm. Every other kiss had been cold in comparison. Closing my eyes, I tilted my head to feel more of his heat suffusing me, a natural reaction to being cold. My arms slid forward around his neck, stepping into him as my body warmed to his touch, to the incredible feel of his luscious lips pinching mine.

Squirming closer to him, I opened my mouth and tasted his lips with my tongue. Making a noise of appreciation, Tynan reciprocated, pulling me tighter as he delved his tongue inside.

The intensity of our kissing grew harder, more passionate, our bodies pressed firmly against each other, still not close enough. Someone started playing the maracas.

A loud smashing sound made me jump back. My eyes were blinking rapidly as the shock filtered through the lust glaze smothering my brain. My god! That had been the best kiss I'd ever had.

Looking just as surprised, Tynan recovered a lot faster, clearing his face of emotion as he turned to watch Trell collecting shards of some crystal ornament from the floor.

"Sorry, Prince Tynan, I can be very clumsy," Trell dramatized. Her tone confused me, my fingers feeling how puffy my lips were, Tynan's warmth still coating them.

Shaking his head at Trell, Tynan motioned Esha forward. When Tynan was no longer looking at her, I read Trell's facial expression. 'He's never kissed me like that.'

Jealousy.

"As promised." Bringing my attention back to him and the sketchbook Esha was handing him, Tynan offered me the sketchbook and a pack of lead pencils. "You'll greet me home like that every day from now on."

Trell hissed over the other side of the room. Eyes scanning me as if he was imagining giving me the same sort of greeting, Esha grinned. Ah, so this is what Mabon meant by jealousy and envy.

Taking them carefully, just in case it was a trick, I hugged them to me and stepped back. "May I go to my room?"

Tynan considered me. After a moment, he turned to make eye contact with everyone else. "I'll have the room." His tone was polite demand. Everyone left without question.

Waiting till the door to the foyer shut, Tynan folded his arms across his chest. "You can hang out in your room during the day. At night, you will sleep in my room, in my bed, naked," Tynan dictated. I opened my mouth to object. "Do it without complaint, Messina, and I will reward you for your compliance."

I wanted to say no, but my instinct didn't agree. "On one condition." Tynan raised his heavy brow at me. "You start calling me Mess. It's what my friends used to call me."

Tynan smirked as he turned to leave. "I've arranged to have your dinner delivered to you. I'll be coming to bed at one. Don't make me punish you instead of rewarding you, Mess."

My cheeks heated when he used my name. God, what was wrong with me? I hated this man. He had hurt me badly, taken me prisoner, and planned to take a lot more from me, and I was blushing for him. Pride walked back in and gave me a discreet nod of his head. Gripping my sketchbook tighter, I made my way upstairs to my room.

9

INTIMATE

❖

Lifting my head from the pillow groggily, I found Tynan looking through the sketches I'd been working on that afternoon. "Hey, you need to ask to see those," I bitched. As requested, I'd come to his bed to sleep, lying naked on my stomach beneath the blankets.

"No, I don't. I own you and therefore own everything you create. These are quite good."

"Will I have no privacy while I'm here?" I grumbled, sticking my face back into the pillow. The bed was quite comfortable.

"No. Privacy allows for secrets. Secrets encourage treachery, and betrayal will get you killed," Tynan educated me as he turned to the next sketch. He frowned. "You saw the food as spoiled, that's why you didn't eat it?" Tynan held the sketchbook and studied me. "You could see the taint on the food. You can sense majick spells." He considered the sketch, then he ripped it out and threw it on the fire in the room.

"Hey!" I objected, sitting up enough to watch the flames devour my sketch.

"It's best no one knows you have that gift, especially the Sluagh and Sidhe." Dropping my sketchbook back on his chest of drawers,

Tynan slid off his suit jacket. Glaring at his back did nothing, so I face planted the pillow again.

Listening to Tynan undressing, I didn't want to watch, and I certainly didn't want to think about what came next. Primarily, because it excited me, and I'd never been excited about the concept of forcing myself to have sex before. Worse still, I couldn't forget our kiss. I'd spent the afternoon drawing the massacre to avoid thinking about how warm Tynan felt.

Darkness descended on the room as Tynan turned the main light off, only for me to hear the click of the bedside lamp. The covers slid across my naked skin as Tynan pulled them back, leaving me exposed. I shivered in both fear and expectation.

Tynan wasn't like the Sluagh. He had pale skin, but it wasn't the chalk white. In fact, Tynan probably had more color than me. He looked Sidhe with his clothes on, only the tribal markings of the Sluagh marking him otherwise.

"Roll over."

Shaking like a mouse, I rolled onto my back, but Tynan wasn't standing above me as I thought.

"Touch yourself," he ordered from the side of the room. Turning my head, I could see his shadow in the darkness. He was sitting in the armchair I'd curled up on earlier to sketch.

"How do you mean?"

"Move your hands over your body. Touch your flesh."

Blinking into the darkness, I moved my focus to the ceiling above me. Unsure, I tentatively placed my hands on my abdomen, then I slowly moved them up to grasp my breasts. "Like this?"

"Yes. Tell me about your lovers."

"Lovers?"

"The men you've been with, how they touched you."

Eyes stinging on the thought, I bit my lip. The memory was cloudy, but I knew it happened. "I, I haven't been with... I mean, I've only been with two men."

"Tell me about your first time. Who was the lucky boy?"

I cringed. "I... I don't want to..." Pain flashed through my wrist. "My stepfather," I hissed, rubbing the brand on my wrist. "I lost my virginity to my stepfather."

The room was deathly quiet. "Your stepfather forced you?" Tynan finally hissed.

"No," I answered a little too high pitched. God, I'd never told anyone. I promised him I wouldn't tell anyone. "I did it willingly." My breath hitched on the admission. Wanting to cover myself in shame, I reached for the blankets.

"Don't!"

Frozen by the ire in his voice, I lay back. He was angry. Very angry. It was okay when he thought I'd given it to some boy I liked.

There were several moments of silence, the weight of judgment crushing me till I couldn't stand it. "You have to understand; they gave me nothing but pain. I wanted something bad enough that I negotiated with the only thing I had to offer," I breathed through the shame. I'd made a decision that benefitted my future and stuck with it. There was no point regretting it now. If I learned anything over the last thirteen years, it was that you need to do what you must to survive.

"What was the deal?"

It hurt to inhale the oxygen needed to explain my circumstances. "They were going to take me out of school. No schooling meant no future. I begged and begged them to reconsider, but his wife wouldn't listen. The night before she went to visit her sister for a week, he took me aside and asked me what I would be willing to do to stay in school till I graduated. I told him I'd do anything. He made me prove it. He told me to get on my knees, so I did."

"Was it horrible?"

While I couldn't remember the act in detail, I did recognize that I hated and loved it. "Yes, more so because..." I cringed. "I liked it. I didn't want to, but I did."

Struggling to swallow after that confession, I licked my lips remembering the look on my stepfather's face. "He was amazed. He didn't think I'd like it, probably was looking forward to hurting and debasing me, but afterward, he couldn't believe how much he enjoyed it." Tracing my lips with my finger, I turned my face to the dark corner I knew Tynan was sitting.

"He walked straight into the kitchen and told the bitch he wanted me to stay in school, that it would benefit them more. He argued if I didn't, considering their social standing, that it would draw attention."

"They were wealthy?"

"He was. He married gold-digging trash. His wife considered every cent spent on me a waste because it wasn't for her. In the end, he wouldn't let her say no to it. The next day when I got home from school, she was gone. A nice dress and my first matching set of underwear were waiting on my bed."

My hands moved over my body remembering the way his hands had touched me that night. "I made good on our deal, and for the week she was away, I secured her husband's promise for me to see out my senior year."

For a moment, my lips turned up in nasty satisfaction. "It was never the same for them after that. My stepfather stopped wanting his wife that way, and she couldn't understand why for a long time."

My smile fell away. "She must have noticed the way he looked at me when I was in the same room. Either way, she took her frustration out on me, not that she didn't hit me before that. My stepfather stopped beating me, preferring to grope or kiss me when she wasn't looking. Since my stepfather was stronger than his wife, only one abuser was better than two.

Silence enveloped us. "Did it happen again?"

"Whenever she was away, which wasn't often enough in my mind," I admitted with melancholy. It's not that I wanted my stepfather, but for that short space in time, life wasn't the worst it could be.

"Mostly, he would corner me in the bathroom or bedroom and have me suck him off. He liked to take his time fucking me, and he couldn't risk her coming home early and catching us. After a few months of things deteriorating between them, he paid her to leave. Then he moved me into his bed permanently. He'd message me at school telling me what he wanted me wearing and doing when he got home. Or he'd send me texts of the things he was going to do to me. Every message made me vomit, but I didn't know what else to do.

"He started taking me out to dinner and making me suck him off while he drove the car. He'd pull me in his lap while his friends were over watching the game and grope and kiss me. He treated me as if I was his girlfriend, not the child he raised, and his friends didn't say a thing. They'd just watch and laugh, and act like it was all okay.

"One night, I needed him to sign a permission slip for an excursion. He was really drunk, and when only his best friend was still there, he pulled me on his lap and told me he'd sign it if I showed his friend how I loved to ride his cock. He stripped me naked and fucked me in front of his friend, and the mate sat there and watched while he drank his beer. Not long after that, I slept with the other guy."

"Was that a boy from school?"

Shaking my head, I became distracted and frowned. "What's that humming sound? Is there a baby rattlesnake in here?" It was faint, but it sounded like someone's mobile was on vibrate in their bag.

"I'm aroused."

"How does that explain that noise?" I'd heard it at the banquet, and this morning when we were kissing, but now my mind couldn't fathom why his arousal made that noise. Maybe it was a Sluagh thing, and they have mini-shakers attached to their cocks.

"Finish the story, Mess. Tell me about the other guy."

Lying back, I couldn't relax because the rattle sound unsettled me, especially as warmth filled my belly and I found myself drawn to the noise.

"It was my stepfather's best friend. The guy who watched him fuck me. I wanted to get my license. My stepfather told me I had to do him and his friend if he takes me to get his license."

"He was willing to share you?" The humming noise got a little louder.

"I guess. Either way, they effectively wanted to live out their porn fantasy. He used my wanting a license to get me to agree to it." Rolling over, I peered at Tynan's shadow. Did I like that he was sitting there getting aroused? Yes. Just thinking about having that effect on him was having a physical impact. My stomach muscles were taut, and my sex was dripping.

"Turn off the bed lamp," Tynan directed as he stood up, staying shrouded in the darkness.

Reaching over, I flicked off the lamp. My fear had left me now; the rattle sound aroused me past logic and sense. I wanted Tynan to use me for his pleasure, wanted to feel him throb inside of me. My heart leaped in my chest when I heard the maracas coming closer.

"Roll onto your back."

When I complied, Tynan used his hands to separate my thighs, the warmth of his fingers igniting fires along the neural pathway of my inner leg. I moaned at his touch. The rattle got louder, still sounding muffled, but there.

Kneeling between my naked legs, Tynan lowered his mouth to my abdomen. My body was trembling with anticipation; my fingers grasped the bedsheet beneath me when a little hesitation broke through the desire. A sob escaped my throat without warning.

"This is about pleasure, Mess. You don't need to fear me right now." Extracting another moan when Tynan's fingers found me moist.

"Protection," I groaned, biting my lip as he flicked my nipple, and leaned further over me to reach my mouth. "I'm not on birth control."

"Take what I give you." The rattle was even louder now.

"Is it going to hurt?" I whimpered as his fingers found that sensitive spot under the hood and pressed down on it.

"Not tonight." He kissed me, just a taste, pulling away and moving something hard and rough against my sensitive bud. I swear I was on fire. The object was vibrating, and I understood the humming rattle sound was coming from it. Fisting the sheets beneath me, my back arched up towards him as I moaned long and hard.

"Do you know how rare the power of satiability is in our kind?" Tynan groaned like he was in agony and pressed the vibrating rod harder against me. "Do you know how much I like that you can't control your power?" It was too much, too intense. I was crying with how fantastic it felt, clawing at the bed sheets.

"You made me so hungry for you with just one glance at my party,"

Tynan murmured in my ear. "I don't get hungry often." He kissed along my jaw. "I suspected it was one of your gifts when I healed you today. I've never felt so satisfied with healing. I suspect you felt it too, a sense of fulfillment?"

"Yes!" Moaning, I grabbed his shoulders to hold him to me as my body climbed to climax. It had never felt this good before. "Ty, I feel like I'm going to explode."

Tynan shuddered above me. "Take what I give." The rod's vibrations picked up. It grew thicker, heavier, and the texture became courser. It was too much. Dropping my head back, I screamed for mercy, my body clutching for something to hold onto, hating that all the pleasure was external.

Tynan roared his pleasure as he thrust his hips forward hard, the vibrating rod hurting with how hard it pressed against me. Looking down, I watched wide-eyed as pale neon-blue liquid spurt out of the darkness and splattered my stomach. It was ice-cold and surprised me out of my lust.

"Oh, God! Are we even physically compatible?" I dreaded the answer. I thought he'd been holding a toy against me, but I could feel it softening as we lay there panting.

Tynan caressed my face. "Tell me the rest."

Swallowing to regain my breath and not freak out about what just happened, I focused on answering his question. "My stepfather drove me down to get my license. Then we drove to his friend's place."

"Did you like his friend?"

"No."

"But you allowed him to have you?"

Peering up at him in the darkness, I felt the tears escaping quietly down the side of my face. "I don't like you and allowed you to do that to me."

"So, your power has been opportunistic, gaining freedom whenever it could."

"Like just now."

Tynan caressed my cheek. "So beautiful, powerful, and naïve to it all." Withdrawing, Tynan rolled off to the side. "Go shower. That stuff will set like glue otherwise."

Shivering with how cold his voice was, I couldn't help the sob that caught in my throat. I didn't understand why his easy dismissal of me hurt so much. It's not like my stepfather had treated me much better. And yet, it hurt more when Tynan did it. I'd expected it of my stepfather, been happy for him to finish with me. "Should I go back to my room after I shower?" I muttered, trying to keep the hurt out of my voice.

"You sleep in here," Tynan growled in warning.

"Yes, Prince." Climbing off the bed, I made my way to the bathroom, his voice stopping me at the door.

"Mess, call me Ty when it's just us."

Warmth bubbled in my stomach. Covering my tummy with my hand as I entered the bathroom, I grimaced in disgust. Pale blue gunk squished under my palm. As I pulled it away, it stretched like a spider's web.

"Gross. I've been slimed!"

10

ANSWERS MAKE QUESTIONS

❖

I was dreaming of him, of what we did together. We were in a bed - not his bed, the room was too colorful and sunlight shined through the windows - when the doors burst open. Sidhe dressed in white and gold uniforms rushed into the room. Tynan tried to fight them, but they used their gold shields to shine sunlight on him, forced him to cover his eyes, then they were on him, dragging him from the bed and me.

They held Tynan in the corner of the room, holding a sword to his throat to force compliance. Some of the soldiers restrained me as I struggled to get off the bed, screaming for Tynan.

"You've tainted our bloodlines enough, Sluagh. You will not taint this one," a woman sneered. Her white dress looked like it was weaved entirely from a spider's web, random gold threads glinting in the light.

Grabbing my jaw to force it open, she spat in my open mouth, murmuring words beneath her breath. Her golden eyes stared into my watering gaze, burning hatred searing into me. I didn't want her hate; I didn't even know her.

Steeling myself, I threw her coldness back at her like a slap in the face. She released me; eyes wide as she touched her cheek. A red bloom in the form of a handprint spreading across her honeyed skin.

Another Sidhe entered the room, golden hair and perfect smile, snapping the woman's attention to him. "The weave is complete. Don't kill the prince. The bond will allow him to feel her distress if she experiences his death here. Use her till your seed takes, then send your men to bring her to us. Don't fail me!" With one last glare in my direction, she checked the bruising of her cheek then stormed out of the room.

The magnificent specimen of Sidhe approached me. "Who are you?" My entire body trembled as he started to disrobe.

"I am Cathal," his forest green eyes shining at me, "Captain of the Solaris, and, once my seed has taken root within your womb, your husband."

"No!" Thrashing against their hold on me, the flesh under their grips tore, pain flaring through my limbs as I fought to get away.

"Don't touch her," Tynan snarled. "Stop! She's untainted. You can't force her choice. You know what happens when you do."

Cathal looked over his shoulder, eyeing Tynan. "Unlike you, I serve my queen loyally. You took what was ours, and now you take from us again. Everything that happens to this girl begins and ends with you taking the Sun King's daughter. What happens here today is a two-hundred-year-old consequence of your actions. All this is your doing, Dark Prince." Returning his gaze to my determination to escape, Cathal stroked my cheek. "I'm sorry it's come to this. If you stop fighting, we can do this the right way. I'll send my men outside and make sure you enjoy it."

Unable to swallow my fear, I gathered it up and spat it on his face. Wiping the spit from his skin, the Seelie Sidhe sighed in resignation. "Hold her down."

"No!" Tynan roared.

When Cathal moved his body between my thighs, I screamed.

Sitting up in bed, I immediately scampered of it, searching the room for any gold soldiers of light. Only darkness wrapped around me. Calming my breathing, I slowly stood, wincing in pain. "Nightmare?" Tynan asked.

"I think so."

"Come back to bed."

My heart raced frantically in my chest. "No." There was a silent pause. "I mean, is it okay if I go downstairs and draw? I won't be able to sleep again for a while."

"Better there than here keeping me awake," Tynan grumbled rolling away.

Grabbing up my dress and sketchbook, I tiptoed out of the room and dressed on the landing before heading downstairs to the lounge. After stoking the fire, I curled up on the sofa. My hands moved of their own accord, lead scratching across the paper, recreating the images of my dream. The fire crackled, dimming in intensity as the light changed in the forest outside. Along with more light, came the feeling of stiffness, my movements slowing, feeling sluggish.

"Do you know that man?" Esha's sudden appearance peering over my shoulder at the sketch of Cathal startled me, but my body didn't move. Attempting to turn and meet Esha's eyes, I realized my body wasn't responding to my thoughts. Trapped in a prison of my own body, I started freaking out.

The morning light was shining through the window as I thrashed and screamed, trying to get my body to respond. Images of the dream flashed in my head, making me paranoid I was still asleep. God, I hoped I was having another nightmare.

With a frown, Esha slipped his hand around my neck, holding me still as he moved my hair to the side. I'd left it down this morning. Internally, I sagged worn and defeated.

"Esha, problem?" Tynan asked from the balcony. Ignoring Tynan, Esha's ruby orbs were intent as he pulled my dress off one shoulder frowning, then again, the same on the other shoulder. "Esha!"

"Since when do you share?"

His rage was a cyclone through the room as Tynan gripped the banister with white knuckles. "I don't, now, get your hands off her."

Releasing his hold on me, Esha turned angrily to his prince. "She's covered in bruises. By the size of the handprints, at least three different men caused them."

Hurdling straight over the railing of the balcony, Tynan landed in front of me, before my eyes even caught up with his movement. Checking my neck and shoulders, his silver light glowing in his eyes. "Esha, turn away."

Esha about faced without hesitation. A second later, I was standing, and the dress was over my head on the floor. Tynan inhaled angrily. "When did this happen?"

In my head, I responded, but my body did nothing. I wasn't even sure I was blinking. Peering into my eyes, Tynan frowned. "Esha, is she drugged?"

Swinging back around, Esha studied my eyes; his ruby irises glowed with intensity as they gazed deep into the void to find me trapped. "Not drugged. Tranced." His eyes drifted down my body. "Who could have done this and not woken you?"

"No one. They would have woken Goyle at the very least," Tynan indicated the statue of a massive nasty looking dog by the fireplace.

Lowering his eyes to my sketchbook, Esha picked it up and started flicking through it while Tynan sat me back down gently. "Ty."

Glancing over his shoulder, Tynan took the sketchbook. "Those are new drawings. Is that me on my knees?"

"And Mess on the bed, being held down by three soldiers of light." Esha frowned and flicked the page over. That's who I think it is, right?"

"Yes," Tynan exhaled. "She had a nightmare last night and wouldn't come back to bed. Find Arachne, see if she'd like to undo her sister's handy work."

With a nod, Esha walked out.

Tynan squatted in front of me. "It's okay, Mess. I'll have those cobwebs cleared out of your mind very soon."

As soon as he told me what it was, I could see the prison holding me. An intricately woven spider's web encased me, keeping me restrained. Ripping and tugging at it with my mind's eye, I stretched the silk netting, trying to create a gap big enough to escape.

"You're fighting it, aren't you?" Tynan whispered impressed. "She's the best weaver the light court has. If you can find your way free of her web, none of them will ever be able to hold you again."

The challenge was in his voice. A dare of sorts. Smiling inside myself, I searched the web determined. It was a thickly layered cobweb, encompassing me entirely. Where would the weak point be? Not at my sides.

Looking up my lips lifted slightly. Shaped like a cursive **W**, there was a thinning of the web. I struck my hand upwards, fingers straight as I drove them through the thinnest part of the silk.

Wincing, Tynan's eyes opened wide as he stared at me bewildered. Wiggling my fingers free of the web, I felt the cold air on the other side, my fingers moving on my living body. That small physical proof gave me hope and urged me onwards.

"My brand is the weakness," Tynan acknowledged taking my hand in his. Steadying his gaze with mine, Tynan's markings pulsed purple. Warmth poured through that small opening in the web, swirling around me.

The brand on my arm began to glow, lightly, but I watched the purple light gain intensity around the weakness in the cobweb and knew how to escape. With all my strength, I dug my nails into Tynan's palm.

Tynan grinned broadly; his pupils dilated with excitement. A moment later, my branding was shining brightly. A purple fire ignited in the sky, the web erupted, burning bright and hot. The fire licked my consciousness, scorching through the middle of my mind in much the same way as a brain freeze.

The opening was visible now, widening slowly. Reaching through the flames, ignoring the blistering pain, I yanked the web down around my ankles. When I stepped out of the spell, the burning in my head cut off abruptly.

Blinking rapidly, tears threatening to spill forward with the immediate relief I felt, I threw myself forward into Tynan's arms. "They are going to kill you." My whisper almost lost to the pounding footsteps as others ran into the room.

Slowly removing my arms from him, Tynan stepped away. "Check her for any other traps by your sister, Arachne. I need to speak to the King." Tynan started to walk out. "Make sure she's safe, Pride."

"You broke free of my sister's enchantment?" Arachne asked suspiciously.

"Tynan used the brand to break me free."

Arachne placed her hands on either side of my head. "She must not have known about the connection, though the question remains how they knew about you at all. Seelie men rarely ever bother with their human progeny."

I didn't correct her theory that my mother was human. "I'm more interested in why they did it?"

Arachne's eyes smiled at me. "That is the right question. Tell me about the dream." When I hesitated, her brow lifted. "That good, huh?"

My cheeks heated and I looked away. "The Prince and I were being intimate..."

"Stop," Pride interrupted, his face full of concern. "Wait till the prince returns."

"Why?" Pride glared at Arachne; she shook her head. "How you know so much about other people's business is beyond me, Pride."

"I've been around a very long time, Arachne. You are not the first dream weaver I've encountered." Pride turned a cautioning gaze on me. "Tell her only what her sister did."

Slightly awed by the tension between Pride and Arachne, I cleared my throat to talk. "She spat in my mouth and muttered under her breath. Then Cathal arrived."

"Cathal? Captain of the Solaris?" Arachne asked suspiciously. Picking up the sketch pad, I showed her the drawings of the dream. "You drew these while tranced?"

"No, that didn't happen until the sun started to rise. That's when I lost control of my body."

Considering the sketches, Arachne frowned. "Messina, did they finish?"

"What do you mean?" Arachne pointed to the picture of me being held down for Cathal. "No. I screamed the moment he touched me, and I woke up." Staring at me, Arachne swallowed with difficulty and stepped away. "I'm guessing that's not good?"

Ignoring me, Arachne glanced at Pride. "Do you know the Prophecy of the Dark Prince?" When Pride nodded his head, Arachne gulped. "Do you know if they have..."

"I assume so."

"Are you sure?"

"I heard him with her, so there is no need for your concern. Esha and all the other Sluagh still need glamor to walk amongst the humans. If you know the prophecy, you know the first thing to happen after the mating was all the Sluagh woke up Sidhe," Pride reminded her.

Nodding, Arachne composed herself. She blurred in my vision and then a shadow that looked arm length and tapered to a point appeared in her hand. "Messina, have you consummated your flesh with the Prince?" Arachne's entire body was tense, ready to pounce.

'Lie.'

Wide-eyed, looking between Pride and Arachne, I followed my instinct. "He had me last night."

The tension in the air dissipated and Arachne relaxed. "Did you enjoy it?"

'I loved it. I lost myself to how amazing Tynan's touch felt that it took the cold of his spunk to bring me back to reality.' Remembering how cold he was when he'd finished with me, my mood sank to the floor. "You were right, the Prince offers coldness."

Arachne smiled in kindness. Coming back into clear focus, the shadow in her hand vanished. "I will report to the prince and King." In a swirl of purple silk, Arachne left.

Tilting my head back, I spied Pride standing behind me. "She was going to kill me, wasn't she?"

"If you hadn't lied, she would have tried. It is best that everyone believes the prince has violated you and that you revile his attention."

Turning to face Pride, I leaned on the back of the lounge. "How did you know it was a lie?"

"I have known the Prince a long time. Unlike the Sidhe, I have seen him naked." Pride lowered himself to whisper to me. "You would not be moving so freely this morning if he had sunk himself within you."

Meeting his eyes, at this proximity, they took up nearly all my vision. "Unless he healed me after."

"He wouldn't. He would want you to feel him every time you moved." Pride moved his large mouth to my ear. I swear it was big enough to bite half my head off. "It is not common knowledge that the Prince can heal, Messina. Best keep that information to yourself." Pride straightened, he turned to leave then paused. "What did the prince do, in your dream, while the Solaris held you?" He pointed to the sketch.

"He told them to stop, that I wasn't tainted, that they couldn't force my choice. He told them not to touch me."

Pride lifted a brow. "Don't tell anyone he said those words. Not even the Prince."

11
————

SOURCES

❖

The forest was strange, not quite how I would expect it to look. No matter how much I tried, I couldn't see the sky. "It's an underground forest," Tynan's voice came from behind me. "We have tubes similar to skylights installed to reflect daylight down without exposing our skin to direct sunlight."

"Oh!"

"Disappointed you can't just smash the window and escape into the forest?" Tynan chuckled at my pout.

"Basically." Turning on my heel, I moved towards where he stood, dressed in his suit for the day. He looked annoyed. "Arachne told you?"

"And the King. We need to discuss last night, but I have a meeting in thirty minutes."

"It's not like I'm going anywhere." Nodding at my observation, Tynan stood watching me as if waiting for something. The image of me kissing him flashed in my mind. Blinking quickly, wondering if that's what Tynan was after, I took the steps towards him tentatively. His pupils dilated as I entered into his personal space, rose on my tiptoes, and pressed my lips to his. It was a tame kiss, compared to the one from yesterday.

Tynan didn't push for anything more. He waited for me to pull back, giving me the control over the kiss. His face was stern, like his talk with the King had stolen all his happiness. "Esha will stay and begin your training today. He is a great warrior, though, a terrible teacher. He has no patience."

"Would someone else not be a better choice then?" Searching for Esha behind him, I was too close to see anything.

"No." Picking up his laptop bag and cane, Tynan turned to leave. "Try not to provoke him to rip your throat out. He's my best friend; I don't want to have to punish him."

Blinking wide eyes at his attitude, I watched Tynan leave. Esha bowed his head to Tynan then turned his attention to me. "Have you eaten?"

"No."

"Then let's go." He waved his hand towards the door. Stepping forward, Pride gave me a discreet nod. Sucking in a breath, I moved to meet them.

Esha led the way to the kitchen, Pride following behind me. We passed several people, a few Sluagh from who I dropped my gaze as Nora taught me.

"Is that her?" A female stared.

"Look at the eyes; she's part Seelie," gossiped her friend.

Several goblins were moving about the corridors, I met their eyes, and they gave small nods of acknowledgment. The Unseelie Sidhe just watched me pass in curiosity. They paid Esha no attention at all, which only irritated Esha more. By the time we reached the kitchen and found Amp, the Captain of the Lunar Guard sitting there eating with another soldier, I was prepared for Esha to rip my throat out just for the pain of being seen with me.

"Margo, please get the Prince's new toy some food. She'll need the energy today." Stalking over to the pantry, Esha came back out with a bag of...

"You eat cheese curls?" I found it somewhat beguiling to see a monster eating human food.

"You think we kill people three times a day?" Rolling his eyes,

Esha shook his head. "Think about it, with how many of us there are to how many humans are out there. We'd exterminate the city in a month. A lot of what you know about us is what we want people to think. If everyone thinks we are vile, twisted, creatures, they fear us and stay out of our way."

"I watched you murder an entire room of people, drinking their blood and devouring their flesh."

Esha glared at me. "That wasn't just Sluagh in that room, and so what? We aren't allowed to have a bit of fun on our Prince's birthday?"

His attitude made me want to vomit. "Fun? I watched my friend have her throat ripped open."

"Your friend was street trash, or she wouldn't have been there."

"Don't you dare! You know nothing about her, what her life was like, what she went through at the hands of others."

"Trash, by definition, is another person's waste. It doesn't matter about the person. She was unwanted by anyone, unloved. No one cared what happened to her. We take other people's trash and use it how we want." Observing the anger and tears threatening to spill down my cheeks, Esha huffed. "I don't know why you are so upset. It's not like she died screaming."

Launching at him, I grabbed him by the throat. Dropping his chips, Esha used my propulsion to turn us, and then slammed me into the wall behind him, one single hand around my throat. "But, of course, that would hurt you. You were the same, weren't you? The humans threw you away like nothing."

Holding onto his wrist, I didn't try and fight him. He wasn't strangling me, just holding me by my neck. "Wrong! They didn't discard me. I chose that life over my other option. Just like Lisa chose that life over being whored out against her will. Not everyone you kill is trash. Some of us are survivors of monsters much worse than you could ever be, monsters who prey on children and their innocence."

Pupils dilating, Esha removed his hand and released me. Sagging a little, I checked my throat before continuing.

"Lisa's father raped her throughout her childhood. When she was fourteen, he started charging others to share the joy. They would beat and rape her every weekend, sometimes for days on end. He wasn't just selling her body; he was selling her soul.

"She survived that, escaped it, only to die moaning while one of you ate her soul. And you have the gall to look me in the eye and call it a bit of fun? Have some respect for your food and what they must have gone through to end up where they did."

Glaring at the ground gritting his teeth, Esha growled and slapped me across the face.

"What the hell...?" Cradling my stinging cheek, I glared at him.

"You made me drop my cheese curls," Esha complained, but the anger wasn't there. "Now, get your breakfast. I have real work to do. I'm not babysitting you all day." Storming out, Esha kicked the cheese curls across the floor as he did. Margo waited till the door shut, then raced forward to clean up the mess.

Watching me quietly, Pride remained tense as I moved to the table. Frustration, grief, and survivor's guilt eating away my insides as I sat down.

"You okay?" Amp reached across from his table to touch my hand. He the other soldier watched the show.

"Yes, he didn't hurt me." My mind was slowly recovering from the confrontation. Spying the plate of food in front of Amp reminded me why I was here. "Margo, do you have toast please?" With a nod, Margo went off to make me some toast.

"You should try the pancakes. Margo is a brilliant cook." Much like when boys talked to me at school, Amp's attention made me uncomfortable. I bit my lip hoping he'd stop talking to me. Pride's eyes narrowed on Amp. Folding his arms, Pride leaned against the door, watching and listening.

"I heard you had an eventful morning. Are you sure you're okay?"

"What part of any of my current situation should I be okay with?" Glaring at him, Amp inhaled and looked away. Huffing, I remembered none of this was Amp's fault. "I'm alive. No one has eaten me or beaten me so far today."

"You spoke to Esha with great passion. Did humans hurt you like they hurt your friend?"

Looking away ashamed, I exhaled hard. "Humans acted like the demons they accused me of being."

The weight of my answer settled over the kitchen. Taking several deep breaths, Amp then stood. "Excuse me." He marched out. The soldier with him met my eyes with sympathy and followed his friend out. Looking at Pride, I found his narrowed eyes now focused on me.

The door swung open, and a troll strolled into the kitchen. The troll's gut was large and hairy where it hung over a tartan kilt. The muscles in his arms and back were massive and bulging. Giant demon green eyes swept over me, and a black tongue slid across his bottom lip. Shifting his position, Pride gained the trolls attention. "Pride."

"Borg. She is the Prince's."

"I didn't ask.".

"I'm telling you, just the same."

Glancing at me one last time, Borg then flinched away as if looking at me hurt him. Moving on, he opened a heavy door, releasing freezing air into the kitchen, the chill tickling my ankles. After thumping around inside, Borg came back out with a human leg on his shoulder. The limb was a chunky thigh, cut from the body at the hip joint, and female if the stiletto heel still on foot was any indication. My eyes were wide watching him shut the freezer door, but I couldn't look away from the ghastly creature hoisting the chubby leg like it was a shoulder of beef.

A plate of toast sliding across the table in front of me drew my attention. Looking at the perfectly cooked toast, I waited to see if the troll left. If the creature planned to sit and eat in front of me, I had no chance of swallowing one bite of toast. Thankfully, avoiding looking at me, Borg nodded once at Pride and left the kitchen.

"Is that normal?" My voice squeaked giving my best impression of a mouse.

Lifting a brow, Pride settled back into his watchful position. "Yes. They enjoy a good spit roast."

My mind tried to replace the typical image of a pig on a spit with a human leg. It couldn't or wouldn't do it. Blinking the encounter out of my head, I returned my focus to my toast. There was a choice of condiments on the table, the jam suddenly not as appealing. I had just finished spreading peanut butter on my toast when Esha came through the kitchen door.

"Margo, I apologize for the mess I made. Please, accept my apologies for messing up your kitchen?" He bowed presenting her with a daisy.

"From outside?" Margo asked awed.

"From the field." Snatching it from his grasp, Margo darted away. Turning his Gaze my way, Esha folded his hands behind his back. "When you were on the streets, how did you survive?" Glaring at him, I bit into my toast. Esha gritted his teeth, taking the seat opposite me. "Pride, help me out here, please?"

Pride stayed leaning against the wall. "Sluagh are unsettlingly polite and have a great love of formality. To ignore them when they ask you a question is extremely rude. The Sluagh react badly to rudeness."

"Oh!" I dropped my toast. "I apologize, I haven't seen behavior that would indicate politeness or formality in my two days of captivity."

"We provided you with a decent room, and we have treated you well," Esha rumbled, holding his temper.

Considering debating that I'd been tortured and forced into a man's bed, I decided not to start another fight. "I lived in the boiler room of the university with Lisa. I was on a scholarship which paid my tuition, and I cleaned the cafeteria tables to eat."

"You were studying? They will have noticed you missing by now."

"Don't worry. Students go missing all the time. No one looks into why they stopped showing up. They write them up as another dropout unless the family reports them missing. In my case, as you so kindly pointed out, I'm unwanted, unloved, and easily forgotten." Picking up my toast, I returned to eating.

Huffing, Esha shook his head. "I have known you a matter of two days, and I would not so easily forget you."

Lifting my gaze, I rolled my eyes. "So full of compliments. What happened to the Esha I first met?"

"I spent six weeks trying to find you, Messina. The day we met, I'd gone five days sleeping in corridors, disguising myself to capture you. A foul mood doesn't cover it. Besides, you are Seelie Sidhe. They are despicable, underhanded creatures." When I raised a brow at his description, Esha looked at my plate. "Is that all you are eating?"

"I'm used to barely having anything. This was a gourmet meal."

"Then let's go."

With a nod, I carried my plate back to the bench while Esha walked to the door. "Thank you, Margo." As I handed her the plate, she stealthily slipped me a piece of paper. Sliding the paper in my sleeve, I went to the door. Pride followed me out, and Esha led the way.

❧

HITTING THE MAT WITH A GRUNT, I whimpered. "Time out."

"Get up. You are part Sidhe; you must have better stamina than this?"

"For running, yes. For having the wind knocked out of me repeatedly, not so much."

Growling, Esha looked at his watch. "It's only been four hours."

"Seriously?" I couldn't believe he thought four hours of fighting was nothing.

Squatting before me, Esha tucked my hair back so he could see my face. "Thousands of years ago we allowed the Unseelie Sidhe to build their mansion above our faerie mound and establish their court. We lived in a tentative peace. Two hundred years ago, our numbers were at their lowest, and the Sidhe tried to drive us out. We fought, nonstop, for forty-one days. It was the prince who rallied us, and after we won, it was the Prince who found a way for us to swell our ranks, to walk amongst humans again, and to thrive again.

"Now, our numbers are three times that of the Unseelie Sidhe. We have our fingers in the human business world giving us access to vast resources and unlimited funds. We have everything we need, and it's all because of our half-blood prince." Esha stared at my eyes, not into them, at them, pressing the importance of what he educated.

"She was wrong. The Unseelie Sidhe may have no loyalty, but the Sluagh do."

Esha stood back to his full height. "Finally, you are catching on." He swung his foot at my stomach. Catching it, pushing my body back to stop impact, I jerked away, taking his foot with me. Esha fell on his back with a grunt.

Rolling, I got to my feet. "Argh! I seriously need a pair of sweats for training. My legs keep getting tangled in my skirt.".

Esha got to his feet. "If they tangle your feet, imagine what they could do to an opponent," he lectured as he circled me. "You will not always be expecting an attack..."

"In this place, I will be."

"...so, learn to use what you have available to you." Esha attacked again. Bruises were blooming on my skin already.

Another three hours later, I was starving and very sore. Pride finally reminded Esha I had barely eaten and already been through a lot this morning.

Grumbling about getting some work done, Esha left Pride to escort me back to Tynan's suite. Excusing myself to my bedroom, I pulled the note from Margo out. It was the same question as last time, the one she never got to read. Smiling, I used my pencil to write the same answer, then hid it back up my sleeve. Looking around my room for a hiding place, I frowned when I realized I'd need to find a method to get rid of Margo's notes straight away.

Going downstairs, Pride materialized out of the hallway instantly. "Is it normal to put a slave in the room next to the owner?"

"That all depends on what type of slave it is. You, however, are not a slave. You are a possession. There is a difference."

"What's the difference?"

"The value placed on the object. The Sluagh are known for their violence, but their nicknames are 'the secret keepers.' They love gathering information. The bigger the secret, the more joy they gain from knowing it."

"They blackmail people?"

Pride shrugged. How could someone so big be so graceful? "Sometimes, not always. Sometimes they trade secrets. I suspect the Sluagh's success in the human world has been through corporate espionage and using their majicks to gain inside information.

Pride took a step closer. "Secrets are not the only commodity they trade in. Any items of nostalgia are of value to them. Strange knick-knacks," Pride caressed my cheek with his humungous finger, "broken toys. Anything that evokes emotion in others makes for an excellent item for trade. It mystifies the Sidhe, the value the Sluagh place on some items, but perversity is the sluagh's trademark."

"I'm a broken toy to them?" My throat constricted on the thought.

Pride tilted his head. "Would you say you are other?"

"No." I shook my head, knowing what he said was true. "I'd love a cup of tea and some crackers. Is there a kitchenette in here?"

"I'll call down the kitchen and have Margo send you something."

"Thank you, Pride."

In my room, I picked up my sketchbook. I needed to remind myself where I was, who I was with, and why I needed to escape. I drew Lisa, and then I sketched Lisa being killed. Every face I remembered during the massacre was detailed, taking the time to perfect the blissful appearances on the victim's faces while they were eaten alive.

My tea was brought in by a goblin. Pride escorted her in, then back out. When I finished eating, I placed the note for Margo under the cup saucer and went back to my sketches.

There was an above ground mansion above the Faerie mound. Maybe I could escape from there? I needed to get back to the garden, to my jacket which held my license. I needed to talk to my mother and find out why her people attacked me.

Taking notice of the sketch of Tynan I'd just been drawing, I stopped and stared at the memory of the surprise on his face after our first kiss. "I need to get away from you."

12

FIGHTING THE UNKNOWN

❖

"You look exhausted," Tynan observed as I removed my dress and laid on his bed. He was sitting in his reading chair, reading, and I was purposefully ignoring the fact he wasn't wearing his shirt.

"I am. I fell asleep in my bed drawing." Thankfully, I'd set the alarm on the clock for midnight, so I could transfer rooms.

Putting his book aside, Tynan switched out the room light. I rolled over to turn off the bedside lamp. "Leave it on. Finish the story."

"Which one?"

"How you bartered for your license."

Unimpressed with the topic, I turned my head and glared in his general direction, the shadows of the room protecting him from my vision. When I heard him undressing in the dark, I realized he didn't want me to see him naked. A new thought entered my mind. Maybe the lack of light protected me. A shudder vibrated through my body like a Mexican wave at the idea.

"Are you going to sit there getting turned on by my sins instead of talking about what happened this morning?" I complained, trying not to think about why Tynan needed to hide his male bits. Every other male I'd known was proud of their appendage.

"Yes. What happened?"

Closing my eyes in shame, I looked away. "They shared me."

"At the same time?"

"Yes."

"They penetrated you simultaneously?" Swallowing a lump of hate and humiliation for something I couldn't even remember in detail; I kept my eyes averted. The baby rattlesnake started shaking its tail again. "Describe it to me, how they shared you."

Since the memory of it was blurry, I gave him the bare details, keeping it short and straighforward. I wasn't going to embellish just for him to get his rocks off.

The maracas grew louder as I talked, filling me with a desire to touch him, and in turn, have Tynan touch me. Finishing my swift walk down memory lane, I sat up and slid off the bed before I even knew where I was going.

"What are you doing?" Tynan's anger a hot wind against my naked chest. The impact of his emotion forced the air from my lungs and startled me to a halt.

Unsure by my actions and confused why that rattle filled me with such desire, I chose to answer honestly. "I want to touch you. I want to see you, and understand how and why your arousal makes that noise."

"Stay on the bed."

"Ty, please. I need to touch you?"

"Stay on the bed!" Silver pupils flashed at me from the dark, the viciousness in his growl ripping through the air, claws digging into my throat and forcing me back.

My bum dropped to the mattress automatically, and my fingers touched the sudden ache in my throat. Wetness greeted my fingers, and when I moved my hand to see them in the lamplight, blood colored them. My breath rushed from me that just the sound of Tynan's voice could harm me.

With wide eyes, I sat very still, adrenaline racing through my blood, heart pounding in my ears, breath short and painful. Taking a moment to calm, Tynan's long inhale and sigh audibly even over the orchestra of terror inside me. The silver glow of beastly eyes faded into the darkness.

"Your needs are not what this is about, Mess. Spread your legs and lean back." Tears leeched from my eyes. I didn't want to cry, but the combination of fear and humiliation was too much. Unable to do this, I shook my head. "You let two men have you at the same time, but you can't expose yourself to me?"

"That was a different situation."

"That's right, you only give it up when you are getting something you want out of it. Fine, I'll give you the rest of your art supplies."

"You're an arse!" Glaring through watery eyes in his direction, the darkness shrouded him while the lamplight exposed my shame for his amusement.

"Lean back and spread your legs, Messina, or I will force you to do much worse," Tynan warned.

For a moment, I considered his threat as just that, and then I decided I was too exhausted to find out the punishment for disobeying. Leaning back on my elbows, I did as he wanted.

"Tell me about the dream last night."

Lifting my face to the ceiling, I blinked my eyes clear of the tears. Of course, Tynan wanted to discuss that now. "We were in bed together..."

"Sleeping?"

Closing my eyes, I sighed at the memory of his touching me in the dream. "Not so much."

"What were we doing?"

"More than we are doing now." My elbows dropped out from underneath me to stare up at the ceiling. "They came, took you away, the woman spat in my mouth and left, and then the soldiers held me down for him."

"Arachne said you broke free of the spell when he touched you?"

"Yes. I didn't like how Cathal felt. It felt like a hundred elastic bands were snapped against the inside of my head when he touched me." The memory of the discomfort made me wince. "I screamed, and woke up."

"That's what Arachne worries about the most. You should not have been able to break free of her sister's weave. I was meant to wake in the morning and think you were dead."

"Why?" I was too tired for this conversation.

"A dead toy is useless to me."

"Why do they care?" The bed was comfortable, pulling me into its warmth, beckoning me to sleep.

"Because they want you back." Tynan's voice seemed closer, but my eyelids were too heavy to check. Warmth caressed the inside of my thigh.

"That's silly," I whispered as I floated into sleep. "They never had me."

SHIVERING IN MY DREAM, I woke cold. I was in bed, the covers pulled over me, but they weren't warming me. Squinting my eyes, I could make out the silhouette of Tynan's sleeping form across the bed. With my teeth clicking under the force of my shaking, I scooted closer to Tynan's warmth and wrapped myself around him.

Tynan's body tensed. "What are you doing?"

"I know I'm just a toy to you, but I'm a cold toy which requires warmth, lest I get sick and die."

"Then stop hugging me."

"But you're so warm to touch?" I whined against his back, already feeling the heat of his skin suffusing my body.

"You told Arachne I was cold to touch."

"I told her you only offered coldness. I was speaking of your heart, not your body." Sighing as my body relaxed against his, my teeth stopped chattering, and I slowly stopped shivering. "She was going to kill me if she thought I enjoyed being with you."

"Why do you say that?"

"Ask Pride," I sighed as I drifted back to sleep. Taking my hand resting on his waist, Tynan moved it up to his mouth. He kissed my fingertips then placed my hand on his chest. I snuggled in closer.

In the morning, I was the exact opposite of cold. Blinking open my eyes, I found my face buried in Tynan's neck, his arms wrapped around me, holding me tight to the front of him. I'd never felt this good waking up in the morning.

Something moved between us under the sheets. Curious, I placed my hand down there and felt something warm and rough brush against the back of my hand. Turning my wrist, I allowed it to slide into my palm, and then I gripped one side of it. That's all my hand encompassed.

It felt different to a human man's; the same sort of texture as skin, smooth and dry, but rough like raw silk. As it grew in my hold, I explored it by touch.

Grooves were running around the shaft in a spiral, much like a flesh corkscrew, but where there should have been a point at the top, was what felt like a bulging cap nearly the size of my fist. A tear escaped my eye as I realized I'd been right. We weren't physically compatible.

Exploring the silky-smooth dome, it was just like a human mans, but where it joined the length of him, there was a ring of nodules. Focusing on these fleshy bumps, I ran my thumb and finger around them, over them. It began to tremor subtly in my hand, and the baby rattlesnake woke up, the muted sound of maracas penetrating the silence.

A gasp caught in my throat. As soon as the rattle started, my body reacted. No longer was my exploration one of curiosity and fear, but one of desire and need.

With my face buried against Tynan's neck, I bit my lip and began stroking him, learning how he reacted to my touch. In my head I prayed to God for how much I loved the feel of his strong hands on me, pressing into my back tightly.

Moaning as my body grew tighter with desire, the rattle rose in pitch, the vibrations had increased in frequency in my hand, and I loved it. Wanting more and knowing it couldn't happen, I whimpered.

Exhaling hard, Tynan pulled me tighter to him. He'd been awake from the moment I touched him. I'd expected him to stop me, but he'd allowed my exploration to continue, and now he encouraged it.

Reaching between us, Tynan moved my hand on him, showing me how he liked to be touched. Moaning his name into the nook of his neck, I complied with his need.

The rattlesnake pulsed in my hand as Tynan groaned. Suddenly, I was on my back, hands pinned overhead, as cold Sluagh lust squirted over my stomach.

Looking down, I hoped to finally see the instrument that inspired my desire and fear equally, but Tynan blocked my view when he dropped his face to mine and kissed me passionately. Moving his body, Tynan covered himself before he pulled away, putting his back to me.

Lying there panting, I trailed one finger lazily through the cold goo on my stomach. "Why do I feel as relaxed as I normally do after climaxing?"

"The power of satiability. Sating me releases your power. It gives you the same endorphin rush as climaxing."

"I kind of like doing this with you."

"You won't like it if I lose control." His tone suggested he nearly did just that.

Considering how good it made me feel and how wretched it felt to be denied, I had to wonder whether giving in would be so awful. "I'm willing to risk it."

Turning quickly, Tynan grabbed my jaw violently. "Are you a masochist, Mess? Only a masochist would even entertain the idea of that happening."

"No! I've suffered enough pain to last a lifetime. You healed me; you know how many broken bones I suffered. You are experienced enough with hurting someone to know how badly they hurt me while they tried to beat the demon out of me. This isn't about the pain. I want how good it feels to be touched by you, how my body reacts to your arousal. I want pleasure that I consent to, and if it's the only thing I'm going to get out of being your possession, then I will take as much of it as I can and worry about the consequences later."

Recoiling as if I'd slapped him, Tynan released his grip on me. Rolling off the bed angrily, I rushed into the bathroom and slammed the door. Tears were streaming down my face. Swiping them away, I was angry that I was upset about his refusal to try having sex with me.

Turning on the shower, I stared at myself in the mirror. "Get a grip, Mess. He's a man. A different species and a gorgeous specimen aside, he is a disgusting male determined to make your life hell. Use him and get the hell out of here."

What made me angrier, was that I knew it didn't matter how much I lectured myself. My body was still high from Tynan's warm touch. I could tell my brain not to care all I wanted; my body was remembering how great his hands felt, how different his...bits felt, and the curiosity of whether the pleasure of sex with the first man to feel right, could outdo the pain of having him inside me.

That's when I burst into tears and sank to the floor of the shower. Of everything that just happened, it's that I was even considering the idea of sex with a monster that broke me.

When I finally emerged from the bathroom, Tynan had his pants on and was sitting on the bed reading the newspaper on his tablet. There was a tray next to him with two cups, a pot of coffee by the smell, and two plates with breakfast foods piled high on them.

Setting aside his device, Tynan patted the bed. "Come and eat while I tell you how this is going to work, Mess."

Ensuring the towel covered me, I set myself down and tentatively took a croissant.

Eyeing the towel tucked around my breasts, Tynan licked his lips. "Where is your dress?"

"It was a bit manky after two days of wear and seven hours of training yesterday. I've hung it up to dry in the bathroom."

"You only have the one dress? What happened to the one you were wearing at the nightclub?"

"Still with my stuff in my hiding place."

"Should I ask how you got that Sidhe dress?" Tynan looked toward the bathroom.

"The faerie mound provided it," I answered around the food I was chewing.

"Of course, it did," Tynan sighed. "It can't be known to anyone but us, that you enjoy my attention, Mess. Most women don't, and it would be a bad omen for you too."

"I figured that yesterday with Arachne." Pouring a cup of coffee, I lifted it to my lips.

"We will enjoy each other here only." He patted the bed. "But, once we are outside those doors, you will act disgusted by my touch. Understood?"

Lowering my eyes, I picked at the towel. "What if I can't?"

"I will hurt you to make it seem like you do."

My stomach was in knots. Anticipation and despair of my situation. Tynan got off on hurting me. I'd seen it when he broke my rib and pierced my lung. The climax he almost achieved from healing me. "Either way, pleasure for you."

Glancing at me out of the corner of his eye, Tynan put his coffee back on the tray. "When we are alone in here, we need to be careful not to lose control of our desires."

"Can I ask why? It can't be about hurting me; you enjoy that, and you get off on healing me, so that's not what is holding you back."

Taking the cup out of my hand, Tynan put it on the tray before he moved it off the bed. "There is a prophecy about a Seelie Sidhe and me. The prophecy says she will be the one to take my coldness, to take my people out of the darkness and into the light."

Sitting with his back to me for a moment longer, Tynan turned his entire body to face me. "There are many interpretations of what that means. Some think it means she will break the spell, grant them the beauty to walk amongst humans as the Sidhe can. Others believe she will remake us in the image of the Seelie. More still believe she will lead us to conquer the Seelie court."

"What do you believe?"

"I believe, that it's all a load of hogwash. We already can glamor, so looking Sidhe is the norm. No one could reform the Sluagh, or incite us to conquer the Seelie court. We follow the Unseelie ways, but we rarely get involved in other Fae business."

"Then why does it matter?"

"Because the others believe it, and they will kill you if they even get a hint that you could be her."

"Her who?"

Sighing in exasperation, Tynan shrugged. "No description is ever given of her, only that she will find warmth where others find cold. That she would find pain, where others find pleasure. She would find pleasure, where others find only pain." Caressing my cheek, Tynan met my eyes intently.

Registering his words, my mouth fell open. "You can't even think it's me?"

"I'm not willing to let anyone else think it is."

"But shouldn't we just, do it?" Tynan raised a humored brow at me. "I mean, that would put it all to rest. No one has to worry I will bring on the apocalypse, and if I do, then we'll deal with it after it happens."

Growling low in his chest, Tynan stood straight. "Maybe you are right." Unzipping his pants, he dropped them to the ground. I'm pretty sure all the blood drained from my face. Observing me, Tynan lifted a brow. "Not so keen now?" I

Shaking my head slowly, I stared at his phallus until Tynan collected his pants and pulled them back into place. How could such a gorgeous man have such a hideous appendage?

Tynan sat on the bed beside me. "Even for the Sluagh, I'm considered monstrous."

"So that's not the norm for them?" I swallowed, still seeing it like it was in front of me.

"The ridges and the nodules yes. The size and texture, no. Like Humans, Sluagh reproductive organs have the same smooth texture as their skin. Sluagh women used to come into heat during intercourse, that's what the ridges and nodules activated, as well as extra pleasure. When the Seelie queen cursed all the Sluagh to hunger instead of breeding, they stopped going on heat, but the pleasure derived from sex is still higher than that with a Sidhe."

"Why are you different?"

Tynan exhaled. "The choice was stolen from me by my birth, as it was stolen from my mother when my father raped her."

"Choice?" My mind was whirring, trying to keep up with Tynan's words, but still stuck on what he brandished between his legs.

"Every Sidhe has a choice, but when someone forces the decision on them, the goddess inflicts punishment."

"Shouldn't it punish those that are responsible?"

Tynan's eyes turned mercurial. "It does. My father's rape led to my conception. My birth denied my mother the choice. This is my curse for stealing my mother's future."

"That's wrong. A child can't be held responsible for their father's actions."

"Someone had to be."

Silence fell between us for several long moments. My brain was filtering through questions and determining which would be a priority to know the answer too. For sure, Tynan's patience and willingness to communicate wouldn't be long-lasting. "Do the others know you are..." Was cursed the right word?

"Some. Rumors got around that I was a monstrous half-breed that even the Sluagh wouldn't bed, and that was that."

"So, you haven't been with a woman for a while?" I queried self-consciously.

Tynan scrutinized me. "Not one who enjoyed it, no. Not one who calls out my name and nearly gets off just touching me."

Heat crept up my neck, warming my cheeks. As the situation dawned on me, I sobered. "It's strange isn't it?"

"That you like it?"

"No, that your people worship you, but not enough that they will grit their teeth and bear your touch. I was loathed and despised as a demon by mine, but they used my flesh every chance they got."

Shoulders tightening, Tynan ground his jaw. "Firstly, they weren't you're people. Secondly, that's because sex to Unseelie is a pleasure always deserved and taken. Sex to humans is debasement and domination. Your stepfather used you for his pleasure, but in his mind, he was also reducing you down to the nothing he thought you were. That's why he shared you.".

"May I remind you, you got off last night with that story."

"I didn't. You were very clinical in the way you described what happened. You got off, but you hated what happened. You've convinced yourself it needed to happen and placed your body and pleasure in a state where it gets you what you need, not what you desire."

Tynan squeezed my hand. "So, tell me honestly, Mess, what do you think you're going to use your body to get from me?" I met Tynan's eyes. "Ah." He stood walking to the bathroom. "No one has ever escaped, Mess."

"That's not true." Frowning, I looked up to meet his gaze. "I've escaped before, and once I remember how I did it, I'm going to do it again."

13
____

HOLD THAT THOUGHT

❖

"*I've escaped before, and once I remember how I did it, I'm going to do it again.*"

Taking one threatening step forward, Tynan snatched me off the bed, his grip biting into my flesh. His mouth closed over mine in a possessive and passionate kiss. His fingers entwined in my hair, gripping to control how my head moved. My body heated with desire, pressing forward, yearning to feel more of the warmth he offered. Sucking my lip into his mouth, Tynan bit down hard. Pain shocked me, a cry escaping my injured lips as I tried to shove him away, but he held me tight, his fingertips leaving imprints in the forms of bruises.

"You belong to me, Mess. I'm not letting you get away from me again," Tynan growled, his irises mercury warning bells. The side of his mouth pulled up in a sinister smile, then he threw me on the bed, ripped the towel off, and sank his fangs into my neck. Choking on a scream of pain, Tynan pulled back, blood staining his vicious Sluagh mouth. His eyes observed the river of tears across my cheeks, then his face fell to my breast, and he sank teeth into flesh again. Tynan bit me in several other places, then he left me crying and bleeding on the bed, and went about getting showered for the day.

~

THE KNOCK on my door startled me from my sketch of a room I remembered as a child here. Not that I'd known it was in the castle, but it was slowly coming back to me in dribs and drabs. Trell let herself in before I could respond to the knock. "The prince would like you to join us downstairs." Pausing, she watched me lick the scab on my lip. "Did he do that to you?"

He did, but I wasn't going to admit it to her. When I failed to respond, Trell frowned. "I guess that's what you get for riling the monster up."

She was still jealous of the way I kissed him in front of her. "If you're not willing to sate your prince, don't get angry when he takes it elsewhere," I replied coolly. "I didn't ask for this."

Her scarlet eyes trailed the visible bruises. Swallowing the distaste on her features, Trell stood tall. "Fate can be cruel."

"Is that your middle name?"

Glaring at me, Trell turned to walk out, but I saw a small smile tilt her mouth. "Come on, Seelie trash, don't keep the Prince waiting."

Groaning, I followed her downstairs and into the lounge room. A female Sluagh stood watching me approach as she talked to Tynan. She wore a black leather corset with gold buckles, red lace covering her breasts, and a dark red velvet mini skirt with splits to her pelvis. The black punk style boots and a top hat decorated with the red lace finished her impressive ensemble. Her lava eyes considered me from head to toe, then returned their attention to Tynan.

Moving to stand in front of the fire, I planned to wait till Tynan finished with her to make my presence known. Turning his head to note my location, Tynan walked over to greet me. Grabbing my chin, he pressed a hard kiss to my mouth. Wincing with pain, I tried to shove him away, but Tynan kept hold of me, releasing a delighted chuckle.

"Brie, this is Messina, she needs a few dresses. A couple of dresses for formal evenings, the rest of her clothes for day wear. She's without any of her former belongings, so you'll be buying everything she needs."

Brie stepped forward, her lips turning up into a grin. "Of course, Prince Tynan. What style am I to follow? Ours or theirs?"

"Theirs. I've always wanted a Seelie doll to play with."

Brie's grin only grew, her eyes mapping me out, already designing my wardrobe. "Perfect. Do you know your sizes, Messina?" She noted down my sizes and request for a pair of sneakers for my escape plans, which Brie found humorous. "I'll have everything you need for dinner tonight."

"Thank you, Brie. I'd like Mess to come to the club tonight, so make sure she has an appropriate dress." Looking me over like a piece of meat, Tynan smirked. "Something bright. I wouldn't want to lose her in the crowd. It took long enough to find her the last time she got away from me."

Smiling mischievously, Brie bowed her head and left. As Tynan sat down on the lounge, I turned to go back upstairs. "Where are you going?"

"Back to my room." Pointing in its general direction, I was unsure why that was a problem.

"Stay here. I want to play with you."

Hating how he said it, I glared at him. Tynan lifted a brow at my defiance at the same time Pride cleared his throat. Exhaling in annoyance, I stayed by the fire.

"Thank you, everyone, you can go." Trell and Pride both bowed their heads and left. Tynan patted the seat next to him as an invitation. Gritting my teeth in annoyance, I moved towards him.

"I'm going to run an experiment, and you are going to cooperate."

"Am I just?" I raised a brow sarcastically.

"If you do everything I ask and give me honest answers to my questions," Tynan picked up a laptop bag from the other side of his seat and placed it on the coffee table, "this is your reward."

Forcing myself to swallow my excitement, I considered him. "With Internet access?" Maybe I could finish my university degree by correspondence, have my qualifications if I ever escaped.

"Monitored internet access."

That still worked. "What's the experiment?"

Shuffling from the hallway caught our attention. We turned around to see Esha hauling a perfect looking man into the room. "Him."

My head swung back to Tynan, unsure how to take that answer. Standing up, Tynan moved towards the man, circling him, eyes studying the specimen of perfection. "This is Nathani of the Seelie Sidhe. He's been our prisoner for...give or take a decade. Today, I'm offering him his freedom. All he has to do is have sex with you."

"Really?" Nathani asked.

"Why are you doing this?" I whispered as he passed by me.

Peering below his low brow at me, Tynan stepped closer placing his mouth to my ear. "By your behavior when we are alone, you're clearly keen for it, Mess. I'm giving you your release."

His eyes danced with joy as he pulled back and touched my sore lip, making me hiss. "Nathani is Sidhe. Human women and other Sidhe find them very pleasurable bedmates. You should be thanking me." Sitting down, Tynan made himself comfortable to watch the show.

Nathani walked towards me. "I'm missing something, aren't I?"

"Hopefully, not what's needed to earn your freedom," Tynan responded dryly, collecting his goblet and taking a sip.

"Does she get a say in this?"

"Show him your wrist." I held out my wrist so Nathani could see the mark. "She belongs to me. My will is her will." Tynan's eyes dared me to refuse.

Moving closer, Nathani touched my face tenderly. I flinched away. "Hey, it's okay. I'm not a brute like him. It'll be nice." Looking up, I met his eyes. Nathani frowned. "Nora?"

My eyes widened, and I backed away. Stepping forward quickly, Nathani grabbed my hair to force me to look up at him. "Tynan?" I begged for him to interfere.

"Nora's dead. I should know. I killed her. So why do you have her eyes?" Nathani growled. "Is this a trick? A glamor to taunt me?" He was yanking on my head with each question.

Esha and Tynan just stood there watching with interest. Reaching inside his elbow that gripped me, I stabbed my nails into the crease. With a yelp, he released me as I stepped into him and kneed him in the bits that mattered. He dropped to the floor.

"Maybe fates a bitch and going to make you stare into the eyes of your victims to earn your freedom." Gripping my hands together, I swung them as hard as I could to thump him in the face. He fell back on the floor. I stalked forward determined to do more damage, to hurt him like I was aching right now. Arms grabbed me from behind, restraining me, and dragged me backward. "No, let me go!" I thrashed against Esha.

Grabbing my forehead with his hand, Esha yanked my head back and put his teeth to my neck. Instantly, I froze with a pathetic whimper escaping my lips.

"Well, she learned something yesterday." Tynan nodded approval to Esha. "Nathani, if you are going to clear the forest before sundown, best you get started."

The Sidhe regained his feet and moved towards me cautiously. He looked at me for a long moment. "The child," he finally said with a sad nod. "The child she helped escape. She betrayed both her family and the King of the Unseelie to help you escape, and you ended up theirs anyway."

Closing my eyes forced my tears to run free. "I didn't know Nora was dead." I felt like a hope I'd always held within me just died.

Nathani moved closer to where Esha held me. He stroked my cheek again; ant bites followed his caress. I hissed from the discomfort it caused. Men touching me always hurt somewhat, but the Seelie seemed to come with a sting to their touch. The only man to have me without pain was giving me to this man. That thought caused a bitter taste to wrap around my tongue and slither down my throat.

My reaction caused Nathani to frown. His mouth turned down, and his eyes narrowed their focus. When he placed his full hand on my neck, I cried out at the pain of it. "I can't touch you without hurting you?"

Still held by Esha, all I could do was drop my head breathing through the sting slowly fading. Nathani turned to Tynan. "Is she bespelled. Is this a punishment of some kind?"

"Something like that. You can go, Nathani. The emotional pain you've caused is punishment enough."

Nathani bowed. I tried to go after him, but Esha still restrained me. "Wait! Why did you kill her?" I needed to know, though, I already knew, I needed it confirmed.

Nathani's eyes were full of sympathy. "Because of you. Your mother died because she wouldn't give them you."

"No!" My anguish rose up inside me, too much to hold. Throwing back my head, I howled it to the room. A funnel of water emerged from my feet, rising to engulf Esha and me where he held me. Darkness surrounded me, a severe storm closing around us.

In the tempest, I saw my mother pleading with Nathani to let her go, to make sure the child was safe before they punished her. There was nothing but her begging, and the howling of the terrifying storm as Nathani showed my mother no mercy. Calling her a traitor, he took her head. I wanted him to suffer the same fate.

The waterspout lifted till it was just a spinning disc of water above my head, then it flew across the room to a gapping Nathani and severed his head from his body. Blood fountained into the room, filling my vision in darkness and scarlet motes. My entire being zoned into his destruction, focusing my sorrow.

The noise of the storm in the room vanished, light returned, the room silent in the aftermath. Esha's slack arms still around me, I stared at the bloody mess that was a sliced and diced Seelie on the floor. The disc hadn't just taken his head; it dismembered him.

"I think I'm going to be sick." Collapsing to the floor, I started vomiting.

"Um, that's a pretty neat power," Esha sounded impressed. "Isn't that an ancient one?"

"If anyone asks, I dismembered him."

"Wait, you aren't going to let her acknowledge her powers?"

"Esha, that is an Unseelie power she just wielded. We will not be telling anyone she has it." Kneeling by me, Tynan placed his hand on my back, rubbing gently. Warmth tickled up my spine, soothing my cramping stomach. "Nora Bayne was your mother?"

Shaking my head, I stood up, avoiding looking at the pile of dismantled flesh while I wiped my mouth clean of puke. "If you've finished playing with me for now?" I was counting to a hundred in my head to keep my composure.

"Answer my question first, Messina. Who was Nora Bayne to you?"

I sucked in a breath to stop from crying. "Nora is the woman who helped me escape when I was five years old." I met his eyes. "I waited years for her to come back for me. Now I know why she never did."

Tynan's eyes held distrust, and who could blame him. His lips pressed together, a light deep in the blackness of his retinas grew, an excitement I couldn't understand.

Esha's brow furrowed, he steeped to Tynan's side. "You say you were five when Nora helped you escape?" Esha turned his face to Tynan, watching his tight leash on his expression. "You knew she was the child from the kitchen?"

Tynan inhaled deeply, his nose flaring as a secret he thought was his became Esha's. "I started to suspect only a day ago. You are free to go, Messina." My eyes went wide. "To your room."

Closing my eyes, I scolded myself. Of course, it was just a dismissal. Hugging myself tightly, I made my way upstairs, shivering from the cold emotions freezing my heart. Like a part of me just died. I can't explain it, but there was an emptiness inside me where there used to be light.

Maybe that was her. Perhaps, I'd kept a flame of hope burning all these years that I'd see my mother again. Now it was extinguished, and I felt like something deep inside me had shifted.

"Can I ask what that was?" Esha's low voice reached me as I walked on the balcony. The sound echoed around my emptiness.

"Manifestation. The user can take any emotion and embody it into a physical force. It's a spirit power."

"So, the manifestation is her spirit. Once you know her hands of power, the girl's secrets will be yours to wield." Esha shook his head in amusement as I reached my bedroom door.

"Not all her secrets, Esha."

When I looked down, Tynan was watching me. Hugging myself tighter, I stepped into my bedroom. I wanted to cry, but there was nothing left in me. Flopping on the bed, I stared at the wall, images of my mother playing with me as a child, of her teaching me how to cast a glamor, the first majick all Unseelie learn.

Sitting bolt upright on the bed, I stared at nothing. "I can perform glamor."

14

———————

REPEAT

❖

The music blared from the stereo system, bodies moved to the beat, grinding and bumping against each other. Scanning the room, I identified shadowed individuals who already started picking up their prey for the night. Bile churned in my stomach at the idea of watching this happen again.

I'd spent the night avoiding Tynan. Once we'd gotten to the club, he'd gone off to make sure things were running as they should be, leaving me in the care of Esha. Esha leaned against the bar, eyes appraising me, flicking to my fidgeting hands. My anxiety was running high, and there was nothing I could do to hide it tonight.

Like all the Sluagh tonight, Esha was covered in shadows, making his appearance blurry to my eyes. Only now, I knew that it was glamor and my powers were trying to see through his magic.

Scanning the room, I'd discovered that several of the Sluagh, while shadowed, still appeared their authentic appearance to me. It took me a while to realize that all the Sluagh differed in how well I could see through their glamor, and it made me understand that their magical abilities impacted on my power. I'd spent the afternoon practicing glamor in my room alone, remembering what my mother taught me.

'It's not enough to build a glamor people can see. The best glamor is the one people can touch and believe.'

"You look like the apocalypse is about to take place." Warm hands fell on my hips as Tynan pressed his body up behind me, heating me, a sigh falling from my lips involuntarily. "Did I mention you look amazing?"

He hadn't, but the way his eyes tracked me when I came into the lounge room this evening, told me he liked the bright purple flared club dress that Brie had picked out for me.

When Tynan pressed his fingers into the bruised flesh of the bite on my hip from this morning, I cringed and tried to pull away. "You keep forgetting that you hate me, Mess," Tynan purred in my ear.

"I don't forget it. My body just likes your body too much to care that your soul is a glob of black tar."

My sneer made Tynan chuckle. "Come dance with me." Taking my hand, Tynan dragged me out onto the dance floor, not giving me the opportunity of saying no.

"I don't want to dance." Trying to push away from where he held me against him, but his hold on me was too firm.

"Mess!" Tynan growled in warning.

"No, seriously, I can't do this. Please, don't make me watch this happen again."

Tynan's smile vanished. "That was my birthday banquet, Mess. If we did that every weekend, we'd run out of business pretty quickly. Tonight is paying customers. They will leave as they arrived. If they wander off from the nightclub, then they are available for the Unseelie to feast their flesh, blood, and souls. Others will invite their predator home with them for a night of pleasure. It is not always about eating. Humans are a delicacy. No one feasts on their special treat day in and day out."

Assessing Tynan warily, wondering if I could trust his words, I still held my body tense in his hold. Sighing in annoyance, Tynan grabbed a wrist of someone nearby. "Excuse me." He held the stamped mark up for me to see. A cursive **U** with bat wings in purple ink on the guy's wrist.

Blinking at the different symbol, I tried to make sense of what I was witnessing. Releasing guy, Tynan watched me look around the room. For the first time all night, I took in the difference in clientele. No longer the homeless and lost souls of the human world, the girls tonight wore fancy dresses and designer shoes, and the men dressed well.

There wasn't a buffet table full of tainted food, only the bar. The entire atmosphere was different, and there was no give for taking here tonight. Slowly, I lifted my eyes back to Tynan's. "I hate this room, no matter what's happening in it."

Eyes softening, Tynan threaded his fingers through my hair. I winced a little, having had my hair used as a leash enough today. My short gasps of pain convincing everyone I hated his attention only made Tynan happier. His mouth brushed across mine tenderly, my breath rushed out of me as a fire ignited in my spine. Crushing his mouth to mine, I groaned in pain, my lip sore from his bite still, but I returned the kiss passionately.

His spare hand pinned my body to his, and I felt his arousal even though I couldn't hear it above the music. My body reacted, desire flooding my bloodstream, and I soughed into his mouth, my hands fisting his suit jacket as I tried to pull myself tighter to him.

Opening my eyes, I saw some shadowed beings watching us. That's when I remembered I was meant to hate it. Biting down on Tynan's lip, I shoved him away. Blinking wide-eyes at me, Tynan touched his bleeding mouth.

Silver lit up in his eyes. Knowing the warning for what it was, I tried to move away from him, shoving my way through the mass of dancing bodies. A hand grabbed my upper arm only a few meters away and manhandled me out of the crowd.

When we reached the dark corner behind the DJ booth, I turned to meet Tynan's angry eyes. "I had to; they were watching us."

Trell and Esha appeared behind him a moment later looking worried. "You bit me," Tynan growled.

"Fairs fair," I replied, pointing to my lip. But I was starting to worry why it was such a big deal. Biting seemed to be the Sluagh's favorite past-time.

Tynan looked frustrated. "Mess, to the Sluagh, biting is a sign of ownership or marking your territory. Me biting you is acceptable; I own you. You bit me, in front of everyone, basically telling every other female in here that I belong to you."

Aghast, I checked to see Esha and Trell glowering in my direction. Swallowing my fear, I shook my head. "That wasn't my intention. I just wanted to get you off me. It was the only way I could think to stop you from kissing me." Turning my pleas to the others to understand. "I didn't know, I swear."

Rubbing his temples, Tynan sighed. "I know, Mess. It doesn't change that you did it." Stepping forward, Tynan slipped his hand around my neck and pulled me towards him, holding me against his chest. He lowered his mouth to my ear. "I have to react, you understand?" Turning, he threw me to Esha.

Catching me by my upper arms, Esha started walking me towards the exit, making sure to be seen by the other Sluagh. Glancing stunned over my shoulder, Tynan watched us leave, his eyes glowing silver.

"Wait!" I tried to stop walking. "What's happening?"

Esha didn't answer just moved his arm over my shoulder and swooped it around to cover my mouth as we got to the door. He held me with my back pressed against the front of him. "Relax, Messina, now we get to play together," Esha whispered sinisterly.

My eyes went wide as his hand slipped under the hem of my skirt and ran up my thigh, coldness chilling my skin beneath his touch. I tried to scream, but his palm muted my voice, and the music hid what sound I did make. Pride emerged from the crowd, face fierce, body tense, his eyes narrowing on the hand assaulting me.

Removing his hand to open the door, Esha dragged me out of the club. Suddenly, I wanted to be there so much more. In the corridor, I stabbed my heel into Esha's foot. When he released me with a curse, I bolted. Running as hard and fast as I could down that corridor, my heart was racing in my chest, setting my pace. Against Sluagh who can fly, I couldn't run quick enough.

Sprinting around a corner, I found Esha was there to catch me. Wrapping me in his arms, Esha laughed when I sobbed and tried to get free again. "Enough, Messina. There's nowhere to run to, is there?"

"Release her," Pride's voice came behind me. "You will not harm her."

"The Prince gave her to me for the night to play with. You can't contradict his orders."

"No, but I can ensure you do her no physical harm, which would contravene my orders." Pride took another step forward. "You would need to drag her back to his rooms kicking and screaming, or unconscious. I will promise her safety and ask her to walk back." Pride placed his hand on my shoulder. "Messina?"

Sucking in a terrified breath, I tried to settle my body which was quaking with fear. Pressing my lips together on another cry of anguish, I stepped into Pride's shadow and protection. Releasing me, Esha allowed his glamor to fade. He stopped being blurry; his olive skin paled till it was chalk white and his eyes glowing like a warning flare.

Turning into Pride's space, like a child beneath a giant oak, I indicated Esha should lead the way. Esha narrowed his eyes, possibly wondering if turning his back on me was a good idea.

"No one will get hurt tonight," Pride assured and gestured for Esha to start walking.

With a nod of his head, Esha led us back to Tynan's suites. Once we were in the lounge room, Esha turned to face me. "Shall we go to your bedroom, Messina? Or do you want to play down here?"

My gaze lifted to Pride, pleading him to protect me. "You'll stay, right?"

"I cannot go into your room, but I can wait outside or down here."

Touching his arm tenderly to thank him for stepping in, I moved forward to Esha. "Here is fine." Pride bowed his head a little.

Esha chuckled and went to stoke the fire. Swallowing my hesitation, I walked into the lounge room. My mind switching to the same state of existence I used for when my Stepfather wanted me. "What game are you planning to play?" I dared to ask.

Esha came back towards me. "Sit." He indicated the lounge. I did so. "Let's get to know each other better, since, it would seem, you will be hanging around for some time."

Moving to a sideboard, Esha lifted up a floating bar. He poured two drinks of alcohol and brought them over to us. "Here."

"I'm underage."

"Not here, you're not." Esha held the glass in front of me till I took it then sat on the lounge next to me. "What were you studying at college?"

"Fine arts." Taking a sip of the drink, I cringed at the pure liquid fire that burnt down my throat. It had a sweet taste, but the burn was horrid.

"Having seen your sketches, I understand how you got your scholarship. Your parents, were you close with them?"

"The people who raised me weren't my real parents and thought I was evil. So, no."

"Did you know your real parents?"

Making a face over from the burn from the alcohol, I shook my head. "I mean, I remember my mother, how beautiful she was, how kind. She always smiled. She gave me up when I left here."

"So, nothing about your father?"

"No, I don't think he was around." Throwing back the rest of my drink, I coughed from the bonfire in my throat and stomach. "What about you, Esha? Are you close with your parents? Any college studies?"

"I have a master's in business hospitality, and in the human world, I'm considered Ty's executive assistant. Trell is Ty's personal assistant."

"And your parents?"

"They died in the War of the Fae. When the queen cursed the Sluagh for joining the Unseelie ranks and defeating the Solaris."

"So, you were born Sluagh, not created?"

Esha grinned. "A hundred percent dark Fae." Taking the empty glass from my hand, Esha placed it on the coffee table. When he sat back, Esha slipped his hand on my thigh, the cold ache of his touch muted compared to earlier. "Do I still feel cold, Messina?"

"You feel wrong."

"It's odd, don't you think, that you couldn't bear to have the Seelie touch you?" Shuffling closer, Esha moved his mouth to my neck. "You're half Seelie, Nathani should have felt like home to you."

"I don't know," I sighed as his lips nipped down my neck. "I've been with humans, and they were fine. I didn't like them, and they felt wrong, but they could touch me without it being painful."

"Like now, with me?"

"Yes," I breathed hard, his mouth wet on my collarbone, his hand moving under my skirt.

"Did you find being with them pleasurable?"

"Yes."

"So, even though I feel cold and wrong, and you don't like me, you're enjoying me touching you, aren't you?" Esha lifted his ruby gaze to mine.

Spit clogged in my throat, I had to swallow it, terrified to answer. "Are you like him?" I almost whimpered.

Esha looked thoughtful. Standing up, he removed his shirt before he unbuckled his pants. Taking my hand, Esha slid it inside to grasp his already vibrating corkscrew before I touched him. His arousal didn't fill me with desire, but it did make me curious. "Can I see it?"

Esha cocked a brow at me. "Did you see his?"

"Yes."

"Did it terrify you?"

"It didn't make me eager."

Laughing, Esha bent forward and captured my mouth. He kissed me ardently as he forced me back to lie beneath him. Placing my hand on Esha's chest, I pushed him back a little. "I don't want to do this with you."

Esha kissed over my décolletage. "I know."

He pressed his hardness into me, I moaned, a feeling I knew too well starting to fill up my veins. "Esha, stop."

"In a moment."

"No, now," I demanded breathless, a combination of excitement and anxiety.

He mouthed my nipple through my dress. "We don't have to stop yet," Esha assured, hands sweeping my skirt up to my waist.

"Yes, we do. You don't understand. Esha-"

His cold lips on mine shut me up, grinding his pelvis against my pubic bone, thrusting into my hand. My fingers gripped him, and Esha's mouth pressed harder against mine. He rocked into my hand, the intensity of his vibrations increasing, he clasped the side of my knickers and started to pull them down.

A growl ripped through the room startling me.

"It's just Goyle," Esha breathed, his voice rough like he was in pain.

Turning my head to the fireplace, I saw the giant scary dog statue was growling, its eyes were glowing red. "Why is the statue growling?" I asked, more than a little terrified.

Grabbing my face, Esha brought it back to his. "He's warning me." He kissed me again, passionately.

"About?" I asked gasping when he freed my mouth. My eyes went wide as a dagger appeared in his hand beside my head.

"The Seelie that is trying to sneak up on us," Esha whispered in my ear.

"What?" I screeched.

15
———

MEMORY BLOCKS

❖

Jumping up, Esha spun, throwing the dagger. Hearing a humph, I sat up in time to watch a blond Sidhe male fall to his knees with the blade embedded in his right shoulder.

Pride was there a moment later, sword to the intruder's throat. "I worried you were too caught up to sense him."

Esha shook his head, eyes ablaze, entirely devoid of any lust now. He met my eyes, a warning in that glance. "Don't move, we'll come back to what we were doing once I deal with him." Walking off, Esha was entirely focused on the Seelie in the room. Crawling to the far end of the lounge, I grabbed a cushion to my chest as if it may shield me from everything in the place.

"What are you doing here?" Esha asked the Sidhe before yanking his blade from the man.

The man cried out in agony and applied pressure to his wound. "I am Maranta, twin brother of Nathani." He lifted his eyes. "I've come to find out how and why my brother died here today."

"Seriously, your brother was missing for thirteen years and you only now come looking for him?" Esha asked, his tone sarcastic. "You expect me to believe that?"

Maranta just glared at Esha. "You are not the prince."

"Observant."

"Yet you have his pet." Maranta's eyes came to me.

Brows furrowed, Esha turned his ruby eyes on Pride. "Did a Sidhe-wide announcement go out about us finding her or something? Why do we suddenly have Seelie sticking their nose in our business about a half-breed?"

Squinting, Pride tilted his head. "There does seem to be an unusual amount of interest."

"The faerie mound is still two halves of the one majick. When the Unseelie court found her, the Seelie court whispered her name too. Ashling has a great interest in the girl and wants her brought home."

"Oh!" Esha looked surprised. "Well, we should give Ashling whatever she wants, since she is the stand-in monarch after she had the last princess of the Sidhe killed." Lowering his dagger, Esha took a step back. "Please, take the girl and give Ashling our best."

"What?" I gasped.

Maranta looked just as surprised, especially when Pride removed his sword and stepped back. Maranta surveyed the room unsure, Esha encouraged him to come and collect me.

Standing slowly, Maranta moved towards me. "Come, let's get you out of here." He offered me his hand. Shaking my head, I cringed into a tight ball. "You don't need to fear me. I'll take you to the Seelie court; no one will harm you there." Getting frustrated when I refused to move, he snatched my wrist.

The pain was the worst it'd been with any other touching me before, like the ants biting me was suddenly scorpions. Screaming, I kicked out my leg to get him away from him. Maranta pulled back shocked.

"Oh, yeah!" Esha pretended he had an epiphany. "I forgot; the touch of Seelie causes her pain." Esha watched the Sidhe's mouth fall open in astonishment. "Boggles the mind really, considering she is half Seelie. We think perhaps she was cursed never to know the pleasure of the Seelie touch."

"I wonder how a woman who finds pain at the touch of the Seelie, would survive in the Seelie light?" Pride offered.

"Perhaps you are right, Pride." Esha stepped closer to the lounge, Maranta retreating away from me. Now that I watched Esha, he had a real cowboy walk and way of talking, reminiscent of the old John Wayne westerns. "That would cause an issue, considering your duty is to keep her free from harm."

"It would also negate your duty to keep her here."

Esha nodded taking it under serious advisement. "You make a good point, Pride. Tell me, Maranta, how did you plan to get her out of here?"

"The same way I came in."

"As a guest of the nightclub?" Esha cocked an eyebrow, then indicated Maranta's wrist. I looked to see the purple U inked on his skin. "But you broke the club rules and drifted into the staff only areas."

"If I don't come back, they will send more."

Esha smiled. "Good, we always need more fun. Goyle?"

The dog statue rose up behind the retreating Sidhe. Wide-eyed, unable to look away, I witnessed the dog grasp Maranta's shoulders as it opened its massive stone jaw. Inside the mouth was gleaming sharp teeth and a bile green tongue. Maranta screamed, like a girl, which would have been funny, but then Goyle closed his jaws over the Sidhe's head.

Blood sprayed out in all directions, splattering the walls and furnishings. Grateful I'd moved to the far end of the lounge, the scene left me struggling to breathe just the same. The high-pitched scream cut off, my ears ringing preventing utter silence. Finally, Maranta's decapitated body fell to the floor, convulsing for several seconds after disconnection.

Staring, horrified by what I'd just witnessed, I started hyperventilating while Goyle returned to his guardian position by the fire. He settled his hind-bones, then opened his terrifying mouth again and belched.

"The goblins are going to think it's Christmas with all the fresh

Seelie meat they've gotten today." Esha walked towards the hallway. "I'll call the cleaners."

With my eyes frozen on the bloody headless body, I couldn't move. Only earlier today I'd lost control of my emotions and dismembered Maranta's brother. This man had come to free me from the prince, so why hadn't I even tried to go with him? He didn't seem to be willing to give me much choice in the matter. Was he also here to take me against my will? I was finding it hard to feel sympathy or even to be upset about the deaths I'd caused and witnessed today.

Perhaps, it was the shock or my Unseelie blood. Either way, my lack of humanity at this moment, scared me more than a stone dog that decapitated people with one bite. One thing was for sure; I was going to need acute therapy if I ever got out of here. "Messina!" Esha clicked his fingers in front of my eyes.

Snapping my attention away from the dead body, I looked up at Esha. "Yes?"

"I told you to go to your room and shower," Esha informed me frustrated.

"Okay." Tentatively rising from the lounge, I made my way upstairs. I wasn't going to sleep. My mind needed purging of what I saw and heard. After showering, I sat on my bed. Picking up the sketch pad, I started drawing out the memories.

"Messina?" Looking up, I was surprised to see Esha standing beside my bed.

"What are you doing in here?" Jumping up, I dropped my sketch pad on the bed.

"Calm yourself." Picking up the sketch pad, Esha appraised the drawing of the headless corpse by the feet of the stone dog. "This is how you cope, isn't it? You draw your life, a way of disconnecting from it, making the bad stuff just a drawing, not something that happened to you?"

"I never thought of it like that. To me, it's a way to keep my memories." Esha scrutinized me, so I cleared my throat. "Since I was young, I've had trouble holding onto my memories, like certain things, or people I encountered disappear while I sleep. One day I realized that if I draw everything, I wouldn't forget it. If I go to sleep first, I lose it."

"Yet, you remember your mother?" Esha asked skeptically, looking through my drawings from tonight.

"My memories of her have been my one constant, but the locations of those memories have always been unidentifiable, the background blurry, so I couldn't even tell you what sort of room I was in." Taking the sketchbook from Esha, I flicked through to find the sketch I'd drawn yesterday. "That's been changing since I came here." Finding the picture, I handed it to him. "This room, I think it was my room as a small child."

Esha frowned. "These windows look familiar." He regarded me. "Messina, do you think you were born here?"

Opening my mouth, I remembered he didn't know, only Tynan, and the King knew. Dropping my eyes, I lied. "I don't know where this room is; I was just saying the memories are becoming clearer."

"It's a beautiful picture. Would you give it to me?"

It felt bizarre that he would want a drawing of a child's bedroom, but at the same time, he complimented my work. Remembering what Pride told me about the Sluagh liking to collect unusual things, I bit my lip and nodded my head in consent. After all, what harm could a drawing of a long-forgotten room cause?

"Thank you," Esha took care in removing the sketch, and set it aside as if it was a priceless artwork. A bloom of pride swelled in my tummy. Esha looked at a few more sketches then held the book up at the pile of flesh that had been Nathani. "Some memories are not good to remember clearly."

Cringing, I looked away. Putting the sketchbook aside, Esha moved towards me, boxing me between the bed, the wall, and himself. I pressed back into the wall behind me as he gave me no room to escape. "Some are worth repeating." Placing a hand each side of my head, Esha dropped a kiss to my collarbone.

"Esha, I don't control my powers." Placing my hand on his chest, I tried to push him away.

Esha chuckled against my neck. "I noticed that already."

"I don't just mean manifestation." I used Tynan's term. "I have a power which is opportunistic when I'm with men. I can't even recognize it happening."

Esha considered me. "You're worried about hurting me?" Licking my lips, I nodded. *'Liar'* my inner voice chuckled. Studying me, Esha used his finger to lift my chin so he could peer into my eyes. "Or are you worried about being unfaithful to your new master?"

"What?" I blinked at him. My situation with Tynan didn't seem to be one that required commitment, after all, he'd let Esha take me for the night. The overall dynamics of my being with Tynan hadn't even crossed my mind, except the need to escape. Though, I couldn't deny I liked how it felt for Tynan to touch me and to be with him. I'd never felt like that with anyone before. Not that I could admit that to Esha.

"Humans are obsessed with monogamy, with morals, what's right and wrong," Esha lectured as he stepped back from me. "You need to understand, Messina, those rules do not apply here. In the Fae world, the rules are not about wrong or right. We exist on loyalty to those who have proven themselves worthy, by duty to oneself and our true natures, and most importantly pleasure, wherever it is found."

"That doesn't convince me to sleep with you, Esha. Your motivations are your pleasure."

"Our mutual pleasure, Messina. Trust me; you'd enjoy what happened between us, far more than any of those human boys you let have you."

Opening my mouth to clarify my previous experience, I quickly closed it. How could I argue with that logic? I did not doubt that Esha would be much better than my stepfather could even dream of being. Esha's brow furrowed, his mouth tilting in concern like he saw something in my eyes. He took my hand. "Do you think you are the only candy the prince indulges in?"

Unable to control my reaction, I looked up surprised. Esha's brows lifted like he was surprised to have guessed my hesitation. "Let me show you something." He moved us toward the door. "You need to be quiet. Can you do that?"

When I nodded, Esha squeezed my hand. Turning off my

bedroom light, he opened the door and led us out to the balcony. As soon as the door opened, I could hear moaning. The heavy breathing of lust echoing through the lounge room.

Moving me to the railing, Esha tucked his body behind mine while the show below captivated me. There was a naked woman on the couch, moaning and writhing on the black leather, Tynan's face hidden between her thighs. A pang of jealousy snaked through my belly, slithering into my lungs, and making breathing painful.

Mouth to my ear, Esha barely breathed his words. "A wealthy human who he picked up from the club. He is a monster even to our kind. Humans are where he has always taken his pleasure. The human women are obsessed with size and love the idea of a well-endowed man, right up until it's pounding into them, causing them agony beyond their belief and irreparable damage."

Esha's hands caressed my hips. "The goddess cursed our prince, but by giving him the gift of healing, she allowed him to take still what he needs and not permanently damage a woman."

Turning my head to see Esha in my peripheral vision, I kept my voice just as low. "You know?"

"We've known each other since childhood. I know most of his secrets."

"Only most?" I teased quietly while the woman downstairs cried out her orgasm.

Ruby eyes gleaming, Esha grinned. "The shows about to get good, though, you know all about what happens next, don't you?"

Focusing my attention on the lounge, I watched Tynan push his pants off before he climbed over the panting woman. Lowering himself between her legs, he found her groove and smiled as she moaned. Taking the woman's hands above her head, he pinned them with his while kissing her passionately.

Looking away wasn't an option, but watching caused the snake in my chest to squeeze my internal organs like a boa constrictor. Sliding a hand up my skirt as he pressed against the back of me, Esha left a cold path in the wake of the touch of his lips nipping along my shoulder. My fingers tightened on the railing, my heart racing in my chest, my stomach felt empty, pure anticipation flooding my bloodstream. I wanted to be that woman.

"Are you ready?" Tynan asked.

Esha's fingers moved my knickers aside, finding my ready heat.

"Yes," she moaned. Tynan thrust forward.

Esha shoved his fingers into me. I cried out, but the woman's shrieking muted it.

Tynan's head lifted, ignoring the woman screaming beneath his pounding body. Instead, his eyes locked with mine and his body moved faster, pushed harder.

Fingers gripped the railing, I was unable to look away, unable to do anything but take what he gave me. Tynan wasn't interested in the woman under him. He was watching me, imagining me being the body he was burying himself in. He wanted me.

Intense pleasure built inside of me, I closed my eyes and released it, Esha using his free hand to cover my mouth to mute my satisfaction. Downstairs, I heard Tynan join me. Despite the distance, I knew my power still reached out to him, dragged him into my euphoria, warmth flooding my core as if he lost himself inside me.

By the time Esha removed his hands from me, and I opened my eyes again, Tynan was healing the woman. "He says to go to bed."

"With you?"

Esha chuckled. "His bed, Messina. You belong to him. Giving you to me tonight was all show for the others. I was getting what I could out of it."

Turning to face Esha, I lifted a brow at his humming groin.

"Don't worry about me. I get her next. My pleasure in return for taking the memory of the pain." He lowered his mouth to my ear. "That's one of my gifts, the taking, and giving of memories. When that woman leaves, all she will remember is the amazing sex she had with two handsome and well-endowed men." Winking, Esha turned to leave.

Before I could think about, I snatched his hand. "Can you unlock my memories?"

Examining my eyes, Esha looked to the lounge. "Not without his permission I can't. You are the prince's toy, Messina. He doesn't have to share, but I won't give you back your memories without getting something out of it myself. I'm Unseelie, not a martyr."

Glancing at the lounge, I flinched at the silver in Tynan's eyes as he observed my interaction with Esha. Tynan jerked his head towards his bedroom door. Swallowing down my fear and resentment, I went to bed. The dark prince's bed.

16

MONOTONY OF CAPTIVITY

❖

Sliding into the bed, Tynan pulled me against him crushing his mouth to mine. Despite my lip still stinging, I moaned and kissed him back just as heatedly. When he rolled me onto my back and pressed his vibrating curse against my sensitive areas, I nearly lost it. "You just had sex," I breathed as his mouth explored my body.

"I know, and I thought that would suffice, but I need to have you too."

I could have melted into a puddle. Between Tynan's words, his kisses, and his touch, I was hot enough to catch on fire. Our breathing was ragged, our bodies heated and craving what they couldn't have.

Like that first night, Tynan brought me to climax with his fingers, and then again while he rubbed his curse against my already sensitive clit. I clawed his back as I came, then Tynan lifted himself enough that his ejaculation landed on my abdomen.

As we lay panting, I drew my finger through the neon blue gunk. "Is it edible?"

Laughing as he rolled towards me, Tynan scooped some onto his finger and coated my lips with it. "Let's find out. Lick your lips."

Eyes locked with his, I did. "It tastes, like nothing. Sort of like plain boiled rice, if a little salty."

Tynan's dark eyes lit up. "Goddess. I want you so much more now." As if to reinforce his statement, his curse started a slow hum.

Reaching between us, I took it in hand. "It's not big, yet. If you enter me now, we might be able to have sex."

Considering me, Tynan moved without warning. From one blink to the next Tynan went from lying next to me to standing beside the bed, dragging me from the mattress. Leading me to the shower, he snuggled in behind me while he washed me clean of his mess. I was still reeling from the sudden change in location, that my head was spinning.

"Don't do that again."

I froze, unsure what I'd done wrong. "Do what?"

"Don't offer to let me inside you. It can't happen. I want you too much to resist you, Mess, and I'm not going too, but we will only do what we have already done, no more."

My heart dropped onto the floor where Tynan squished beneath his toes in his rejection. Tynan would be intimate with strange humans, but not me. It wasn't hurting me that was the issue, not since he already proved he could do that without a guilty conscious, so why was having sex with me such a horrible thing for him to consider. "Why?"

"Because we can't," Tynan growled spinning me to push my back against the shower wall. He caressed my face as he repeated tenderly. "Because we can't."

He kissed me heatedly, our passion hotter than the water pouring over our skin. His fingers delved inside me, searching out the place that made my eyes roll back into my head and call his name. Barely able to hold myself standing, Tynan slotted himself between my legs, pinning me against the wall, and thrust his textured manhood against me until I came again, Tynan painting the wall with neon blue cum a moment later.

When I burst into tears, Tynan stepped away, his eyes checking me over for injury. Turning my back on him, I hid my dejection in the water. "Did I hurt you?"

"Yes," I answered honestly.

"I was too rough?"

"No, that's not it." How could I explain the sudden sadness that came over me?

"Tell me. Look at me and tell me why being intimate with me makes you cry, Mess. Am I a hideous monster not worthy of touching your flesh? Is that what depresses you?"

"No," I whispered. "It should, but that's not it. It's not even that I'm a toy to be used to your liking."

Tynan's heat radiated across my back. Reaching past me, he turned off the taps for the shower and wrapped my towel around me. Forcibly turning me, he tilted my chin up to meet his eyes, then stepped back. "Tell me. I won't hurt you for being honest, Mess."

Biting the inside of my cheek, I took a moment to consider my words before I swiped at my face and cleared my throat. "Being with you is the only time I'm warm. The feeling when you touch me, the intensity of our chemistry, is such a high, that when it's over, and I return to being a prisoner and a toy, it hurts. Coming down from the high of being with you is like falling through the floor into dark despair, and it's getting worse with every hit."

Tynan assessed me for a solid minute before he stepped back. "Come to bed. It's late." He left the bathroom. Left me standing there, cold and hungry for his warmth.

By the time I climbed into the bed beside Tynan, I was physically and emotionally exhausted. When I cuddled into Tynan, he lay there awkwardly, but I'd didn't care. He was the only person I liked touching me.

"Tomorrow we will practice controlling your powers. From Monday onwards, I want you to spend your mornings practicing your control. I'll send Esha home early to practice hand to hand combat with you. We'll eat dinner together and then you can have the evening to yourself until I come to bed."

"Are you really two hundred and fifty?"

"Yes."

"Does that mean you are immortal?"

"Yes."

"But I watched two Sidhe die yesterday." It was past midnight, closer to dawn and the emotional and physical drain of the day was about to bury me.

"They are also immortal, but not in the sense humans believe." Tynan held me a little tighter, his body relaxing beneath mine. "We can live for centuries and still look youthful. However, Sidhe are still susceptible to fatal wounds, hence why they became great warriors. It's hard to get close enough to one to kill them."

"But we killed two in one day?"

"Nathani has been imprisoned for thirteen years. He was weak and lethargic. Not that anyone can protect against a manifestation of your magnitude. Maranta was stupid or egotistical. I'm not sure which one." Tynan caressed my arm tenderly. "Sluagh are harder to kill. We can lose limbs and will heal quickly, even grow them back. It is why the Sidhe fear us, and why we were required to become the better warriors."

Rolling me onto my back again, Tynan nestled himself between my hips. "Again?" I asked half asleep. The roughness of his curse highlighting how tender I was.

"Again."

"Okay, but tomorrow you better come home with a big tube of lube. I'm getting a serious case of friction burn."

Tynan tilted his head. "You've needed lube before?"

"I took two guys at once remember?"

Tynan considered me. "I'll get some." He rolled off me.

"What? Now?"

Rolling me back in to cuddle; his eyes focused elsewhere. "No. Sleep now. I can wait till we've rested." I wasn't going to argue. My eyes closed, and I dreamt of warmth and Tynan smiling at me while we made love.

~

THE NEXT DAY, I spent my morning with Tynan trying to get me to bring on my manifestation. It didn't happen. Then he went on to try and get me to recognize when my satiability power was activating. That also wasn't working. Each time we'd both end up lying in a panting mess of goo.

Monday, Tynan went back to work, and I began the monotonous routine of trying to learn my powers in the morning and getting my arse handed to me by Esha each afternoon. He broke my arm the first night, accidentally. Annoyed as he healed it, Tynan finished the training early to give Esha a serving.

They kept me in Tynan's suite, not even taking me to the training room anymore. Goblins delivered my meals to me - Margo and I used the food trays to exchange notes - and the only time I was allowed out was on Friday afternoons.

There was no fighting on Fridays, just running. Esha would open the large glass window and tell me to run as far as I could, then turn around and run back as fast as I could. The underground forest was eerie even in daylight, but I didn't mind because it got me out of the suite, allowed me to stretch my legs, and most importantly, allowed me to scope out the forest and if there was a chance of escape.

Do you know what happens when you run in one direction as far as you can? You run until your legs are sore, your lungs are burning, and the idea of running another step is the thing of nightmares. That's what Esha made me do going out. I had to run till I couldn't anymore. Trying to be smart, I thought to save some energy for the return run, but Esha wouldn't let me. He made me run until I was barely able to stay upright. Then, I had to turn around and sprint back.

As a seasoned runner, I didn't run five minutes and turn around. We crossed the forest for over sixty minutes before Esha determined I'd run far enough. "Now run as fast as you can back."

"You've got to be kidding me?"

"Every time I catch you, I will hurt you," Esha warned, showing me his dagger. "I'll give you a five-minute head start."

Taking him at his word, I gulped in a lungful of air, pushed through the muscle tiredness and bolted for the return path. Tree branches slapped at me, hindering my pace. Fallen logs created hurdles, and tree roots tried to trip me. Esha caught me ten minutes later. The first I knew of his nearness was the slash to my right arm. Crying out, I pushed harder. My heart pounded in time with my feet to the forest floor. Another slash across my shoulder sent me sprawling to the forest floor. Lifting my tear-streaked face, I saw Esha landing not far away. That's when I realized why I didn't hear him coming. He wasn't running.

"Get up! If you lay down, I will take it as an invitation and fuck you while I feed on you," Esha snarled.

Arms trembling as I pressed my hands into the dirt, feet searching for purchase on the leaf-covered ground, I ran for my life. A second later, I was running through the trees, cutting a path not marked, desperate to find the window. A sudden gust of wind was the only warning I got before the blade sliced down my left triceps. Agony seared up my shoulder, into my neck, and a scream escaped my mouth.

Gritting my teeth to prevent wasting my oxygen, I powered forward. A blur of greens, browns, and pain, surrounding me, my brain not even sure I was running the right way, but I wasn't going to stop and get my bearings.

By the time the window was in sight, I'd lost track of the cuts on my arms. A meter out from the window, I was crash-tackled to the ground. I didn't have the energy to struggle against Esha. Laying there, I waited for whatever hell came next.

"Not too bad." Standing up, he walked inside, leaving me there exhausted in the grass. The relief of not being violated slowly filtered through my system. Big arms collected me, carrying me up to my bedroom, where Pride placed me gently on the bathroom floor. He ran a bath for me before he left me to undress and crawl into the soothing water.

Waking beneath the water, lungs burning, and no energy to sit up, I hooked a leg over the edge, then an elbow. Spluttering as I levered my body out of the tub and fell to the floor, I lay there cold and wheezing for several minutes.

Eyeing the bed through the door, I tried to stand only to fall when my legs refused to hold me. Sucking in a hard breath, I combat crawled painfully across the floor, the use of my arms opening the clotted slashes and leaving a blood trail across the floor to the bed.

My bed. I didn't care it broke Tynan's rules. It was the closest bed, so that's where I went. Fatigue pulled me into unconsciousness the moment my body was lying flat on the mattress.

Still exhausted, I barely woke up when Tynan collected me from my room and carried me to his bed. Just enough to sigh with happiness when he healed my slashes and cuddled me into him.

That became my life. Training and the best near-sex I'd probably ever have in my life. Day in and day out for six months. I never forgot I was a possession, the Sluagh wouldn't let me, and I never forgot my plan to escape. I did forget I hated them.

17

MEMORIES AWAKEN

❖

"You promised me! It's been six months!" My voice ricocheted around the lounge room making me wonder if Tynan designed the acoustics of the room for torture.

"As I have said every week for the last six months, the time is not right." Pride never got angry. I could yell and scream and rant, and he just sat there reading whatever flowery romance novel he was reading this week.

"This is bullshit!" Picking up the coffee pot from the tray, I threw it at him. Swatting it away with his book, it smashed on the floor. "I need to get my stuff." The plate containing my uneaten breakfast went next.

"What the Unseelie is going on here?" Tynan's voice cut through the lounge room.

Turning around surprised by the voice, I found Trell and Esha were right behind Tynan. Pouting, I dropped my butt on the sofa in a huff. "Nothing." Collecting my cup of coffee, I drank it sullenly.

"Trell, can you chase up that information for me please?" Tynan requested.

While Esha was privileged to the secrets about my power, as far as Trell knew, I was a useless toy. *Just a pretty Seelie to be used and abused.'*

Her words, to my face. Though, I think she was starting to like me. She was laughing now when I gave Esha shit.

Once Trell was gone, Pride closed his book and stood from where he sat in lotus on the floor. His flexibility was disturbing. "Mess is frustrated that she still can't control her powers. She was trying to make herself angry to see if that activated it." Bowing his head, Pride left.

If Tynan was in the room with me, Pride went elsewhere. He wouldn't tell me where, but as soon as Tynan was leaving, Pride would appear again. He used to stay while Esha was there, but he now trusted Esha with me and didn't feel the need to watch us tease each other.

Yes, I flirted with Esha, and he teased right back. That's as far as it'd gone, and that suited me. We were just comfortable around each other now. "You're home early," I scowled into my coffee.

Taking a sip, I put it down, went to grab a slice of toast and remembered it was all over the floor across the room. Groaning in annoyance, I threw my coffee cup at the fireplace, the smashing sound somewhat satisfying. That lasted until I noticed my breakfast was gone again; I was starving.

Walking towards me, Tynan dropped his bag by the end of the lounge. "I didn't leave. Unseelie business kept me here today."

Pretending to care, I nodded my head once. Tynan cleared his throat. Looking up in annoyance, I observed Tynan's intense gaze and stood reluctantly. Stepping into him, I kissed him just as grudgingly.

For once I didn't have to fake it. The fire of our chemistry started to ignite, causing me to yank away from him. I was annoyed and frustrated, the last thing I needed was sexual frustration on top of it all. "I'll get out of your way," I murmured, starting for my room.

"Stay." Grabbing my hand, he sat on the lounge and pulled me down to straddle his hips. "Esha, go organize someone to clean up." Bowing his head, Esha left. Tynan caressed my face and neck.

"Ty..." I breathed, his touch heating me up.

"I like watching you react to my touch. Maybe, we've been focusing the wrong way to activate your powers. Just because anger activated your manifestation once, does not mean that will be the emotion to train you. Perhaps, we need to try a different emotion."

"I think if lust were going to work, I'd be a master of my power by now." Caressing his hand with mine where he palmed my breast through my dress, I moaned.

"Continue to think about it."

My fingers started to unbutton his black shirt. "I also don't think this is working with controlling the satiability." Spreading his shirt, I let my fingers trace the tribe markings over his muscular chest.

Sliding my skirt up, Tynan nipped my chin with his teeth. "I have been thinking about that. We have a strong connection, a powerful attraction to each other. Perhaps, if you were intimate with a stranger, you might better feel the difference when the power kicked in?"

My hands paused where they were opening his fly, keeping my eyes downcast. "You want me to have sex with a stranger?"

"I think it could work, Mess. Once you feel the switch activate that first time, you'll be able to feel it each time after that. Then you can control it, instead of your power controlling you."

My chest felt tight, making breathing painful. "If that's what you want?" Removing myself from his lap, I stepped further away to adjust my clothing.

Peering at me, Tynan's brow furrowed, confusion by my withdrawal shining in his eyes. He opened his mouth, but the door opened, and we heard the distinct sound of goblins entering the foyer.

Moving to Goyle while Tynan quickly rebuttoned his shirt, I rubbed my hand over Goyle's head petting back and forth behind his ear. A contented rumble sounded through the room. The goblins cleaned up the shattered crockery, plus the food.

"Will you require a fresh breakfast?" One of the goblins asked.

"No, I'll come down to the kitchen and make my own," I answered before Tynan could. Tynan raised a brow at me. "If Prince Tynan permits?"

"I'll escort you personally."

The goblins left, bringing my attention to Pride standing back beneath the balcony. How he knew when we weren't alone baffled me.

Striding into the room, Esha whispered something in Tynan's ear causing his brows to lower and his eyes to glower. "Pride, take Mess to get something to eat. I'll meet you in the kitchen. Don't leave the kitchen till I get there."

Bowing his head, Pride regarded me patiently.

"Wait! Why don't you trust Pride to walk me back?"

Raising a brow at me, Tynan turned to Esha and Pride. "Wait outside."

Watching Esha's sympathetic gaze as it swept over me, I became more confused. Shaking his head sadly, Pride left and fear dropped into my stomach.

A wall slammed against my back, Tynan's hand around my throat. Squealing in fright, I clawed at his wrist to get free out of natural reaction, but I didn't try and get free how Esha had taught me. That would only make it worse.

"You've grown too familiar, Mess. That you question my orders at all should get you punished, but to do it in front of others..." Tynan stepped closer to me. "You've been training with Esha. He's told me how fast a runner you are. You will not go anywhere without Esha or me, that has been the case for six months now, it will not change."

When he released me, I fell to the floor coughing. He said it so definitely, with so much permanence. "I have a question. When you tire of me, what happens to me?"

Appraising me where I lay gasping on the floor, Tynan blinked his silver beacons demarking the entry to hell. He didn't answer me, just stormed out. Crouched there on the ground, I squeezed my eyes tight. I died. That's what he didn't say. When he was bored with me, he'd kill me. Probably in the most horrible way I could imagine.

"You eat too little," Margo fussed as she put two slices of toast with peanut butter in front of me.

"I eat enough, Margo."

"No. Look at you. Skin and bone. You need more meat."

"You are not fattening me up to eat me, Margo."

Glaring at me like I'd insulted her cooking, she huffed and stormed off into the pantry. The truth was, I'd gotten thinner since I'd come here. All the workouts with Esha had been building strength, and the Friday afternoon runs had impacted my physique. I didn't mind, and Tynan certainly seemed to like the change.

Groaning, I dropped my forehead to the table. He wanted to let someone else have me. Six months of enjoying me every night and morning, and suddenly, I was about to start being shared candy.

The kitchen door opened and two Sluagh females walked in. I recognized Brie; the other was new to me.

"Morning, Messina. Need me to go shopping again for you yet? I had a ball finding your clothes." The other Sluagh looked appalled that Brie would offer to shop for a Sidhe.

"You'd have to ask the prince that. It's not like I get a say in anything."

Brie's eyes were the kindness I'd get from the school nurse when she saw my injuries as a kid. Well, as kind looking as lava could look. Moving closer, she touched a particularly sore part of my neck causing me to wince.

"He's in a temper today, as you've already found out. Probably not the best day to hit him up for a shopping spree."

"This is the pet?" The other girl asked awed. "I heard she was dark, but I expected her to be like the other Sidhe. She's not at all. She's not light or dark. She's like the moon itself, light when full, invisible in the darkness when there is no light, but always covered in shadows that change in intensity. You don't belong with any of the Sidhe."

Brie looked at her friend gobsmacked.

"Is your friend alright?" I asked, noticing her eyes were unfocused.

"Um, Sauvignon has what we call soul-sight," Brie answered slightly panicked.

"You're so cold, like the surface of the moon. Even we would feel warm to one as cold as you."

That comparison made me laugh, thinking of Esha. "Trust me, I feel how cold you all are."

"So cold, and alone. The forest is no place for a child. So much pain to forget, so much to forget, always to forget."

"Brie, she's freaking me out."

Brie, still wide-eyed and shaking a little herself, grabbed Sauvignon and dragged her out of the room. "What was all that?" I heard Brie almost screech outside. "You've never talked to someone like that before?"

"She's different to anyone I've seen before," Sauvignon replied as the door started to swing shut. "I think she's a...." The door slammed.

Leaving his corner, Pride dropped his plate on the table a little too loudly as if he wanted to make sure I didn't hear her finish that sentence. "You are trembling, Messina."

"Am I?" Staring at the door as if it may swing open and let me hear everything else Sauvignon had to say, a shiver ran through my body.

"You must be very hungry. Margo, I believe Messina needs more toast to eat."

Margo bustled out of the pantry and made herself busy. "I suppose you want another bowl of custard?"

Pride grinned ear to ear. "I will never say no to more custard, Margo. Thank you."

BRIE WAS RIGHT, Tynan was in a foul mood today. When he walked into the kitchen an hour later, I was sitting sketching Sauvignon and the look in her chili-pepper eyes. "Have you eaten?"

"Yes."

"Good, let's go. I have more important things to deal with." The room blurred when Tynan turned his head to murmur to Esha.

"Messina, don't stare." Nora's voice chided me as Tynan and Esha spoke to Margo.

"But it's him." A little girl answered.

"The prince?" Nora asked. "Yes, I know, but you shouldn't stare."

Turning to look at Nora, a small scowl creasing Tynan's nose, then his eyes came to me, and all emotion vanished from his face.

"Not the prince. My prince."

"What?" Nora paled as I slid out of my seat and walked my child legs over to Tynan who just watched me in shock. "Messina, don't!"

Taking Tynan's hand, I smiled up at him; I barely reached his waist. "I am your light in the darkness," I told him proudly.

Smirking in amusement, Tynan squatted to be eye level with me. "Oh really? And what am I to you?"

Stopping to think about it, I felt my smile grow as my certainty cemented. "Home and hearth."

Tynan chuckled. "Do I feel like a warm, safe place to you?"

Placing his hand on my cheek, I sighed and smiled. "Yes. I'll always be safe with you."

Tynan blinked in confusion. Nora grabbed me up quickly, taking me away, rushing out the door, tears gushing from her panicked eyes. "They must never know. I'm sorry, Messina, you need to go."

Jerking back to the here and now, a sting filled my cheek. Blinking through tears, I rubbed where Tynan slapped me. Not hard, just enough force behind it to bring me back to reality. "I told you to get up." His black obsidian eyes showed he was annoyed, not angry. His eyes looked immune to light, blocking it all from his dark soul.

"I'm your light."

Tynan jerked as if I'd hit him at the same time a loud gasp filled the silence in the room. Margo stood covering her gaping mouth. Slowly, she took her hand away. "The child."

18

———

OUTSIDE LOOKING IN

❖

The night was clear, stars twinkling overhead, the breeze cool after a warm day. Tynan loved nights like tonight, walking around the mansion to problem solve or contemplate whatever responsibilities he held.

In the past, he spent many nights roaming the woods of the estate to escape the buzz of the mound. The faerie mound spoke to him since Tynan was a child, always whispering, just out of earshot when it didn't have something for him in particular.

Over the last six months, he'd barely stepped foot outside the mound if it wasn't for business in the human world. Anything that took him away from Mess, Tynan hated, and he trusted very few to keep her safe.

Still, even when he was in the castle, he avoided her except at bedtime. The warmth of her flesh, the invitation in her big aqua eyes, the hunger for her Seelie blood, almost drove him beyond his restraint.

Watching her flirt with Esha goaded him. Esha knew it and enjoyed watching his friend quietly seethe. Of course, Esha thought Tynan was using Messina entirely; all the Sluagh believed the same.

Only ever watchful Pride was wiser. When he saw Tynan's anger was beyond resisting what Messina so willingly offered, Pride would run interference, distracting Tynan with news of another Seelie attempt. The reason Tynan was yet again called from Messina's warm body tonight.

Now Esha wanted a private word, and the time it took away from lying Messina beneath him, ired him. "Why did you want to meet out here?" Tynan asked Esha as he approached him in the forest surrounding the mansion.

"Is Messina's dark half Unseelie royalty?" There was a look in his eyes that Tynan knew too well, an examination of which to be cautious. Esha had found a secret and was ready to unravel it to gain a more critical thread.

"Why do you think that?" Tynan couldn't outright deny it, Messina's powers were as Unseelie as they came, and ancient in their origins.

Esha indicated the top story. "That's the King's suites, right?" He pointed out the Kings bedroom window.

"Yes."

"So, that set of leadlight windows to the left of his bedroom, that's his concubine's rooms, correct?"

"What does this have to do with Messina?" Tynan asked, knowing Esha already knew who those rooms belonged to, or who once occupied the place.

Esha took a piece of paper out of his pocket, unfolded it and showed it to Tynan. "Those are the concubine's windows, aren't they?" The sketch he showed Tynan was one of Mess'. "Messina keeps drawing this room. She says it's the room she spent her childhood in before her mother sent her away." Esha looked at his best friend. "Messina is King Mabon's daughter, isn't she?"

Tynan stared at the drawing. How had Esha gotten hold of that drawing? Tynan was sure he burnt all the potentially dangerous pictures before he went to sleep each night. "Her parentage is unknown," the prince answered honestly.

"But if I'm right, if she is, that makes her just as cursed as you."

"No! The birth of Messina was not the action that stole her mother's choice. I did! I forced Titan to relinquish his daughter as a hostage, and I gave her to Mabon for his concubine. The blame was never Messina's. Just like it would be mine again if I do to her what my father did to my mother."

"It would explain her powers."

"And why the Seelie want her so badly," Tynan exhaled frustrated. "Still, perhaps Nora was just caring for her."

"She's the child from the kitchen that day, isn't she? The one you went looking for after meeting her? The girl who went missing that same day. The child the Seelie court killed Nora Baynes for hiding from them."

Tynan had known the moment she told him he warmed her. He'd looked into her eyes and recognized the child who said he was her home and hearth, but she hadn't remembered Tynan till today.

Esha blew out a breath when his friend didn't answer. "I want her."

Tynan looked at him, glared really. Esha knew he couldn't have her, Tynan had been clear on that the moment he decided he was keeping Mess, permanently.

"I know you've been enjoying her to the limits of your physical abilities, but I know you haven't taken it beyond that. I've not once heard her scream while with you, seen her tender the next morning. You can't have her the way I can, and I want her."

"No." Tynan turned to walk away.

"Are you jealous that I could satisfy her in a way you can't?"

Glared at his best friend, Tynan gritted his teeth. "Jealous? No. Possessive? Yes. You can have every other woman in the Unseelie court. Leave me this one."

"I can't help that my passion draws me to her."

White knuckles curled into fists around his cane as Tynan's anger was reaching a new height. Gaze flaring with his rage as his spirit power rose to the surface, turning his pupils' silver in warning to those around him, Tynan watched Esha take a step back. "Messina is mine! I don't want to hear another word on it." Taking a breath,

Tynan relaxed just a touch. "It's *her*, Esha. I can't share her, and I won't."

Esha licked his lips, a gesture Tynan had worked out as children. It was what Esha did when he planned to disobey his parents. He wasn't going to back away from Messina. Opening his mouth to warn him off, Esha cut him off.

"Do you think the King knows her lineage? He placed Pride to protect her."

"I'm sure he does. I'm also sure he has plans for her that do not involve me."

"We can't let him have her. She belongs with us."

Assessing his friend, Tynan wondered when Messina had become a shared possession. Instead, he turned and went back inside. Tynan wasn't going to have this fight with his best friend. He didn't want to have to choose between them.

There was one thing he could do to end the debate, but the prophecy scared him as much as others. There was also the issue of hurting Messina that way. He'd never taken pleasure from punishing her, just a necessary behavior to prove to the others she wasn't the one the prophecy spoke of, or to have her behave.

Over the months, he'd found the idea of hurting her harder to stomach. Even this morning, he'd held her against the wall and been unable to do any further damage. She'd spoken the truth. She was his light. She'd brought him out of the darkness of his upbringing and reminded him that he wasn't all Sluagh.

The look in her eyes when he'd told her to practice her power of satiability on someone else. It hurt her that he was willing to share her. That hadn't been his intention. Tynan only planned for her to be intimate to the point of knowing the satiability took hold. He was sure that would happen long before they got naked, especially with a stranger.

Time was running out. Ashling wasn't one to give up lightly. As a male, she'd have used Messina's dreams to get what she wanted, but Ashling, as a female, could never genuinely hold what she desired, and so she sought to abduct Messina instead.

The Seelie were getting too cunning in their attempts to take her. None had gotten close for months thanks to the procedures he'd put in place. However, only last night, two had made it as far as his lounge room before Pride caught them.

There was no way to deny it any longer. Someone was helping the Seelie enter the Unseelie court. Tynan's eyes flicked to the Kings residence. He had a good idea of who. The thought annoying him the entire trek back to his suites.

By the time Tynan stood in his bedroom watching Messina sleep, his eyes were burning orbs of silver rage. Undressing, he pulled the sheet away to expose her naked flesh. Bruises from her training, and Tynan's prior attempts at restraint like violent artworks on her paleness.

The sound of his arousal filled the quiet room. Messina moaned in her sleep, her thighs drifting apart, Tynan's name on her lips. Kneeling on the bed, Tynan hovered his body above Messina's, her heat radiating across his skin, beckoning him to touch her, pleasure her, take his pleasure from her molten core.

Trembling with ferocious need, Tynan grabbed his rough shaft, directing it to spread the folds covering Messina's sex, pressing the vibration against her hood, before dragging down to the pleasure he denied himself.

"Please?" Messina whimpered.

Checking her face, Tynan found she slept still, but her breathing changed to match his need. He wanted her so badly, to make her his entirely and prevent the disgusting Seelie, or King Mabon taking her away. Worst still, Esha.

Tynan's supporting arm shook, his hand gripping the sheets. It would be so easy to end all possibility of anyone taking his light.

Eyes finding the tube of lubricant besides the bed, Tynan pulled back from the temptation, grabbed it from the bedside table, and coated his shaft. Gazing upon her beauty, Tynan gripped his lubricated cock and rubbed it against her folds.

"Ty!" Messina's hand finding his shoulder.

This time, when Tynan checked, her eyes were open, still half asleep, but the aqua irises pushed out by the desire of her pupils. When he met her eyes, she observed his anger and her body tensed, thighs trying to close, to push him away. He hated forcing her to act as if she despised him around the others, and he wouldn't have it now.

Shoving his hips forward, Tynan forced her legs open and pressed his head inside her. Messina's mouth and eyes opened wide, her breath catching, fingernails biting into his flesh. She couldn't draw blood, his skin was too tough, but he felt her pain just the same.

"Take what I give you." The sensation of her heat encompassing his dome was magnificent. He wanted to press deeper, to see how much she could take before she screamed, the rage in him yearned for it, but he wouldn't. Not to Messina. Not to the girl who had looked at him with innocent eyes and called him her home and hearth.

Instead, he dropped his hand and strummed her pearl till her eyes closed, her inner muscles relaxed, and he slipped a bare millimeter forward.

Messina's panting filled the room, the vibrations in Tynan's shaft growing, his need demanding more. Needing a distraction, Tynan moved his right hand to her abdomen and pressed his power into her.

Messina groaned, her eyes blinking rapidly. "What are you doing? I suddenly don't feel well."

It made sense that if she were able to see through glamor, her power would object to someone watching her abilities come alive. Still, it was important for Tynan to stop them both enjoying this too much. "Take it!"

The compliance of her body always amazed Tynan. As his words growled past his lips, he fell that touch deeper into her, stretching her more than he ever had before.

A sound of pain escaped Messina's lips, and then her satiability bloomed, opening like the bud of a rose, stealing her pain, exchanging it for pleasure, before it hurtled towards Tynan like a bullet.

Flames of pleasure licked his entire body, surrounding him in her power, and caressing his shaft as her body should be. Tynan moaned and thrust that little bit forward before he could stop himself. Only Messina's whimper reminded him he wasn't inside her, that her power mimicked the sensation to protect her.

Looking between them, Tynan could see he wasn't even close to having his head entirely buried, let alone his shaft, and yet, he felt her muscles contracting around him, squeezing him tight.

Eyes dilated with pleasure, his anger dampened as Tynan watched the nodules around the rim balloon, like pus-filled pimples, and the first hint of the delicate hair-like tentacles peaked out. Tynan's breath rushed out of him.

Affected not only by the view of their bodies joined, but to know he was fertile. Tynan waited two hundred and fifty years to see even the hint that he could father a child. Few Sluagh and Unseelie reproduced now because of the Seelie queen's curse. But the Seelie had no troubles producing offspring.

Tynan's head jerked up; eyes wide. He and Messina were both half Seelie. His body shook, Messina cried out as his engorgement stretched her further, and then Tynan felt his orgasm burst from every extremity, shooting to his groin and escaping in a rush of ecstasy. Stars exploded behind his eyes, his body entirely encased in the sensation of touch, stealing sight and sound for those few seconds in time.

Slowly opening his eyes, Tynan withdrew, checking to make sure the delicate tentacles had retreated. His breath blew out in relief when everything was how it had always been. There was no potential for a child between them now. Tynan was fertile, Messina wasn't, at least, not this time. He would need to be more careful of where his temper led him. For sure, his thoughts about stopping other's from taking his light caused tonight's doing.

Taking a deep breath, Tynan lifted his attention to Messina. Her eyes were wide, breathing short, staring up at him, a mixture of fear and awe covering her features. Releasing where he held her wrists pinned by her head, Tynan wondered what she'd done to cause him to hold her down. "Mess?"

"You didn't pull out."

"It's okay. I didn't plant a seed."

"Because we're not compatible?"

Was it hope or despair asking that question? Would it do any good to point out if a Seelie and Sluagh couldn't breed, he wouldn't exist? No, not tonight. Her withdrawal from their intimacy caused her enough emotional unsteadiness when the high dissolved.

Kneeling back, Tynan ignored her question to examine the damage. There was blood, only a trickle, but it stood out in the dark to him like a neon sign to his sense of smell. "It's okay, Mess. I'll take care of you."

His stomach was growling with hunger as Tynan lowered his face between her thighs and licked the injury clean, bringing Messina to orgasm on his tongue. As she recovered from her climax, Tynan called forth his healing power and healed her of his anger.

When he pulled her into his arms to sleep, he felt her tears fall quietly across his chest. Tynan came too close to losing control tonight. The next morning, she was unlikely to remember more than them having an intimate encounter, just like every other time he'd gone too far. But Tynan would know how much further it went than any time before.

Tynan knew she took his cum inside her for the first time and she hadn't been disgusted by the idea. He would remember he could be a father and claim this girl the Sidhe way if he wasn't careful.

As he lay holding her, pretending to sleep and ignore her tears, he was painfully aware that if he told her to grit her teeth, take the pain, and let him have her, she would comply and probably find some pleasure from it. That knowledge was dangerous. Thank god Sluagh's did nothing better than keeping a secret.

19

DARK STORM

❖

"Ow!" I grunted as I hit the floor. Groaning, I rolled just in time to miss getting kicked in the stomach. Jumping up, I blocked Esha's approach before he could get another hit home.

Feigning a punch, Esha swiped his leg, but seeing it, I jumped back, straight into the window. With another grunt, I stumbled forward, straight into Esha's approaching fist. Opening his hand at the last second, Esha grabbed my top, tripped my leg and came down on top of me.

"The fighting has improved immensely, but you need to watch where your opponent maneuvers you."

Grabbing my hands, Esha pinned them over my head, his eyes flicking up to scan the room. It was empty, Pride having wandered off like usual these days. Cold lips pressed to mine when he kissed me, forceful and determined. It felt wrong after kissing Tynan for the past six months, which felt oh, so right.

On instinct, believing it to be another test, I lifted my knee to his groin. Esha rolled free from me before I could make contact. Going the other way, I got back up ready to fight. Esha stood glaring at me.

The annoyance on his pulled me up. "That was just part of the training wasn't it?"

His ruby orbs glared at me a moment longer, then grabbing his shirt, he stormed towards the door. "Of course, it was. I'm just sick of that being your fallback defense."

Staring at the hall he'd disappeared down; I was unsure what to make of what just happened. I had a moment to realize I was alone in the room for the first time in months. Biting my lip in hesitation, I assessed all the doors and then the clock, Tynan wasn't due back for hours.

Without bothering with shoes or a jacket, I picked up the towel and bottle of water, wiping the sweat off myself as I walked, and throwing the towel aside just before I entered the hallway.

Opening the door to the suite, I took one step outside and stopped. Shadows were swirling all around the hallway. I wasn't sure if it was guards with glamor or some other type of majick, but I wasn't taking the chance.

"Pride?" I called hesitantly.

After six months cooped up in Tynan's suites except for occasional kitchen excursions and my Friday runs, I'd developed slight agoraphobia. Anxious, I turned back around to go inside. Pride stood behind me; a suspicious brow raised in my direction.

"There you are. I'm starving. Do you think we can go to the kitchen?"

"No." Crossing his arms, Pride stepped back to indicate that I should return inside.

Pouting, I took one step towards the suite but froze when I heard what sounded like a gale force wind blowing down a tunnel. Spinning on my heel to face the corridor, my eyes went wide as a massive black shadow storm rushed down the passageway towards me.

"Get inside!" Pride yelled over the noise. Stepping out, Pride grabbed me and threw me inside the suite doors. He went to move after me, but the black storm surrounded him. "Run!"

Frozen in fear, I stood there watching as the storm surrounded Pride, Black tentacles entwined each wrist and ankle, Pride fighting his way free only to be ensnared again and again. Ink splattered the walls where Pride dismembered the creature, but no matter how many black tentacles he ripped apart, more appeared.

"Messina, it's a seeker. It won't stop till it finds its target, then it will do whatever it was created to do. You need to run."

Pride's words were heard, processed, and understood, but my feet wouldn't move. "Pride!" Seeing the creature change its tactic before Pride did, I tried to warn him.

While Pride defended its attempt to restrain him, the creature thrust one giant tentacle forward, penetrating Pride's chest, blood, muscles, and bone splintering and separating as the thick limb forced its way through Pride's torso.

My eyes were filling with water as Pride froze, his mouth hanging open agape. Scarlet spit expelled from his lips. My brain was processing that Pride bled red like me when the tentacles of the creature secured Pride's elbows and knees.

Unable to look away, I watched horrified as Pride was stretched in every direction, that thick trunk holding him pierced. With a sickening popping noise, Pride screamed his agony as the creature tore Pride's limbs from his torso like he was a gingerbread man. Instead of crumbs, blood and fragments of bone and cartilage hailed through the air like bits of confetti at a goblin wedding.

"Run!" Pride choked out one more time. His head was turned right then rip back left, leaving his body hanging spraying blood in five directions. The thick tentacle jerked left, then right, dislodging the lump of flesh from its end, then disappeared back into the shadow storm.

Swallowing in fear, knowing I was doomed, my feet finally obeyed my brain. Spinning around, I ran into the suite as fast as I could. It wasn't soon enough.

Pain ripped through me as something gripped me around the waist. There was a moment where everything froze, the view of Tynan's suite imprinting into my memory forever, and then I was ripped back into the storm of pain. Screaming Tynan's name into the darkness with my last breath.

SCREAMING STILL, I sat bolt upright in bed. "Mess, what is it?" Tynan took my face in his hands and looked deep into my eyes as if searching for my source of pain.

Touching his face, I knew he was real and dived forward into his arms. "Don't let them take me. Please, don't let them take me."

Sobbing against his chest as the images of the dream continued flashing behind my closed eyelids, the sound of a storm still roaring in my ears. "They killed Pride. Tore him apart like he was a paper doll."

"Mess, stop."

"Please don't let them take me. It hurt so much, too much pain to stay sane. God, Tynan, you can't let them take me."

"Mess! Stop!" Tynan yelled, throwing me away from him. Thumping into the bed head stunned me when my head flung back and connected with the stone wall above it. Slumping onto the bed, I grabbed the back of my head and blinked through my tears at Tynan wondering why he'd do that when I was distraught.

Looking to be in agony, Tynan reached over his shoulder, and his fingers came back smeared with blood. "By the goddess, you're powerful, Mess. No one has physically harmed me like that in centuries."

Blinking down at my hands, I found my fingernails covered in blood. Eyes stretching wide, my breathing came in shorter gasps as the panic and fear built in me. Tynan would punish me for this, and I couldn't even fathom how bad it would be. Probably on par with the pain of my nightmare. "No, Mess, calm-" The funnel of water started at my feet.

Surging forward, Tynan grabbed my face in his hands and joined our mouths. Kissing me fiercely, his lips passionate as if he could never kiss another as he did me.

Falling into that kiss wholeheartedly, I put my heart and soul into kissing Tynan and making the pain go away. I knew he could do that.

He could make it all go away. If I gave him everything I was, he would make all the pain stop.

Throwing Tynan on his back, I straddled his thighs. Tynan moaned, his hands gripping my hips as I kissed him and rubbed my body over his. When I lifted my lower body, his curse sprang up in search of its prey. Using my hand to guide his hunt, I moaned when I fed him his desire.

As the vibrating head of him pressed against my entrance, Tynan's fist gripped my hair. He ripped my head back just as I pressed myself down, forcing him a millimeter deeper. His head lifted to watch how he impaled me, pupils dilating with need when I cried out at the stretch of his opening me to him. I'd dreamed of this moment many times, and now it was happening.

Without warning, Tynan threw me on my back. Tynan's body pinned me to the bed with my hands above my head. His mouth worried at my nipple, then swapped to the other while he rubbed himself on my hip.

Aggressively, Tynan pulled back and looked down between us again, a growl vibrating through his chest, matching the rattle of his snake. Lifting his face, he just watched me, as if waiting for something.

"Ty?"

"You don't know what you're asking for."

"Yes, I do!"

"No, Mess, you don't! This is bigger than just sexual satisfaction." Releasing me, he moved to the bottom of the bed, covering his lap with the sheet. Tynan waited for me to pull myself to sitting and swipe at the endless tears. "Tell me what happened in the dream. Every detail, Mess."

He listened and waited patiently, eyes flashing silver when I told him the part about Esha kissing me. Even when the dream ended and I admitted how much I wanted him. He knelt there and heard it all.

Only when I had fallen silent for several minutes did Tynan move. Standing up, he walked away from me towards the bathroom. Blood streaked his back where the flesh was clawed open.

"What happened?"

"You woke terrified and your pain manifested and served it up to me," Tynan explained before entering the shower. Biting my lip, fear of the dream, of Tynan's punishment crippling me. "Get your arse in here, Mess. I'm not the only who needs a shower."

With shaking legs, I stood slowly and moved into the bathroom. Standing with the hot water pouring down on his back, Tynan held out his hand to me. Moving to him, he pulled me into a hug.

"So now we know intense emotions activate your power of manifestation, we just have to teach you how to recall those emotions to use it."

Caging my face in his hands, Tynan peered into my eyes for several seconds. I felt like he was searching my soul for some truth, but I was helpless to stare back into those obsidian orbs. As long as his pupils were black, I didn't fear him.

Licking his lips, he kissed me passionately. Moaning into him, I didn't realize he was pushing me down till I was already on my knees and he broke the kiss to stand straight.

"You want me to lose myself inside you?" Tynan growled as he guided his curse to my lips. "Let's give you what you want."

"Ty..."

Tynan smacked my cheek with his thick hardness, just with enough force to let me know he wasn't playing. I'd hurt him physically; now I was going to pay it back.

Meeting his eyes, I opened my mouth. He wouldn't fit, but he knew I could use my tongue just as efficiently. My eyes stayed locked with his while I licked and sucked the lollipop given me with all the enthusiasm I could muster - which wasn't much to start with, but as the first taste of precum passed my lips, I suddenly couldn't get enough of him. There was at least that benefit from my power of satiability.

~

SEVERAL HOURS LATER, I watched Tynan getting dressed for the day.

He'd tucked me into bed after the shower, no pleasure for me this time, and then he went elsewhere. He was back in bed with me by the time his alarm went off. His back healed, not a hint that I'd injured him, and part of me wondered if I'd dreamed the entire thing.

"Can you heal yourself?"

"Yes, but I have to take the energy from another."

"You did that last night?"

"We've seen a great influx of Seelie Sidhe trespassing of late. Some are currently prisoners of ours." Tynan met my eyes in the mirror he was using to knot his tie. "We have one less this morning."

"Oh." Biting my lip, I sank a little further under the covers.

"Practice your manifestation this morning. Remember what it felt like in your dream last night, or how you felt confronting your mother's killer."

Closing my eyes, I focused on blocking those memories before they could manifest.

"Mess?"

Opening my eyes, I found Ty standing over me.

"Do you want Esha to make a move on you?"

"No. Why would you think that?"

Tynan lifted a brow. "Because dreams tend to manifest our subconscious desires."

"So, I want Pride to be ripped apart and to suffer unimaginable pain?"

Again, Tynan just cocked that damn brow over is black eyes in a question of my attitude. With a huff. I rolled over, putting my back to him. "I want you, Ty. I'm just sick of feeling empty when you've finished wanting me."

Staying quiet behind me for a moment, my eyes shuttered when he patted my hair, brushing it over my shoulder before he dragged the sheet down my body so he could see it. His touch burned a trail of madness beneath my skin.

"Ty, I can't take much more." My breathing was already ragged, my body crying out for desecration.

Tynan's hand snapped away as if I'd stung him. "You're going to have to. We can't be together that way. I'll see you tonight."

Covering my mouth to hold in a sob, I didn't want Tynan to know I was on the verge of crying.

"Don't leave the suite, Mess. My rooms are the only place you are safe."

After watching the door close, I buried my face in the pillow and groaned in frustration before flipping on my back and sitting up. Slipping my robe on, I headed to my bedroom.

Out on the walkway, I looked down to see Esha talking with Tynan. Both their eyes tracked me back to my room like predators. Closing the door on their hunger, I grabbed up my current sketch pad from the small pile and started putting my nightmare on paper.

I didn't draw as often now. Not just because I spent all day training, but because my life was the same day in, and day out. I only drew anything new or different, or the dreams which seemed too real to be a dream.

When I finished drawing what I remembered, I considered getting up and dressing for the day. I was meant to practice my power, but I just didn't have the energy. Instead, I lay down on my bed and went back to sleep.

20

THWARTED

❖

My door opening dragged me from my sleep. Yawning, I rolled over to watch the goblin place my usual tea on my side table, bowing before he left. Famished, I ate the tea cakes Margo had sent up and drank the tea. After I finished, I sat hugging my knees against the bed head, chin resting on my knees as I made plans in my head.

"You're not dressed?" Esha's deep voice brought me from my plotting. "Have you been in bed all morning?" With a huff, I squirmed back down beneath the blankets, putting my back to him. "You were meant to be practicing." Esha moved closer to the bed. "Get up; we have training."

"I'm not well, and I need to rest," I murmured, cuddling my pillow.

"Sidhe don't get sick, Messina."

"Maybe those who don't mix with humans regularly, but I've gotten sick plenty of times." Truthfully, other than the injuries I'd received I'd never once had a cold or flu.

"I heard you screaming last night. Did he...? Are you hurt?" Esha was quiet for a minute when I didn't respond. "Is there something you need?"

"To be left alone." Bowing his head, Esha went to leave. "Esha, can you tell the Prince I'm unwell and would prefer to stay in my room tonight?" Not that I believed it would do a shred of good."

"I will let him know your wishes."

Exhaling, I rolled to stare at the ceiling. I had to escape, but to do that, I had to remember how Nora got me out of here the first time. Esha could unlock memories, but he wouldn't do it without Tynan's permission and trade of pleasure. Giving him my body was nothing, I'd done it before to get what I needed from my stepfather. It helped that I knew that I'd barely remember the experience. I knew I'd done it, what happened, but I had to focus hard even to remember how it happened.

Esha, however, would grant me back those memories, and I didn't want a lot of my childhood again, just the way out of here. My other option was to get to the garden and ask Nora how she got me out the first time.

Just as the thought occurred, my door opened, and one of the goblins who worked for Margo came in to collect my tray. Sitting up watching her, when she met my eyes, I smiled. She snarled a little. It made me giggle which made her hiss at me. Turning her back to collect the tray, I decided now was as good a time as any to try my glamor.

Focusing on how my mother taught me, I joined my fists before me, concentrating my energy. When I could feel the pressure between my body and fists, I unclenched my hands and swept them up in front of me, passing over my face, and then sweeping back and over my head. My skin tingled all over, my hands blurry when I looked at them. A smile pulled at the side of my mouth.

When the goblin turned around, her mouth dropped open in shock. I waved my goblin hand in front of her face, pushing my energy towards her, painting the goblin in my mind till she grew and morphed into a blurry version of me.

Snatching the tray from her hands before she could drop it, I practiced a snarl. "Enjoy being Sidhe for a day. Esha will love to spend it alone with you if you desire the company."

Staring at the mirror, the goblin focused on me looking like a goblin for a minute, and then to the reflection of her, now looking like me, utterly mesmerized. I left the room quietly.

Downstairs, Esha sat working on his laptop, ignoring the goblin walking passed. Pride appeared as I reached the hallway, but I kept walking for the door. "Where is Messina? I sensed her presence."

"Still in her room. Did you hear her screaming last night?"

"How could I not?" Pride replied mournfully. "But I shouldn't have felt Messina if she was still in her room." Reaching the door, I opened it.

"Go check for yourself. I can't stand being near her when she's so miserable."

Closing the door, I walked down the hall. No shadows were hiding here, no dark storms rushing to take me. Making the first turn without issue, I went around the corner. The hall was empty, so I quickly changed my glamor to look like Brie, and hid the tray as a package of clothes. I was halfway down that corridor when I heard yelling from the Prince's end of the hall.

"You go that way, and I'll head for the kitchen," Esha directed Pride. "Look for the goblin."

Walking casually, Esha flew by me, not even paying attention to the Sluagh female down the hall. As soon as he passed, I placed the tray on the floor and let the glamor around it dissolve.

Moving a little quicker now, I turned the passageways until I was nearly at the garden. Once I hit the corridor of the garden, I bolted. All that training with Esha paid off. I was able to sprint the hallway quickly, finding the garden and pulling the door open, stepping inside, and relaxing when the corridor was still clear of anyone.

Closing the door, I let my glamor dissolve, returning to the true me. It was daylight in the garden, and it looked as I'd left it. Thanking the garden for still allowing me entry, I moved up the path I'd learned well to my mother's hammock in the tree. "Where are you going to run to?" A woman's voice asked me as I prepared to climb the tree.

Turning, I discovered the silhouette of a woman, the light shining from her too bright for me to see her detail. Instantly, I knew that the light was of her soul, but at the same time, I felt the need to adore and fear her. "Who are you?"

"Who are you?" The woman returned the question.

"I'm Messina Doe."

The woman tilted her head. "You are wrong. Messina Doe never existed. She was born of fear when you escaped this place and died the moment you returned to the Unseelie court. So, I'll ask again. Who are you?"

Biting my lip, I dropped my gaze to my hands. "I don't know who I am anymore, or what."

The woman chuckled. "But, of course, you do. You are a Sidhe, born both of light and dark, like the goddess herself."

"If I'm born of light, why does the Seelie touch cause me pain?"

The woman's light seemed to fade slightly, making her more visible. Her dress was silvery silk, her hair shiny and silver also, her smooth wrinkle free skin was alabaster, and her eyes the deepest, coldest, black I'd ever seen. Her eyes chilled me to my bone.

The woman stepped to the side. "That was unfortunate, but not unwelcome. Because of your powers, the touch of any not worthy of you will always make you uncomfortable, but the pain was your mother's doing. Nora, with her last breath, cursed the Seelie never to hold you. The curse took her words literally."

She turned to face me again. "No matter how it came about, the curse protects you to some extent as it prevents the Seelie interloper's plans for you. For this reason, I will leave it be."

Unsure what to think of her words, my mind stopped paying any attention when Tynan's mark on my wrist started glowing. He wasn't due home for hours, so he shouldn't have been here to locate me.

Suddenly, fire sizzled the nerve endings through my entire body like a vineyard inferno, a gash opening across my inner arm. Screaming, I clutched my sleeve to me. "How do I get out of here?"

The woman took a breath frowning at Tynan's way of forcing me out of hiding. "Messina, you belong here."

"No, not like this, not with him." Holding up my arm as another gash appeared, I cried out and huddled over my injury.

Through watery eyes, I watched her sigh and look away. "True, this is not how it should be between you. So much has gone off course and it is trying on my patience to bring it back on track."

"Will he hurt me if I stay?" *Please, tell me no.*

"Of course, he will. He is cursed as much as you." The woman rolled her eyes, then focused on me, her cold gaze burning into mine. "That, Messina, is the point. The fates can be cruel. You must bear his curse if you wish to find happiness." Turning her back on me she disappeared into the garden.

"Wait! What does that mean? He will hurt me; how does that make me happy? It's killing me to be with him and not be with him."

"You are fated to be lovers, let it happen," her voice drifted back to me dismissively.

"I've tried to be with him; he won't have me."

"Jealousy is a strong motivator, even among the Fae," the woman's voice reached me even as her light vanished altogether.

"Jealousy?" I muttered, entirely lost by her meaning. Trying to puzzle through it for several minutes, I analyzed her words until the brand on my wrist flared bright purple, telling me Tynan was close by, and a third gash opened across my arm making me collapse in pain.

Giving up, I made for the tree. I would leave. I would find out from Nora how to escape, and then I would get out of here. Locked away in Tynan's suite as his plaything was not how I wanted to spend the rest of my life. Even when Tynan wasn't hurting me, his touch tortured me with how much I desired him.

Reaching the tree, and despite the pain in my arm, I started climbing. The air in the garden broke apart with a loud crack and lightning flashed across the sky impacting with the tree.

Thrown off by the force of the strike, the air forced from my lungs when I landed hard on the ground, my head reverberating with a crack as it impacted rock. My vision blurry, lungs burning, and body aching, I lay there.

The woman crouched above me, worry in her eyes. "My will is not thwarted twice, my child. You should have been raised here, always in his grasp. You will not remember how to leave because I won't allow it." Her hands were tender as they stroked my hair.

In a blink, she disappeared. Groaning, I cringed in pain as I sat up straight. The sound of a roaring fire surrounded me. Looking at the tree, I sobbed as it burned.

Stumbling towards it, the fire was too hot on my skin; the heat stung my eyes causing them to water, but the tears evaporated before they could fall. Coughing on the smoke, covering my mouth with the front of my dress, I searched for a way to climb the tree.

A loud cracking sound made me look up to see the branch holding the hammock snap. Smoke stinging my eyes, I leaped out of the way to avoid further injury as it crashed to the ground.

Scrambling to the burning hammock, I snatched the edge of my jacket, which bundled the last of my belongings, and scampered free of the fire. Crawling away from the tree, I stayed low until the heat above me wasn't searing, then I stabilized my feet beneath me, and ran.

Safely at the door, I turned back to witness the burning garden, spreading as if a fire demon raged through it. The destruction of the most beautiful place in the entire court brought me to tears.

Coming back here would never be a possibility again. That's why she did it; I understood that. This garden was never my place, but Nora's, and Nora was dead. Now that my heart knew the truth, she'd never come to me again.

Stumbling out the door, I fell to my knees, my chest was tight, lungs shriveled, and heart breaking. Smoke billowed out into the corridor as shiny black shoes stepped in front of me, reflecting my pale, soot-smudged face back up at me.

"Oh, Messina," Tynan stroked the side of my cheek, "my trust is not to be broken, for I never give it twice. I thought we understood each other, that we passed this." His fingers threaded through my hair, searching for that perfect grab spot.

Pain seared along nerve endings from where I'd knocked my head forcing me to cry out before he even curled his fingers. His hand froze.

Withdrawing his fingers, Tynan observed my blood smearing his fingers. "How badly are you hurt, Mess?"

What a question. The pain of losing my last connection to my mother went beyond the physical. We'd be delving deep into the abyss of my soul to find the real impact. Sobbing harder, I curled over the rescued bundle of my past.

Growling in frustration, Tynan stepped away from me. "Pride."

Picking me up from the floor, Pride settled me in his arms. Gritting his teeth, Tynan pried my jacket from my arms.

"No!" Sobbing, hurt from his gashes, the movement needed to fight him was agonizing, and I didn't have a chance of holding on to it.

Once Tynan had my jacket, he nodded to Pride, and Pride walked with me in his arms.

"Do you think she was attacked?" Esha asked Tynan behind us.

"I don't know. At least she knows her safe place isn't safe anymore. That should end the need to escape there."

"It doesn't make sense otherwise. Mess knew we'd be waiting when she finally came out. She didn't even try to fight us just now, and she could put up a much better resistance now. Something happened behind that wall."

"Since her injuries are more extensive than I intended, I would agree."

With tears still streaming down my face, I sobbed against Pride's chest. "I'm sorry, I couldn't wait any longer."

With a shake of his head, Pride lowered his face to my ear. "They knew you were biding your time, Messina. They've been waiting for you to try and run for some time now. I should have known last night would set you off." His arms held me tighter.

My crying escalated at his gentle words. Denying the need between Tynan and I was becoming unbearably painful. Tynan kept drawing me into this chaotic emotional vulnerability with his lust. If I couldn't escape, I needed to get control of my satiability.

Tynan wasn't my boyfriend; I owed him no loyalty, and since he was still fucking human women, there was no commitment between us. If learning to control my powers meant letting someone else have sex with me, then that's what I'd do.

21

DARKNESS AND LIGHT

❖

"Take her to her room please, Pride."

"Will you heal her?" Pride queried respectfully.

"No," Tynan's tone was final. Not waiting for an explanation, Pride carried me upstairs to my room and placed me gently on the bed.

"I need my sketchbook." I tried to sit up.

Placing his large hand high on my chest, Pride pressed me gently back to the bed. "You need to rest. The pain of your injuries won't be his only punishment for your disobedience."

"No, I need to draw it. If I sleep before I do, I won't remember in the morning. I need to draw the memory before I lose it."

Frowning, Pride collected my sketchbook and pencil and handed it to me, helping to prop me up before he left the room. At my door, Pride studied me quietly for a moment, serious contemplation on his face before he closed the door.

My hands drew everything I could remember from the garden. The woman, the tree as struck by lightning, some of the words she said to me, and the garden ablaze. I drew until my hand seized, my eyes refused to open anymore, and I passed out.

When I woke, Tynan was sitting on the chair beside my bed looking through my sketchbook. "Did she tell you her name?"

"No," my voice croaked, barely audible.

"An effect of the smoke inhalation. Breathing will be difficult for a few days." Standing, Tynan dropped two pills on my bedside table beside a large glass of water. "For your headache, and keep your water up."

"Ty?" I called as he dropped my sketchbook and yanked open my door.

Turning his head, silver orbs of anger stared back at me. "She could have killed you, Mess. You do something stupid like that again; I'll kill you myself, then I'll bring you back and kill you twice more for the fun of it."

"I needed to try. I needed my stuff."

"You have not needed for anything the entire time you have been here."

"I've needed you to make love to me!"

"I've taken care of you better than any other would, and you use majicks to try and escape me," Tynan continued, ignoring my complaint.

"Glamor is free."

Tynan's jaw tensed. "Have I not given you everything you asked for?"

"She said we are meant to be lovers." Painfully, I eased up to sitting.

"I've had you trained up like one of us, I've fed you, clothed you, pleasured you..." Tynan was yelling at me.

"I want you to fuck me!" Nothing but the sound of my hitched breathing. "It hurts," I whispered. "The empty pleasure hurts. My body reacts to your arousal, but your very presence is starting to bruise, making my flesh tender and sore, and each repeated exposure leaves me feeling beaten and hollow."

If I couldn't see Tynan's shoes in my peripheral vision, I would have thought he left, it was that quiet. "Release me!" I pleaded with a barely-there voice. "You're torturing me, and I can't take it anymore."

Stepping out of my room, Tynan slammed the door. Closing my eyes, I lay back and slept, my dreams plagued with nightmares of being eaten alive, of soldiers of light taking me, of Lisa dying. Every imagining caused me suffering.

Now, I was locked in an onyx jewelry box, a precious item that Tynan kept locked away and only took out to play with on occasion. As the years passed, he took me out less and less, until one day, he stopped coming back. He left me alone in that cold dark stone box for eternity. That's when the voices started.

"Messina?" a gentle voice tugged at me from outside the box. "She's feverish. Esha, call the Prince; he needs to heal her."

"He won't do it, Pride. Her pain is her punishment."

"It's been a day already. She's not waking. If he doesn't heal her, he risks losing her."

"Sidhe don't die from fever induced nightmares."

"Tell the prince to heal her or I will go over his head."

"The prince gave an order. We follow our orders," Esha warned, then a door slammed, rattling the lid of the box.

"Let me out!" Hopeful someone might hear me and let me see the light again. "Please, let me out! Please? Release me! Kill me! Torture me! Just don't leave me alone in the dark."

The lid remained closed, no sound penetrating it again. "No! No, please, don't leave me here." Scrambling to climb the walls, I was determined to see if I could force the lid open. Scratching and clawing, I tried to climb, but the walls of the box were too smooth to get a hold.

Sliding down to the cold stone floor for the hundredth time, I trembled, tears streaming down my cheeks. Hugging my pained fingers to me, I could make out the smears of my blood lining the walls. The silence was deafening.

"What happened to her fingers, Pride?"

"I don't know. It happened two days ago. I came back, and her fingers were bloody and raw to the bone. The fever is getting worse. Three days have passed since she's woken, Esha. We need to intervene."

"I'll speak to him."

"What's happening in there, Messina?" Pride sounded close to the lid of the box.

Screaming until my throat strained again, I begged him to help me. Curled in a ball on the floor, I called continuously until my voice broke and refused to work anymore.

That's when hope died. The last glimmer of light in the deathly dark box, which had allowed me to at least determine the walls and roof. It snuffed out.

Despair crushed upon me. A tidal wave of loss and doom hammered me into the cold stone floor, breaking all my bones, stealing the air from my lungs. I was suffocating, but I couldn't care. There was no strength to fight for my life anymore. No will to live. I had nothing. There was nothing but darkness and pain.

Even the pain faded eventually until it was just darkness and emptiness. I was a hollow, broken vessel. Nothing to anybody, not even myself. There wasn't a name for who I was, no memory of what I looked like, or what form I was meant to take.

The box was timeless, floating, no longer weighed down by my skin and bones anymore. Hovering in the box like a dark cloud of nothingness.

Randomly, I drifted into the wall and found a gap in my onyx prison. Tentatively, I pressed into the hole. There was no resistance to moving into it effortlessly, and I felt freedom on the other side. Beneath me, the sack of skin and bones released a final breath, the last tether to that being, snapped.

"Call the prince!"

The air trembled, the box shaking under the force of the pained demand. Fear coursed through me. A long-forgotten feeling, unwelcome in my emptiness. Racing through the gap, that sudden burst of emotion slowed me down.

'Get out, get out, get out, now!' a child's voice encouraging me to float faster, to escape the gap and the box for good. Since, I lacked substance, the air currents, and the vacuum caused by air rushing past the outside of the box controlled my escape.

"What is it!" Anger raged like an inferno, pushing me back a little from the end of the tunnel. "No!"

Panic.

"You are not getting away from me."

Fear.

"Messina, don't you dare."

Anger.

Every hit of emotion slowed my escape. Buffeting against me, confusing me, stalling me as I tried to remember which way I was floating. Which way was out?

'*Get out, go, now,*' the child urged, panic rising in its voice

"Messina?" a man whispered, an unknown emotion pushing in at me.

"Messina," a female echoed him. "You have to run. Don't stop, for anyone or anything." Turning towards that voice and the fear in it, I found myself in a forest that seemed familiar. Thick and green, heavy with underbrush, and the tiniest sliver of light through the dark canopy. "Run and don't stop, Messina. Run until you find the light. Then you climb into that light and never look back. Don't ever come back."

Pushing me away from her, she repeated her words until my little feet started running. Running from my mother, fear, and confusion making my heart beat faster than it should have been.

I ran until I found the light, high above me, then I stopped and focused on my fear. Letting it build within me, I waited till my skin felt tight, then I shoved it out of me through my feet. The water and wind combined to create a twister around my ankles. Holding my power down, it had no choice but to lift me up.

A horrific storm was raging around me. The twister lifted me towards the light, and once I was high enough, I reached up and grabbed the rim of the skylight and pulled myself up and inside the tunnel.

Warmth and light surrounded me, only brightness ahead. I felt at peace.

I felt.

22

—————

SUNLIGHT

❖

Blinking rapidly against the light that was too bright, too pure, I struggled to see. Six months underground my eyes had forgotten the strength of the sun. The air around me felt warm. Not the warmth of a building, but the heat of the sun upon your naked skin.

It had been winter when I'd left the human world, now it was the height of summer. Stretching out on the comfortable bed I was on, I exposed as much of me to the sun as I could, soaking up its light.

Bed?

Sitting up, I peered at my surroundings. A room, decorated in the purest whites and golds. The bed was placed beneath a large window which was faceted in a way that during the day, sunlight channeled towards the bed.

"The King's consorts chambers." Turning my head, I found a familiar Seelie Sidhe, dressed in the white and gold uniform of the Solaris, lounging across the room. "The King had a Seelie consort for a very long time, and a Seelie needs sunlight."

"So, I'm still in the Unseelie court?" My voice croaked from disuse.

Standing casually, Cathal moved towards me. "Yes, and you are still a possession of the dark prince. I'm here at the King's doing."

"Why?" I gently lifted the messed sheets of the bed to cover my nudity.

"Because the Unseelie, in their ignorance, nearly killed you." Fisting a handful of the sheet, Cathal tugged it back. "Don't do that. You need your skin to soak up as much light as possible. You've been too long in the dark."

"I'll burn."

"No, you won't." When I released the sheet, he tugged it back to the base of the bed and dropped it. "You don't need to fear me; I would never harm you."

"You tried to rape me."

"Ashling was impatient. The fastest way for us to get you back was for you to be pregnant with a Seelie child. I am a soldier; I take my orders from my superiors." Cathal sat on the side of the bed. "When you return to the Seelie court, I will take my orders from you, Queen Messina, and no other."

"Queen? What drugs are you on? I'm not a queen, I'm not even full Seelie."

Cathal looked confused. "No one has told you?"

"Told me what?"

Cathal made himself comfortable. "When the Dark Prince brought the Sluagh to join the Sidhe war and defeated the Seelie, he took a trophy and gave it to King Mabon as a peace offering." Cathal met my eyes. "He took King Titan's only child, Princess Nora Bayne, and gave her to the Unseelie King with the formation of peace being that the princess was kept safe and treated well.

"Titan died over a decade ago now. Ashling stepped up as our leader while we negotiated Nora's return with her child. King Mabon didn't want to let either of you go. The next thing we knew, you went missing from the Unseelie court, and no one could find you. The former captain of the Solaris, Nathani, was sent to question Nora. The questioning got out of control, and he killed Nora."

"He was ordered to kill her."

Cathal looked surprised. "No, she was our queen, we would never have..."

"He told me directly that she was killed for refusing to hand me over. His twin brother, Maranta, confessed that Ashling ordered Nathani to kill their princess."

Cathal looked worried. "That doesn't make sense. Nora was a sane and good Seelie. We'd only kill royal blood if they threatened our existence."

Watching the confusion on Cathal's face, I shrugged my shoulders as I planted a notion. "Maybe Ashling got used to her faux-royal status and decided Nora coming home threatened her existence as ruler."

Cathal stood and paced the room. After a moment he stopped. "You said Maranta confessed. How do you know that?"

"I was in the room."

Cathal's eyes were filled with suspicion. "Maranta was here?"

"Yes. Maranta came to take me back to the Seelie court on Ashling's orders. Sadly, for him, he lost his head. We've had a massive influx of Seelie assassins being caught around the faerie mound."

Grimacing as if in pain, Cathal turned his face away and started pacing again. Sick of watching him, I stood up and moved into his path. When Cathal turned around, I was there, and it brought him up short. "What killed me?"

"You were exposed to a poison." Palming my elbow, he led me back to the bed. Ants bit along the nerves of my arm, the discomfort radiating out from his touch. He walked to the bedside table and collected a branch of a plant, a beautiful pure white cone-shaped flower hanging from the end.

"It's Fae's Betrayal. In this form, it's harmless. However, if you ingest or inhale it, it will poison us. Without treatment, you die in a matter of days." Cathal made it sound like this was common knowledge.

"Why didn't Pride know?"

Cathal put the plant down. "It only grows in a Seelie garden. The Unseelie have never encountered it before. When you exhaled your dying breath, Pride was able to get the prince to you fast enough to hold you to life, but the poison was still in your system.

Pride called the King, the King called me. I knew what it was immediately."

"Is that because you poisoned me?"

Shaking his head, Cathal made himself comfortable at the end of the bed. "No, but I'm fascinated by herbology, and the King knows I have a thorough knowledge. Once I was told your symptoms, I rushed over with the antidote."

"If it only grows in a Seelie garden, how was I poisoned."

"By the severity of your reaction, you inhaled a strong dose of the burning plant. Have you seen that flower anywhere recently?"

"I'd have to check my drawings, but at a guess, it was growing in Nora's garden when it burnt."

"Nora has a garden here?"

"Had. Past tense. Some crazy chick burnt it to ashes the day I got sick. I was standing in the garden at the time."

"That would probably be the source then. Do I get a thank you for saving you?"

Lifting my arm, I traced Tynan's mark on my wrist. "No." Cathal's brows jumped in surprise, and his eyes told me he'd expected me to be grateful. "What did you get out of saving me?"

Cathal's eye drifted down my body, reminding me I was exposed. "I bargained for a night with you." He moved his upper body forward as if he was about to kiss my stomach.

"Don't," I flinched. "Seelie touch causes me pain."

"It didn't hurt you a moment ago when I led you back to the bed?"

"Yes, it did. I've grown used to the discomfort of men touching me and don't always show it."

"The Prince hurts you too?" Cathal placed his lips on my abdomen. It felt awkward, small sparks of hurt, but not painful enough to scream.

"Not at first, but the pain after he touches me is the worst." Shoving on Cathal's shoulder, I squirmed away from his lips. "Seelie touch is unbearable from the first instant."

"But not right now?" Cathal placed his hand tentatively on my abdomen. I waited for the searing pain, it didn't happen, but the ants were nipping. "Tynan said something when Ashling sent me to take you by force. Do you remember?"

"He said I was untainted. That you couldn't force me to choose."

Cathal's smile lit up the room. "That's right. Do you understand what he meant?" He waited for me to shake my head. "It means you haven't completed the coming of age tradition. Until you do, it goes against the goddess to force you to leave your home. A choice that would be taken from you if I forced a child on you unwillingly. I believe that you react badly to anyone trying to take you from your home, Messina."

"This isn't my home."

Cathal lifted his eyes to me. "I know that; I just wasn't sure if you knew that."

"Trust me, I'm never left in doubt that I'm a prisoner here."

"So why not come with me?"

"Because I don't trust the Seelie to treat me any better." Sitting up, I moved away from Cathal. "You came into my dreams, forced yourself upon me, and imprisoned me in my body so the prince would think me dead. Do you know what they do with dead Seelie here?" When Cathal shook his head, I wanted to slap him in his stupid forehead. "They feed them to the goblins. Had your plan worked, I would have been eaten alive."

Cathal's face hardened. "Ashling's plan, not mine."

"Are you that hard up for sex in the Seelie court, you would rape me to get some?"

"No!" Shoulder's tensing, Cathal screwed his face up in disgust. "I'm the captain of the guard, I'm expected to bed our Princess."

Remembering his words in the dream, I frowned. "Bed, not wed?"

"I would only become your husband if I succeeded in filling you with a child. You are of the royal line. We cannot risk you not carrying on the line, so it would be expected you take multiple suitors and whoever seeds your womb would become your husband."

Processing all he was telling me, I narrowed my eyes at him. "And since I am in line to become queen, that makes you King."

"King consort."

"You can leave now."

"Messina..."

"I don't want to be stuck with a guy who doesn't care about me, simply because he got me pregnant. I'm not having sex with you, now get out."

Shaking his head, Cathal stayed where he was. "We would learn to care for each other, Messina, but we can't do that while you are the Prince's pet. Come with me, and we can get to know each other in the light court."

"I may not be home here, but I definitely don't belong there." Closing my eyes, I let the melancholy of that thought sweep by me. "I think you have your wires crossed. I'm no queen. I'm not even good enough to be a princess. I don't even truly believe that I'm one of you at all."

Opening and closing his mouth like a guppy, Cathal seemed to be trying to find the right words. "I understand you were raised as a human?"

"The word raise suggests that at any time the people caring for me tried to support me, to lift me up. All they did was beat me down and drag me around."

Turning his face to the window, as if the sun may show him how he could convince me to put my well-being in his hands, Cathal pursed his lips.

"If I'm to be honest, Cathal, I've never been treated better than I have by the prince. I won't go with someone who has tried to force me to do anything against my will." Collecting the sheet from the bottom of the bed, I covered myself, turning so my exposed back was to the window and could absorb the light for me.

"The Prince has forced you against your will."

"He's also tortured me, and yet, staying in his cold-hearted care is still more appealing than going anywhere with the people who killed their own princess."

"What would convince you to trust me?"

Looking over my shoulder, I lifted onto my elbow to face the

Seelie Sidhe. "Don't try to take me where you want me. Help me escape and leave me be. Let it be up to me."

Clenching his jaw, Cathal narrowed his gaze to pinpoints before he looked away. "I can't do that. There is no escape from here, Messina. You need to choose us."

"Then I'll stay here. Thank you." Closing my eyes, I lay back down, so my back was still exposed to the sun.

It took a few minutes before I felt Cathal's hand skim over my back, my nerves firing painfully in response. His body scooted in behind mine naked. I tried to move away, but his arm encircled my waist. "Let me show you what you are missing, Messina," Cathal murmured seductively.

Before he could get a good grip, I bucked my body and rolled away. Cathal came after me. Emptying my mind of everything, I pretended he was Esha, and that this was another training session. Esha never held back. If I didn't want to get hurt, I had to defend myself well.

"Goddess!" Cursing when I got a good punch in, Cathal stumbled back holding his jaw. "You're stronger than you look."

There was no holding back my pride at his compliment, my lips turning up in a smile. "Thank you."

Cathal smirked. "That was a Sluagh move. They've taught you to fight?" When I gave a single nod, Cathal came at me. "Let's see what you've got."

Blocking his attack, I backed up, defending against his plethora of punches and kicks. Energized and alive, I was riding a natural high. Attacking as much as I defended, anything I could use in the room was utilized.

It's fair to say, a fair bit of the furnishings were damaged or smashed in our fight. Vases were thrown, I was tossed around, landing on coffee tables which crumpled beneath me. Throwing what I could lift, I did my best to keep Cathal from getting hold of me.

The fight encompassed every inch of the room. Esha taught me to use what was on hand, so I did until there was nothing left. Circling back to the bed, I used the sheet, wrapping it around his striking wrist as I turned and twisted in behind him, wrapping it around his neck at the same time. Cathal pivoted and used my own weight to throw me off balance, so I either let go of the sheet or fell.

Releasing the sheet as he turned, I lifted my knee to try for his family jewels. Blocking it, Cathal grabbed my throat and forced me back on the bed.

"Now, that's just fighting dirty," he chuckled as he knelt over me. "Two of us can play that game." Jamming his hands between my legs, he rubbed. His touch was uncomfortable and unwanted, but heat flared, a spark igniting, catching my breath.

"Like that?" Dropping his mouth to my breast, Cathal kept that other hand firmly restraining me at my throat. Arching automatically into his mouth, a sob escaped the confined airway of my throat. Heat stirring and cycling through my body, despite the pain of his touch. Recognizing how my body always reacted to my stepfather touching me, I whimpered and tried to push Cathal away to explain.

"Let me show you how good it could be between us, Messina," Cathal murmured while swapping to the other breast.

Despite the pain and discomfort, his touch was the sun caressing my moonlight skin. Alight, I was growing lighter with every suck of his lips, every swipe of his tongue. For the first time, I understood my satiability was doing precisely as Tynan suggested, and being oppor-tunistic.

"Wait!" I tried to plead, feeling the heat swirl beyond what my body could hold. From one moment to the next, I recognized my power for the first time, and the next it took over me, sweeping me away in need of flesh and lust so intense I didn't stand a chance in hell of pulling it back.

Releasing my throat, Cathal leered down at me with pupils show-casing the drug of lust that my body was pumping out. Rolling us, Cathal lifted me to straddle his naked hips, then he was pushing inside of me.

Tears brimmed my eyes, a war waging inside of me to control this power, but I didn't have a hope in hell of winning. Why couldn't Tynan be the one filling me?

As soon as I thought of Tynan, the tears flowed. Rising up on his elbows, Cathal reached up and wiped my cheeks. "I won't hurt you." Reaching behind my neck, Cathal lowered my face to his.

Kissing my cheeks, he drank my tears, then pressed his lips to mine. Tasting the salt of my tears on his lips, his desire pulsed hard inside me.

"You don't feel right," I whispered against his mouth.

"Give me a second, darling, and you'll never have felt better." Thrusting up with his hips, causing me to moan, he opened me to him entirely. Cathal was right. It felt amazing having him pound into me. If it felt this good with someone who felt wrong, I could imagine how good Tynan would feel.

Tynan.

My eyes dropped to his mark while Cathal paused, his breath heaving as he held me so he was buried as deep as he could go.

"He's coming."

Following my eyes to the mark on my wrist, Cathal noticed the slight glow around it and used his hand to turn my face back to him. "We have time. I'm not going to rush this. Ignore him, you're mine right now."

Kissing me intently, his hands rocked my body over his, increasing speed as our kisses became frenzied. The satiability was eager for more, taking control like I'd gone without vital sustenance all this time, and finally, it was getting what it needed.

Sex for me had always been a way of getting what I needed, had always been about the man's pleasure, never mine. Yes, I got off, but it was their desire. This was no different, and like every other time, the satiability took away my distaste for what was happening.

I didn't care that Cathal's touch didn't drive me crazy like Tynan's did, he was inside me, soothing the itch that had been building there for months.

Engulfed in sunlight; wrapping around me like an electric blanket in the middle of winter, the orgasm came from nowhere. One moment I was riding Cathal, the next I threw my head back and cried to the goddess. No empty pleasure for once.

Rolling us, Cathal rose up and pinned my hands above my head. "I told you, Messina, we are fantastic together." He picked up the pace, I clutched his hands and moaned my continuing pleasure. Cathal's eyes lifted to my wrist, then to the bedroom door, his hips thrusting harder as he reached for his own rapture.

"Messina, bite me. I love being bitten." Kissing his shoulder, I pressed my teeth into his flesh. "Harder!" he groaned, thrusting into me with all his strength.

Curling up to gain leverage for the bite, the angle of my body changed his impact, taking him deeper. Unable to hold it, I dropped my head back to moan at how wondrous the slight pain of his forceful thrusts felt.

"Bite me and draw blood."

He was just on edge, his cock pulsing with eagerness with every pause between thrusts, and I suspected he was holding himself back now, drawing it out. His grip on my hands was starting to hurt now that my satiability was winding down.

"Ow, you're holding me too tight." Struggling to breathe between the massive thrusts of his body into mine, and the pain in my palms, I whimpered.

"Bite me!" Lifting my mouth to his shoulder, he pressed my mouth to his skin.

Ignoring the pain his body was causing me, I started to sink my teeth into him. The change in angle on my body was too much this time. Throwing my head back, I screamed as I came again.

"No!"

Cathal's body pulsed strongly in mine. Unable to resist my climax, Cathal released his own and flooded my body with sunlight. The summer sun was shining right through to my very core.

By the time Cathal stilled, my tears were falling freely. Ants were biting all over me, and I hated my power and myself, just like every time my stepfather had me. My thoughts were dark with despair like the day my stepfather shared me with his best friend, and I came down from the high of satiability to the pain of having them both inside of me, knowing they physically hurt me.

What was worse, was for some reason, those memories were flooding back in with high definition clarity. Not the act, just the memory of lying there with men I hated impaling my body. "Oh god, get off me!" I pleaded, wanting those memories to escape me again.

Cathal's attention was on the loud yelling and noises at the door, but his words were for me. "In a moment, Messina. You feel too good for me to move right this moment."

Pain shot throughout my body, wherever our skin made contact. I cried and screamed for him to get off me. Smiling at my angry eyes, Cathal placed a peck on my lips. Without my power of lust, I jolted back from the sting of his kiss.

Unhindered, Cathal moved his mouth to my ear. "It was amazing, wasn't it? It was nearly the best sex I've had. If only you had been willing instead of me having to induce your power to force you.

"Did you know that's one of my powers? I can take another person's power and activate it, even use it against them. You have so much power, little Princess. That satiability of yours is ravenous. So much so, that I failed to get you to bite me before I finished. Had you willingly ingested my blood, you'd be in love with me right now and begging to come home with me. Still, there's a good chance I can still make you mine. After all, it's not like you will remember this all tomorrow."

My eyes were wide, fear and despair choking me. "How do you know about my memory?"

Teeth bright white in his full smile, his joy filled the room with direct sunlight. "The curse is there for anyone willing to see it, Messina."

The door burst open, drawing both our attention to the intruders. Through watering eyes, I watched Tynan storm in with Esha and Pride. There was a pile of injured soldiers on the other side of the threshold. Tynan's sword was dripping blood, and his eyes were silver orbs of fury as he took the scene in before him.

"Get off her!"

23

———

DESPONDENT

❖

"**G**et off her!" Tynan's voice was colder than the Arctic.

"Settle yourself, Prince Tynan. It's not like you can undo what's been done," Cathal replied bored. Keeping my hands pinned as he pulled himself from my body. There was a dribble of something warm following him out, the feel of it caused me to whimper. As he knelt back, he released my hands.

Sitting straight up, I raked my nails across his chest, blood blooming in the gouges causing him to hiss as I shoved him back off the bed.

Gathering the sheet around me, I moved back to be pressed against the head of the bed feeling violated beyond anything my step-father had ever achieved. To know it wasn't just my body he used, but my powers too, took the rage and disgust I felt to an entirely new level.

Finding his feet, Cathal dabbed his fingers in the blood on his chest. "That's going to scar."

"You deserve worse."

"Oh, Darlin', don't pretend you didn't enjoy it. Your power was basically begging me to dump my load in you." Winking as he turned, Cathal started dressing. "Get lost, she's mine for the night."

"I didn't make that agreement." Narrowing his eyes, Tynan assessed me where I huddled, his sword still dripping blood on the floor.

"The King made it as an exchange for the antidote. I saved her; I get her." Picking up his drink, Cathal took a sip. "You better not have mortally wounded any of my men."

"The King had no right to make that deal with you. She belongs to me."

"But he did. Now, leave." Cathal struck out with his left hand, but Tynan held up his right hand and whatever Cathal intended fell as ash to the floor. Wrinkling his nose in disgust at whatever Tynan did, Cathal lifted his right hand. Tynan tried to counter with his right again, but stumbled back two steps and leaned forward. Tynan's exposed skin was turning green like algae were smothering him.

"The girl is mine for tonight, and with any luck, for the rest of her life." Smirking, Cathal leered at me, taking his eyes off Tynan. "When you get such a powerful girl with a hand of satiability, you don't even need to force her physically. All I do is switch her power on and watch her come apart on my cock."

Heat flared between my thighs, I whimpered realizing he'd done it again, triggering my satiability to steal my control and will. "Tynan, please!" The idea of spending the night having my power and body violated nearly broke me.

The smirk died on Cathal's face when Tynan flicked his hand. That's all Tynan did. Just a quick movement of his sword hand. It barely looked like he'd moved. Cathal's arm dropped to his side, his eyes blinking.

With effort, Tynan straightened, the green algae still there, but not hindering him any longer. A line of blood bloomed directly up the center of Cathal's torso. "I told you, she belongs to me," Tynan sneered.

The bloodline grew into a gash, Cathal's clothes fell open, and slowly, so did his abdomen, tearing open slowly, revealing glistening intestines and other organs. "I would have protected her," Cathal mumbled. The skin separated further, and Cathal's entrails slopped out onto the floor at his feet.

Covering my mouth to prevent screaming, my eyes were wide open, seeing it all. I wanted to look away, not to see anymore, but I couldn't.

Cathal's mouth moved, but no sounds came out as he dropped to his knees. Tynan took a step closer. "Don't worry, if she bears you a child, I'll send it to join you before it even draws its first breath. I won't have your filth cluttering up my household."

With a whimper, I hugged my knees tight to my chest. Tynan jammed his sword through Cathal's eye and into his brain, a whine leeching from my throat as I watched Cathal's body fit, impaled on the sword.

Yanking his sword free, Tynan spun and severed Cathal's head from his body. Blood splattered all over the white room, raining down on the already trashed furnishings. Cathal's head rolled a few feet away and stopped, staring up at me blankly with its one remaining eye.

I wanted to pass out, but my brain wasn't letting that happen, so with great effort, I lifted my eyes to Tynan. He stood watching me with those silver orbs, wiping his sword clean with the other end of my sheet.

"I was informed Solaris were guarding your door. I suspected the King was dealing with the Seelie." Sheathing his sword back into its walking cane scabbard, Tynan tilted his head. "Now, I know he is."

Trembling with fear, I pressed my lips closed on the sobs trying to escape. Really looked at me then, Tynan scanned my body and noticed the bruises that were blooming all over my skin from my fight with Cathal. His head swiveled to take in the state of the room. "You fought him?"

"Y-Ye-yes."

"You obviously gave it a good effort. I doubt there is anything salvageable in the room." Lifting his face to the window with the dying sun, he closed his eyes and enjoyed the feel of it on his skin.

"The sun doesn't bother you?" I queried quietly, voice still trembling.

"I'm half Seelie too, remember?" Opening his eyes to study me, Tynan sighed. "I think you've had enough light for now. Let's go." Turning, Tynan marched out of the room.

Stopping by one of the groaning guards in the doorway, Tynan held his right hand above him. Black smoke rose from the Sidhe soldier, faded to grey in the open air, and then to the purest white as it funneled into Tynan's hand.

With a shiver, Tynan rolled his shoulders, the green algae receding until you wouldn't even know he'd been injured. The guard slumped to the side, empty eyes staring into the world he'd left.

When Tynan's silver orbs focused again on me, I knew better than to try and plead my defense. Gulping down my fear, I wrapped the sheet tight around me as I stepped off the bed. I cringed at the muscle soreness in my, well, everywhere, but my legs were yelling the most. Pride stepped forward to help me.

"Don't! Carrying her won't work the muscles. The best thing she can do for the pain is to walk through it." Tynan waited, observing me as I gritted my teeth and limped forward. "Leave the sheet, white doesn't look good on you."

"You want me to walk naked through the faerie mound?" My voice was rough trying to restrain my emotions.

Glaring at me, with a deep exhalation, Tynan gestured at Esha, then turned and stormed off. Esha came forward removing his suit jacket and holding it for me. I tried to cover myself as I slipped one arm in, and then the other.

"He's not angry at you," Esha whispered in my ear as I wrapped the jacket tight around me.

"Lier."

"Well, it's mostly not you. You put up a good fight. If you hadn't, Ty would have made you walk back naked. Let's go before his anger gets the better of him, and he kills the king for allowing a Seelie to rape you."

That term, that one word, swiped my feet out from under me.

Never before had it been that. I'd always chosen to let a man use me; it'd never been that.

Esha caught me, half cradling me, his ruby eyes swimming in my vision, the darkness of despair closing all around me. "Shh, Mess. Whatever happens now, know that the Prince is angry he failed to protect you. He is bound to lash out, but it's not your fault. You are untainted. Very few of us master our powers before we come of age. There is no way you could have stopped Cathal from using your powers against you. He's older than the Prince. You saw what he managed to do to Ty. Few have ever harmed the Prince, that was the strength of the Solaris Captain."

"Everything hurts. Cathal woke my memories of when others used my satiability to their gain. Not just the emotional, but the physical pain of those memories is fresh again."

"Is that possible?" Pride queried, his bulk close behind me.

Changing his grip on me, Esha observed me, a vibration sweeping through my body like an electric current, his eyes unfocused.

A loud noise of something breaking came from outside. Only Esha's hold on me stopped me from jumping up and running from the rage tumbling along behind that noise.

"Settle, Mess. We're here to protect you now." Lifting his eyes to Pride, Esha straightened me to standing. "The prince says we shouldn't underestimate Cathal, and her memories may not be the worst he leaves her with."

A sob caught in my throat, my body trembling violently as I tried not to give in to the pain, to my emotions, to show just how weak and pathetic I felt in this moment.

Watching the tears fall down my cheek, Esha reached out and wiped them away. "I told you I would never give your memories back without payment. I never said I couldn't take away your pain."

As his thumb moved across my skin, I felt the memory of being trapped by the body of my stepfather and his friend tug towards it, a magnet drawing the shards of hurt from my head. As Esha's thumb fell off the side of my cheek, those recollections, even the one from moments ago, slipped from my grasp too.

My breath rushed from my lungs, relief filled me from head to toe, and I closed my eyes to take a moment to let my body catch up. I never thought I'd be so glad to forget anything in my life. Still, I knew it happened, but already, the details were blurring.

"Let's get you home." Walking ahead of me, Esha's shoulders shifted as if he was uneasy. Pride fell in behind me, catching me whenever I stumbled.

As we stepped out onto the landing, I noticed many armed Sluagh standing over the injured Solaris. Waiting till we were past them, Esha stopped before the last Sluagh. "Feed them to the goblins."

Wincing, I squeezed my eyes closed as I heard the first guard's plea cut off with a grunt and the slick sound of a blade being yanked out of a body. Yelling downstairs stole my attention. Tynan stood with several more armed Sluagh facing off with the King and his guard in his lounge room, Amp among them. Eyes tracking me, Amp turned away, closing his eyes before stepping towards Mabon.

Amp whispered to the King, Mabon stopped, his eyes widening as he watched me hobble across the landing and down the stairs.

"Yes," Tynan growled, "it looks like Cathal took excellent care of her. I guess the Seelie are no different to mongrels who walk the halls of this castle."

"Remember, you are one of them," the King snarled.

"I don't walk around claiming goodness and then do that to a woman!"

Pride caught my elbow as my legs weakened beneath me again. He held me up, made sure I was back on my feet before he released me. "You'll need a hot bath and a cup of tea."

"Food might be a good idea," Esha suggested.

"No," Pride objected. "She's gone too long without food; it would shock her body. Tea and a few dry biscuits will suffice tonight. We can add to that tomorrow."

Intent on staying upright and moving, I stayed out of the argument. The pain in my legs highlighted externally with bruises and welts from the fighting.

It took forever to travel down the several flights to the prince's level and the other side of the castle to his suite. Well, it felt like forever. We passed all manners of creatures on the way, everyone stopping to stare at my brutalized form.

Brie and Sauvignon gave me sympathetic looks as we passed. "Did the prince do that?" Brie asked Esha disgusted. Esha didn't answer with words. He shook his head slightly. Exhaling with relief, Brie used her large lava eyes to portray sympathy for whatever happened.

The further we walked, the more torturous each step became. Outside of the physical pain was the utter humiliation of being seen by others in this state. Hiding wasn't an option, Esha and Pride demanded attention with their presence.

The constant scrutiny was a violation in itself, chastening me with their judgment and sympathy alike. The shame built with every passerby, weighing me down, siphoning my strength and sense of self-worth. By the time we were approaching the suite, I was crying without restraint and using the wall to hold myself up.

My legs were swept out from under me when the doors came into view. Strong arms lifting me and holding me against a warm hard body. I expected it to be Pride, so I was surprised when I blinked through my tears to see it was Tynan. "I'm sorry."

He wouldn't look at me. "The Seelie are known for their fertility, Messina. You are part Seelie, so we need to assume you carry his child until we know you don't."

This wasn't happening. The last thing I wanted to think about was the events in that sun covered bed leading to me getting pregnant. Remembering Tynan's last words to Cathal, I started bawling into his shoulder. "You wouldn't really kill a baby, would you?"

Tynan's jaw tensed, but he didn't answer me. Carrying me to my room, he set me down in the bathroom. I expected him to leave me there, to walk away and forget about me like he did last time, but that didn't happen.

Pouring my bath for me, Tynan swept me into his arms again, then gently lowered me into it. Not wanting to seem weak, I bit my lip on a whimper when the water hit the open grazes and cuts so he wouldn't know how much it hurt me. Not that he looked to be happy, but I didn't want Tynan to enjoy my pain.

Watching me for a full minute, Tynan eventually met my eyes. Silver orbs burned into me, maximizing my hurt and shame. When I looked away, tears falling silently, he walked to the door.

"Yes. At the very least, I would take his baby to the Seelie court and let them fawn over their new Seelie prince or princess. Either way, you would never hold or see that child."

My heart wrenched in me. I tried to keep calm, but a little wail escaped my lips before I clenched my jaw shut. Closing my eyes, the tears fell quickly across my cheeks. "Is that for any child, or just if it is his?"

Tynan was quiet. Opening my eyes, I thought I could try and guess the answer from his facial expression, but he wasn't there. His absence made whatever resilience I had left, shatter across the bathroom floor.

When I crawled from the bath, moving was a little easier. Snuggling into my bed, I drank the tea left on the tray with a handful of freshly baked cookies.

Beneath the teacup was a slip of paper I knew was from Margo. The question made my breath stop in my chest for a moment. The words teasing me from the page. I knew Margo didn't intend to hurt or humiliate me, but at that moment, it felt like it. Staring at the question, I tried to fathom an explanation, but I just kept coming up with the same answer.

'I don't know.'

24

ISOLATION

❖

Tynan wouldn't allow me out of my room for a week. No training, no socialization, nothing. Everyone stayed away from me except for delivering my meals. Flipping through my sketchbooks achieved nothing because I had no inspiration to draw anything. There was a memory niggling to be remembered. A child and a tunnel of light, but I couldn't grasp it. The harder I tried, the faster the memory faded.

Food was delivered by Pride, goblins no longer trusted in my presence. This I knew. I'd performed glamor to escape. Not only on myself but someone else. Pride informed me that it took a remarkable Fae to throw a glamor over another, and the goblins now, rightfully, feared me.

Every day, I took Margo's last question and looked at it, but I still couldn't add to my three worded answer. It wasn't enough, so I hadn't sent it back.

My door opened, and I shoved the paper under my pillow. Pride came in carrying my dinner tray. "You should try dressing; it would make you feel better."

"I'm not going anywhere; clothes would be pointless. Besides, it's stuffy in here."

I'd been naked waking up seven days ago. While I bathed twice daily, I hadn't seen the point for the past five days of doing more than changing my underpants. It's not like I was exposing myself, I had the sheet over me, but once Pride left, I could throw that off as well.

"Too much sunlight." Placing the tray down, Pride turned to consider me. "Your injuries seem mostly healed."

"Yeah, about that. I don't remember getting this banged up when I fell out of the tree." Raising a brow at Pride, I waited for an explanation.

He frowned at me. "The tree?"

"Yes, you know, when I went back to the garden to get my stuff. Speaking of which, where is my jacket?"

Pride took a step closer. "Messina, what is your last memory?"

"What do you mean? The crazy bitch burning the Seelie garden. Right before Tynan found me and you carried me back here." Pride's face closed down, and my stomach disintegrated. "Something happened after that?"

When Pride continued to watch me, I threw back the sheet and searched through my notebooks, throwing them across the room when nothing new was in them. "Did I use a different notebook? I must have drawn it. I never sleep without drawing what occurred, I know I'll forget if I do."

Continuing to search the notebooks, I was desperate to find what happened to cause these injuries. Then a thought occurred to me. I turned to look at Pride.

"Did he do this to me? If he tortured me again, then I might have passed out, and that's why I don't remember. Tell me, Pride. What happened?"

Pride gritted his teeth, eyes glistening with anger. Shaking his head in dismay, Pride walked out, locking the door behind him. Crumpling to the floor, I looked over the scattered notebooks. I hadn't drawn anything since the garden burned. I didn't even know how long ago that happened.

What if this was Tynan's punishment? Taking away my sketches, and along with it, my memories.

No, that's not how it worked. As long as I drew it, I remembered it. I never had to see the sketches again unless it was the smaller detail. So, that could only mean, I hadn't been able to draw my memories.

Even then, some memories stayed, invading my dreams, like Lisa's death had, or my first meeting of Tynan. In fact, from the moment I arrived in the Unseelie court, holding memories without drawing them had been easy. So why had I lost them again? If this was Tynan's new way of torturing me, he might have Esha removing my memories.

Tears filled my eyes. Anything could have been happening to me, months could have passed, and I wouldn't even know. Frustration built to bursting. Anger exploded from me in the form of boiling water. It combined with air and churned around my feet.

The pressure built up within me again, a violent storm cocooned me in a cacophony of thunder and lightning, so loud it shook the marrow in my bones, and the teeth in my jaw. Throwing my head back, I screamed my agony of unknowing. I cried till my voice cracked and died.

"Messina." Tynan walked through the hurricane, his hand held in front of him, glowing like a beacon in the darkness of the storm as he trudged over the waterlogged floor. Tynan's eyes were deep and black, wariness shining in them as he knelt before me.

"What have you don't to me?" I whispered, tired and angry.

Tynan tilted his head to assess me. "I haven't touched you."

"I don't believe you."

Ignoring my accusation, Tynan assessed the storm around us. "You're growing more powerful, or maybe your emotions are more unstable."

Reaching out, Tynan traced my jaw with his finger. My eyes fluttered at the warm sensation of his touch. Tynan's breath rushed out of him. He moved his entire hand to touch me, his eyes closing with sadness.

"You shouldn't still feel this good." He withdrew his affection. "Can you shut it down?"

Looking around me, I sobbed as I shook my head.

Tynan closed his eyes in defeat. "I thought so." He opened his eyes and met mine. "I'll heal you; I promise."

Opening my mouth ready to argue, a gasp escaped instead as pain burst to life in my shoulder. Looking down I found a blade protruding from my right shoulder. Following the thin edge back to Tynan's hand, I slowly lifted my shocked eyes to his again. "Free me!"

Clenching his jaw, Tynan pulled his sword free, and as he did, I screamed. The storm crashed to the floor. A wave of water swept out away from us and splashed up the walls of my already trashed room. More concerned with my blood dripping into the water from Tynan's sword, I barely noticed.

Watching my blood, I focused on it, blocking out the pain. Directing my rage towards it, I wanted my blood to etch away his sword, to make it rust and break. The drops started to slow, then they began to bubble on his sword.

Holding out his glowing left hand towards my shoulder, Tynan focused on my wound. Anger raged in me. Lashing out, I knocked his arm away. "No! I don't want you to heal me."

Frowning down at me, Tynan bunched his brows. "The wound needs treating, Messina."

"Not by you!"

Silver orbs of moonlight bloomed within Tynan's eyes. "I'm the one who should be angry here, Messina. You betrayed me!"

"I owe you no loyalty! I'm just your toy, your plaything for you to torture and gain pleasure from. Soon enough you will be bored with me, lock me away, and forget about me." Taking a breath, I begged him with everything in me. "Free me, please?"

Turning away from me, Tynan walked to the door. Ripping the door off the hinges, Tynan let it fall to the floor. "Esha!" Esha appeared in the doorway, red eyes full of concern and awe as he took in the room. "Take Messina to room five."

Esha looked alarmed. "Like that?"

Tynan observed me, kneeling in just my knickers, holding my ruined shoulder. "As she is. Then organize for this room to be renovated, and get me the book of powers." Lifting his sword, Tynan studied the oxidation of the metal tip that had only moments ago been covered in my blood. "I'll be needing a new sword too."

Esha shook his head. "She's not ready for..." Tynan walked out without a backward glance, and Esha hung his head.

After a moment his eyes came back to me. There was no hiding his concern. Coming towards me, his throat swallowing convulsively as his eyes stayed locked on my bleeding shoulder, Esha lifted me into his arms. "Save your energy, Messina. You're going to need it."

"What's happening now?"

"Room five has many uses, but it is usually the holding cell before the gauntlet run," Esha explained as he walked me down corridors I'd never seen before.

"Gauntlet?"

"He's going to make you run for your life, Messina."

Dropping my head to Esha's shoulder, I closed my eyes. "Will he free me if I survive?"

"No."

"Then what's the point?"

"You get to live," Esha explained as if that was a great outcome.

"Without freedom? Just to return to being his toy? It's not worth even trying."

"The gauntlet is a rite of passage for the Sluagh. All the ranked Sluagh have run it. It proves our strength and superiority as warriors. If you survive, you will have a place as one of us. This will become your home, and we will become your people."

"You did this?" Esha nodded. "Has any Sidhe done it?"

"Many."

There was a strange look in his eyes. "Did they survive?"

"One survived." He looked down at me in his arms. "The King ran the gauntlet and survived. It's the only reason the Prince respects him, and he respects the Prince for it."

"Why?"

Esha licked his lips. "Because the Prince ran it and came out the other end with barely a scratch on him. The King, however, crawled into the safe zone and was badly injured."

"I don't have a chance at surviving this, do I?"

Approaching a heavy door, a guard all dressed in black opened it. Esha carried me in and placed me on the cold stone floor. Something about the black stone walls of this room tugged at my memory but escaped me again too quickly.

Esha looked at me, then back to the guard. "Give me your shirt."

It was a direct order. The guard instantly removed his black tunic and handed it to Esha before leaving the room. Esha helped me into the tunic.

"I've been training you for this every Friday afternoon, Messina. The runs through the forest were training you for this gauntlet. I have faith you can get through this," Esha tried to reassure.

"That's not what you told the Prince."

Esha sighed. "I would have preferred more training, and for you to be at your strongest running it, but you are powerful enough to get through it."

Taking my face in his hands, Esha made me meet his ruby orbs. "You get through this, you'll still belong to him, but not as his toy anymore. Do you understand what I'm telling you?"

Shaking my head, I couldn't understand how belonging to Tynan could be any different to what it was already.

Esha gave me a sad smile. "Then I suggest you survive it and find out." Standing up, Esha stepped away. "There is no set date. When all the competitors are in place, the window will open. You will have from complete dark till the beacon dies to reach the safe point."

"How will I know where the safe point is?" I trembled in the cold stone room.

"Trust me, you can't miss it."

25

GAUNTLET

❖

Time was absent in the cell. Food was brought in at intervals and left on a tray on the floor. Unable to just lie there, I got up and ran on the spot for as long as I could after every meal, then I'd run a little longer before crashing back on the bed. At least I had a comfortable mattress.

What I perceived to be two days later, I was woken by the door opening and soft light entering the room. One of the guards and a Sluagh female came into the room, already heavy petting. He pushed her against the wall while he helped remove her knickers. "Hello! The room is occupied," I waved at them.

Ignoring me, they proceeded to fuck in front of me. At first, I blushed furiously, but as the guard pounded into her from behind, I became obsessed with the sound of them having sex. Ever heard cats mating? The excessively loud mewling, and carry on that always makes you think the poor pussy, excuse the pun, is being tortured? That's what I was listening too.

The woman looked to be enjoying it, but the mewling, especially when they reached the crescendo, was enough to make your ears bleed. Pulling the pillow over my head, I tried to ignore them until he roared the blowing of his trumpet.

Disengaging their bodies, the guard stepped outside, handing the female a bag and soft lamp. "Keep the light low, and away from her, so you don't ruin her night vision," the guard directed. "Her chances of survival are already pretty low."

"Thanks, Damk."

Sauvignon's was still ringing in my head after her little soul sight moment, making it instantly recognizable. She left the light in the corner and came towards me, pulling clothing out of her bag. "You need to look the part for the gauntlet."

"What are you doing here? If the prince..."

"I kept seeing you running the gauntlet. Sometimes you wore this outfit, and I watched you reach the beacon. Other times, you wore a guards tunic, and I watched you..." Sauvignon shook her head. "I knew the goddess was telling me to help you. Strip and let's see your shoulder."

A little concerned, but willing to go along with this, I tentatively pulled the tunic over my head. Sauvignon hissed when she saw my shoulder. I couldn't blame her, it looked horrible and infected.

"This will weaken you. Everyone else is at best health running the gauntlet. You won't be, but I can prevent you from being at your worst."

Pulling out ointments and other first aid looking things, Sauvignon went to work cleaning and applying some smelly cream to the wound before bandaging it.

"Leave the bandage till the window starts to open, then rip it off, or it will hinder your freedom of movement."

"Have you run the gauntlet?"

"For the Sluagh, it's a coming of age ritual. Only the strongest survive."

"Are you allowed to tell me about it?"

"Don't be the first to run into the forest, but don't be the last. After that, just run. Keep running. Don't stop running towards the beacon. Once the first person reaches the beacon, the light begins to dim. You have an hour from that point to make it, or you'll be left to the Devils. The Devils will try to delay you. Don't let them." Sauvignon stood up.

"That's all I can tell you. Get dressed and rest. The gauntlet is scheduled for tomorrow, so save your energy now, and make sure you eat."

"You aren't meant to be here, are you?"

Standing up, Sauvignon collected the lamp. "You're lucky Damk and I have a thing. I could bribe him to let me see you."

"About that, did I have to see you?" I asked, indicating the wall.

The heat in my cheeks made Sauvignon laugh. It was a beautiful sound. "Where'd you want me to pay him? In the hallway?" She kept laughing as she tapped on the door. "Good luck, Moon Child. I'll be waiting for you at the other end."

After Sauvignon stepped out, the room returned to darkness. Picking up the clothes Sauvignon left me, I got dressed. There wasn't much to it. A short flared black skirt, and a tight black top to go over the bra and joggers. Over everything, I was grateful for the joggers.

Once I was ready for the gauntlet, I laid down and rested, remembering my training with Esha. I ate when the food came, and I slept in-between. My eyes became accustomed to the dark, which is the only reason I even noticed the heavily tinted glass slowly slide open. There was a rush of humid air into the room, and then a shrill howl of either an emasculated animal or some type of high-pitched blow horn.

Taking a deep breath, I walked towards the window as I unwound the bandage from my shoulder. As soon as the window finished sliding all the way open, it started to close again, forcing me to scurry through into the forest. The window shut, and only then, did I consider just staying in the stupid room. What would Tynan have done then?

Others were hovering on the forest edge to either side of me. A few Sluagh who stood tall and ready. Two trolls, one at either end, who only had eyes for the forest, and two Unseelie Sidhe, one who was watching the Sluagh, the other, the captain of the Luna guard, was moving towards me.

As far as I could see, I was the only female. All the men were shirtless and carried weapons, but there was no point me having one; I'd probably hurt myself trying to use it.

"Nice outfit, Messina." Amp, who'd come to stand beside me smiled as he bowed his head slightly. "Should we get going?"

Looking to both sides, I noted that no one had moved yet. Peering ahead, I understood why. "Not till the beacon goes up. That way we know where we are heading."

Amp looked out over the forest. "Do you know what we are in for?"

"I was told to run. Not to stop running no matter what, that the devils would try to delay me."

Amp's brow rose. "So, this is where those bastards live." He looked back at me. "What else?"

"When the first person reaches the beacon, it will start to dim. We then have an hour to reach it, or we get left to the devils."

"Great! I'm going to stick by you princess and make sure you get to that beacon."

My brow cinched in suspicion of the title he used. "Why?"

"Because I want to be the first Sidhe since the king to make it, and my instincts say if I stick with you, I will."

"What about your friend?" I indicated the other Sidhe.

"That is Ashok. He's not even a ranked Sidhe. If he makes it, I'll make him my second, but he has to make it on his own."

"There it is," someone yelled.

Amp and I turned to see the Beacon shining brightly into the sky, calling us northwest, Amp studied the area, getting his bearings. "That's the amphitheater if my directions are right."

Two trolls started running straight for the beacon. "Where would the prince's suites be from here?" There was more chance of making it if I ran a familiar path. Amp considered the forest below and pointed northeast. "That's where we are running."

"That won't be a win," Amp argued.

"Call it female logic, Amp." Several Sluagh ran for the forest, so I took my cue. "I was told not to be first, and not to be last. Let's go."

Running into the forest, I kept the beacon forty-five degrees to my left. It would slowly tick like a clock hand turning anticlockwise, but it would give me my direction.

'Run as far as you can, then back as fast as you can.' Esha trained me to be exhausted doing this run. I could get to the prince's suites in under an hour. Even if the first person crossed the line in that time, it should give me plenty of time to circle around and reach the beacon. Of course, that wasn't allowing for Devils, whatever they were.

It took twenty minutes of jumping fallen logs and dodging around trees to understand the outfit Sauvignon had given me. It was unrestrictive, allowed for freedom of movement and was lightweight. A lot less restrictive than the ankle length, full skirt Seelie dress I'd worn for training.

Smiling, I pushed harder. Behind me, I could hear Amp running, his boots making heavy footfalls through the forest. Yelling and fighting could be heard off to my left. Ignoring it, I kept running. Suddenly, pain lanced across my shoulder. Falling forward, I wondered if Esha had caught up with me. Catching myself on a fallen log, I turned my head to see something big and black in the branches of the tree above me. With wide eyes, I got my feet under me and started running again.

The beast laughed with a shrill voice before it burst through the branches of the trees and raked its claws across my exposed upper back. Crying out, I lurched forward again.

"Get up!" Swinging his sword, Amp beheaded the creature.

Getting up, I started running as fast as my legs would move. If that was a devil and that's what they were going to do to delay me, I wanted out of here even faster.

On track for Tynan's suites now, I was running the part of the forest I'd come to memorize over the past six months. Becoming more confident with every footfall, my feet knowing exactly where they were going, I pushed myself to my maximum.

Amp cursed behind me, and I heard him stumble. "We're nearly there," I called over my shoulder to encourage him forward. No reply came from him, just the panting of someone exerting themselves. It was enough though. Reassuring, until it wasn't there.

Glancing over my shoulder, Amp wasn't there. My eyes went wide when he suddenly fell out of the sky and landed on the ground with a heavy thud.

"Amp?" I stopped running ready to go back for him? He'd already helped me once, maybe more, I hadn't been paying attention.

Something big and black landed on the ground between Amp and me. Slowly it unfurled, growing taller until what I already knew was a devil, stood before me.

It was tall, at least seven foot. It was a black human skeleton, but over the bones was thin black skin. From its back hung two large wings, the frame of which was clearly visible, and like the rest of his skeleton, covered in black furry skin. The cross-section was a brown membrane that looked more like webbing, than wings.

"A human bat?"

Lifting his skeletal head, he assessed me with pure black eyes. He inhaled deeply, his nose flaring. "Hmmm, I could smell you across the forest. You are running the wrong way pretty thing."

"Am I?" I asked, stepping backward.

He smiled. Well, it looked to be a smile. His skull while human, didn't have the muscles and flesh to work the same as ours. "I've been hearing you run this forest for months now, smelling your sweet blood, hungering for a taste of you."

"Really? That's the best pick up line you've got, Batman?"

The devil paused to consider my comment. His confusion was an opportunity I needed. Spinning on my heel, I bolted. It was like training. I was running as fast as I could, but instead of exhaustion, fear was what was trying to bring me down.

The devil came after me, laughing as he slashed at me with is claws. "Now, I understand why the Sluagh did this with you. It's fun," the devil announced joyously.

Recognizing why Esha wouldn't allow me to fall or give in, I stayed upright and running. If I collapsed from the pain with the devil chasing me, I doubted I'd ever get back up again.

"Run rabbit, run rabbit. Run! Run! Run! Run rabbit, run rabbit. Run! Run! Run!" The devil sang off-key behind me. A swish of air ignited pain across my back and stole the air from my lungs causing me to fall on all fours. "Go rabbit, go. Better get started. Get on your feet. Better go in full retreat. Or you'll just be rabbit pie." Launching to my feet, I kept running. The devil hissed and cackled behind me.

Racing into the clearing just before Tynan's suite, I banged into the window, turned immediately, and put my back to the window to watch the devil. My blood smeared the glass as I slid along it towards the west, eyeing where I had to run next, but the devil blocked my path.

"So, rabbit, oh, rabbit, come right here," he stated instead of singing this time. I shook my head. "Defiant little rabbit." His eyes raked my body. "Such a pretty little morsel. I don't have to eat you, you know. We could be...friends?"

"Usually, a man suggests we be friends like that, he means he wants to fuck me." Dropping my gaze pointedly at his Ken doll pelvis. "Looks like I don't have to worry about that being the case with you, Batman."

The devil laughed. A shrill cackle that reminded me of bats at night. Suddenly, it cut off. "You want to see it, do you?"

My eyes widened as he opened his mouth, lifting his little tongue. From beneath it, a long bright pink muscle emerged. It grew longer thicker till it filled his mouth and he couldn't close his jaw at all.

He stepped towards me, the bright pink raspberry calippo pointing right at me. The end closest to me was weeping a gooey opaque liquid. Cringing as he moved closer, then as he came within reach, I stepped into him quickly and slammed both palms up into the bottom of his jaw.

The devil stumbled backward with a smothered scream opening the path, and I bolted towards the beacon. This terrain was foreign, but I didn't care. The beacon just dimmed, and there was no chance I was getting left behind with the devils.

"Bitch!" The hiss sounded just before his wing collided with the side of me, throwing me sideways and slamming me into a tree.

Groaning, I pushed to my feet and ran faster. My left arm was screaming at me that it was injured, but I wasn't listening. It could tell me how bad it was after I crossed the finish line.

Clawed hands grabbed my shoulders and shoved me forward, staying with me as I hit the ground, cutting off my cry of alarm when the wind rushed from my lungs.

"You're not escaping, little rabbit," the devil spat on my cheek. "I'm going to make you beg to be bled dry." Rearing back, he sank his fangs into the side of my neck. I screamed.

With the devil drinking my blood, I clawed the ground, desperate to get out from underneath him. Removing his mouth form me, the devil stood up a little wobbly.

Crawling forward before turning to look at him, my hand going to the blood dribbling from my neck. The devil had a massive smile on his face, his eyes glazed. I could be wrong, but he looked drunk. Observing my blood coating his mouth, the way he licked his lips, I focused my attention, seething hate for my blood being anywhere but where it should be.

Like with Tynan's sword, slowly my blood began to bubble. With a frown, the devil scratched where my blood was. His mouth, his throat, all the way down to his stomach, and I understood, even my blood inside him was bubbling. "You should be more careful what you eat," I snarled as I imagined my blood catching fire.

Peering at me confused, the Devil opened its mouth as if he was about to vomit, and screamed like a tortured rat. Smoke rose from his open mouth like a chimney, then the flames erupted in his mouth. The devil fell to the ground rolling around in agony. I got up and ran.

Feeling weak and lethargic, I dug deep for my reserves and pushed on as fast as I could. The beacon was dimmer. I doubt you'd be able to see it from where we started now.

Drawing myself up, I did what Esha told me. Ignoring everything around me, I ran until there were no more trees, nothing between myself and the dying beacon other than a small stretch of clearing and the knee-high wall of a window sill.

On the other side of the wall stood Sluagh with weapons drawn. Amongst them was Esha. He saw me and shouted. "She's here!"

I didn't stop running. A bloody mess of a Sluagh was crawling over the wall ahead. To the right, I saw the other Sidhe, Ashok, the one who was doing this to get on the Luna guard, running for the wall, sword drawn, bloody and beaten.

Tynan was suddenly at the wall, his eyes peering into the darkness. "Don't stop running," he murmured, but I heard him.

Ashok turned to look at me. His eyes went wide. "Watch out!"

Pain ripped through me, my legs crumpled beneath me and I fell to the ground shocked.

"Air ar oo oing abbit?" A mangled mouth hissed behind me.

"No!" Esha gasped.

Lifting wide eyes towards the beacon, Tynan's face was ashen. I tried to get my legs under me again, but they wouldn't move, I couldn't even feel them. A scream of defeat was building in my chest, I was going to die here, like this, with that creature doing god knows what to me.

No! That wasn't my fate. I didn't go through everything I had to die at the hands of Batman.

Refusing to give up, I dug my hands into the soil and pulled my body forward. Footsteps were running towards me, lifting my eyes, fearing what would come next, I found Ashok coming to my rescue. Sword razed he attacked the devil.

"Et ost!" The devil swatted with his wings, the dagger edges backing Ashok up. Then there was a second Sidhe, as Amp arrived, bloody and limping and attacked the devil from his other side.

Focusing on pulling my body forward, I reached the wall and reached up. Without asking, I knew that I had to get myself over. It didn't matter if I died when I got there, I damn well wasn't dying out here.

"Move!" Tynan growled somewhere above me.

My hand gripped the top of the barrier. A hand grasped mine and warmth flooded me. "Ty," I sobbed.

Arms grabbed me on either side and hauled me over the wall and onto the cold stone ground of safety.

"They've never attacked once past the tree line before," one of the

Sluagh complained to Esha. Two bodies hurled themselves over the wall just as the beacon died, barely missing landing on me.

"Can't grab it. Oh, my dear. What will I do for my fun this year? Guess last year's goat. Dang rabbit, that rabbit can run." The devil sang off key again as the windows slid shut with a thud.

26

MISTRESS

❖

"**G**oddess, he didn't want her to make it," someone exclaimed above me.

"He severed her spine," Tynan murmured.

"Will she make it?" Amp enquired a little off to the right.

"You need to declare, Ty, everyone is waiting," Esha advised him. "Not many are still standing, and they all saw how close she was to finishing still on her feet."

The shiny black shoes beside me moved as Tynan walked away. All that mattered was I was safe in here, not out there. I couldn't feel my legs, breathing hurt, my arms ached from pulling my body across the ground, but I wasn't out there with that creature.

"My friends, the gauntlet is run. We have our proven warriors..." Tynan mentioned a handful of Sluagh names, then I might have passed out for a moment.

"...For the first time in centuries, we have Sidhe who made the beacon. Captain Amp of the Luna Guard, Ashok, and our first ever female Sidhe to try the gauntlet, Messina." The crowd roared their support. "Tomorrow we will gather and feast in their honor. Let our warriors have tonight to heal."

With that, everyone started to depart. Shiny black shoes came back to stand in front of me. "You want me to carry her?" Esha asked quietly.

Tynan met his eyes, something passing between them before Tynan knelt by me and wiped the tears from the cheek he could see. "You made it, Mess, now you are one of us for all eternity." Patting my hair, matted with sweat as it was, back from my face, he saw the bite on my neck. "He drank from you?" Blinking confirmation forced more tears to escape.

"Everyone's gone," Esha knelt by us. "There are no witnesses."

Placing his hands over me, Tynan closed his eyes. A pure white glow filled the space around me, too bright to keep my eyes open. Suddenly stiff, my entire body went rigid. A shock, then another, then too many close together racking my upper body to start, then the convulsions of electric shocks slowly spreading to my lower limbs.

Esha held my head in his hands to stop me smashing it against the stone floor, such was the force powering through my body. The electrocution stopped only for the ghosts of magic to pass through me, cold chills combating the heat as each one dove through me, faster and faster.

As the last ghost left my body, they grabbed my wrists and ankles pulling my limbs in every opposite direction as molten magma poured into every wound. Gritting my teeth, I tried to take it, but when the lava seared all along my spine, it became too much. Opening my mouth, I screamed. Heat tickled between my thighs and in my womb, then my satiability stole me away.

With a loud snap, everything stopped, and I fell listless to the ground, panting, but whole. Warmth trickled through me; Tynan moaned as if we'd just had the most fantastic sex. The boneless happy feeling of a great orgasm was covering me like a warm blanket. "Thank you."

Rolling me over so I could look up at him, Tynan caressed my cheek. Esha gave me a quick smile, then moved away. "I was so proud when I saw you still running from the forest. When that devil sliced your spine, I felt like my world ended." Stroking my face lovingly,

Tynan placed a delicate kiss on my lips. "I won't fight fate anymore. Anything you want, it's yours."

"I want to go home," I whispered, tears stinging my eyes. "And, I really want a shower." The taste of dirt was in my mouth, and I was covered in forest muck and blood.

Tynan's smile was a gentle relief. He offered me his hand, and I let him help me stand, stamping my feet a little to celebrate being able to feel them then followed Esha and Tynan our into the warren of halls.

"Where did you get the outfit?" Tynan's eyes glinted dangerously.

"Seriously? I've just run the gauntlet, had my spine severed, and crawled my sorry arse to safety, and your concern is who gave me this outfit?"

"You're right, my apologies, that's a concern for another day."

Turning to face him, I brought our procession to a halt. "No, it's not. I ran the gauntlet, I'm not your toy anymore. You can't torture my secrets out of me," I bravely proclaimed.

Lifting a brow, Tynan peered past me to Esha who was whistling as if nothing happened, and glanced back to me. "You are right that you are not my toy anymore, but you are still mine."

"How does that work?" I challenged.

Taking my elbows in hand, Tynan moved me up against the stone wall. He glanced at Esha. "Keep watch. Let me know if anyone approaches." His gaze came back to me as he kissed my chin, along my jaw, down my throat. My heart thudded in my chest, blood boiling with need.

"How to explain it in a way that you're human upbringing can understand?" Tynan murmured as his hands roamed over my body. My hands automatically came to his shoulders as he kissed over the mound of my breast, pushing his tongue beneath the confines of the top to lick my nipple. Moaning, I gripped my fingers tighter.

"You are equal to every other Sluagh now, but me." His fingers found my pubic mound, slipped a little lower, and started rubbing me through my knickers. "You are higher ranked than any who have never run the gauntlet, which means all but three Sidhe, and all goblins." Biting my lip with a whimper, I refused to beg him for release.

"The thing is, you already bear my mark, Mess. I'm now officially your prince, which means you are not just any other Sluagh. It's giving you a title, like your mother when she was Mabon's concubine." Tynan smiled widely, and his face was the most handsome I'd ever seen. "Like the mistress of a King. Not formally his wife, but granted all the same privileges."

"Kings put their mistresses aside," I panted. My body was hot and sprinting for the pleasure Tynan summoned from me.

"Not this prince," he whispered in my ear. Removing his hand from my body, Tynan grabbed my jaw and forced me to meet his eyes. "Not this princess." He kissed me deeply, heatedly. His body pressing into mine so I could feel how much he wanted me. "Do you want me, Mess?"

"Yes," I breathed.

"Then cum for me without me needing to touch you."

Closing my eyes, I pictured him pressing his misery inside of me, imagining the feel of his cold climax painting the walls of my core, fantasized about him loving me.

It was enough. Opening my mouth, I came. Clamping his hand over my mouth, Tynan moved his other arm around my waist holding me to him to prevent me crumbling to the floor.

"That's it, give yourself to me." Using his hand at my mouth to turn my head, Tynan sank his teeth into my neck. I screamed, but his palm muted my mouth.

His teeth buried into me, summoning my pleasure and dragging it through my body like a worm on a hook to my neck, where he sucked it out of me. Or was that something else? My head spun, my body went limp, and my eyes fluttered closed. I was vaguely aware of Tynan lifting me into his arms and carrying me down the corridor.

"I can't believe you just did that without her consent," Esha grumbled unhappily.

"You're just upset you couldn't manipulate her to it yourself. I told you from the start, she's mine."

"Goddess, you're a sly one, you only did that to stop any other from trying."

"Tomorrow night, at the festival, you and those two Sidhe who fought the devil for her would have been all over her. Don't deny it. She's not my possession any longer."

"Was that wise while Mess remains untainted. She can't stay that way forever, Ty, you know that. She has to choose eventually," Esha sighed. "She may not choose us."

"That's why she needs time. Time as one of us, so she can make an informed choice."

"How much time? The wisp walk usually occurs the week preceding the gauntlet. You didn't give her that option. Everyone will expect it to be done within the week."

"Everyone can go to hell."

We stopped moving. "Pride is waiting in there to know if she made it," Esha warned. "He couldn't bring himself to watch the windows shut and know she was never coming back. I think he was worried he'd charge into the forest to find her if she didn't make it. It's probably a good thing he wasn't there to see what happened."

"He really cares about her. Highly unusual for one of his kind to care for one of hers."

"She's kind of infectious with her messed up innocence and determination to survive. Should we mess with him?"

Tynan chuckled. "On your head."

The door opened, Esha going ahead. "No!" Pride thundered. "I told you she wasn't ready. I should have gone and taken her from the room, we shouldn't have allowed it. Why are you smiling at me?" Pride yelled furiously.

I knew the moment Tynan walked us into the lounge room. "Let me put her down, Pride. Examine her then," Tynan offered.

The cool leather of the lounge touched my back, Tynan removed himself from me, leaving me cold causing me to whimper. "Shh, it's okay."

"But, Esha looked so heartbroken."

"Oh, I am, but for another reason."

"She's not so badly torn up. I expected worse," Pride announced as his large paws checked me over.

"So, did we," Tynan admitted. "A few wing clips, claws in the shoulders, and...one of them drank from her."

"Drank from her? They never drink during the gauntlet, they always wait till they have their victims and take their time," Pride argued.

My body came back online, and I was able to slowly open my eyes. I felt like I'd slept for days and was ready to rerun the gauntlet. No, not really, but that's how I would be comparing my energy levels from now on.

"They also never breach the clearing and attack someone before the wall," Tynan shook his head before he relayed what happened.

Pride stood outraged. "Who?" Tynan met his eyes. "Lucifer?" Tynan nodded his head.

Swallowing the lousy memory, I sat myself up slowly, just in case feeling fine was a lie. Everyone watched me, waiting, for what, I wasn't sure. With nothing to offer to the conversation, I stood. "I need a shower. Do I still have a room here, or do I go elsewhere?"

Tynan raised a brow. "Use my bathroom, Mess. Your old room is still being renovated. I'll organize your clothes and things to be brought in."

Bowing my head, a little, I made my way upstairs.

"Is that a bite on her neck? I thought you healed her?" Pride worried as I walked upstairs.

"I did," Tynan smiled, watching me walk across the landing, "that's my bite."

There was a moment of confusion, Pride's bushy brows bunching, and lowering over his eyes till they became dark caves. The moment passed, Pride's forehead smoothed tight, eyebrows high. "You didn't?" Pride appeared horrified. He looked to Esha. "She agreed to it?"

Esha huffed as he sat hard on the lounge. "No, he didn't even ask her. Like usual, he just took what he wanted from her and gave her no choice in it."

Tynan's eyes were all for me. Swallowing nervously, I kept walking. I wanted to understand, and at the same time, not. Tynan's smile grew into a Cheshire grin.

My eyes went over Tynan's head to the window. The sun was dawning, making the forest visible. The window was still covered in the smear of my blood from the night before, and there, written into my blood, or possibly, licked into my blood, was a single word, written for those inside to read.

Rabbit.

27

HOME & HEARTH

❖

After washing three times, it still wasn't enough. Spending four days in a cold, empty cell, left me dirtier than I'd ever been before I even ran the gauntlet. I don't know how Tynan could touch me like this, let alone kiss me.

"Are you planning to stay in here all day?" Waltzing into the bathroom, Tynan joined me in the shower. My body temperature rose just at the sight of his nudity.

"Why are you the only thing on earth to make me feel hot?" Tilting his head, Tynan studied me like I was something he'd never seen before. With arrogance, he pressed his body against mine. "Ty," I breathed his name.

Tynan placed his finger to my lips. Knocking his hand away, I pulled him close. His mouth crushed against mine was the same feeling as coming home after a long time away. Wrapping my arms around his shoulders, I lifted one of my thighs around his hip. His curse rubbed that place that made me religious.

Lifting my other thigh around his waist, Tynan put my back against the cold stone wall of the shower. It felt even colder with the inferno in my blood. I was a supernova, radiating so much heat I could scorch the earth. "Ty, I need you."

"I know, Mess. I need you too." He lifted my hips till his misery was freed from between our abdomens. "Put me where you need me."

Reaching between us, I slid Tynan through my moist lips till he was nooked in my holy place. Torn between fear and relief; if he dared to refuse me this time, I think I'd lose it and kill him, or myself. Tears stained my cheeks, my eyes staying locked with his as I positioned him.

Watching me, his eyes full of enough heat he could turn the water cold, and I wouldn't notice, there was wariness in Tynan's eyes that added to my fear. Tynan wasn't exactly known for his emotional stability.

Drawn to the intensity of his look, I locked my mouth to his as I removed my hand and Tynan settled his weight against me, pinning me between him and the wall. Holding his body a little out from mine, he slipped his hand to my prayer bead and strummed me to his own harmony.

As he played me, my body grew wetter and ready for him. It slowly loosened, opened, allowed him to slip just a few millimeters inside of me naturally. Panting his name, I cringed a little with that first pull of stretch. God, it was like losing my virginity all over again.

The vibration of his hardness, his fingers rubbing me, it was already enough. But, as he stretched me enough that just his head was entirely inside me, and I got to feel those large nodules that marked the beginning of his length, it all became too much.

Breaking from our kiss, I cried my pleasure to the ceiling. My body tightened, sucking Tynan's cock a little further inside before I clamped down around his shaft, pressing one of those vibrating nodules right against the spot inside a woman that makes heaven feel real. My eyes sprang open and my voice choked off as the clenching and pulsing of my body became more intense than it had ever been.

Holding me tight while I recovered, Tynan moved his hand north, lifting my breast so he could suck the nipple. My body tightened again.

When I met his eyes, Tynan swiped the tears from my face. "Did I hurt you?"

"No, I've never felt anything so good before."

Visibly swallowing, his black eyes glassy with his lust, Tynan caressed my cheek. "I thought my heart stopped when the devil sliced your spine, Mess. I've wanted to sink into you for months, but I couldn't do that to you, not while you were just a plaything. I wanted you to be more in everyone else's eyes when I took you as my lover."

Lover? Was that like being his girlfriend? I'd never had a boyfriend, or even been interested in one. I'd spent the last six months trying to escape Tynan, but all that time, I knew I never wanted to leave him. Cupping his face, I stared into his eyes. Why did I want him so much? Whenever I thought about it, the same words replayed in my head. "You're my home, my hearth."

Tynan's eyes lit up, a mischievous smile playing through them. Kissing him, my tongue searching his mouth, his probing mine, while his curse vibrated harder between my thighs. When I started winding my hips a little, he sank a little bit deeper. Tynan's grip on my hips tightened, vibrating out of control inside of me.

"Goddess, Mess," Tynan panted against my mouth. "Mine for all eternity. Promise it."

The small amount of pain from having Tynan inside me was worth how amazing it felt to be with him. With Tynan, I experienced warmth for the first time in my life. The answer was easy. "I promise!" I cried out, peaking my next orgasm, feeling the best I'd ever felt in my life.

A moment later, Tynan jerked inside of me so hard, I felt like I'd been punched, then ice filled my womb. Staring wide-eyed at the ceiling, I bit my lip as his ice cooled the meltdown his touch caused in my core.

Clinging to him while he kissed all around my neck, I was in awe of the sensations creeping through my body. I didn't even notice when Tynan bit my neck gently, and again, dragged that something from me. Unlike the first time where I resisted the sensation, I gave it willingly. I'd give him anything if he did that to me again.

Withdrawing, Tynan settled my feet gently to the ground. I couldn't entirely focus my mind. His holding me, washing me, and then carrying me to his bed, was all a bit of a haze. A beautiful, pleasant, haze of happiness.

"I want you again," Tynan whispered in my ear when he woke me a few hours later. His hands were already readying me. Rolling me onto my back, Tynan set himself between my thighs. My heart danced in my chest as he brought me moaning to my first pleasure, ensuring I was slick for him, all the while kissing me with more passion than I thought he was capable of showing.

Sliding himself to my opening, Tynan put his weight behind it so that he would sink only as deep as my body allowed, then he pushed a little further. Gripping the sheets, back arching from the discomfort with a pinch of pain, I bit my lip to prevent mewling.

"Too much?" Tynan breathed.

Meeting his eyes, I wanted him to see I was stronger than that. I wanted to be the woman who could withstand his curse and be with him in every way. I needed the feeling of home to never stop. "I'll take what you give me," I assured him, repeating his words from our first encounter in this bed.

Tynan's eyebrows lifted in amazement, his eyes glazing in lust. He kissed me long and intent, then started rocking. He didn't go any further than his body had already forced to open for him, I understood he was taking this in steps, breaking me in, as it were.

Clinging to him as his pleasure mounted, my nails gouged his back when he swelled, making the pain a little more than bearable. Tynan groaned, cooling my molten core with his ice and inciting my body to exchange the sensation of pain for my own climax.

After my body stopped seizing, I dropped to the bed exhausted. Kneeling back, Tynan brushed my sex with his finger. Darkness smothered the head of his curse. "Is that blood?"

"I've torn you a little, you'll heal naturally. I'm going to clean up, do you need to shower?"

"Probably," I yawned closing my eyes, "I'm just too tired to stand."

Brushing my hair from my face gently, Tynan kissed my temple and went to shower. The blood didn't bother me. My stepfather and his friend had hurt me a lot worse when they got rough sharing me.

The tear they'd caused ulcerated, and I'd needed to see a doctor for treatment.

God, the memory of letting a doctor inspect down there and trying to avoid admitting how it happened was suddenly fresh in my head. The transparent look of sympathy while she asked if I'd willingly let a man do that to me. When I told her it was two men, the doctor really pressed things and kept asking if I wanted her to call the police or my parents. It didn't help she was our family doctor, and I was barely seventeen the first time it happened.

My brows knitted. First time? I thought for sure it only happened once, but suddenly my brain was swelling in my head, trying to force other memories at me. "Esha!" I sobbed, holding my head in my hands, not wanting those memories to escape.

"Mess?" Tynan took my face in his hands, forcing me to meet his eyes.

"The memories are trying to break free. It hurts."

Pulling me close to him, Tynan planted his lips to my third-eye center. The tribal tattoos started to glow on his pale skin, his lips growing hotter as he glowed brighter. Suddenly, white light burst from his mouth. I closed my eyes as burning heat pressed into my skull, smothering my brain, shrinking it back to its standard size.

Gasping for breath as Tynan drew back, I blinked away the tears and stared up into his silver orbs. "You don't need Esha to take away the pain of your memories, Mess. I can take your curse, just as you were made to take mine." Adjusting his seating, Tynan held me snuggled against him as we returned to sleep.

Waking with a smile on my face despite the overwhelming heat cocooning me, I found Tynan was wrapped around me. His solid chest was pressing against my spine, one hand cupping my breast, the other over my womb, his legs entwined with mine. It reminded me of Golem when he had his precious ring, and I expected him to start snarling *'my precious'* possessively at any moment. The thought made me giggle.

"What?" Tynan murmured, placing a kiss on my neck, as his curse awoke between us.

"Have you ever heard of Stockholm syndrome?"

"Of course." Tynan shifted his hips, and his still growing appendage sprung between my legs, finding what it sought immediately.

"Do you think I have it?" I breathed as he slipped into me. I was sopping wet, my womb still flooded with his desire, and his sizing right now was that of the average man, so he slid into me entirely with ease.

"The fact that you're asking is no, Mess. What you feel right now is not a syndrome."

"All I can feel is you," I answered, biting my lip as he grew thicker, longer. "Ty, I don't know..."

"You'll take what I give you." He dropped a kiss right before my ear.

Squirming as the ache mounted, I moaned. Tynan kept his pelvis hard to mine as he grew. The discomfort was increasing to the tipping point, and I couldn't stay still.

Gripping my hip, Tynan allowed me to squirm but not move away. "My fluid inside of you will relax those muscles and lubricate you, Mess. Unlike when I first enter you, my secretion will assist your body to adapt to me."

Biting my lip on a moan, I realized it wasn't hurting. As uncomfortable as it was, Tynan was right, it wasn't painful.

"We're meant to be together, Mess. Your body was designed by the goddess with me already in mind. Don't fear it." Massaging my breast, he nipped my neck, helping me relax against him. Then Tynan started circling his hips, encouraging my body to open to him.

Gripping his hand that held my hip, I bit my lip harder. I could feel him pressed hard against my cervix. "Fuck, don't stop." My body racing to a more profound climax. Tynan told me the texturization of a sluagh's penis was to provide a higher level of satisfaction, but this, this was beyond pleasure. "Ty, I..." I gripped his hand harder, pressing it harder into me, trying to pull away so he could thrust into me.

"Not yet, Mess. Baby steps," his voice deep and guttural.

"Cum!"

"What?"

"I need you to cum in me."

Gripping me harder, Tynan pulled me tight against him. He bit my shoulder, not enough to draw blood, just to have something between his teeth. I think Tynan was trying to mute his desire, but it was pointless. He was balls deep in me and experiencing pleasure without a woman screaming in agony for the first time in his life.

Throbbing hard in me, Tynan threw back his head and roared his happiness to the entire faerie mound. His coldness flooded me, took hold of me, and I cried out as my body convulsed around his. We'd both yelled so loud that my ears were ringing. My body was buzzing, and it felt like there was so much electricity around me that every hair on my body ought to be standing on edge.

Content and smiling, I relaxed, snuggling against Tynan, glad he wasn't moving away from me straight away. Then my eyes bulged open as something started swirling inside me.

Tynan's grip on my hip was bruising. "Don't move. Goddess, Messina, don't move, I beg you."

"What is that?" Placing my hand on my lower abdomen, I could feel something was moving around inside me, just below where he butted against my cervix still.

Tynan kissed my shoulder, and I could tell, whatever it was, was causing him immense pleasure that wasn't to do with climaxing. It was having a similar effect on me, relaxing me, hormones flooding into my bloodstream like the best drug you could buy.

"Before the Seelie queen cursed us, the nodules of our reproductive organs contained soft spurs. When we mated with our Sluagh females, those nodules would emerge after our climax, bind our bodies together, and encourage the female to release an ovum."

Horrified by what he was saying, I double checked my comprehension. "You could force your women to get pregnant?"

"Only after mating with them. The female had to willingly give you what we call her desexo. Her desire."

"Ty, I'm eighteen, I'm not ready to be a mum." I wanted to cry at the thought, but the hormones in my body refused to give way to sadness. Only good feelings were permitted right now.

"You're not Sluagh, Mess." Tynan gasped, his body pulling hard to mine and trembling. My womb opened to him entirely, and I clawed the sheet in front of me as a feeling better than climaxing, better than... Goddess, there was nothing to compare this too. Gripping the bedding, I moaned long and hard as it seized my entire body.

Tynan's markings glowed purple on his skin as he alternated between swearing and moaning, his fingers gripped and released my hip like a cat kneading a place to sleep. I felt it when it happened. My satiability exploded out of me, embraced Tynan and me in its majick, and took what was happening to an entirely new level.

"Oh, goddess, Mess...!" Tynan bellowed my name to the room. I yelled my own response, and then, like a flash, it was over.

We were left panting and wheezing on the bed. Sweat dripping from us, the entire bed beneath us wet. It took me a while to recover enough to even assess our surroundings. The only movement inside me was Tynan's receding curse. I felt like I'd traveled through time I was so disorientated, but I felt so damn good.

The hesitant knock at the door made us both jump. For once, the door didn't just open. Kissing my shoulder, Tynan pulled away. "Can you walk?"

"I...I think so," I frowned wiggling my toes.

"Go shower. I'll deal with this first, and then we should probably talk."

Smiling, I made my way to the bathroom in a daze of post-orgasmic bliss. If we arrived at the festival tonight and the Sluagh suddenly had skin color and eyes so they could pass as human, we would have to do some serious explaining.

28

FESTIVAL

❖

"**I** need you to understand what's happening," Tynan informed me from where he stood in front of the empty fireplace.

"Can we discuss that first?" Pointing to the windows where my blood had been smeared last night. Tynan bounced on his toes a second, then settled and nodded his head. Noticing the tense line in his jaw, I worded my question carefully. "I thought the Sluagh are what the humans mistake as vampires?"

"They are."

Perplexed by the answer, I let my hand drop to point at the dark forest outside the window.

Tynan exhaled. "The Devils are descendants of the Sluagh. The bastardization of a Sluagh and a Seelie faerie."

"So, there are such things as pretty little fairies that fly and grant wishes?".

Closing his eyes, Tynan pinched his brow. "They perform glamor, but they are horrid creatures with sharp teeth and a penchant for mischief."

"How are they Seelie then?" Instead of clarifying things for me, this conversation was making me more confused.

"They are beautiful in appearance. The light court isn't so interested in personality as the outer shell. The only reason we have Sidhe in the darkness is that they either do not have an interest in the political machinations of the light court, or they prefer the dark."

Moving to the window, Tynan looked out. "We are all children of the goddess, Mess. She holds both the light and dark within her. We all carry a mix of both." Tynan turned to look at me. "Most carry one more than the other, but there are a few who hold the aspects of the goddess in balance."

"So, the Devils, are vampire bats?"

"The humans have myths about vampire bats. They see them as normal bats which feed on blood, but it's the Devils casting glamor."

Closing my eyes, a shiver tremored through my body at the memory of the Devil with his teeth in me. Deciding my question was answered, Tynan slipped his hands into his pockets and appraised me.

"You've found all your powers now, Mess. You're spirit power, and your two hands of power." Returning to the fireplace, Tynan opened a large book on the table. "We already have seen your spirit power, manifestation. Your left hand is satiability, and now I know your right hand is blood." Tynan turned the book to face me.

Shifting forward on the lounge to read the page, I peered at the book, but it wasn't in English. "I can't read that."

Frowning, Tynan's heavy brow shadowed his eyes. "You can speak our language, but not read it?"

Lifting my eyes to him unsure, I tilted my head. "Um, I only speak and read English."

Raising a skeptical brow, Tynan studied me. "Messina, we are currently speaking Eirnish, and you quite often switch to Albanic for some words. Considering your mother was Seelie and their court mainly descends from the Scottish and Welsh, that's to be expected."

My eyes blinked at Tynan astounded. He gestured back to the book. "Look again, focus a little and see if you can recognize any words."

Peering down at the book, I tried scanning the page to see if anything stood out, but nothing did. "I was five when I left, and my memories got left behind with me." Pushing the book away, I slumped back. "I can't read that."

Clenching his jaw, Tynan retrieved a folded piece of paper from his pocket. It looked scrappy like coffee had been spilled on it. "Yet, you could not only read this, but you could respond in Eirnish." On the table, Tynan dropped the last question Margo sent me. "What is this thing humans crave called love?" Tynan read out. "In your handwriting underneath, 'I don't know.'"

Frowning, I studied the handwriting. "How did you find this?"

"We are renovating your old room, thanks to you trashing it. I personally removed your sketchbooks that could be saved myself. When I found this, I thought it might have been a sketch. I didn't realize you were still communicating with the person who helped you, Messina."

Oh, he was using my full name; I was in trouble. Folding my hands in my lap, I focused my attention on the feel of the velvet evening gown Brie had brought me to for the festivities tonight.

"They didn't help me escape; I swear. They warned me not to eat the food at the nightclub - not that I would have - and told me to get out before the clock struck three."

Narrow eyes observing me for any hint of a lie, Tynan pressed his lips together in a straight line.

"I helped her. She fell, and I stopped her from falling to the ground and caught what she was carrying. That's the only reason she helped me.

Folding his arms behind his back, Tynan looked sophisticated as usual. "Margo has been asking you the questions?"

Avoiding eye contact, I watched my fingers fidgeting with the silver rope that hung as a belt from the purple dress. I wasn't going to confirm it for him, but I didn't want to lie to him either.

"I should have known it was her. She's always wanted to know more about her human half."

Lifting my eyes to the book, I tried focusing on the text again, but it was all gibberish. "I don't understand. I swear I wrote my responses in English. I swear the questions were in English. Why can't I read the book?"

Eyes flicking between the book and me, Tynan tilted his head and held up his right hand towards me. Something moved through me, causing a violent quake in my internal organs, and I covered my mouth to prevent vomiting all over the book.

Tynan stood straight. "You're not allowed too."

"What?" I wondered if I looked as green as I felt.

"There is no spell on you, but every time you look at the book, I see a veil wrap around you, so something doesn't want you reading this book." Tilting his head again, Tynan moved towards me, closing the book as he did. "Something or someone wants you to remain ignorant, Mess."

Lifting my eyes to him as he brought his face closer, I elevated one of my brows in consideration of how debonair Tynan looked tonight. "Probably the same someone that steals my memories."

Placing one knee on the lounge next to me, Tynan cupped my cheek and drew his mouth close to mine. "Mess, we need to talk about your power, need to train you, but we also need to discuss us."

"I don't think I'm meant to know about my power, so let's talk about this thing called us."

Smiling, Tynan moved closer, I leaned back to keep him from kissing me, but that just ended with him hovering his entire body over me, and me lying on the sofa beneath him.

"Mine for eternity, Mess." Dropping kisses to either side of my mouth, his hand lifted my knee, sliding my dress up.

"Brie is going to kill you if you ruin this dress."

Tynan's eyes flared with humor. "Only if I ruin it before the festival." Mouth to mine in a firm but restrained kiss, Tynan pulled away quickly when the apartment door opened and Esha's voice drifted towards us.

Wanting to blow off the festival and go back to bed with Tynan, I quickly righted my dress, my cheeks just as hot as the areas Tynan had just been touching and kissing.

Offering me his hand, Tynan helped me stand. "Which it is time to attend."

Esha walked in with Trell, and they both looked us over suspiciously. "What do you think? Was he about to fuck her or kill her?"

Raising a brow at us, knowledge in his eyes, the side of Esha's lips twitched upwards. "He can't kill her now without cause; she's one of us."

Snickering, Trell's eyes lit up. "Guess that leaves fucking then."

Placing his hand against my skin, the backless ball gown providing easy access, Tynan once again checked my spine was intact for the third time since I came downstairs this evening while he spoke to the others. "Are we ready?"

"Festival is happening, just waiting for our warriors," Esha smiled. "You look perfect, Messina."

Rolling her eyes, Trell turned to leave. "It's like you've all have never seen a Sidhe female before. Get over it already!"

"Hey, I earned the right to a bit of self-pride, and this is the best I've ever felt or looked since I was five. So put a glamor on it!"

Everyone stopped and looked at me shocked, then they all burst out laughing. "I've never heard that one before," Trell chuckled, "I'm stealing it."

We made our way out towards the amphitheater and the banquet hall attached to it. "You will wait backstage with the others until your name is called, then you will enter the hall and take your seat at the table," Trell instructed as we walked.

"How will I know which seat is mine?"

"You will be announced last. Therefore, it will be the only other empty seat," Trell answered sarcastically.

"It will also be the seat to my left. As my..."

"Mistress, lover, other?" I offered when Tynan hesitated.

"Yes, that," Tynan swallowed, "you'll always be seated next to me at any formal occasion now."

Trell gave Esha a surprised look, Esha put his finger to his mouth indicating silence. Trell's eyes came to me, and something in them told me I'd been lied to.

My feet came to an abrupt halt. "Wait! Is there an oath or something that you can make a Sluagh take to force them to be honest?" I asked Trell.

She opened her mouth, Tynan glared at her, she shut it. "I'll see you at the banquet." Trell stormed off.

Waiting till she was away from us, I turned to face Tynan directly. "What are you keeping from me, Ty?"

Tynan didn't look impressed. "Many things, Mess. That's what Sluagh do."

"What are you not telling me about us, about me?"

Ty cleared his throat. "I wanted to talk to you about this, but we ran out of time. We'll talk about it tomorrow." Taking my arm to escort me forward, Tynan cursed when I pulled back.

"Wait. Will anything happen tonight that I should know about. Any gestures, behaviors that I shouldn't do? Like biting you? I'm sick of you leading me into situations unprepared and then punishing me for doing something harmless, which means something entirely different here."

"The only thing tonight is that when you are introduced, it will not be the name you are used to being called."

He was kind of cute when he got all huffy, but I needed to keep my mind on the conversation, not how much I wanted to touch him naked. "Why?"

"Well, for starters, we know your real mother's name now," Tynan explained as he started us walking again. "Females carry their mother's name so you will be announced as Messina Bayne. Fae also use a precursor before the surname to denote sex, Ui for female, Ó for men. Then, there is a title added to the surname to denote rank or title. It tells people where your bloodline comes from."

"Ty," I growled, "no one is meant to know." Tynan kept walking. When I appealed to Esha, he purposefully refused eye contact. "Pride?" I begged him to help.

"You are a princess of the first line. I agree with the Prince. Since he has made you his, your title should be known. You are no longer half-breed street trash that the Prince was given as a toy. You are the lost daughter of a princess, heir to the Seelie throne, and the-"

"Thank you, Pride. People need to know why I allowed you to run the gauntlet, Mess."

Sighing in exasperation, there was no point wasting my breath. Nothing I said or did, would change Tynan's mind once it was made up.

Bringing us to a halt, Tynan cupped my face in his hands. "Mess, the Seelie know, the Unseelie Luna guard know, or did you think it coincidental that the time you run the gauntlet was when the captain of the Luna guard chose to try it? That he and the other came to your defense when that could have lost them the challenge and their lives?"

Meeting his eyes, I accepted his reasoning. He was right. Noting my non-verbal acceptance, Tynan kissed me, firmly and restrained.

"Okay, what's with the sudden control when kissing me?"

Lifting a brow, Tynan moved his mouth to my car. "If I kiss you any more than that, Mess, you'll have your back against that wall and be screaming for mercy a minute later," he whispered. "I haven't been inside you for six hours now, and it feels like six centuries."

Just the suggestion made me press my body closer to his. "Whoa!" Stepping forward, Esha pulled Tynan back, Pride moving me further from the Prince. "Let's keep it PG till after the festivities."

When Tynan physically growled at Esha, Pride literally stood between us, blocking my sight of the two, and possibly Tynan's view of me. "This is why the Sluagh does not mate any longer. You turn into feral, possessive, nymph-beasts until life is sourced, and since that isn't possible, you all start acting like cavemen."

"Not possible for the pure breeds," I countered Pride's assessment.

"What?" All three looked at me then, Tynan sidestepping to see me around Pride, seemingly back in control immediately.

"Well, the Seelie curse only seems to affect the Unseelie if they are breeding with their own. Tynan was conceived after the curse, Margo is a half-breed goblin, I'm half Unseelie. So, the curse only stops you breeding with your own kind. Stick your wick in something foreign, and you get babies." The three men stared at me. "It's kind of in your face here guys. Did no one cotton on to these little mishaps as your solution before now?"

"We believed it was divine intercession. That the goddess blessed a select few."

Laughing at Tynan's answer, I shook my head. "Well, obviously not. My dad and mum where both Sidhe, but from different courts, so even that was enough."

Considering me a moment longer, Tynan smirked when he turned to Esha. "There are two female Sidhe in holding, correct?" Esha nodded, his eyes lighting up. "After the feast, take our warriors who just finished the gauntlet down to holding and let them celebrate with the Sidhe. Tell the women, it's their ticket to freedom. The first one with child lives."

Esha was happy as can be. "So basically, we get to tag team the bitches till they conceive?"

"Basically," Tynan agreed.

"Ty! You don't have a right to their bodies." The look on Tynan's face drew me up.

"You sold your body for your education and freedom, Mess. These girls get the same option."

He did not just compare my circumstances to this. "I'm fucked up, Ty. My situation was fucked up. It was when I let you touch me the first time too, remember?"

Eyes flashing silver, Tynan cocked a brow at me. "Those two women you are heartily defending were part of a team of Seelie assassins sent to kill you, Messina. They are in prison pending death by goblin or troll. I'm giving them the option of freedom by getting pregnant, but if you think I'm going to make it pleasant for them, you are wrong."

The admission left me staring wide-eyed at Tynan. "How many people have been sent to kill me?"

"For a couple of months there, we had regular attempts at least once to twice a week. We currently have thirty Seelie Sidhe assassins in holding who survived their capture."

Swallowing that uncomfortable revelation, I considered how

much Tynan had protected me behind the scenes, how he'd trained me, prepared me for more than my so-called human parents ever did.

Remembering witnessing Sauvignon and Damk in my gauntlet cell, I turned my gaze to Esha. "Make the bitches mewl." Esha winked. When Tynan lifted a brow at me, I held my head high and met his eyes. "You should have some of your women volunteer to go ride a Sidhe and see if they can get knocked up as well."

Esha laughed. "You do know Sluagh male to Sidhe male is seen as a downgrade."

"You would say that."

"Well, I guess you can compare."

"Esha!" Pride scolded.

"It's okay, Pride. I've never done Sidhe to compare, only human. Trust me, that wasn't so great."

"You have so-" Esha cut off when Pride reached over and grabbed him by his collar reeling him back before snarling angrily in his face. Esha was pale as he nodded.

"What's that about?"

With a shake of his head, Tynan got us walking again. "Nothing you'll want to know."

Reaching a door, Tynan opened it, and we went inside. Trell was waiting and led us to a dark back room where the five Sluagh and two Sidhe who survived the gauntlet were waiting. Amp and Ashok instantly had their eyes and smiles for me when I entered.

Growling under his breath, Tynan pointedly swept my hair aside before he caught my mouth in a deep, languid kiss. My body moved into his, but Pride's arm came between us. "Unless you plan to do her on the festival table, pack it up," Pride whispered harshly.

With a mischievous smirk, Tynan backed up. "I'll see you at the feast table, Mess." Tynan and Esha left with Trell. Pride stayed, moving to stand to the side.

Amp approached first. "You healed? I was worried about how deep that cut was..." Amp's eyes moved to my neck and froze there. "Was that from the devil?"

My hand reached up to feel the two different bites in my neck, both from Tynan yesterday. "Oh, the devil bit me, yes."

Amp shook his head. "It's strange, isn't it. That the devil chose you to change the game with?" Tilting my head, I considered him. "I mean, hundreds of years of the gauntlet, and only now do they drink from someone during the run. It weakens them. They become blood drunk and are vulnerable. Why would he do that?"

"Or that he broke the accords and attacked outside the tree line," Ashok joined us. "That too was a first."

"Messina was also the first female Sidhe to run the gauntlet, and half Seelie," Pride chimed in behind me. "Many firsts occurred at yesterday's gauntlet run."

Amp bowed his head respectfully. "Right you are, Pride. I was just concerned, after all the attempts on the princess's life..."

"Princess?" I heard one of the Sluagh whisper to another. Bloody-irises congealed in wide-eyes appraising me.

Taking a breath, I exhaled to relax my shoulders. It just didn't seem right to have become a princess overnight. "I'm sure it's as Pride said. I can't see the Seelie risking time with a devil to have me killed."

Amp bowed his head to me. "As you say, Princess."

"It's starting!" Trell buzzed through the room excitedly. "Line up."

The Sluagh formed a queue, the Unseelie Sidhe next and I joined the end. "Will you be walking out with me, Pride?" There was an itch between my shoulder blades that made me suddenly self-conscious.

"Right behind you, but out of sight, Messina."

"Trell, announce Messina directly after me. Don't allow time for me to walk away from her." Glaring at the Luna Captain, Trell was about to refuse Amp's plan.

"It's a good idea," Pride agreed. "To be safe."

Rolling her eyes, Trell glanced at me. "Does this get annoying?"

"Live a day in my shoes. Your feet and snatch will be killing you."

Amp and Ashok choked on their spit. Trell's brows lowered, eyes flicking around as her brain tried to understand me. "Snatch?"

I pointed to said anatomy. "Your girly bits."

Trell's eyes went wide. "Does it really...?"

"Trell!" someone called her back out front. Shutting up and

focusing on her duties, Trell left. Soon the names of the Sluagh were being called.

Pride put his mouth close to my ear. "Did he do damage?"

Leaning my head back onto his shoulder, I sighed remembering last night. "He was gentle. I loved every second of it, but he hasn't..." I stopped as Amp turned his head to watch us, his eyes glaring at the bite on my neck.

"Try not to fall over, Messina," Pride murmured as Ashok's name was called. His big paws on my upper arms setting me to stand straight.

"Amp Ó Macha-Mór," Trell's voice called. Amp stepped through the curtain.

"Messina Ui Bayne-Ard," Trell called again immediately, not leaving the space she had for the others. Stepping through into the candlelit festival hall, I followed Amp. "Consort of Tynan Ó Wane-Ard."

Gasps were already audible after my name was announced, but now shock and whispers were near deafening. Immediately following was the sound of chairs being pushed back as everyone at the table stood to watch me approach.

"It is respect for royalty," Pride whispered from the darkness to my left. "You are ranked higher than them all. They must acknowledge it."

At the table, Amp took a seat one down from mine and waited for me. Walking to the empty chair, my eyes going to Tynan at the end on my right.

Tynan gestured for me to sit, then he sat immediately after me, and everyone else sat after us. Tynan looked down the table, Trell handing him a microphone.

"Welcome warriors," Tynan began before standing again. "Everyone at this table has run the gauntlet. Tonight, we welcome eight new warriors amongst us. Our strong Sluagh." Tynan indicated the five Sluagh. They stood. "I am proud of every one of you. Brought into our fold from your human life, you have trained hard to sit at this table. Welcome."

The table moved as everyone thumped it in applause. When the thumping stopped, the Sluagh sat.

"For the first time in centuries, we welcome new Sidhe males to our table. Captain of the Luna guard, Amp Ó Macha-Mór and Ashok Fiachdubh."

The thumping started again as Amp and Ashok stood to take the praise, a few Sluagh throwing teasing insults about wooing the Devils to let them pass instead of fighting.

When the applause finished, and everyone was seated again, Tynan set his eyes on me. "For the first time, we had a female Sidhe run the gauntlet. As you heard, for my birthday half a year ago, I was given a half-breed Seelie as a toy. The joke was on the giver. By the end of the first night, I knew that my toy was full-blooded Sidhe, born within the Unseelie mound."

Murmurs of astonishment drifted down the table.

"It took a little more digging before I discovered, that my toy, was not only full-blooded, but the daughter of King Mabon's Seelie consort, Nora Ui Bayne-Ard, and that Messina was the missing heir to the Seelie throne." The room was suddenly dead silent.

Reaching down, Tynan took my hand urging me to rise. He waited until I was standing beside him to continue. "Warriors, tonight, not only do we welcome a Seelie princess, first in line to be the queen to our table, but we also welcome my consort and my mate."

Every Sluagh stood and yelled their support, thumping the table with both fists, the impact of the sudden noise nearly making me jump out of my skin. Amp and Ashok stared up at me unhappily. Esha, he stood, but his heart wasn't in it. Lifting my hand, Tynan kissed it before indicating I should sit.

Moving my hair aside, Amp brushed his thumb across the bites on my neck. "One of these is his?" I nodded, keeping my eyes on my lap. "No one ever said the prince was stupid, but he forgets, marks mean nothing to the Sidhe. To us, you are still available until a child is growing inside you."

29

AFTER PARTY

❖

Alcohol flowed like a tsunami at the banquet. When my glass was initially filled, I avoided drinking, focusing on eating and listening to the stories of the Sluagh who passed the gauntlet. However, after every story, we all cheered and toasted their bravery.

The first toast, Tynan moved my shot glass in front of me and ensured I knew to drink from it. Lifting the glass to my lips, I took a long sip of the plum flavored liquid.

Five shots down, it was Ashok's turn. He'd seen which direction Amp ran off with me and worked out what I was doing immediately. "I figured, all the devils would be chasing our pretty princess here," Ashok teased, and everyone laughed. "Let's face it, if you have the choice, we'd all have chased the half-naked Seelie princess. Am I right?" Everyone cheered making my cheeks flame up. "So, I ran as far from her as possible, and, I believe, that's why I got through the gauntlet."

"Did you fight any of the Devils?" Esha teased.

"Aye, there was a lass of a devil," Ashok grinned, and the sparkle in his eye told me he was about to take the mickey. "Ugliest thing on two legs, I ever did see. She attacked me, and tried to mount me, would you believe?" Ashok looked appalled. "A bastard Sidhe like me, when a lord was running the gauntlet not far away," Ashok whacked his hand on Amp's shoulder. "I told 'er there were a lord and captain of the Luna guard chasing the princess. She told me she would get to him later. She wanted me to give her a baby. So, being a respectable bastard as I am, I asked her where she wanted me to stick it."

Mockery ensued about the Sidhe not being true warriors. Ashok raised a brow. "Think what you like, but I tell y'all, worst five seconds of my life was with my pipe in that Devil's mouth. Clearing that forest and seeing the finish line was pure relief." The Sluagh turned their mockery to his prowess as a lover. Laughing, Ashok lifted his hand as his face turned serious.

"But, none of what I encountered in that forest came close to when I saw our beautiful princess still standing, running for that finish line, and then that devil came into the clearing and cut her down with only meters to go.

No one laughed now. "I knew I couldn't cross that wall and leave her there. Not because Messina was a woman, not because she was a princess, not because she is more beautiful than moonlight, but because she dared."

The entire banquet was quiet. Ashok frowned down at his drink. "I ran the gauntlet because to my own, I'm a bastard, not worthy of a title. For the Sluagh, it's a rite of passage, to show you are good enough." The Sluagh nodded.

"Unlike the rest of us, Messina didn't choose to run the gauntlet to prove herself worthy. She ran it to survive. From what I've heard about our princess, that has been her modus operandi since she fled the Unseelie court at five years of age, to survive.

"So when I heard the princess was being forced to run, I knew, if ever I was going to do this, it was now. And there she was, still running at the end with barely a mark on her and that devil cut her down? Did our princess give up? No. She pulled herself, bloody and body uncooperative, to the wall and over. There is not a single one of us who would have expected she'd make it, let alone still be running at the end, is there?"

Ashok waited while everyone shook their heads. Ashok nodded. "So, I didn't care if I made that wall in the end. Just as long as the princess, my princess, did."

"To the bastard Sidhe," someone toasted down the table. "He fought the Devils with his willie, then defended his princess with his sword. A braver Sidhe I never did meet." Everyone roared their support, and everyone drank.

Amp was next. "Unlike this brave bastard beside me, I chose to run the gauntlet with the Princess. To be honest, the hardest part of the gauntlet was not fighting off the Devils, but running behind the princess in that skimpy outfit and not stopping for a roll in the grass. I was about to suggest we do just that when that devil picked me up, flew above the treetops and dropped me, just to get me away from her.

"A testimony to our princesses bravery was that she stopped to help me, only for the devil to attack, and for her to have no choice but to run.

"Keen to get back to watching the princess run in that outfit, I recovered quickly, got to my feet to give chase, but was engaged by another devil. Sadly, I didn't catch up to the princess again until just before the clearing. I too knew I had to defend the princess until she was over the wall because the devil had broken the rules. Watching her crawl across that grass and drag her injured body to safety only confirmed her worthiness to me. As soon as Messina was safe, the Devil wasn't interested in our pretty faces, and Ashok and I were free to jump the wall. So, not only do we get to claim the honor of running the gauntlet, we get to say we defended our princess with our lives."

"To the captain of the Luna guard," a Sluagh called in a toast. "He ran hard, literally!" Everyone snickered. "Another great warrior we greet."

After everyone drank, their eyes turned to me. Touching my elbow, Tynan indicated I should stand. Swallowing nervously, I used the table to support me, the room spinning as I stood.

"I ran. I fell several times to the slash of a devil's wing. I smeared my blood across the prince's window. I was bitten..." Everyone cringed. "...I was propositioned, and I made a devil bite his own dick."

The men cringed, and the women cheered. I smirked, but then sobered.

"I cannot tell you the relief I felt to see that wall, but I wasn't slowing down for anyone. Even when that devil took my legs, I wasn't stopping, and I didn't until I was in our Prince's arms."

Murmurs of support went down the table as I turned to Ashok and Amp. "I owe my life to Captain Amp of the Luna guard, and his second in command, Ashok." I watched Ashok's eyes widen in surprise and look to Amp for confirmation. "Since I cannot give them my life, I offer them my thanks, my gratitude, and a kiss, for taking on that devil, which got me to the wall."

Leaning passed Amp, I kissed Ashok's mouth, then as I pulled back, I kissed Amp. Neither of the kisses was interesting, but both of them looked at me with shining eyes.

Standing straight, I raised my glass. "I survived, and I'm alive. This rabbit can run," I smiled, knowing they all heard the Devils song.

Everyone laughed. Esha stood raising his glass. "To Princess Messina, so beautiful and brave, the Devils broke the accords to try and get her." Esha raised his glass to me. "May she never need to run again. Welcome home, Princess."

Everyone cheered. Drinking my shot, I swiped at the tear escaping down my cheek as I sat. Taking my hand in his, Tynan moved his mouth to my ear.

"Light in my darkness."

THE MUSIC WASHED through the room. Heavy beats reverberating through our bodies as we danced. I was dancing with Sauvignon and Brie, and anyone else who came and went from our circle..

Hands grabbed my hips as a body pressed against the back of mine. I didn't care, I was warm, heated through from the alcohol, and alive. Amp danced with his body rubbing against mine, his hands roaming freely.

"She's mated," Brie warned Amp, "come dance with me."

"She's Sidhe. She's not mated until there's a child," Amp countered. "Plus, I doubt Tynan gained her consent."

Brie shook her head. "Barking up the wrong tree, Captain. She's in love with our prince. She'll give him whatever he demands, and that was before he mated her."

Ignoring them, I spotted Esha gathering up the five Sluagh who ran the gauntlet with us. Stepping away from Amp, I wound my way through the crowd to reach Esha. "Messina. I thought you were busy dancing?"

"I want to come," I yelled to get over the music.

Esha's eyes widened as he looked around. "Well, you're mated now. You need to see Ty about that."

"I meant to the dungeons. I don't know where Ty is," I clarified, still dancing, unable to stay still.

"He's on a business call, he shouldn't be too long."

"I want to come with you." Esha stared at me. "I want to watch you fuck the Sidhe."

"Who's fucking Sidhe?" Amp yelled in my ear, wrapping his arm around my waist.

Nose crinkling and ruby eyes flashing promised violence, Esha snarled. "Get off her."

"You are," I answered, turning around and moving Amp to stand by Esha. "For this experiment to work, Unseelie Sidhe should be included."

Esha's left eye twitched as he eyed Amp. "Fine, get your friend and meet us at the exit." Glaring after him when Amp winked at me and walked off to find Ashok, Esha took my shoulders in his hands. "You need to stay here, where it's safe."

"I'm meant to stay with you when Ty isn't around. But, if you think I'm safer here among all these drunk people, then okay." I turned to leave.

"Wait," Esha sighed catching my elbow. "You know you are one of the drunk people, right?" I nodded. "Are you sure you want to come down for this?"

"Yes."

Esha studied me. "You can't let Amp seduce you, Messina. Tynan would hurt you both badly."

Rolling my eyes at this nonsense, I took his face in my hands. "Ty is the only one who I like touching me. All the others don't feel right."

"I didn't feel right, but when I got you drunk, you nearly let me have you."

"That was before I was with Ty. Now, nothing compares, and I don't want anyone else."

Esha dropped his face to the ground. "Amp's been pawing you all night..."

Lifting Esha's face, I met his eyes earnestly. "Esha, I would do you before anyone else here, but I love Ty..." Covering my mouth with both hands, I stared wide-eyed at Esha. He observed me, eyes flitting over my face, carefully taking in my reaction to my own admission. "I didn't mean that," I blurted. "I'm drunk."

Glancing around the banquet, Esha made eye contact with someone then tilted his head towards the exit as he took my wrist and pulled me along. "You stand and watch. You let anyone touch you, I'll rip their heads off."

"You sound like Ty," I rolled my eyes. "And like Ty, you should know better. Plus, Pride will keep everyone away. Won't you, Pride?" I smiled over my shoulder where I could feel a large shadow suddenly.

"Yes, Messina," Pride chuckled behind me.

"This goes wrong, I'm not taking the fall from the prince."

"It would have been worse to leave her drunk and alone with the Luna captain," Pride suggested.

"Which is the only reason I'm letting her come," Esha returned as we reached the exit. The five Sluagh and two Sidhe were there. "Let's go have some fun!"

"Where are we going?" Brie and Sauvignon appeared by my side suddenly, eager to be in on mischief.

Esha smiled. "The after party in the dungeon. You keen?"

"Will there be fucking?" Brie simpered.

"That's the idea," Esha chuckled.

"Ooh, we are so in, on, ready," Brie chuckled looping her arm through Sauvignon's and stepping to the front of the line.

The Sluagh led the way, Esha kept my hand in his as we moved through the maze of the Unseelie court, Pride staying behind me like a barrier. After sinking deep into the earth, we came to the place I'd been taken to wait for the gauntlet. "Bringing back memories here," one of the Sluagh murmured.

Gripping my hand harder, Esha kissed the top of my head. He knew I'd been injured and naked when he brought me here last. Not exactly the best memories.

We reached another corridor, this one was dark, not a single light on. "Turn on fifty-three and fifty-four," Esha ordered the guard at the door.

Keeping hold of my hand, Esha led me down the corridor to where the faint glow was emitting from one side of the wall. Through full glass windows, I could see the Seelie Sidhe females in each cell. They looked exhausted, drained, and very naked. Brie and Sauvignon huddled either side of me. "Watching or interacting?" Brie whispered to me.

"Watching."

"Do we get to play?" Brie asked Esha.

"There is a goal to this mischief, but afterwards, sure," he didn't refuse them. Moving to the wall between the cells, Esha pressed two buttons, the breathing of both women in the rooms suddenly audible. Esha pressed and held another button. "I have a proposition for you..."

30

———

MEWLING

❖

One of the women said yes, the other said something that could be politely summarized to a stern no. Esha pressed two buttons. The first opened the door to the cell of the woman who said yes. Waving the two Unseelie and two of the Sluagh in, Esha shut the door.

In the other cell, the blacked-out window to the devils' forest was opening. "What are you doing?" The naysayer called panicked.

"You won't dance with us; you can dance with the devils. We have no use for you and Lucifer was after a female Sidhe."

The woman's eyes went wide. She started trembling, watching the window slide like a devil might not wait for it to be open. Watching her, Esha indicated the others get ready to enter her room before quickly glancing at Pride.

Hitting a switch, the lights went out in both rooms, leaving even the corridor in darkness. A woman's blood-curdling scream, sinister laughter, and then the moans from the first room filled the hallway. The light in the first room with Amp and Ashok came back on. Looking around, everyone else was gone, and Pride now stood at the control panel.

"What happened?" Pride leveled me with a look. My eyes went to the darkened room. "Turn the lights on."

"No," Pride refused plainly.

"Turn the light on!"

Catching my shoulders in his large hands, Pride moved me back from the controls and lowered his giant head to be right in front of mine. "You can watch the room with the lights on, or I can take you back to your room. Those are your choices here, Messina."

Glaring at Pride, I swung away quickly when a movement to my right caught my attention. Stepping out of the shadows, Tynan kept his eyes locked on me. "You don't have to stay, Pride."

Pride considered Tynan. "You mean I shouldn't stay."

The side of Tynan's mouth lifted. "As you say." Tynan placed his cane against the wall in easy reach.

"Goodnight, Messina." Bowing his head, Pride farewelled and walked off into the darkness.

Wrapping his arm around my waist, Tynan pulled me tight against the front of him, his warmth spreading across my back. My eyes lifted to the room with the light on, Amp currently having his turn with the Seelie assassin. Becoming aroused just watching, I bit my lip. The two Sluagh was sitting in the corner snoozing, Ashok was watching and laughing at something Amp said.

Lifting his arm to the control panel, Tynan hit the button so we could hear what was happening in the room without lights. "Listen to one, watch the other, Mess," he urged as male moans, joined with the feminine in the darkened room. There was a noise that wasn't quite moaning, but the others drowned it out.

"What's happening in there?"

Tynan moved his mouth to my ear. "Absolute debauchery." My breath hitched in my throat, the darkness his voice alluded to making me shiver with want.

"She said no." My breath rushing out as Tynan's hand found my breast.

"She's not part of the trial, Mess." Squeezing my breast as if it was fruit and he was checking the ripeness, my nipple tightened, and Tynan flicked over it, my knees nearly buckling.

"This would have happened no matter what. She will be used for our wants and then used as a bargaining chip," his voice still deep, dangerous.

"Ty..."

"Yes?"

"Fuck me?"

Stepping around in front of me, Tynan threw me against the wall, his body slamming against the front of me so hard, my breath rushed out of me. Eager hands scrunched my dress up, then yanked my knickers free. Dropping his own pants, Tynan lifted my thighs to either side of his waist.

"Guide me in, Mess."

Complying, I was desperate to feel him inside me. It wasn't till he was shoving into me that I remembered there'd been no foreplay, and there was a reason we'd always taken it slow. My fingers gripped his shoulders as I clenched my teeth on a yelp. Pulling back, Tynan thrust again, barely gaining any ground, my body too tight over his curse.

"Relax, I don't want to hurt you, Mess," he murmured as he kissed up my neck.

Moaning, I moved my hands up to thread through his hair and yanked his head away from my neck so I could meet his eyes.

We stood there, staring into each other's gaze, and I felt how much I wanted him flooding my system, warming me through until I was boiling inside, needing Tynan and the pleasure he could give me.

Tynan was watching me, studying me, his eyes like a dark mirror shining my own lust back upon me. My need filled to bursting, and then it flowed out of me in a rush, passing over my skin like warm honey, and rushing into Tynan.

His eyes lit up as they closed and he hung his head back with a moan. My body relaxed, my clutch pulsing as I sunk over Tynan, opening and letting him slide as far in as he could go. It was uncomfortable, but those nodules and the ridges of his length felt marvelous as it moved into me.

Tynan moved his mouth forward suddenly, finding mine with a pang of hunger I couldn't explain. His tongue thrust against mine. Circled, and tasted me. He shifted his hands for a good grip, then he pulled back and drove forward forcefully. I swore. Tynan groaned out loud. He pushed into me again, and again, over and over, my back slamming into the wall, making it difficult to draw breath, but it didn't matter.

My satiability had taken over, lust and need making everything Tynan did to me feel amazing. Crying out, my nails gripping the back of Tynan's neck as he swelled bigger. The pain broke the power of my satiability. When my body couldn't stretch anymore, I gripped him inside me, and Tynan whimpered as my body clenched tight, holding him, squeezing him, rebelling against his size.

"Mess..." Tynan pleaded me for release. "Do it again, more."

Biting my lip, I resisted acknowledging how much it hurt and concentrated on my need. Focusing on my womb needing to relax, wanting to enjoy it, demanding to god-damn cum.

The satiability resurrected itself, sweeping Tynan and me into its wave of power, smothering us so that sight was lost. We were wrapped in a cocoon of darkness where everything had to be felt, intensifying every single sensitivity.

Digging my nails into Tynan's flesh, I came the hardest I ever had, the plunging of his sculpted curse, bringing a new pleasure I'd never known before. Tynan swore, his grip tightening at my hips as he pumped harder and faster into my body and cried out his own release, pinning me against the wall as we panted into each other's shoulders.

Slowly, tenderly, Tynan withdrew. Cringing on the discomfort of my sudden emptiness, the cramping through my lower abdomen made me double over. Now the satiability had found its release, I had to live with the after effects.

"Mess, are you okay?"

Nodding over gritted teeth, not entirely meaning it, I noticed my fingers and blinked at the blood covering them. "Are you?"

Reaching behind his neck, Tynan brought his fingers back to assess the blood on them. "I'll be back in a second."

When Tynan helped me to rest against the wall, I flinched, the bruising already starting to emerge. "Next time we do that, it happens in a bed," I grouched. "A very soft bed."

Kissing my cheek, Tynan moved down the corridor where he pressed a buzzer to open a door. He went into the cell, a purple glow came out of the room, and then a man started screaming, over and over. It lasted maybe thirty seconds, and then suddenly stopped. The screeching, the glowing, all just ended mid-scream. Tynan emerged, shut the door, and moved towards me.

"Do you want to stay and watch some more?"

Lifting my eyes to the room, Amp was finished, dressed, and seemingly looking at me, unhappy. "Can they see us?"

"Not really, more just a shadow," Tynan explained.

Observing the room again, I was sure Amp was looking right at me. Ashok was bringing his turn to an end. "How long were we at that?"

Tynan looked at his watch. "I've been down here close to two hours now."

"Jesus, no wonder I'm sore. It felt like ten minutes."

Tynan quirked a brow at me. "I think I'm insulted?"

"It's the satiability, it steals the perception of time."

Cuffing my chin, Tynan forced me to meet his eyes. "Because you want it to go faster. When you are hurting or wanting something to be over quickly, the satiability zones you out, so time becomes insubstantial."

"I love being with you, Ty."

"I was hurting you, Mess. You consciously brought the satiability on because you needed its power to protect you."

I blinked up at him. "I consciously used my power?"

Tynan's lip curled up. "Yes, Mess. You are learning to control your power."

"Ever since the garden and the woman," I whispered in awe.

Tynan's smile vanished. With a huff, he moved a step back from me. "No, Mess, there was something that happened after that. You were poisoned in the garden, you became very ill, and I nearly lost you."

Staring up into Tynan's eyes, a spark of silver flashing through the darkness like lightning, causing me to be wary. "I don't remember any of that."

"You were unconscious for most of it." Surrounding me with his body and heat, Tynan turned us so we could both watch the room.

"This is what I came to see," I admitted as the first Sluagh took his turn between the woman's thighs. I couldn't hear it, but the woman's face told me she was feeling it. A small drop of satisfaction made me shiver. My toes curled, and I pushed back into Tynan, my back twinged with the pressure.

"You're a voyeur, Mess. Did you know that?"

"Oh, yeah, I love to watch."

Out of nowhere, Tynan stepped forward and hit the button for the door to open on the other woman's prison. Esha came out, followed by the two men and female Sluagh. "That was fun," Brie skipped towards us. "Can we play some more?"

"Pick a cell, any cell," Tynan encouraged.

Brie smiled, held her hand out for Sauvignon to join her, then they played Eeny meany miny mo, to pick a room. They disappeared into it, laughing like school girls.

Shaking his head, Esha looked at Tynan. They did that speaking without speaking thing, and Tynan nodded his head. "Make sure you all have a go at the trial tonight. Then set up a roster, so there is someone with her every day and night. They fuck till they can't, then they call the next shift."

"She gets no rest?" Esha asked with a grin.

"Meal breaks and recovery time only." Tynan's arm around me tightened.

"Sorry," I mumbled when I realized I'd been grinding my bum

against him, in time with the pump of the Sluagh's hips in the room opposite us.

"Come on, Mess." Tynan squeezed me a little. "Let's get you into bed before you invite me to retake you."

"Fifty says you don't make the room," Esha bet.

He lost. Only just. We made it to the apartment before we started kissing and pulling each other's clothes free. Foreplay occurred between the lounge room and stairs, but he didn't push into me till I was lying beneath him, on our bed, staring up at him like he was heaven.

He was so gentle this time, the strokes even, and restrained. He coaxed me slowly to give myself over to him and then lost himself in me. His body did that mating thing again. The tentacles in his nodules swept around inside me, inducing us to pleasure too unique to describe.

When it was done, we slept in each other's arms, and I dreamt of Tynan and this place as my home.

31

HEARTH

Tynan wasn't happy about having to leave Messina alone at the festival. She already had a sexual appetite to match his own, and now that they were mated, Tynan felt a perpetual need for her. He knew he shouldn't have done it, but Esha had been touching Messina more and more, and Tynan knew it was just a matter of time before their friendship stopped preventing Esha from acting.

Then the way Amp looked at Messina after she survived the gauntlet, there was no way to avoid it. Cathal used Messina's satiability to rape her, and the concern Tynan held that someone else might do that and successfully plant their seed, stealing her away from him, tore his soul in two.

His rage over Cathal's actions caused diplomatic issues as it was, and Tynan spent the week after making sure Mabon knew that if he pulled a stunt like that again, the Sluagh would be the ones to drive the Sidhe out instead of the Seelie.

More importantly, he'd needed to stay away from Messina just to prevent doing worse to her than Cathal did.

Had he mated with her before she ran the gauntlet and been accepted by the Sluagh, she would never have had their respect.

Tynan didn't want her to be known as the toy consort; she deserved more than that.

"Why am I down here?" Tynan asked the goblin waiting for him.

Drail bowed his head, the tuft of hair on top flopping down in front of his face. "Prince Tynan, we thought you should see this." Drail scurried ahead, leading Tynan to the holding room Messina had occupied before the gauntlet.

Stepping through the door, the room now filled with light for the goblins cleaning the rooms ready for their next use. The walls were full of paintings, some were scratches in the black stone, others were dried blood.

Most of the artworks contained Messina and the encounter in her old room that brought her here. Not that she wasn't always going to end up here, he was just hoping to have time to explain why it needed to happen first. Instead, she'd lost control of her power, and he'd done the only thing he could think of to bring her back.

Truthfully, he could have found a way that didn't harm her, but he'd been furious that Cathal touched her, and the potential of her bearing a child to him. Tynan hadn't let her attend the Wisp because he needed to know if she was pregnant before she ran the gauntlet. And Mess, she didn't remember a damn thing about it and blamed him for her injuries.

Shaking his head, Tynan focused on the other drawings. A child climbing towards what looked to be a bright light; two Sluagh embraced in physical pleasure; a child in her mother's arms; and the one his eyes kept coming back to, a child holding his hand.

"My home and hearth."

"Sorry, Prince?" Drail asked not understanding.

Tynan shook his head. "Memories. Clean the walls as best you can, but have photos taken first and deliver them to me."

"Yes, Prince," Drail bowed and left the room.

The sharp sound of steel being dragged across glass made Tynan's head snap to the window. Closing his eyes in annoyance when it ended in three steel to glass taps, Tynan turned back to the door and turned off the lights. Taking the time for his eyes to adjust before he opened the window, Tynan breathed through his annoyance of just another thing keeping him from his mate.

The glass slid open, a breeze from the forest floating in, Lucifer squatting by the window, smiling at him. "Prince." He gave a slight bow, his mouth tilting up slightly.

"You broke the accords."

"The girl angered me. She has the blood ability, and turned my food to acid, made it burn within me, then made it catch fire."

"You shouldn't have drunk from her."

Lucifer cocked his head. "She would not give up," his beady eyes came to Tynan. "She upset me."

"Because she made you bite your own-"

"I want my rabbit!" Lucifer's eyes burned with envy.

Stepping forward menacingly, Tynan held his cane in his hand ready. "She survived the gauntlet, despite your breaking the accords. You cannot have her. Besides, she's worthless as food to you."

"There is always the fun."

"She survived the gauntlet, and we are mated."

Raking his finger across the ground in a fit of rage, Lucifer seethed as clumps of dirt and rock sprayed the room and forest behind him. "You mated with a Seelie?"

"I mated with an Unseelie Sidhe who happens to have a Seelie mother," Tynan scowled, setting Lucifer straight. "Her mother just happened to be Nora Ui Bayne-Ard."

Standing slowly, peering down at him suspiciously, Lucifer stretched and fisted his hands. "That would make her father..."

"Yes. She is the reason I granted your people this forest to live permanently, instead of just visiting for the gauntlet," Tynan explained further.

Lucifer's eyes traveled to the drawings on the wall. Barely visible in the low light, but for him, they would be brighter. "She's the child who escaped?" Tynan nodded confirmation. "You found her? Does she know what she means? Or has your seduction of the queen been," he flourished his fingers in the air, "one of romance?"

"Neither. The girl is smart and not fooled by empty gestures. All that matters is that you won't be getting the girl."

Lucifer considered him. "What would you have done if she hadn't made the gauntlet, Prince?"

Tynan lifted his eyes and glared at him. "Then she wouldn't have been worthy, would she?"

Tilting his head, appraising Tynan, Lucifer laughed, high-pitched squeaking and shrill like a bat. "You don't fool me, Prince. You had to have a plan in place, or some knowledge to risk the last queen."

"My plans are not your business," Tynan returned as he turned to walk towards the door.

"I want," Lucifer breathed angrily, "my rabbit!"

Pausing, nose flaring in annoyance, Tynan considered that Lucifer's tantrum could become problematic. Cocking his head, Tynan reached out to Esha through their bond of loyalty.

'I need one of the Seelie women. You can't have them both.'

'Easily done, one said no.'

'Good, she just became a bargaining chip.' Smirking to himself, Tynan watched Lucifer who was observing him intrigued. *'Use her then throw her in the forest.'*

'Might be difficult. Messina is here with us. She was too drunk to leave alone with the lunar captain,' Esha almost whimpered, awaiting Tynan's anger.

Pinching the bridge of his nose, Tynan counted to ten in his head. Amp had been going out of his way to try and run into Mess in the kitchen since she arrived. Pride kept him informed whenever Amp just happened to stop in at the same time Messina was there. Then for Amp to sign up for the gauntlet, and to be one of the two who saved her... there was a reason Tynan dragged Messina's desexo from her by force.

'I'll be there in a moment. Distract Mess and make sure that Seelie bitch screams.'

'Might be hard with her mouth full, but at least Mess won't hear it.'

Breaking the link, Tynan studied Lucifer. "What would you do for a rabbit?"

"Obviously, not the princess?" Tynan answered that query with a cold stare. Lucifer crouched again. "What did you have in mind, Prince?"

Smirking, Tynan found a secret weapon in this new war. Lucifer was always hungry, and starving people are easy to manipulate. That thought made him think of Messina and how her hunger for food and warmth brought her home. Now, her desire for him would bring Tynan the crown. All he had to do was put a child in her womb, and even the Sidhe would need to kneel before him.

As he watched the window close after telling Lucifer where to find his rabbit, Tynan considered Messina's panic only this morning when he'd educated her what his body was doing to hers. Yes, he evaded her anxiety by reminding her she wasn't Sluagh. Yes, he'd lied to her, and not for the first time.

He'd need to keep her from discussing it with the others. All he'd need is for one of them to point out that being mated was enough to stimulate her body to conceive, and Messina would flip out. That wasn't something he wanted to deal with this week. It would be bad enough when King Mabon found out Tynan mated with the woman he planned to barter to the Seelie with, and not just for that reason.

Moving further into the holding cells, Tynan made his way to death's hold. The corridor where those waiting to die were kept. Of course, the prisoners weren't aware that was necessarily their fate.

Messina looked beautiful and fierce facing down Pride as Tynan walked down the dark corridor of the prison. She was so determined to see the atrocities she couldn't prevent. She was naive, but not from lack of trying. Tynan admired how well Messina had dealt with becoming a toy. Perhaps the state of her time with the humans trained her for that outcome.

Tynan's fist clenched around his cane at the thought of what the humans had done to his beautiful princess. Nora made a mistake sending her daughter away for fear of Tynan taking her. At least, in the Unseelie court, she would have been untouchable as the future princess.

Of course, the Seelie were trying to take Nora back, and Tynan had been involved in the negotiations to send the child to the light court instead of Nora at the time. The moment he knew who the child was, he was never letting her go to them. He would have given the Seelie her mother back in exchange for a new Seelie consort for Mabon, but Messina would have stayed. The child would have been the new hostage.

Tynan would have been there to train her, raise her the Unseelie way, to make sure she was ready for where she was always going to end up from the moment she took his hand and whispered home and hearth to him. A hostage was better protected and more respected than a toy.

Oh, what a present she'd been. She hadn't been Tynan's first toy, but she was the first to love him for it.

Love. Messina claimed she didn't know love. Her eyes and body told Tynan that wasn't true. Even now, as he stepped into the light excusing Pride for the night, Messina's pulse throbbed in her neck, her chest rose short, her eyes glistened, and pupils dilated.

Messina didn't need to tell him she loved him, she showed it each and every time they were in a room together. This girl had started out a toy, become a pawn, but very early on, Tynan had to admit to himself, the love wasn't all hers.

It didn't change his ploy, just made him adjust how he took what he wanted. What he wanted was her crown. Not only the Seelie throne but that of the Unseelie as well.

He could never understand the prophecy around him. Now, with Messina in his life, with him buried inside of her warmth, losing himself in her, he perceived with clarity.

She will be the one to take his coldness.

She will unveil the Unseelie darkness and show them light.

She will unite what should never have been broken.

The daughter of the moon will teach him love, and the radiance of the sun.

32

INVESTMENT

❖

"What are your plans today?" Tynan asked as he dressed in his suit for work.

"I'm allowed to have plans?" Sitting up in bed, I was deliciously sore all over from another night of passion.

"Mess, you've been one of us for two weeks now. You can make plans, do things, have lunch with friends. You just have to stay in the castle."

"Why? I don't need to cast a glamor, and everyone else is free to roam."

Tynan's eyes found mine, a warning held in their blackness. "The Seelie are still after you, Mess."

"I'll go out with some other guards. Amp offered to escort me on his days off," I suggested, excited about the prospect of going out. If I thought Tynan was secure in our relationship, I was wrong. I was suddenly pinned to the bed, Tynan hovering over me, eyes silver orbs of suspicion.

"Amp? When did you see Amp for him to make that offer?"

"Two days ago, in the kitchen," I whimpered.

"What else did you discuss?"

"The Faerie mound, the Luna guard, that the Seelie prisoner is pregnant."

Tynan released me, the gates of hell still burning mercury in his eyes. "Pride is your bodyguard. I don't trust anyone else to keep you safe." Turning his back, Tynan started dressing again.

"Surely you don't doubt my loyalty?" I queried, rising to my knees.

"You are a lustful creature, Mess. A side effect of your satiability, I suspect." He turned to face me, and his eyes dropped to my naked body. "You wouldn't mean to cheat on me, but I know you are easily manipulated and lead astray. In that, your innocence is to blame."

Reaching out, I helped tuck his collar over his tie. Tynan's fingers found their way to my waist. "You still think I'm innocent after everything we've done together in this bed?" Pulling him a little closer, I rubbed my hands over his chest.

"Yes." Tynan raised that brow at me. "Though, perhaps naive is a better word." His eyes were black again and glazed with lust.

"If I'm naive, it's because people like to keep me in the dark. I can't be expected to know what I was never told."

Tynan looked between our bodies. "You've made me run late every day for two weeks, Mess. I need to get to work on time today."

Smiling, I moved back, pulling the sheet up over me. "I'm pretty sure I didn't even touch you yesterday, and you still chose to go in late."

Taking a deep breath, Tynan stepped away. "Well, I actually do have meetings I can't run late for today. I'll see you tonight."

Turning on his heel, he walked out. With a sigh, I stretched my body long, smiling at all the places my body felt tight, sore, loved. I missed Tynan when he wasn't here, but my body needed the reprieve. Still, the thought of waiting hours to see him took some of the joy out of the day. Gingerly, I made my way to the shower, as I did most mornings now, and got ready for the day.

When I went downstairs, Pride was waiting for me. "Pride, can you see what Brie or Sauvignon are doing today? I'd like to hang out with them."

With a bow of his head, Pride went to the phone while I went to the window and looked out on the forest. A shiver went through me as I remembered my blood covering the window.

As if my fears came to life, I stepped back as the nightmare of the gauntlet stepped out of the forest and towards the window. "Pride." My voice a mere whisper choked by fear.

The devil held up his hand in a gesture of peace. Then he bowed low. "Princess Messina, I have a message for your consort."

"So why are you here, when you know he is not?" I doubted.

The devil smiled that misshapen mouth in my direction, his beady eyes glassy and focused. "I see why you survived the gauntlet." He rubbed his chin as if the memory of the night wasn't just haunting me. "Tell your prince he was right; your father betrays us." With that said, he turned and walked away.

"Wait, what?" I stepped forward to the glass. "What does that mean? How do you know my father?" He kept walking away.

When I moved to open the window, Pride was suddenly in my way. "That would not be safe, or wise."

"What did he mean?"

"I do not know," Pride looked worried, "his words were for you, not my ears. Those creatures can be in a packed room and make it so only one can hear them scream. It's quite unsettling."

My brows furrowed, trying to understand that only I heard what Lucifer said. Pride tapped the window. "The glass is soundproof, Messina. His message was beamed directly for your ears only."

Eyes widening, a kind of envy of that talent filtering through my mass of confusion as I shook my head. "The message is for Tynan."

Pride watched me, unsure. "I can call him for you if you like?"

That I couldn't even make that decision for myself annoyed me. "Tynan has been my consort for two weeks now. I have no way of contacting him should something go wrong..."

"That's my job."

"...and he still tells me where I can go, and who I can go with. I thought I was his equal now?"

Pride was watching me. "You can't let him get to you."

"That happened half a year ago."

"I meant the devil," Pride argued. "He came here to mess with you."

"Well, if his goal was to make me angry, he succeeded." Storming towards my room, I needed shoes and a jacket. No matter what Tynan thought, I was his equal and I was going outside today to feel the fresh air and get some sunlight again.

Pride was waiting when I came back down and got in my way. "Where are you going, Mess?"

"I need fresh air and sunshine. I need to go outside."

"In broad daylight, when the Seelie are at their strongest and the Unseelie weak?"

"Because the sun isn't up at night, Pride. I am born balanced. I need sunlight."

Assessing my words, his eyes darting back to the window before Pride bowed his head. "Okay, but we do this my way."

Happy just to get outside, I nodded my head in agreement. Opening the door, Pride indicated I walk ahead of him. Stepping outside, I waited for him to join me, then took his arm as he led me through the corridors.

When we exited the door into the underground car park, I was surprised. There were quite a few of those luxury sports cars still parked here. The vehicles I thought belonged to the nightclub guests that night, but now I knew, belonged to the residents.

Pride stopped just outside the door. A moment later, a large chauffeured SUV pulled up in front of us. When Pride opened the back door for me, I slid in, the seating allowing for maybe six or seven people inside the back area.

"Move to one of the side seats, Messina."

Shifting forward, I sat side on in the back of the car. Maneuvering his way inside the vehicle, Pride took up the entire back seat. His legs were stretched in front, and his head brushing the roof. No one was getting to me quickly. The door closed and the car drove forward.

The gates to the outside world opened taking us through a tunnel then out onto a road surrounded by trees. I tried to see the house, but the forest here was deep. Reaching forward, Pride pressed a button.

The roof of the car slid back to reveal a glass moonroof, stopping halfway open.

Sunlight beat down upon me. Closing my eyes, I lifted my face to the light. Stretching out on the seat, I raised my skirt to expose my legs and as much skin as I could decently get away with.

Lying down on the seat, I soaked up the light. My breathing calmed, making me acknowledge how worked up I'd been after the devil's visit. Slowly, as the vehicle sped along the road, happiness seeped back into my body, easing the tenseness of my muscles. The exposure to the sun leaving me energized and healthier.

We only drove for a short time, less than an hour. When shadows started passing over me, I opened my eyes to see tall city buildings floating overhead. As we entered another underground car park, Pride closed the roof. Sitting up, I was surprised when a human looking man in a black suit and black sunglasses sat watching me. He looked the epitome of a bodyguard.

"Pride, you're kind of hot." Gifting me a smile, Pride blushed a little. "Where are we?"

"Somewhere safe for you to frolic outside in the sun."

When the car stopped, pride moved out of the car and waited for me to take the arm he offered. When he closed the door, the car drove away, and Pride led me to a set of elevators. Stepping inside, Pride swiped a card before hitting a button for the executive lounge.

After a quick ascent, Pride led me out to a foyer and swiped his card again. The receptionist on the other side of the doors beamed in our direction. "Pride, what brings you here in broad daylight?" Shadows swam around her, revealing she was Sluagh casting glamor. It made me wonder why I could see Pride so clearly, not a hint of obscurity around him.

"The Princess needed fresh air and sunlight. Brie was going to drop something off for her."

The woman lifted a bag from under the counter. "I'll let the Prince know you are here."

With a nod, Pride led me through the empty lounge and bar to a bathroom. "You can change in there."

Giving him the stink eye of suspicion, I took the bag he handed me but didn't question him. I trusted Pride to keep me safe. In the bathroom, I opened the bag to find a bikini and a sarong. Unable to repress the joy the items elicited, I changed, leaving my dress hanging in the change room.

Stepping out of the bathroom, Pride escort me to a set of French doors. "I'll wait here. I'll be able to see you through the window."

"Thank you," I kissed his cheek, Pride blushing as if he was sun-kissed.

Pushing open the door, the sun radiated down on me. The place was set up for entertainment. Chairs and tables in a garden type setting to the left, a pool and outdoor bar, that was currently closed, to the right.

Leaving my sarong on one of the sunchairs, I dived into the sun-warmed water of the pool, swimming laps with enthusiasm for an activity that wasn't training or painful.

Taking a break, I sun baked in the sunchair, breathing the re-energizing deeply, and healing fresh air. When I felt full to bursting, I dived back into the pool and burned some of that energy off again.

As I climbed out the next time, the French doors opened, and Tynan came out carrying a towel. He had sunglasses on, but lifted his face to the sun and soaked it in as I took the cloth and dried myself. "Feel better?"

"Much."

"What was the message?"

"You were right. My father betrays us."

"They were the Devils exact words?" Tynan asked pulling out his phone.

"Yes."

"And your need to leave hit immediately after this encounter?"

"Yes. I needed fresh air and sunshine."

Tynan put the phone to his ear. "Check my suites and all the places Mess regularly goes." He hung up, silver orbs shining through the dark lenses of his glasses.

"You think the devil made me want to leave because of an imme-diate threat?"

"I do. Lucifer needed you to leave in a way that didn't create suspi-cion. He knew Pride would know your immediate need to escape was planted and would satisfy your need as a precaution."

"Precaution?"

"Your natural instinct to survive, Mess. Pride is very aware of how strong it is for you. He has watched you change your mind about wanting something to eat, only to discover later there was a Seelie assassin lying in wait for you to go to the kitchen."

Handing me my sarong, Tynan folded his arms to watch me. "You suddenly needed out of the castle. Pride understood that need wasn't psychological, or selfish. It was survival. You couldn't have explained it if you needed too."

"I asked you this morning to leave. You refused me."

Taking my hand, Tynan placed his lips to my wrist, his tongue flicking against my pulse. My eyes shuttered, the sun was suddenly cold in comparison to Tynan's touch. "I am not as aware of your moods as Pride. I am too distracted by my need for you."

Tugging on my hand, Tynan led me back inside. "Since you are here, we should eat lunch together."

Waiting for me to change, Tynan led me into the lounge and sat us at a table. After taking our order, the waiter left us alone. There were a handful of others in the bar now, eating and talking with each other. One got up and came to speak with Tynan. Esha appeared out of nowhere, covered in shadows, and headed him off with some quiet words. "He's human?"

Tynan looked across to where Esha was keeping the man away. "Yes. Most of my employees are Unseelie, but to exist in the human world, you must have humans in your company too. Most of our marketing team are human. That man is the marketing director."

"And what is it you do here?" Taking a sip of the drink in front of me, I surveyed the room. There were a lot of nice suits.

Tynan tapped his fingers on the table considering me. "This is an investment bank."

"People invest money with you? That is your business?"

"It's one of my businesses, yes." Looking down at his buzzing phone, Tynan picked it up from the table. "I'll be back in a moment."

Moving over to the corner to take the call, Tynan gritted his jaw, his eyes were silver orbs of hellish anger. I shivered uncontrollably. Without thinking, I stood up and moved to the window where the sun was shining through to absorb the light.

"Hello, I'm Michael Baird, Marketing Director of Wane Investment," a man's voice called my attention to where he stood next to me. He held out his hand. "You look familiar. Have we met before?"

"Messina," I responded without offering my hand. The man looked familiar, but I couldn't pinpoint why his name was also ringing a bell. Looking over his shoulder to where Esha was talking to another employee, I tried for a polite smile. When Esha spotted Michael talking to me, his jaw clenched. He quickly excused himself and headed towards us.

Michael let his hand drop, his eyes lighting up, a hidden knowledge shining within. "Are you a new client, Messina?" Pride was suddenly at my shoulder, Michael looked him over and became more intrigued.

"Messina," Esha cut in, stepping between us and taking my arm, his arm landing on Michael's shoulder, forcing him back a step. Esha's eyes widened for a moment, and then they turned feral, the ruby irises nearly breaking through his glamor. "Mr. Wane asked me to escort you to his office. You can eat lunch there."

"So, you are a client?"

"No," I answered as Esha turned me away, Esha's eyes finding Tynan and going into that blank far off stare for a moment, then he was back and leading me away, his grip bruising on my arm.

"Then what is your business here?" The man got in our way, a sly grin turning up at the side.

"Michael, I warned you to stay out of this," Esha hissed. We had the attention of everyone in the lounge now.

"I just want to know why she is here." His eyes were all over me the way my stepfather was from the time I developed breasts. The comparison made me shiver with disgust.

"She's my wife," Tynan's voice cut through the whispers around us. "Step out of her way, Mr. Baird or her bodyguard will break your leg."

"That's a bit overboard, don't you think, Mr. Wane?"

Tynan didn't, he stepped forward menacingly. "I am very protective of my possessions, Mr. Baird; my wife more so. She has been hurt in the past when those who should have protected her failed at their jobs. I will not let that happen again. If you continue to harass her, Pride will move you for me. Esha." All the men stood tense as Esha took my arm and led me to the elevator.

"Well, I hope you got a prenup. That girl is too young to be serious about you?" Michael challenged. "The next big dick to come along and she'll be all over it."

The man was suddenly up in the air, Tynan holding him by his throat. "Her age is irrelevant. Don't approach her without my consent again," Tynan replied coolly. "Unlike her, you are replaceable." With a shove, Tynan threw the man across the room, watching him land with a crash into a table. No one looked surprised by Tynan's hostility. I wondered how many had been on the receiving end of Tynan's anger before.

The receptionist held the door of the waiting elevator for us. Esha stepped us in while she blocked the entrance for Tynan. When he stepped into the lift, the door closed on all the watchful eyes with raised brows.

My heart sank with the descent, knowing this wasn't going to end well. "Did you enjoy the swim, Messina?" Tynan asked unhappily.

"Yes, thank you," I mourned, understanding that tone.

"Good, because you won't be coming here again."

"Because another man was attracted to me?"

"You would never leave my bedroom if that were the reason I didn't want you here, Mess." Sighing, Tynan turned to face me, his finger tracing my jaw, lifting my eyes to his. Finding his irises black was a relief. "You are my mate. My nature is to protect you. Knowing someone has hurt you, that it was out of my control to stop them, takes my anger to a level that could expose us to the humans around us. Do you understand?"

"I do," I pouted, thinking about the way he'd thrown him across the room. "Though, that man didn't hurt me. I'd never even met the man before."

Tynan's eyes went to Esha's, a silent communication taking place between them. Exhaling, Tynan brought his eyes back to me. "Mess, your memories were stolen from you when you left the faerie mound, but the spell that stole them isn't why you forget all the horrible things that were done to you in the human world. You have blocked out those memories yourself. It is why certain events trigger your recollection."

"You're saying I knew him?"

Tynan looked to Esha again. Esha cleared his throat to gain my attention. "When I touched Michael, I was able to access his memories. Are you sure you don't know him?"

"He was familiar, his name rang a bell, but I don't remember him." Seeing the look that passed between them, I leaned my head on Tynan's chest. "I don't want to remember him, do I?"

Tynan's fingers massaged across my back. "If I said he was a friend of your stepfather's, would that answer your question?"

A violent tremor passed through my body from my feet to my head. '*The first time*,' I remembered thinking. It was only the first time he shared me with his best friend. That wasn't my stepfather's best friend, but the sudden need to vomit told me I shouldn't know the truth. "I don't want to remember."

"We know, Mess. I may not have been able to protect you then, but I can protect you now," Tynan assured.

The elevator dinged. Wrapping his arm around my waist, Tynan walked me off the lift into a sleek executive level office floor. "Pride, take Mess to my office, I'll be just behind you."

Offering me his arm, Pride escorted me down the hall. "I'm going to need a new marketing director," Tynan spoke to Esha as they walked behind me.

"I've already messaged Trell to let her know."

"Good. Who do you recommend should break the news to Michael that we are letting him go?"

"The Gemini twins always love terminating an abusive man's employment. You know how they feel about those kinds of men."

"Set it up," Tynan agreed as I stepped into his office. Warmth flowed over my back a moment before Tynan's arms wrapped around me from behind. "If you don't mind, Pride, I think Messina needs reminding how to smile. Could you help Esha organize the twins while I have my wife for lunch?"

The wording snagged the side of my mouth, lifting the corner slightly. Looking over my shoulder, I caught Pride murmuring something to Esha as they closed the door, shutting themselves on the other side. Even in human form, Pride was imposing, but he'd always be my gentle giant. Tynan's mouth nibbled at the back of my neck, his body guiding me towards the sofa in his office.

"You know I can't be quiet."

Sitting on the sofa, Tynan guided me to straddle his lap. "Trell and Esha are running errands. There's no one here to listen. Even if there was, so what? I'm the boss, and I have a beautiful wife. Why shouldn't I enjoy my lunch break?"

The grin on Tynan's face was all-encompassing. Tracing the outline of his lips with a fingertip, I wondered how a man could make me feel for him with equal amounts of conflicting emotions. "Thank you for wanting to protect me."

"You are my mate. You are my light in the darkness. Without you, the sun will never feel warm again, Mess."

Those words heated me in a way he had only ever done physically, reaching a part of me his touch couldn't. As our lips clashed, expressing our needs in a non-verbal manner, hands and bodies communicating with senses, I knew there would never be anywhere else for me, but in Tynan's arms. He was my home and hearth. The prince of darkness was my reason for being.

The impact of that awareness hit me like a slap in the face. Opening my eyes wide, bright white light shone from the corner of the office behind the sofa. While Tynan's lips pinched my neck, and his hands raised my skirt, my eyes met the abyss like eyes of the woman from the forest.

For a moment, my mind flashed to a collection of trees that glowed blue and the image of this woman taking my hand and walking me through it as she whispered my destiny in my ear. Her words were silent, but I knew what it was she was telling me. I was born for a purpose, and Tynan was the key to my fate.

33

PLARYERS

❖

"Brie dresses you well," Tynan purred coming into the bathroom where I was just finishing getting ready.

"How was work?" I laughed as he wrapped me in his arms and buried his face in the crook of my neck.

"Annoying. I wanted to be here with you. Take it off."

"Ty, we'll be..."

"Don't make me rip such a beautiful dress, Mess," Tynan growled. Stepping back, Tynan dropped his clothes to the floor as he peeled them away. Finding the zip for the dress, I swallowed nervously as I tugged it free. Tynan was hungry for more than sex; I'd learned to recognize that over the last month since the gauntlet.

"Bed," I pleaded as he wrapped my legs around his waist and sat my bum on the bathroom bench. It fell on deaf ears. Tynan sank into me, my nails dragging across his back with his impatience. He was rougher than usual, less restrained in his demands of me.

Opening my mouth, I pleaded for mercy, only his name crossing my lips before my instinct yelled for silence. Forcing myself to quiet just a moment before Tynan's hand grabbed my neck and slammed me back into the bathroom mirror, holding me restrained. The sound of cracking glass instigated the sting of it against my shoulders, making me cringe and whimper.

Silver orbs greeted me. His anger was there, but as I watched, they filled with the fires of hell. First golden, then burning red, like that of the Sluagh, but with more heat then I'd ever felt in any of their touches. "Okay," I gasped, understanding.

Cringing in pain, I twisted my head to the side to expose my neck. The shattered glass of the mirror I was pressed against slicing into my skin as I offered him relief from his hunger.

Growling, Tynan moved his hips harder and faster as his teeth sliced into the tender flesh of my neck. Mewling, I gritted my teeth on the pain until I couldn't bear it anymore. Reaching into myself for the first time in weeks, I pulled my satiability forward, built it to bursting, then freed it. My power swept me away into a tight pleasure, and then nothingness.

"...NEVER felt the need like that before. I didn't mean to hurt you."

Opening my eyes, I found Tynan sitting beside me, fully dressed, holding my hand. Meeting my eyes, he caressed my face tenderly. Sitting up, I studied him. "Did I sleep in?" I asked looking at the clock. "Damn, I meant to be ready by the time you got home from work. I'm sorry."

When I tried to get up, Tynan kept hold of my hand. "You were ready. I desired you, but I lost control and hurt you," he confessed, his eyes watching me for any hint of emotion.

Taking a moment, I realized I felt good, too good. "What happened?"

"I took you on the bathroom counter. We broke the mirror."

Blinking wide eyes at him, I thought of how to respond. "Oh! I'm guessing I didn't fare well from that?" Closing his eyes for a second, Tynan was expecting my anger and hurt, but I couldn't remember any of it to get too upset about it. "Are we too late for the club tonight?"

"No. We are not too late." Standing up, Tynan handed me my

dress and underwear. "The bathroom is safe, but there isn't a mirror. You should shower first."

Understanding, I went to shower and dress. Ignoring the blood running off my back, I focused on the night ahead. Tynan was waiting in the lounge when I came downstairs, whispering with Esha and Pride.

Turning towards me, Pride smiled. "Our beautiful princess." The sentiment in which he said it made me blush.

Taking my arm, Tynan kissed my cheek. "Let's go."

We headed towards the nightclub, but Tynan took us into another room first. Here, were a select group, including Amp and Ashok. As I entered, they all turned and yelled, "Happy Birthday, Messina!"

My entire being froze on the spot. "What?"

With a gentle smile, he kissed my cheek again. "I found your birth certificate. Today is your birthday. Today, you turned twenty."

Giving me a gentle hug, Pride kissed my head, Esha held me a lot tighter, then I was passed around to everyone wanting to wish me a happy birthday. Food was brought in, and we ate while we talked.

After an hour, Tynan collected my hand, and we all headed to the nightclub. It was different now; I wasn't his toy. I wasn't some Seelie half-breed who had foolishly entered the Unseelie court. Now, I was a princess, the rightful queen of the Seelie, and the wife of the Sluagh Prince.

Kissing Tynan while we danced, I purposefully bit his lip. Eyes wide with surprise at first, Tynan then laughed and kissed me deeply. "I'm going to go get a drink and do some business. Will you behave unsupervised?"

With a shrug, I smirked at him. "Nothing much you can do about it now, since I'm your wife, not your toy anymore," I teased.

Shaking his head with a quiet smile, Tynan put his mouth to my ear. "Well, if you must misbehave, make sure I receive the invitation."

"You know you're the only one who feels right to me."

Kissing me passionately, Tynan disappeared into the crowd of dancers. Hands wrapped around my waist almost instantly. "Dance with me."

Turning to face Amp, I mounted my hands on his shoulders and created a little distance. "Find a single girl worthy of you, Amp. It's never going to be me."

Amp smirked, his eyes twinkling. "We'll see." He pinched my bum as he moved away, staying close while he chose a human dance partner.

Moving through the crowd, I spied Brie and Sauvignon dancing together, their glamor making them a little hard to find initially. "Are you two always together?"

"There isn't much we don't do together," Brie winked.

"Sex?"

"Always! With each other, or sharing another, we are always together."

"Poo?" I raised a brow.

Brie winced at the suggestion. "Evacuating the waste is always better done alone." We laughed. The three of us danced together till I was thirsty as hell, then we all headed to the bar.

There were lots of guys holding the bar up, and they all checked us out when we approached. "Mess?" A familiar man called across the bar.

Stopping dead, my heartbeat racing in my chest, I lifted my eyes to meet my stepdad. Chris smiled with delight as he came around the bar, his best friend in tow. "Wow, look at the difference a year makes to a girl," Chris, my stepdad, purred as he surveyed me. His thumb rubbed across his lower lip, a gesture I knew well. "Are you going to introduce us to your friends?"

"Chris, this is Brie and Sauvignon," I introduced. "This is my stepdad and his best friend, Wayne."

Brie eyed them, both dressed in their suits, her eyes assessing their clothes and mannerisms. It was apparent she wasn't sure what to make of them. I'd been homeless when I came here, but a blind man could see Chris was well off.

"Nice to meet you," Brie answered politely. "We'll go find Esha," she excused, her eyes intent when they met mine before she took Sauvignon's hand and abandoned me.

"So how you been, Mess?" Chris leaned on the bar. Jesus, he was flirting with me. "I've missed you at home."

"I've had a few hard times, but I've found a home where I belong, and I'm happy. You?"

"Oh, we separated a few weeks after you left," he informed me. "Things haven't been the same since you left. I really us, the fun we had together." Chris indicated the space between us.

Wayne moved around to my side boxing me in. "We've really missed you. We can't stop thinking about those nights we all spent together," Wayne murmured in my ear, his hands encircling my waist.

My throat convulsed over the plural in his statement. I knew it was more than once, only through small slips in memory, but it didn't stop it disturbing me any less that I couldn't remember even a reference to any other time. Maybe a lot more happened with Chris than I remembered.

"Remove your hands." Lifting my eyes, I found Pride standing behind Chris, glaring. He was in his human bodyguard form, a reason I could never find him in the club. It was like he turned invisible when we walked through the doors. "Messina belongs to another."

Wayne and Chris looked surprised and lifted their brows at me. Taking a breath, I raised a finger at Pride asking for a second. Pride took a step back.

Relaxing, I smiled, touching Chris's shoulder. "That was a hell of a night. My two friends, they like to do group sex. Perhaps, you two might want to try taking on three of us at once?"

Chris and Wayne stood straight with interest. "We can go back to my place," Wayne offered.

"No need, the girls and I live here. There is a residence behind the club."

"Like a brothel?" Chris asked, unsure if he was going to have to pay for it.

Asshole. "Not even close. No money needs to be paid for sex here."

"Lead the way," Wayne suggested eagerly.

"Hold your horses, Wayne. I have to find the girls first. We'll leave by a door to the right of the dance floor. You'll just have to wait till we are ready." With a wink, I walked into the crowd.

"You just offered for those men to come into the mound," Pride accused as he followed me.

"I did no such thing. I told Warren and Chris they could fuck us, that we live here, and that we would exit via a particular door. I never invited my stepfather and his friend into the faerie mound, or told them to follow us."

Pride relaxed a little. There were rules about entering the faerie mound. If I had invited Chris and Wayne in, I would be responsible for protecting them. If they enter uninvited, they were food.

"Where are Brie and Sauvignon?"

Turning his head, Pride pointed me to them.

"Thanks, can you tell Ty where to find me?"

"He will be pissed."

"He will understand when you tell him it's my stepfather. Trust me."

Pride's eyes darkened. "Your stepfather?" He must have missed the introductions. "The one who abused you?" When I stayed quiet, Pride nodded and walked off into the crowd.

Locating the girls dancing will Trell, I made my way over to them. "Up for some fun?"

"Always," Brie answered excitedly.

"Good, let's go to your rooms." The confusion on all their faces made me chuckle, causing suspicious looks to be cast my way. "Fun is going to follow us, uninvited."

Tilting her head in consideration, Brie looked back to the bar, a smile blooming across her face. "Trell, you up for a gang bang?"

Trell grinned. "With a tasty ending? For sure."

Looping arms, we headed for the door. Pride was there waiting already. When I lifted a brow to check on Tynan's response, he gave a single nod.

Stepping in beside me, Esha put his arm around my waist. "I heard there is a private party being had, and I wasn't invited?"

"You can come." As we went through the door, I kissed his cheek.

"You better carry through with that promise," he teased, giving me a squeeze.

Out in the corridor, we started towards Brie's room. A room, it turned out, she shares with Sauvignon. The sound of the music grew louder for a moment, then disappeared indicating the door to the nightclub opened and closed behind us. Stopping, we all waited for my past to catch up with us.

A cold shiver passed through my body, making me cringe at the recognition of my actions. Esha held me a little tighter. "You okay?"

"I just did this," I breathed, guilt itching across my chest. "I just sentenced these men to certain death."

Turning me to face him, Esha cupped my face. "They are predators, Mess. This time they just jumped into a pond with bigger fish. That's all you have to remember. For what they did to you, your stepdad specifically, they are going to enjoy this way more than they deserve."

"Ty told you?"

"When he first healed all those old injuries of yours, Mess," Esha kissed my nose. "He was disgusted for how you had been treated. That hasn't changed in the least. He wouldn't allow this if he didn't feel they earned it."

Chris and Wayne caught up. "So..." Wayne clapped his hands together.

They were attractive for middle-aged men. Offering Wayne her hand, Trell pulled him into her, kissing him without hesitation. She moaned when his hands grabbed her arse and pulled her tight against the front of him.

"A few other friends decided to join us," I explained happily to Chris.

He was eyeing Esha and the way he held me with doubt. "Is this your boyfriend?"

Esha shook his head. "Nah, I work for her husband."

"Husband?"

"Yeah, Tynan Wane," Esha dropped the name on purpose, a familiarity in Esha's eyes as he appraised my stepfather.

"You're married to Tynan Wane?" Chris asked astounded. "And he's okay with you having gang bangs?"

"Well, I won't be having sex with you, just watching this time, and maybe a little playing," I purred brushing my lips over Esha's.

Esha laughed his eyes alight as he met mine. "Only a little?"

Brie caught Chris's hand. "Come on. I promise it will be the best night of your life."

34

PLAYED

❖

My breath came out in a pant. Kissing me, Esha ground his hips against mine. The bed was full of the other five, kissing and touching, so Esha and I were on the sofa watching. Esha pulled me side on into his lap only moments ago so he could feel and kiss me.

Slipping his hand under my dress, Esha left a trail of discomfort up my thigh. Grabbing his wrist, I pulled back from the kiss. "You're distracting me from the show."

"Okay." Turning me to face forward, Esha took my hips and rubbed me against him, so his erection stimulated us both. If it weren't for his pants being in place, Tynan would so be killing him right now.

Things were heating up on the bed. Clothes discarded, and mouths were exploring naked flesh. Rising to his knees to relieve Trell of her underpants, Chris's eyes found me, moaning and sighing from Esha's attention. Grabbing Trell by the hair, he shoved her mouth around his cock, where she happily started sucking away.

Wayne and Brie were sharing Sauvignon, lavishing her with attention. Sitting back, Brie looked over to me. With a smile, she climbed off the bed, whispering something to Sauvignon before coming to me.

"Fast or slow?" Sitting on the lounge beside us, Brie watched the show just as keenly as I was. Sauvignon pushed Wayne to his back and sat on his face.

Pointing to Wayne, I considered what little I remembered, how he never said a word about his friend touching me inappropriately, or when he sat me on his dick in front of him. Not once did he remind his friend, he was meant to be my father. "Fast, and uncomfortable."

Turning my finger to my stepfather, I added all those years of beatings onto the scales. "Very slow, very painful."

"I love the way you think, Mess," Brie grinned.

"Brie," Esha gave her a warning look. "They hurt her a lot when she was still a child."

Brie's smile dropped, her eyes glowing red even through her glamor. "We're going to need props." Standing, she walked to a trunk on the other side of the room and started collecting items.

My eyes returned to the show. "I want to be inside you," Esha whispered in my ear.

"You know it doesn't feel right for me," I reminded him, not allowing him to distract me from the scene on the bed as Brie handed Trell a set of handcuffs before returning to Sauvignon.

"I can make you forget them, Mess."

"Tynan would kill you," I dismissed his offer, barely paying it any attention.

Turning my face to his so that I was forced to meet his eyes, Esha caressed my cheek. "Tynan offered this. He said if it's what you needed; he will allow it this once. If you let me have you, I'll take this pain away after you get your revenge."

Returning my gaze to the bed, I watched as Trell handcuffed Chris to the frame. "I already have my revenge. I had it the moment they left the nightclub." Standing up, I created a clear separation between Esha and me. "Thanks for the offer, but I've spent my life trying to hold onto my memories, no matter how painful. I'm not about to hand them away."

Blinking up at me, Esha watched me as I moved further back in the room to be by myself. Brie returned from the trunk with more toys. Whispering something to Trell, she then handed her a strip of cloth.

Rising up, Trell placed a blindfold over Chris's eyes. "This will make your senses come alive." Smiling, Chris let it happen. The same when she set earplugs in his ears, securing them in place with the blindfold. Kneeling either side of his head, Trell sat on his face before returning to blowing him.

"I'm going to make you scream," Sauvignon purred to Wayne.

"I can't wait," he responded eagerly as she used leather cuffs to tie him up.

Once he was secured, Sauvignon licked his lips. "Say ah," she flirted. "Show me that tongue of yours." With a laugh, Wayne stuck out his tongue. Sauvignon caressed his jaw. "Open your mouth wide," she encouraged, as Brie sat over Wayne's legs. "I want to suck my juices from it."

When Wayne stretched opened his mouth, Sauvignon placed her mouth over his and sucked his tongue into her mouth, going as far down his tongue as she could.

Making a noise of pain, Wayne reefed his arms against the cuffs, Sauvignon gripping the join of his jaw to prevent him from closing it. Then Sauvignon bit down. Clenching her jaw hard, she continued biting.

Wayne was screaming as Sauvignon chewed his tongue off inside his own mouth, blood spitting out around where their mouths joined, Wayne thrashing and screaming. Covering my mouth horrified, I blinked rapidly as tears spilled from my eyes.

Wrapping his arms around me, Esha turned me to him, so I didn't have to look. I didn't, but I did. It's one of those moments that you don't want to watch, but you can't look away either.

Sitting up abruptly, Sauvignon spat Wayne's tongue to the side. Kissing him again, she swallowed the blood pulsing up into her mouth hungrily, Brie patting her head tenderly, encouraging her.

They dropped their glamor now, no longer caring to hide what they were.

Lowering her mouth to Wayne's waning erection, Brie dropped her mouth over it, only to treat his manhood like a chew toy. Digging her teeth into the base, she started tugging and yanking like a dog trying to pull a tasty worm out of the ground.

Keening in agony, Wayne thrashed, but the two Sluagh pinned him down as they fed on his blood. Brie dug claws into his shins and dragged them up, scarlet rivers of pain flowing free from his skin.

Abandoning sucking Chris's cock, Trell moved down his body and sheathed his hardness inside her. Grabbing one of Wayne's thrashing legs, Trell pinned it to the mattress and dropped her hungry mouth to the wine of pain he served up.

Jolting, Wayne mewled anew when Trell sliced her teeth into his flesh, finding a vein which delivered her wine in pulses of his racing heartbeat.

Licking his lips next to my ear, Esha was lowering his mouth to my throat before I even thought of the effect it was having on him. Pride pulled me out of Esha's grasp as his teeth scraped my neck.

"Join the feeding frenzy. The prince offered her memories, not her blood." Esha's lust glaze eyes appraised me, then in a blur, he was at Wayne's neck, feeding.

"God, stop, or I'll come," Chris moaned, Trell's hips fucking him eagerly as she sated both lusts.

"Let me take you back to your room," Pride requested. Meeting his eyes, he too had let his glamor go. "You've delivered your abusers to their doom. You don't have to witness it."

"Where is the satisfaction in that?" I asked, trying to brave the violence of the room.

"Mess, where is the sanity in causing yourself more horrible memories?" He challenged. "You have enough pain inside you to last multiple lifetimes. You are light living in darkness…"

"I am born of the dark and the light."

"You are balanced, but you will not stay so if you subject yourself to unnecessary brutality," Pride urged. "You are not Sluagh. Not any part of you. You are entirely Sidhe, and even the Unseelie Sidhe would not watch a Sluagh feeding frenzy willingly."

Daring a glance at the bed, I felt my eyes itch when I noticed Wayne wasn't thrashing anymore. Returning my eyes to Pride, I found his face blurry in my watery vision. "I did this."

My chest restricted, and breathing felt painful. Yes, these men hurt me, and they enjoyed it, but other than small glimpses of blood in my underwear, snippets of memories of the pain their bodies caused mine, I was still alive and mostly unharmed. Was this vengeance fair? My compassionate heart was at war with the darkness in my soul that demanded it still wasn't enough.

"Let me take you home, Mess?" Pride tried again, his voice tender and fatherly. Unable to balance my emotions, I nodded. Using his arm around my shoulders to turn me from the room, Pride led me out to the corridor. He kept his arm around me as he walked me to Tynan's suites, taking it slow as if I might break on the way.

"I said uncomfortable and fast," I murmured somewhere along the way. "I went to Wayne willingly, and while he wasn't gentle, nothing he did to me deserved that."

"That was fast and uncomfortable for the Sluagh, Mess. What your stepfather is going to suffer..." Pride fell quiet. "They will be hours in comparison to the swift death his friend suffered."

When we reached the lounge room in Tynan's suites, he was standing by the fire, staring into the flames. The window to the forest was open, and Lucifer was sitting on the window sill, enjoying a glass of wine, watching Tynan's silent contemplation. Lucifer moved the glass from his lips and swallowed. "Hello, Rabbit."

My body shivered as a natural reflex. Tilting his head to confirm my return, Tynan cursed under his breath. "You're back earlier than I anticipated."

"I got what I needed," I answered, understanding I wasn't meant to see whatever was happening here. "Did you need me to go elsewhere?"

"Not at all, rabbit. I could use a little rabbit with my wine."

Opening his mouth, Lucifer lifted his tongue till the tip of his penis poked out, and he waggled it at me.

"Put it away before I make you bite it again," I hissed angrily. "I've already watched one man have his dick chewed off tonight, it won't bother me to see another."

All the males winced in the room. "That would be the Gemini's I gather," Lucifer cringed uncomfortably.

"Undoubtedly," Tynan agreed. "Only Brie takes satisfaction to emasculate a man that way."

"Not the best role models for your wife, Prince, if you know what I mean."

Tynan smirked. "I don't have to worry about that with Mess." Turning to face Lucifer, Tynan tilted his head to the forest. "I'll contact you when I have a plan."

Lucifer stood, stepping to the table to place his glass down. As he moved back to the window, he paused and crouched to the ground. When he stood a woman hung limply in his arms as he carried her out the window. Stepping forward, I was about to object when Pride put his arm out barring my way. "Goodnight, rabbit," Lucifer called, climbing outside and walking into the forest.

The window slid shut silently as I looked to Tynan for an explanation. "She followed me out of the nightclub to hit on me," Tynan informed me mildly. "She entered the mound without invitation."

"Two men entered the mound without invitation too, but they wouldn't have done so if I hadn't suggested they'd benefit from it."

Tynan peered at me, his eyes flashing silver. "I did not lure her if that's what you are suggesting."

Swallowing my argument at the sight of the silver orbs glaring at me, I fidgeted under his gaze. Turning back to the fire, Tynan contemplated the flames jumping within. Summer was over, fall was here, but it wasn't quite cold enough for the fire.

Inhaling deeply, I lifted my eyes to Pride. "Good night, Pride. Thank you for watching out for me tonight." Bowing deeply, Pride turned to the door he always disappeared into.

Moving to Tynan's side, I relieved him of the scotch he was holding, but not drinking. "Do you want to talk about it?" I asked, eyeing the remnants of some of my sketches as they curled and burned in flames.

Anger licked at my insides, wondering how many he destroyed over the months. Throwing my head back, I skulled what was in the glass, letting the burn of it wash into the pit of distrust. Tynan didn't answer me. Placing the glass on the coffee table, I walked away from him. "Goodnight."

"Mess."

"Don't!"

Making my way into the bathroom, that was still devoid of a mirror, I undressed. Trying to wash the conflicting emotions from my mind, I stood in the shower for longer than was necessary. Hands caressing my hips jolted me back to the room.

Tynan's mouth kissed the side of my neck as his naked body pressed in behind me. "I do it to protect you, Mess." His hands explored me, preparing me for his attention. "There are things you put in your drawings that no one should ever find out about you."

Keeping quiet, I closed my eyes to the sensations his touch evoked in me. "You offered me to Esha."

"I offered for you to be rid of painful memories. It was for you to negotiate the terms."

"You knew what he'd ask for. You know you're the only one I've ever felt right touching."

"If you needed it, I wanted it to be an option for you. It's your birthday, Mess. I just wanted you to be happy. You do that to me, make me want to only see you happy."

"You make me happy, Ty. The way you touch me, the way you make love to me, and the way you care for me. When you're not an asshole, you are my happiness."

Kissing my shoulder, Tynan pinched and held my clit. I squirmed from the discomfort that quickly swelled to pleasure. "Do you love me, Mess?"

"I wish I was brave enough. I just feel like you are playing a game with me still."

Releasing my clit, Tynan checked my readiness causing me to gasp with his roughness. "You don't trust me?"

Pressing my palms to the wall to stay upright, I breathed through the pleasure. "No," I answered determined and honest.

"Good, you shouldn't trust anyone." Turning me to face him, Tynan lifted me to his waist and slid his curse just inside me, watching as I bit my lip and gripped his shoulders. "Don't trust a living soul." He thrust forward hard. Crying out, I dug my nails into his flesh, discomfort pushing beyond the threshold of pain. "Me especially."

35

BETRAYED

A small stack of pancakes was placed in front of me. Blinking down at the smiley face made up of syrup and butter, I frowned as I lifted my eyes to Margo who stood watching me.

"You haven't smiled for weeks. Maybe you need to be reminded how to?"

Not wanting to cause issues, I forced a small smile just for her. "Thank you, Margo."

Instead of appeasing her, my smile made Margo frown and consider the others in the kitchen. She clapped her hands loudly. "Out!"

Without question, but with a lot of grumbles and complaints, the population of the kitchen dwindled to three. Turning to look at Pride, Margo pointed to the door. "She is not going anywhere."

"I am not to let her out of my sight when she leaves her room, Margo."

"Pride, if you ever want me to make black sesame ice cream again, you will leave this kitchen and wait outside," Margo challenged.

Pride looked hurt. He glanced at me pleadingly, but I concentrated on the smiley face on my short stack and stayed quiet. With a curse, Pride reefed the door open, nearly pulling it off its hinges, and stepped out.

Margo, satisfied, turned those big black eyes on me. "You were happy for weeks after the gauntlet. That has all changed since your birthday?"

"It's nothing you can help with, Margo."

"Does the Prince not make you happy?"

"Sometimes, Margo. Sadly, I don't trust the Prince. Therefore, he can't make me truly happy."

"Trust is not something anyone in the mound has, Princess. We respect instead. We admire the King, we venerate our prince who protected us from the Seelie, who developed ways for us to thrive in a human-dominated world. We respect each other. If we do not, we die."

Standing up, Margo put her small pale hand over mine. "Don't trust the Prince, idolize him for being the man to save your life. Adore him as your husband. Respect will keep you alive longer than trust ever will, no matter where you live. Humans are stupid to trust; nothing good ever comes from it."

"Love comes from it."

"What is love?"

My eyes became blurry as they filled quickly with tears. "I don't know," I lied and escaped for the door. As I charged out, tears spilling down my face, Pride fell in beside me.

Lying about my feelings for Tynan was useless, he probably knew exactly how I felt. The truth was, I'd known I was in love for weeks now and I learned something else too. Love was dangerous.

Love was a blindfold you apply before entering the maze of the Minotaur. It was foolish, and more than likely, you would end up fatally wounded, bleeding your heart out in a dead end where no one could hear you screaming for help.

Tynan saved my life, but loving him was going to be the death of me, and I would be a fool not to know he had an agenda for keeping me alive. He had been plotting from the moment he realized I was more than just a half-breed Seelie.

Sometimes, I wondered had I not escaped that first night and managed to hide, had he taken me in the club amongst all the blood and gore of his birthday massacre, would he have realized before he killed me?

"Mess?" Tynan touched my shoulder gently. Turning from where I was staring out the windows in his lounge room, I took in my surroundings.

Pride sat in his usual spot, lacking his typical steamy romance book. Instead, he watched me with eyes that worried. Caressing my face, Tynan wiped the tears away gently.

"You're home early."

"Pride called me after you cried for two hours staring out this window. That was an hour ago."

Looking at the clock, I frowned at how many hours had past since I left the kitchen. Stepping away from Tynan, I sighed. "Sorry, I was lost in my thoughts." Moving to sit on the lounge, I collected my sketch pad and pencil and started drawing.

"What thoughts held you so captivated?" Sinking onto the sofa next to me, Tynan angled his body to face me.

"The night we met." Lifting my eyes from my sketch pad to meet his, solid and black, no anger at my confession. "I was wondering if you would have killed me that night if I hadn't had escaped."

"No," Tynan answered easily, but his eyes were studious in my every reaction. "Even a half-breed Seelie would be worth a couple of weeks of fun to me. However, I wouldn't have been gentle, I wouldn't have taken my time with penetrating your body, and I wouldn't have wasted my energy in healing you."

The tears seemed to run faster as the thoughts of pain beyond my imagining teased my consciousness.

"Being able to hide from me as long as you did, intrigued me. Even when I found you and recognized you were half Unseelie, it was the King's protection that truly saved you, Mess. Not because I obey the Unseelie King, but because he gave it. Unseelie or not, Mabon has never interfered in my business before. The moment he told me you were not to be fatally or permanently harmed, I suspected there was more to you than appearances. Mabon's interference saved you from the worst of my darkness."

Closing my eyes, I tried to breathe through the torrent of emotions I was feeling. Slipping closer, Tynan moved my hair back so he could see my face.

"It saved you initially, Mess," he murmured quietly as if he didn't wish another to hear, "but you prevented me from disregarding his wishes. Not just because of your bloodline, but because you are the only person to ever crave my affection. The way you react to me..." When he groped my breast, I cringed with discomfort. Tynan stopped. "Are you hurt?"

"No," I assured placing my hand over his as he relaxed his grip. "They are just really sensitive. They've gotten bigger, and I'm not quite fitting in my bras anymore. I think it's time I went up a size."

Tynan was observing me, more so my bigger bust. He looked unsure and humored at the same time.

Squeezing his hand gently, my eyes fluttered on the gentler grop-ing. "I still enjoy you touching me, Ty, just be gentle around the maturing breasts this week."

"Are there any other changes I should be aware of? Anywhere else you need me to be gentle?"

It was an odd question for him, and it made me confused. "No."

Taking the sketch pad from his hand, eyes flicking over the drawing of Margo trying to advise me, Tynan smiled placing the pad on the table and slipping his suit jacket off. "Good."

My eyes canvassed the room, we were alone. When they came back to Tynan, his chest was bare, Sluagh markings on display, faintly glowing purple. Fascinated, I reached out to run my hand over them. I'd never seen them just glow purple before without him using his power.

"What do they mean?" While all Sluagh bore the markings, they were all unique in design.

Tynan moved forward, laying himself over me as he pushed me back on the lounge. "They are birthmarks." Taking my hand, he placed it over his heart. "The pattern here denotes my tribe, joining my mother's and father's markings into one."

Examining the swirls which looked like a native depiction of the sun during an eclipse, I admired the artistry. "Your mother was Seelie."

"Exactly, but even the Sidhe have markers in the Sluagh." Moving my hand to another design over his right chest that I didn't understand, I traced the design hoping to get an idea of what it was, but it looked chaotic and dangerous. "This is one of my spirit powers." Indicating both his shoulders, Tynan smiled down on me. "They represent my hands of power. It is the same with every Sluagh."

"What are your powers?"

Freeing my right breast from my dress and bra, Tynan smiled as he wrapped his tongue around my nipple.

"Guess."

"Healing, and you can block other's powers or something."

"Something like that," he teased. Yanking the sleeves of the dress down my arms aggressively, Tynan exposed my other breast, still barely held behind the material of my bra. His mouth latched onto the nipple through the lace as he continued to tug and yank my dress down my body.

"Ty, there's a zip."

Growling, Tynan gripped the dress and tore it. He continued to rip and growl, tearing at the cloth as a five-year-old does wrapping paper hiding his birthday present. When the clothing and underwear were in shreds, my body completely exposed to him, Tynan licked from my clit to my heart in one long stroke.

Squirming beneath him, I gasped as his fingers tightened around my hips. He mouthed, sucked and kissed my breasts till I was breathless. "Please, Ty," I begged, tugging at his pants desperately.

Allowing me the time to release his curse, he watched with a pinpoint focus in his eyes, but once it was free, his patience was worn. Using his fist in my hair, he demanded my mouth and kissed me deeply as he inserted his body into mine.

Finding the catch, he released my mouth and pushed forward

slowly, but without recoil. He demanded my body open for him, and it submitted, unable to resist his authority.

When he was buried as deep as he could go, he took my hands above my head and looked down at me intently. That look terrified me more than any he had cast my way before. "Please, don't," I sobbed knowing whatever was about to happen, I wasn't going to like.

"What I'm about to do is only going to hurt because of your power to detect majicks, Mess, but it is important you know that I'm doing it to protect you, to protect us," Tynan confessed, his markings growing brighter as his power smothered me.

"Ty..."

Extreme cold poured over my body like I'd submerged into liquid nitrogen. Screaming as his power burnt along my skin, I thrashed under the weight of his body, the only part of me not appearing to burn was where he was inside me. In comparison, his curse seemed to heat my insides in gentle warmth while the outside of me burned cold.

The purple light dimmed, and the cold stopped, but my skin felt raw and cold as ice. Unable to voice any longer the pain I was in, I blubbered incoherently, wanting to know why he did this to me.

"Ty, what did you do?" Esha asked coming around the sofa.

Removing himself from me, Tynan kept my arms pinned over-head. "Take it from her, now."

Esha's eyes widened in surprise, his mouth falling open slightly, but he didn't refuse the offer. Pulling his clothes off in seconds, he fit his body to mine. I couldn't breathe to protest; I couldn't think to understand. Esha pumped his body into mine, uneasiness creeping beneath my skin where he touched me.

Unable to take any more, my power of manifestation yawned open wanting to make it all stop. Light encompassed me just as the darkness consumed me, blocking it from growing or protecting me. Pulling it back, my psyche turned to my next power, and the satiability spilled over us.

Tynan's light retreated, permitting this power to have its way. It crashed over me like a wave, and I cried out in combined pain and pleasure.

"When you are done, take your part out of this too," The only response was Esha's grunts. "I'm sorry, Mess," Tynan murmured sadly. His voice echoed in my head, the room blurred beyond my watery vision, Esha's face as he reached ecstasy faded and disappeared. Closing my eyes, I felt the world swept away from me for a moment.

Opening my eyes, I discovered Tynan was kissing around my neck as he lay within me. Confused, I blinked, my forehead frowning as I remembered we were making love. Wondering how I had blacked out during sex, especially with Tynan, I lifted my arms and caressed his shoulders.

"You're back?" Tynan murmured against my neck.

"What happened?" Kissing his shoulder, I wrapped my arms around his neck.

Lifting his face above mine, Tynan smiled gently. "Your satiability stole you away."

Wondering if this is what had happened those other times I couldn't remember with Chris and his friends, I averted my eyes.

"Hey," Tynan brushed my cheek, "don't feel bad. If I hurt you bad enough for your power to protect you, then that's on me."

"You like hurting me."

"I like rough sex, yes, but I don't fuck you with intent to hurt you." Lifting me as he sat back, Tynan settled himself to have me straddling him. When he brushed my hair back from my face, the rivulets of sweat ran down my body. Was I running a fever?

"I care very deeply for you, Mess." My heart stuttered in happiness hearing him speak those words. "It's important that you know I care for you."

Gazing down at him, I couldn't lie to myself or him any longer. "I'm in love with you."

36

THE END OF HAPPINESS

❖

"Something wrong?" Tynan asked coming into the bathroom.

Frowning as I considered my body in the mirror, I rubbed my hand down my abdomen. "Does my body look different to you?"

"You look more beautiful every day. Why?"

"When I touch myself, I feel like my hand follows a contour my eyes aren't seeing, and this morning I tried to put one of my favorite dresses on, and I can't get it to do up. It was suffocating me, but I don't understand why?"

Tynan's false smile dropped. "Well, your breasts have grown significantly bigger. I'll get Brie to buy you some new dresses, ones with a bit of stretch for your maturing body."

Hands sliding around my waist, Tynan caressed my stomach adoringly. Again, his hands didn't follow the contours they should. It was like my body was out of alignment with my soul. Watching his hands in the mirror, my eyes blurred.

Frustrated, I moved out of his reach. "Something's wrong, I feel out of touch from my body, I have for over a month now, and I don't understand why the sudden change."

Observing Tynan's annoyance, I bit my lip and stepped towards him, running my hands over his muscular chest, tracing the lines of his markings.

"I'm sorry. Things have been so good between us these past two months. You've been so attentive and loving and treated me like a princess. But this disconnected feeling is getting worse, and I hate it. I feel like these months of happiness are just setting me up for a bigger fall, that something is slowly eating away at it, that it can't last."

Tynan caressed my waist, his eyes severe and resigned. "You're right, I need to tell you something." Tynan pulled me closer, so our naked torsos were pressed together. "I have never cared about anything or anyone like I do you, Mess, and two months ago, I realized your life was in more danger than ever before. I did something to protect you without your permission."

"What?" Frowning, I wondered if he had more guards following me.

"Ty, we need to go if we are going to make your morning meeting," Esha's voice came from the bedroom.

Cupping my face, Tynan met my eyes. "I put a glamor over you." Stepping away, Tynan went out to the bedroom to start dressing. "I'll be there in a second, Esha."

Following him out to the bedroom, I watched him stunned. Tynan kept his back to me while he dressed, a classic avoidance tactic of his. There was more to it.

"What sort of glamor?" Did I appear different to everyone else? Wouldn't my being in Tynan's apartment give away who I was?

"I told you, one to protect you," Tynan answered as he put his tie in place and knotted it.

"Ty, we've known each other a year now. I know when you are evasive. What does this glamor appear as to everyone else?"

"You look just as you always have to everyone else, including yourself."

"Then why the glamor? What are you hiding from everyone including me?" Grazing my hand over my stomach tenderly, a vision of the pregnant Seelie being held as a prisoner in the dungeons flashed into my mind. The Sluagh markings wrapping around her abdomen, a lot more faded then the Sluagh, but there.

Observing my hand, Tynan picked up his briefcase. "You already know, Mess, you have since it started. You just didn't want to face it."

The world tilted on its axis, throwing everything off-center, making the ground I stood on unstable. Feeling for the bed, I carefully sat my bum down, so I didn't fall down.

Focused on the tears shaking loose from my eyes, Tynan kissed the top of my head. "We'll discuss it tonight. I have to go." Moving to the bedroom door, Tynan stepped out. Pausing, he looked back at me. "Mess, I'm just trying to protect you. That's all."

"Protect me? Or protect this?" I accused rubbing my belly. Now that I knew, I could see the faint purple like markings in my skin, and the slight bloating of my stomach.

"Both," Tynan answered. "Because you mean more to me than you realize."

"Do you love me?"

Tynan's eyes burned silver for a moment. Closing them, he looked away. "More than you could imagine." The door shut and he left me there to deal with this.

Sitting there stunned, I rubbed my belly, tracing the lines of the fetus's tribal markings. The pattern of Tynan's markings from his heart was mixed with something else. Swiping the tears falling down my cheeks, I tried hard to control my sudden out of control breathing. He knew I didn't want this, so he had hidden it from me.

There was a knock at the door, bringing my attention back to my surroundings and the fact I was still naked. "Mess," Pride's voice reached through the solid timber like it wasn't even there. "You've been summoned to see the King."

"Crying out loud! Of all the days." Standing, I pulled my clothes on, choosing a maxi dress to allow for breathing room and a cardigan for the cold weather above ground. Pride waited for me outside my bedroom. Confused by the expression on his face, I looked below to see an unhappy Amp and six of the Luna guard. All anger at Tynan vanished as I turned to Pride. "Am I in trouble?"

"I do not know," Pride replied, his voice tight.

"Has the Prince left?"

"He left two hours ago, Mess," Pride looked even more worried now. "I've called him, but he's not local today. I had to leave a message."

Starting to walk down the stairs, I glanced at Pride over my shoulder. "What do you mean Tynan's not local? The city is half an hour away."

"He flew to Newcastle for his morning meeting. If he's on the helicopter heading home, they probably can't hear the phone," Pride whispered as we reached the lounge room.

Meeting Pride's concerned eyes, I swallowed painfully before turning to face Amp. "Is something wrong?"

"For your protection, Princess, since we know the Seelie have tried to abduct you many times," Amp told a half-truth. We were friends, hung out in the kitchen regularly, and I knew he was uncomfortable with whatever the King intended.

"Do you know what the King wants?"

"My understanding is that the king wishes to discuss your relationship with the prince."

"A bit late, isn't he?"

"I cannot tell you any more, I'm sorry, Mess," Amp looked genuinely apologetic.

"I get the feeling you are not going to be as sorry as I will be."

Bowing his head in silent acknowledgment, Amp gestured to the door. Three of his guard went ahead of me. "You are not needed, Pride," Amp informed him as we moved to leave.

"I am to stay with the Princess whenever she leaves these rooms," Pride objected.

"That was not your orders from the King."

"His orders were to keep her safe. The prince ordered I go with her. The King hired me; the Prince has my loyalty."

One of the guards started to withdraw his sword. "I wouldn't do that if I were you," I warned.

Amp put his arm out to gesture the guard to stop. "As far as the King's door, as always?" Amp offered.

Bowing his head, Pride offered me his arm. We started walking down the corridor. "What a shit fucking day this is turning out to be."

Pride lifted surprised eyebrows at my colorful language. Pride was the epitome of an English gentleman and vulgarity was unnecessary in his mind.

"Whatever happens, try and delay, Mess," Pride whispered. "Hold off whatever the King has planned till Tynan gets here."

"What do you worry it is?"

"Whatever he plans to do after, his first move will be to break the bond. He won't want the Prince to be easily able to find you."

"We are mated."

"To the Sidhe, you are available until a child is inside you," Pride reminded me. It was on the tip of my tongue to argue there was when Pride continued. "Be glad there is not, they would kill it and the Prince to undo that bond if that was the case."

My jaw jammed shut. The double doors to the Kings suite approached. My mouth was dry, and I clung to Pride's arm. "Tell the prince," I murmured as the guard stopped and the doors opened. "I knew the happiness couldn't last."

Amp gestured for me to follow. Lifting up on my toes, I kissed Pride's cheek. "Tell him I'll be waiting for him to come and save me."

Falling back to flat feet, I stepped away from a miserable Pride. Amp led the way in, the exterior doors shutting off my view of Pride, closing on the best months of my life. "I'm sorry, Mess," Amp mourned in the antechamber. "I personally would prefer you with the Prince, if given the option. You understand, though, Mabon is my King."

Understanding completely; I nodded my forgiveness. As the internal doors opened, I lifted my wrist to my mouth and kissed Tynan's mark on my wrist. "I'll miss you with every beat of my heart."

37

MISSING MESS

❖

"Where is she?" Tynan raged as he stepped out of the car in the underground car park. He felt the bond break, a year of feeling Mess under his skin, stolen away by a bond breaker. Mess would be in agony.

"The King's suites," Trell informed, nearly running to keep up with Tynan's stride, Esha right by his side. "Pride stayed with her, but they didn't let him inside. I've sent some of our warriors to meet him and wait for your arrival."

"I'll kill him for this," Tynan threatened. Trell, smartly, remained quiet.

It took several minutes to get to the corridor outside the King's residence. Several minutes too long in the Prince's opinion. When Tynan turned the corner, the passage was full of Lunar guards and Sluagh facing off. Nothing was being said, but it was evident that once the Sluagh arrived, the Kings guard had called reinforcements.

"Let me pass," Tynan bellowed, his order echoing off the stone around them. Everyone stepped back. The two lunar guard at the door, looking anxiously at each other as Tynan stormed towards them, begging each other to be the one to stand up to the Prince. Had it been anyone else, they would have stood their ground and risked death. The prince was different. There were worse things he could do to a soul than death.

"Move," Tynan snarled, his eyes glowing silver orbs of rage. The guards stepped aside but didn't open the door. Turning the handle, Tynan threw the door open. Marching through the antechamber, he ripped the next door off its hinges as he yanked it open.

Too much time had passed since the bond had been broken and the pain it caused Mess could impact on their child. Worry clutched at his heart faintly, but his anger churned the fire inside him as he stormed down the corridor ready to sever the King's head from his traitorous body.

Tynan's feet halted at the opening to the lounge. The room was a chaotic silence. Furniture was strewn across the room, most of it destroyed. Some of it still floating in the air, held in slow motion. Truthfully, it looked like a hurricane had swept through the room, dismantling and destroying everything in its path.

Searching the debris as he slid his sword back into his cane. Blood and flesh riddled the mess, a random arm cut from a body floating past him.

Amongst the wafting ruins bobbed the King's severed head, hanging isolated in the center of the dormant storm. Gasps split the silence behind him as the Sluagh and Lunar guard tried to make sense of what happened.

"Did the Seelie do this?" One of the guards queried quietly.

Stepping into the room carefully, Tynan hit the wall of the remaining majick. A vibration ignited through the chaos like a mallet rubbing around a cymbal, growing louder as it passed towards the center of the room till it hit the King's head. Blood, bone, and brains exploded from Mabon's head like a grenade in the center of the deafening impact and brought the majick crashing down.

"Mess?" Tynan called carefully, just in case she was hiding and scared, or unconscious somewhere. This was the wreckage of her spirit power; he remembered what her bedroom had looked like after she'd lost control of it.

"She's not here," Pride murmured. "I can't sense her nearby."

Now that the room was safe, Tynan used his cane to move the debris out of his way. He stopped when half of Ashling's face looked up at him, fear and shock set permanently in place. "They thought taking her would be easy, that her inability to control her powers would make her easy prey."

Pride and Esha peered down at the dissected bodies as they moved carefully through the room. Shifting a piece of table aside, Tynan observed the dismembered arm of a Solaris, the badge on the sleeve labeling him the new captain. Clamping his teeth shut on the anger burbling within, Tynan once again scanned the room for any sign of his wife. She hadn't been dressed this morning when he left for him to even know what to look for.

"There is a Seelie woman, or what is left of her, over here." Picking up the remnants of her head by her hair, Esha lifted it for his prince to see the precision of the cut slicing diagonally from car to mandible. Mess's discs of pain, like the ones she used on Nathani when she reacted to the news he killed her mother.

"An exchange. The King made a deal to gain a new consort in exchange for Mess."

Tynan looked down at the remnants of the King's body. "He sold her, and he sold the rest of us out by doing so." Trell came back to the lounge from upstairs and shook her head. "Where is she?" Tynan raged into the room. No answer came, everyone, looking at the debris, searching for another head, for her head.

"Move," the order came down the corridor and the Sluagh and Lunar guard alike, moved aside to let the second in command, the man who had saved Mess at the gauntlet, march through. Entering the lounge, Ashok's eyes went wide.

Tynan pointed to Mabon's remains. "Your King is no more. Now, Messina is the last of the Royal line for both courts."

Awed by the turmoil, Ashok scanned the room. "Is she alive?"

"We cannot find her, dead or alive," one of the Lunar replied.

The second in command took everything in, then with a deep breath, Ashok went to a knee, his guard followed his lead. "Prince Tynan, as the prince of the Sluagh, and the queen's consort, we ask you to witness, the Lunar guard pledges their loyalty to queen Messina Ui Bayne-Ard."

"Find her," Tynan snarled. "Search every inch of this castle. Send men to the Seelie court and search for her there in case they took her. As her consort, I am king there too. Messina rules both courts equally, and I rule until my wife is found and crowned." Tynan thumped his cane on the ground.

The castle shook, the entire building trembling and a sizeable crashing sound could be heard far below. Confused and off balance for a moment, Tynan worried Messina had lost control entirely. It wasn't unknown for a Fae to go insane and kill their own kin when their power went wild. Having seen Mess lose control before, his concern was rational, particularly worrisome with the evidence surrounding him.

A whispering started around the room, too soft for Tynan to hear, but, as he listened, he understood it was only one word being repeated over and over again.

"Reunited," someone shouted down the corridor. The sea of guards parted as a goblin raced into the room panicked and bowed before Tynan. "The faerie mound has reunited."

The whispering shut off as Tynan recognized what it had been telling him. "United under the blood of the last queen," Tynan muttered, relief spread through his chest, revealing how tense he'd been. "Which means she's alive." He lifted his eyes to Ashok. "Find her."

Commanding his men to search the castle, Ashok organized them into groups and locations. Stepping up next to Tynan, Esha spoke quietly. "They broke the bond, she would have been in agony, and you remember what she was like the last time she lost control of her power. She could barely stay conscious."

"I'm aware," Tynan responded dryly, searching the room with his eyes.

"Who do you think carried her out of here?"

"Pride," Tynan called the Red Cap over.

"Yes, my prince," Pride bowed his enormous head. He was

worried about Messina; it was there in his eyes. He'd become very protective of her very quickly when he was assigned to her. The fights they'd had about her...and Messina never knew how much Pride had looked after her as if she was his own daughter. Tynan had never seen a red cap act so fiercely protective, especially of a Sidhe.

"You said Amp escorted you here?"

"Yes."

"Did he escort her inside?"

"Yes."

"Did he come back out?" Pride quietly shook his head. Tynan looked to Esha. "Search the debris for the Lunar captain's head. If it's not here, we know who got her out."

"Out?" Esha queried.

"Yes," Tynan scowled as he walked towards the door. "Out of the faerie mound. Mess isn't here. Pride would sense her proximity if she were."

"There is one place I would not, if she was still here," Pride challenged.

Tynan considered him. "Esha, organize this hodgepodge to be cleaned up, the bodies are to be cataloged, and every person in this room accounted for. Pride and I will search the forest."

"You don't want me to help?"

Esha knew the forest better than most, Tynan acknowledged that with a nod. "Meet us there once you have this lot organized."

Tynan stormed out with Pride by his side, everyone moving out of their way instantly. No one messed with a red cap, even less messed with the prince of the Sluagh, especially when his eyes were pure silver light.

Pride kept his mouth closed the entire trek back to Tynan's suites. Once inside, Pride searched the suite while Tynan went to the window. It was closed, and it was daytime. "She's not here, and none of her stuff has been taken," Pride informed as he returned to Tynan's side. "She's not leaving of her cognizance, my prince."

"You were with Mess whenever Amp was with her," Tynan began. "Did you get a sense of his interest?"

Pride turned his head to assess his prince. "He was overly friendly."

"I mean, was his interest of the heart, or did you feel it was a power play?"

Pride turned his eyes to the window. "Either way, the result would be the same," Pride muttered unhappily. "To destroy your claim, there needs to be a child."

Tynan felt what might have been insecurity, anxiety, fear, for only the second time in his life. It was the same twisting in his gut he'd felt waiting for Mess to run the gauntlet, being forced to watch Lucifer slash her spine, and not be able to rush out there and save her. "She carries my child," Tynan revealed. "She is mine, Pride."

Mouth falling open, Pride took a moment to contain his reaction. "How far?"

"Three months, thereabouts," Tynan's eyes pierced the forest. He knew she wasn't out there. She wasn't in the mound. Either of them. He'd felt his son growing within her through the bond, and now he couldn't perceive either of them.

"She would be showing beneath her clothes," Pride frowned. "If he sees there is a child, he may return her unharmed." Pride turned his face. "Does Mess know?"

"Yes," Tynan acknowledged but failed to add she only became aware this morning. If she hadn't drawn it and had fallen unconscious, she may not remember when she woke next. "I've placed a strong glamor on Mess so that no other could see the changes in her body. He may not be able to see."

"Surely, Mess would tell him?"

"I gave her reason to fear others knowing, Pride," Tynan grizzled. "Very valid reasons. She may not tell him until she goes into labor, at which point, she will be too weak to protect my child by herself."

"If no one knows there was a child, you have no claim if he then puts his child in her womb," Pride warned. "You should not have hidden it," Pride admonished. "We could protect her against the Seelie, and the Unseelie would have acknowledged your claim. Now, you have no grounds, now, the Seelie are not the threat."

The door opened, and Esha came in. "The captain of the Lunar guard has been located," Esha announced immediately.

Turning, eyes suddenly focused on this news, Tynan's anxiety grew. "He was killed?"

"No, he was in the Seelie court. He was there when the mound reunited, several Solaris account for his presence. Amp was sent ahead to ensure Messina's safety. Effectively, he went to the Seelie and informed them of Ashling's murder of Nora and her attempted assassination of Messina."

"But Mess isn't there?" Pride asked.

"No," Esha mourned. "She is not anywhere."

"This is worse than Amp having taken her," Pride worried. "At least we had a suspect. Now, we have no clue who has her."

"Esha, order every Lunar on duty questioned. I want to know who went into that room or if there were other means in or out. Search their memories. Especially the Captain's." Bowing his head, Esha left. Tynan focused his eyes on Pride. "There is something wrong with this picture, Pride. I want the missing pieces."

"What are you thinking?"

Silver balls of hellfire shining out from within Tynan's eyes making Pride hesitate and step back. "When we know everyone who came and went from that room, I want a list of their powers."

38

A DIVIDED COURT

❖

In the months after Mess vanished into thin air, everyone searched non-stop for her. Tynan even let Lucifer hunt her, but no one could find a trace. Soon, the Sidhe decided their last queen had died with the others. In fact, they believed Ashling attempted another assassination that went horribly wrong.

Either way, the Sidhe gave up hope, only the Sluagh still searched, but even that was waning. Tynan kept faith steady for six months. He held the belief in his heart, that when his son entered the world, somehow, he would know and be able to find them.

He counted the months, and then the weeks, then the days, and he did so for another thirty days past when he suspected she was due. Then he counted weeks again, and now he counted the months once more.

"There was an incident at a hospital two hours south three months ago," Esha informed, placing a printed news article in Tynan's hands as they walked.

The picture gave a glimpse of a hospital room in chaos, bodies of nursing staff and orderlies lying limp and lifeless, the shape of a female patient strapped to the bed also unmoving. The face couldn't be seen, and the bodies weren't eviscerated; could it be his queen?

"What is the story?"

"A woman was brought in by the police with severe stomach cramps, and on examination, they discovered she was in labor. No one can tell anyone what happened next because everyone who was there is dead. The patient, Jane Doe, was the only survivor. She was drugged and restrained. That's all the facts they revealed."

"What wasn't revealed?" Tynan stopped his march to the throne room, waiting outside the doors to hear Esha out.

"The police report states the woman was found wandering naked and delirious. They said it was obvious she had been drugged, and there were indications that she had been kept prisoner somewhere."

Esha showed Tynan pictures of bloody rusted shackles around one of the girl's ankles. The blood had eaten away at the metal, his heart lifted with anticipation they might have found a lead, finally. Tynan continued to be handed evidence photos while Esha talked.

"There were wounds from being tied up, and her feet were bloody from walking over broken glass," Esha read from notes. "They took her to the hospital where this happened. From what they could piece together, whoever was holding her found her at the hospital, came in and killed everyone and took the baby. The patient was rendered useless by whatever drugs they gave her and just kept muttering about a prince of the monsters, and a traitor."

The next picture Esha handed Tynan was a finger painting in blood on the sheets. A crude depiction of a person walking away with the baby in their arms, and the viewer reaching for the child.

"She drew it so she'd remember she had a baby," Tynan understood what the painting was for. "They held her down and took her baby, so she lashed out."

"Possibly, but that doesn't explain that she was still there, and the baby wasn't. Plus, Mess is normally more violent than this."

"Remember her room? No discs of pain then, just a sea of emotion. She wouldn't want to hurt the baby by accident," Tynan considered. "But, you're right. Who took the child? Did hospital security give the police no leads?"

"Nothing, the cameras all conveniently went down during the

time this happened. The police think Messina was held prisoner and repeatedly raped and somehow managed to escape when she went into labor."

Rage burned in Tynan's soul. "Where is she now?"

"The police can't tell me. With how quickly the girl was found and the hospital staff murdered, they worried someone powerful who ran a sex slave business might have been behind it. Since I work for someone rich and powerful, my questioning about the incident didn't go unnoticed. They finally revealed the victim was moved to another undisclosed hospital in case the attacker came back for her."

Creating fists with his hands, Tynan struggled to hold his worst power in. "Did you remind them my pregnant wife was kidnapped nine months ago?"

"Did you miss the part where someone killed eight people and stole a baby from the hospital but left the patient unharmed?" Esha raised a brow. When Tynan's silver orbs burned in his direction, Esha sighed. "It's the first lead we've had. It's the best I could do, but they've given me nothing. The only reason your place isn't swarming with the police right now is that we called and asked."

"I was a suspect?"

"Initially, yes, but when I kept pressing to know where she was, if she was safe, to know if they found the baby, they accepted I didn't know what happened after, which cleared your involvement."

A swish of metal brought both their attention to the fact Tynan's sword had half left its scabbard. Gritting his teeth, Tynan sheathed his power and the sword. "Tell me."

"She disappeared from the undisclosed hospital. A nurse put her to bed and left the room to get her a glass of water to take her pills. She was out of the room for maybe two minutes, and the door was in sight the entire time, but when she went back in, the girl was gone and hasn't been seen since."

Watching Esha's face fall, Tynan realized he wasn't the only one annoyed. Esha just had time to cool his temper before passing on the news. "She vanished into thin air at night?"

"Yes."

The sound of Tynan's jaw cracking filled the space between them. "There is only one creature that can disappear in plain sight in the Fae, Esha. Go find him."

Bowing his head, Esha ran down the corridor. The Fae they sought didn't live within the confines of the mound, preferring large human dwellings, but it was Unseelie, and extremely old. With the right spell, someone could summon the Urisk and beg a favor, but you had to have something it wanted, or it may just kill you for disturbing its rest.

Pushing through the doors to the throne room, Tynan made his way to the dais and his seat; those gathered parting the way for him. Once he was settled, Tynan gave a nod to Trell.

"Welcome all, on this fine Beltane we gather to celebrate the creation of new life. All those who have received the Goddess's favor may present your child to the King for naming."

The naming day was held once a year to celebrate the birth of any children born. Too few were observed over the last two centuries, but this year, for the first time, there were several. A tightness constricted Tynan's chest as he thought of the fact his son should have been one of the babies brought forth today.

The first to approach the dais was Máel, the Sluagh warrior who successfully impregnated the Seelie assassin. "My King, I present my son, Tanish Ó Máedóc-Sleá."

"The first child born of the merge," Tynan lied, his eyes considering the assassin mother. With grace, she gave a short curtsy, her hands caressing her growing belly.

When the child was born, she'd been given a choice to have her child raised a bastard or mate with the Sluagh father. Surprisingly, she'd chosen the mating. The Sluagh summed it up to their sexual prowess over the Sidhe. Since they mated after Tanish's birth, there was already another child on the way.

"Welcome to the Fae, Tanish Ó Máedóc-Sleá. May you be as brave as your father, and cunning as your mother," Tynan welcomed the babe. Continuing to do so for the next five brought before him without issue. After the formalities were over, Tynan bided his time with the Beltane celebrations, watching the clock for Esha's return.

Feeling an itch between his shoulder blades, Tynan adjusted his stance, his sword slipping an inch from its scabbard in readiness.

The air shifted when the assassin lunged, Tynan spun, his sword flying into the air and securing itself in his hand as he swung. The music and festivities died as all eyes watched the assassin's head dance through the air, blood arching from the cleanly sliced neck, to land with a thud amongst the circle of young troll children in attendance.

"Ball!" one called and raced forward to use the Seelie head for a game of football.

Wiping his blade clean on the clothing of his would-be assassin, Tynan addressed the room. "The courts are merged. I am the king. I respect that I am not the king the Seelie would choose, but, considering your leaders in the past, when have you ever had the choice?" Silence echoed his words. "Even if the queen is found, I will remain king. Accept it. Stop wasting lives to undo what the goddess has fated. If she didn't want me as the throne, I wouldn't be."

Waiting long enough for the message to sink in, Tynan waved everyone back to their celebrations. While the Goblins collected the body, Esha made his way to Tynan and bowed. "What took you so long?"

Without words, Esha handed Tynan his phone, a picture already loaded for his viewing. The Urisk they were seeking was dead; its head separated from its body and eyes gouged out. "How long?" Tynan asked, his stomach sinking.

"Months. Stealing Mess from the hospital was probably the last thing it ever did. Whoever hired the Urisk, made sure it could never reveal them to another."

"So, my wife disappears into the nothingness once again?"

"But we know she lived long enough to birth your son, and she wasn't killed, she was taken. I believe she's still alive, Ty. Being held captive, but alive."

"By who, Esha? Who gains from taking her and keeping her prisoner? To the human's she is nothing and those who know her worth need her healthy and safe to claim the crown. From what we saw in that police report, she is neither."

When Esha couldn't answer the question, Tynan stepped around him and left the festivities. Not knowing what befell her was eating away at him. Knowing someone took his son; possibly killed the child before it could draw breath was more than Tynan could bear.

Stopping still, Tynan opened his mouth and yelled his rage into the empty corridor, a tornado of pain and suffering impacting the surrounding area.

He'd let Messina think that it was the mark that allowed him to hurt her from any distance, and, in some ways, it was, but only because his hand to heal could also harm. Anyone else with their mark on her pale skin could never have damaged a hair on her head without finding her first.

When the air stilled, Tynan stood, head down and breathless, the stone walls around him bleeding from the gashes of his rage. The faerie mound shrunk in on itself, whimpering its pain in his head. "You can't punish the mound for what another has done."

Lifting his eyes, Tynan spied the white-haired goddess with dark orb eyes. "Where is she?"

"I cannot control another's actions. If I could, Messina would never have left the Unseelie court to begin with."

"You can bring her back to me."

"I'm trying. To do that, I need Messina to listen, but she is lost in the fog."

"They have her drugged?" The goddess turned her face away in an answer. "What about my son?"

"He is safe."

"Why did you allow this?"

"I did no such-"

"You let this happen to her," Tynan raged, his anger buffeting against the goddess and her light. "Again, and again, she has been harmed because you allowed it. Are you jealous of her? Is that why you punish her? Mother?"

The Goddess shrank back from his anger, her brightness dimming, her eyes closed, a tear glistening as it cascaded down her white cheek. She took his pain, held it, and tried to ease it. Tynan exhaled in frustration, but he calmed as he faced down the lady of light. "If I lose her, I will never forgive you."

Lifting the lids that covered her darkness, the Goddess appraised him. "If it comes to a choice, the girl or your son, what would you choose?"

"That's an impossible choice."

"Is it?" The Goddess sashayed closer. "Is it really?" Her voice faded as she disappeared from sight.

Tynan heaved a breath, his eyes glancing around him. The mound was healed, the Goddess tending her child before she left. Closing his eyes, Tynan sent up a prayer to see Mess and his son again, to be able to hold them both and watch his son grow to be a man.

Then and there, if the Goddess forced a choice, he knew what it needed to be. He would hate making it, but Tynan knew she'd been right. It wasn't a choice at all.

39

GET A CLUE

❖

"We have no business there?" Esha questioned the directive Tynan had just given him.

"We never used to before the faerie mound reunited and I became the King of all the Fae. Now, our business extends into the previously dominated Seelie areas."

The Unseelie were very analytical, so their business tended to revolve around banking and industry. The Seelie were more your creative souls and therefore managed to make their way in the human world under the guise of actors, musicians, and artists.

Of course, the Seelie was also very political, so they tended to try and control human politics at times too, never as the leader, but as someone with clout. They were the shot caller behind the scene. The Kingmakers.

Now, Tynan ruled both courts and Fae business quite often crossed over into the human domain. Today was one of those days.

"I need that file delivered to Kyrenic by midday. He runs a yoga studio in East district, so that is where I need you to go to."

"This could be another power play."

"It always is," Tynan dismissed Esha's concern. Tynan turned his attention to his desk calendar. "Twelve months to the day."

"Do you still believe she's out there?" Esha queried quietly. He hoped she was, but it had been so long now.

"I know she is. I won't stop looking for her," he vowed.

Esha said no more. He understood Tynan had kept Mess for the crown, but at some point, early in those first few weeks, Mess had gotten under Tynan's skin like nobody else could ever hope too. Tynan had the crown now, in essence, he didn't need Mess anymore, but that didn't keep his bed warm, and it didn't sate his lust in a way no other woman could without screaming in agony. The crown didn't give Tynan his mate.

Bowing his head, Tynan took the papers. If it was general business, a courier would have delivered them or a lesser employee, but not for Fae business, only Tynan's most trusted employees, Esha or Trell, ever handled those.

Watching the city streets pass by, Esha thought about Mess. She belonged with Tynan, but Esha would be lying if he denied being in love with her also. She lit the same fire in him that she did his prince. If it had been any other Sluagh who had her, Esha would have challenged them for her, and he would have won.

Not the prince though, he'd never challenge Tynan. Esha put his case to Tynan once, let him know he felt for her, but Tynan wasn't willing to share. For the first time ever, Tynan had kept something that Esha wanted. That was the moment Esha understood, Mess was more than fun or a crown, but he hadn't given up wanting her.

Letting his head hang low, Esha remembered the one-time Tynan had allowed him to have her. He couldn't say no. Not for Tynan needing him, and not for his own selfish reasons. Esha never expected to see what he had in her memories. He flipped through them to rip out the pain Tynan caused her, but grown confused as to why Tynan casting a glamor on her was torturing her. So, Esha went looking for the answer.

That is when he deepened his understanding of the royal bloodline, of Messina's power, and of her curse. Her memories showed him the woman who set fire to the garden and Esha had taken longer than he needed so he could watch that entire encounter unfold.

He hadn't told Tynan initially. Stewing on it, Esha demanded to know why Tynan cast the glamor. Not till she was gone, had Tynan revealed Messina's vulnerable state.

The Seelie challenged it, stating there was no proof, but Tynan held the amulet of truth as he vowed to the court Mess was legitimately his, by Sluagh law and Sidhe, he and Messina were married.

Now, Tynan was crowned the King. It still bugged the Seelie, a half-breed Sluagh as their King, but so far any challenges had kept the goblins well fed.

When the car arrived at his destination, Esha stepped out. "I can't park here, Esha, I'll find a park and text you where I am."

Nodding his head to the driver, Esha walked into the yoga studio. "Are you here for a class?" A human staff member enquired flirtatiously.

"To see Ky." He was dressed in a suit; did she really think he would be bending and flexing in that. The receptionist toddled off to find her boss. Esha enjoyed the human women perving on him. If only they could see the real him, they would scream, and he'd love every second of it.

The receptionist returned and escorted Esha back to Kyrenic's office. He stepped in, and both waited for the door to close before Kyrenic held out his hand. Esha handed him the documents. "What are you hoping to find?"

"A lead," Kyrenic muttered as he started reading through it. "This was written by the Lunars; I trust them to have done a thorough job."

"We have followed every lead in that document. It got us nowhere."

"Still, fresh eyes couldn't hurt," Kyrenic dismissed. "There were six bodies amongst the debris."

"The three Seelie, Mabon, and two goblins."

Kyrenic flicked through the pages to look at the photos of the body pieces. They had been collected and reassembled as best they could be for identification. "This goblin doesn't have the same outwardly appearance as most goblins."

"Margo was half human. Except for her eyes, she could pass for human, albeit a short one," Esha mourned. He missed Margo. Missed the stash of cheese curls she always kept for him, the way she smiled at him, and the food she cooked. The kitchen had been hers, now, she was gone.

"Her head is more...desecrated then the others."

"Messina and Margo were friends." The Lunar had already detailed and investigated the slight difference in how badly cut up Margo had been. "Messina couldn't control her powers, but we believe when she realized she had killed someone she cared about, it cut her up emotionally. Since she was using a spirit power, we believe her power manifested that emotional pain physically on the poor creature."

"Did she feel the goblin betrayed her?"

Esha looked to his feet. "Her father was selling her into a life of misery and pain for his own personal pleasure. I think it is safe to say she felt betrayed by everyone in that room. It was just unfortunate that the goblins were there serving food when the emotional turmoil became too much to bear."

"I guess the Sluagh would consider living in the golden court miserable," Kyrenic gritted.

"No, Messina was cursed by her mother. The touch of the Seelie literally caused her extreme agony. I saw what it did to her first hand." Esha held out his hand. "I can show you the memory if you would like to understand."

Kyrenic considered Esha's hand. "You expect me to trust you?"

"No more than I trust your hand of leprosy."

Considering Esha, Kyrenic nodded before folding up the sleeve of his jacket. Esha put his arm on Kyrenic's and passed the memories of Messina being touched by Seelies. It is not something Esha would freely offer usually, but Kyrenic was basically the head of the Seelie now, after Ashling's demise. If they were to stop the challenges against Tynan and learn to coexist, they needed his support.

Esha stepped away, Kyrenic staying locked in the memory a moment longer. Blinking, he shook his head. "The poor girl, to be denied her own kind," Kyrenic sighed.

Esha rolled his eyes. "I also witnessed when Tynan first met Messina when she was five. Would you like me to share when she recognized the Sluagh prince as her home and hearth?" Esha offered sardonically. "I witnessed a lot of their passion. I assure you; it was not made up on either side. They are truly made for one another."

Kyrenic grimaced. Esha understood. What he had shown Kyrenic cemented the fact that killing Tynan would not win anyone else the crown.

"Even if we get her back, the most you could hope for is an Unseelie King in the Prince's place, but they would never be half the king Tynan will be," Esha promised.

Huffing, Kyrenic closed the file. "Is there anything else that could assist us that you have left out of this file?"

"Nothing," Esha lied. There was the woman from the garden, but Esha didn't think sharing the fact the goddess herself had condemned Messina to be the Prince's plaything would benefit anyone. He was curious if she was behind Mess disappearing off the face of the planet. If all she wanted was the child...

Kyrenic scrutinized Esha. With a deep exhale of acceptance, he held the document. "May I keep this?"

"You may." It was a copy, not the original. With any luck, after a year, the Seelie and Unseelie may just start to coexist peacefully. Now, if he could only find Mess.

Walking outside, Esha pulled out his phone to locate the driver. It was overcast today, so he wasn't worried about walking in the sunlight. Following the directions to his left, Esha put away his phone to watch where he was going. Stopping at a crosswalk for the lights, he took in his surroundings.

He'd never been to this part of the city before, with its alternative medicine, yoga, Pilates, alternative bookstores, music shops, hipster cafes, and art galleries. It wasn't the sort of place a Sluagh would come to hang out, nor any sort of Unseelie really. So, it surprised him, even more, when he looked through the window of a shopfront diagonally across from him and saw Pride standing there.

Pride had been so withdrawn since Messina's disappearance,

Esha half expected to find out Pride was in love with her also. Frowning as the light turned green, he crossed to the storefront, wanting to know what Pride was doing here. That's when it occurred to him, he looked too small, and he was in his natural form. Even more discombobulating, right behind Pride stood another Pride in his human appearance, looking debonair in a tuxedo.

Esha was more confused with every step. Pride, like most red caps, had a human form. It meant he didn't have to cast a glamor to walk amongst the humans. For this reason, a lot of red caps joined the army. Where else could you keep your hat bloody with the life of your enemy?

In front of the store now, Esha looked in the window at a very life-like painting of Messina's former bodyguard. Esha felt his jaw drop as he spied a few other depictions on the internal walls. Taking several steps back, Esha looked at the name of the store and pulled out his phone texting his driver before pressing the call button.

"Is it delivered?" Tynan asked.

"Yes, I think he will come around. That isn't why I called."

"Is there a problem?"

"I'm looking at Pride through the window of a store."

"In the east district?" Tynan sounded concerned.

"And in his natural form. I'm also looking at myself running through the devil's forest, chasing a scared girl. Brie and Sauvignon are naked, markings on display, making love in their bedroom as they decimate the men who abused Mess."

"What are you talking about?"

"And right at the back of it all, I'm looking at you, shirtless, in bed, making love to your wife, and it is your bedroom I'm looking at, Ty," Esha clarified.

"Where are you?"

"An art gallery. The poster by the door is promoting gothic art painted by M. U. B. Ard."

"Messina Ui Bayne-Ard?" Tynan breathed.

"The car is on the way to get you," Esha informed as he pulled open the door. "I think you want to buy some art."

Tynan arrived faster than expected. He was angry. If Mess was selling her art, painting them, then she remembered and was hiding from him. Esha was already inside browsing. A painting holding his attention.

"Esha," Tynan murmured taking in the painting of Esha and Tynan in the kitchen. It was a fantastic painting, the detail almost perfect. Tynan's face slightly different practically set to make him unidentifiable to anyone but those that knew him well.

"This is from the day we first met her," Esha murmured. He pointed to the cane Tynan held in the painting. "That is your old cane before you broke it fighting that red cap ten years ago. She was five, but with the detail, you could believe it happened yesterday."

Tynan remembered that day like it was yesterday. "I am your light in the darkness," Tynan whispered, emotions boiling in him. Anger, grief, the anxiousness that they finally had a lead. "Have you spoken to the owner?"

"Told her I was looking for a piece for my boss and that I thought you would like that one," Esha pointed to the one of him being intimate with a female who looked a lot like Mess. Tynan's features were blurry, but his Sluagh markings were clear. There was no mistaking it was meant to be him.

"I told her I'd called you to come and approve the purchase. It is the most expensive piece by the way."

"Mr. Cargella," a woman in a bright pink professional style dress moved towards them, her heels slapping against the polished cement floor.

"Your show now, boss," Esha explained as he turned to the woman. "Simone, this is my boss, Mr. Wane."

Simone's eyes lit up. "Mr. Wane, what an honor."

"Can you tell me about this piece?" Tynan pointed to the scene of intimacy.

"The artist is obsessed with monsters. But in this piece, other than the markings, both subjects seem normal."

"This character tends to repeat in a lot of the artworks," Tynan said of himself, pointing to all the other pieces he starred in, even with his back to the artist.

Simone's eyes dulled, sadness filling them as she looked over the painting. "He haunts her dreams. At least, that's what she tells her carers."

"Carers?" Esha and Tynan asked simultaneously.

"Sadly, the artist is talented, but not entirely sane," Simone explained sympathetically. "Such a shame, she's such a pretty little thing."

"Could you explain more?" Tynan requested.

Simone hesitated, eyes flicking to the painting, then back to Tynan before she forced a smile. "No, it's such a sad story, and I don't know all the facts. I'd rather discuss the art."

"Simone, I plan to buy at least three of these paintings today," Tynan took his unhappy tone, "but I want to know everything you know about the artist, starting with her name."

Simone's eyes lit up at the thought of the sale. "Well, I actually don't know her real name, I've never met her, just seen her in her room through the door. I've been working with the local mental health network to help promote the work of artists with mental health issues. Once a week, I pick up the paintings from the outreach coordinator. The money from the sales go to the artists, or in this case, towards clothes and supplies, she needs for her therapy. The coordinator brought Mess to my attention some months ago now."

"Therapy?" Tynan asked confused.

"The coordinator tells me the artist was registered as M. U. B. Ard and goes by the name Mess. She never talks to them anymore because they won't believe her about the monsters. I only know she's pretty because of the paintings."

Moving to a cabinet on the side, Simone opened a drawer as she kept talking. "The poor girl, she is so sure these monsters are real, she kept trying to run off into the woods. I have no idea how it came about, but she's institutionalized now."

Simone walked back to the painting with a magnifying glass. "Initially, the paintings were all like that," she indicated the one of

Lucifer, large and scary and very lifelike. Tynan imagined Lucifer would quite like that painting of himself. "Then she started painting him," Simone admired the painting of Tynan and Mess being intimate.

"The intimate ones always sell the best, but knowing the real story behind them takes some of the beauty away, so I prefer not to share it." Simone pointed to a mirror in the back of the room and placed a magnifying glass for Tynan and Esha to see. "Instead, I prefer to focus on the amazing detail."

There in the mirror, painted so small you wouldn't automatically see it, was Mess. It looked like she was banging against the mirror trying to get out as if she was trapped inside of it. "She's crying," Tynan murmured.

Simone nodded before she stepped to the painting of Tynan and Esha. In this one, the fridge caught her reflection. Again, too small for the naked eye to make out, Mess stood holding a baby. She smiled down at the naked chubby thing, crying, her eyes sad despite the smile on her face. The child bore the Sluagh markings.

"She has the child?"

"I'm not sure if she does or it was a dream. I asked the coordinator about it, that's how I found out about the girl's story," Simone sighed. "The poor girl, so talented, but so lost in this terrifying world inside her head. Her way of coping with what was done to her."

If Tynan asked what Simone meant by that comment and the answer set of his power, it wouldn't end well for anyone. Gripping the magnifying glass, Tynan decided Distraction would be safer.

"Do you know which institution she is in?" Tynan queried, using the magnifying glass to study the marks on his son. Best to focus on what his son's abilities were because if Mess painted them accurately, he would be a force of nature just like his father and mother.

"There is only one private one locally," Simone sighed. "The sanitarium, it's half an hour out of the city on the Northern Distributor."

Tynan looked to Esha who quickly pulled out his phone and started looking the place up. "She is an amazing artist." He considered the paintings around him. "I'll take all the ones with him, plus those three over there." Tynan selected the ones of Lucifer, Pride, and Brie.

Simone's eyes were glistening sapphires. "Of course, Mr. Wane."

"Simone, considering the investment I'm making, is there anything else you could tell me about this girl, about her family perhaps."

Simone nodded as she started sticking sold labels next to the artworks. "Not much, but I did hear that it was her sister who had her committed."

"Do you know the sister's name?" Tynan asked while she was busy.

"Margo."

40

KIN BETRAYAL

❖

abon stood by the window whispering in a Seelie's ear. The woman looked unhappy as he feathered her golden hair. By the lounge stood Ashling and a Solaris soldier. On seeing me, Ashling smiled warmly. Contradictorily, her eyes looked at me with absolute loathing. "And here she is, in the flesh," Ashling sashayed towards me.

"She has the Unseelie coloring," the Solaris muttered unimpressed. His golden eyes appraising me like livestock.

"You obviously weren't around during the age of Titan, Glarald," Mabon smiled coming towards us, happiness radiating from him. "She is the image of her grandfather."

"That she is," Ashling agreed. "Though, she holds her mother's beauty and radiance."

Mabon took my shoulders in his hands. "Messina, it is time."

"No. You left it too long."

Mabon's smile slipped a little. "You talk of the mating? True, I did not expect that of Tynan, but it matters not to the Sidhe. A woman is not married until a child grows in her womb."

"It matters to me. I am the Prince's mate. There is nothing to be done about it now." I turned to leave.

Grabbing my arm, Mabon yanked me back to him. "Don't you dare turn your back to me. I am your King," he snarled.

Meeting his glowing eyes without hesitation, I showed no fear. Honestly, Mabon had nothing on scary after a year with Tynan. "I have run the gauntlet and crossed the wall, and I am the queen of the Seelie. You are my equal."

"You are not crowned our queen," Ashling sussurated.

"If you had your way, I never would be. How many Seelie have you sent to their death to assassinate me, just so you could remain ruler?"

The other Seelie looked at Ashling horrified.

"None, I sent our people to their death trying to rescue you."

"Lier. I was told to my face by your would-be assassins what your orders were. I know you had my mother murdered because her assassin confessed his sin to me before he died."

"She speaks the truth," the female Seelie by the window informed everyone, her expression aghast. "Dear gods, Ashling, you have been killing the Royals for decades."

"Shut up, Nexxis," Ashling raged.

Looking horrified, the Solaris Captain moved forward, and a moment later Ashling cried out in pain as she fell to her knees on the ground. Her arms were restrained with iron shackles behind her back, but her panting breath indicated she was in pain. Glarald bowed to me. "Ashling is charged with treason against the crown and her people. I will ensure she never harms you again."

"Bring in the bond breaker," Mabon called.

"No!" I fought against his grip on my arm. Using a move Esha showed me, I managed to break free.

"Restrain her," Mabon ordered.

Amp grabbed my arm, Glarald the other, his grip like acid pouring over my skin causing me to scream from the pain Glarald's touch caused me. A Seelie stepped before me, placing his hand over my wrist and the tattoo of my bond with Tynan. Gut-wrenching agony pierced me, two Seelie touching me was ten times worse than one. It only got worse as a thousand needles stabbed at Tynan's mark and started twisting and turning through my skin and tendons.

The pain was driving me out of my mind. "Stop, please, stop! Let me go, you're hurting me! Tynan, please help, please," I cried. "Stop! Mercy, please, mercy. Let me go!" I screamed. They heard none of it. The pain went on, and on, my mind trying to break free from my body and escape this torture.

The needles gave one final spin and stopped. There was a minor fleeing sensation, my blood fleeing through my veins, trying to get away from my breaking heart.

"Let the princess go, your touch makes it worse," Amp ordered. The Seelie let me go, and Amp supported me as I fell to the floor dizzy and disorientated. "Mess, I'm sorry."

Pain radiated up my arm. Through water-filled eyes, I could see Tynan's mark was gone. In its place was an ugly red welt, burst open, bleeding and weeping pus and serum onto the floor. Unable to tell which way was up, and which way was down, I sat there sobbing on the floor. Hurt like never before, I acknowledged my heart ached worse than any other part of me.

"Amp, go to the Seelie court, ensure they understand Ashling's betrayal and that my daughter will be safe," Mabon ordered. Those words echoed in my head.

Daughter.

He was my father, and he was selling me out to the Seelie for his own personal gain. A flash of anger and hatred more potent than any I'd felt before overcame me.

"Ah, here is tea," Mabon clapped his hands happily.

"Tynan, please," I begged the stone floor. "I love him."

The silence stretched through the room. "Don't be foolish, Messina," Mabon recovered first. "You are young. Soon you will realize he was just using you to gain your crown."

"No. Tynan loves me."

"Such naivety," Mabon mourned. "A hundred years from now, you will know better."

My anger boiled over, rose up around me like a tornado of pain. "The Dark Prince loves me!"

SITTING UP, I was suddenly wide awake, heart pounding, and sweating from the memory of my pain. "He loves me." The room was foreign to me; it blurred, and then came back into focus. Slipping from the sheets, I looked out the window. There were bars on the outside of the glass, and beyond that, a clearing before a forest of trees. "Where am I?"

Going to the bedroom door, I eased it open and checked the living area. Everything was dark, the only light coming from outside through the curtained windows.

"Hello? Tynan? Esha? Pride?" My heart raced in my chest. I hadn't ever stepped out of my room and not found at least one of those three waiting for me since Tynan found me.

Moving into the open space, I took in the timber furnishings, the simple accessories, and the humanness of my surroundings. My heart started beating frantically, struggling to draw breath as I panicked about where I was. "Ty? Hello? Anyone?"

A door opened and closed. I stopped. Everything in me stilled in wait, my feet pressing into the floor in case I needed to run. A drum was beating in my ears as I waited to see who was here with me.

A small female walked around the corner, her large goblin eyes wary as they took me in, her clothes so different and human compared to the outfits she wore as the cook in the Unseelie kitchen. "Margo?"

"Messina, you're awake. How do you feel today?"

"Confused. Where am I?"

Pressing her lips together, Margo huffed. "You give me the same answer every day, and every day ends the same way. Could we try for something a little different after all these weeks?"

"Weeks?" Stopping to consider Margo, I looked around the house. Flashes of a storm of blood and pain pierced my vision. "Mabon tried to trade me," I breathed. Margo's face floated above me, the memory of her helping me to stand and leading me down a dark stone passageway. "You helped me escape."

"You killed the King. You committed treason. The heir or not, you would need to be punished. I saved you."

"Saved me? Where are we?"

"I'm sick of explaining, Messina. You need to remember." Turning her back, Margo walked further into the house, then the clutter of pans banging in a kitchen started. Following the noise, flashes of sitting on the lounge, in the yard, in the kitchen and Margo talking to me filtered through my memory.

As I entered the kitchen, I looked her over. "Is that a school dress?"

Margo lifted a brow at me. "Is it? Rupert likes me to wear it while we fuck."

"Rupert?"

"He's the human who owns this house. We met on the internet. We met a few times, and he brought me a pretty pink dress to wear for him, while I sucked his dick. When I told him I wanted to leave home and be with him, he offered for me to live here in his cabin. He was worried at first when I turned up with you, but when I told him you were my sister and our father hurt you, he was happy to let you live here too. He brings me clothes to wear, food to eat, and we have sex."

"Are all the clothes childlike?"

Frowning, Margo looked down at her school uniform. She looked all of ten dressed like that, especially with her tawny hair in pigtails. "I don't know what you mean?" Her face clearing, Margo continued to make some food.

"It doesn't matter. I have a job at the hospital now. I have to use glamor to appear more human and older because no one believed I was an adult, but once I start getting a regular paycheque, I won't need to keep fulfilling all Rupert's dirty fantasies. I'll just eat him. Until then, Rupert wants to bring a friend of his over to meet me, said you might be interested in him."

"No, I want to go home to Tynan."

Margo stopped. "You can't. To the Fae, we are dead, Messina. We died in the manifestation you killed your father with, just like everyone else in the room. This is our home now."

"But, I'm not dead. Tynan will be happy to find me alive."

Growling under her breath, Margo put a bowl of food on the table for me. My stomach cramped in hunger. Sitting down, I started eating. Margo waited until I was several mouthfuls in, and then argued her case.

"Messina, he captured you as a toy, hurt you, and treated you like a plaything. The fact you were a princess didn't stop him, and he let everyone think you were a nobody until it suited him for everyone to know the truth. Then he forced you to mate with him just to steal your crown. As soon as you were declared dead, that's what he did, Messina. He took your throne and claimed the crown of both the Unseelie and Seelie courts. He could never have done that if you weren't mated to him. He doesn't care about you now. In fact, if you show up, he will more than likely kill you."

"No!" I shoved the nearly empty bowl away. I must have been starving to eat that quickly. "Ty loves me. I know he does."

The world tilted a little, I grabbed the bench to stop from falling out of my seat. Blinking at the bowl, I tried to lift my eyes to Margo, but the room spun out of control. "You drugged me."

Sighing, Margo walked around the bench and helped me out of the chair, taking me towards my room. My brain was fuzzy, my eyes wouldn't focus, and I was too weak to fight her off. "One day, you'll wake up and be willing to hear me out. Until then, Messina, I'll keep you safe."

The memory of Margo walking me into this cabin the night Mabon broke the bond trickled into conscious thought. In too much pain, my brain bleached out and jellied, I didn't realize where we were until Margo tucked me into bed in the little house.

"Tynan," I begged.

Patting my hair, Margo gave me a reassuring smile. "Rest, Mess. Our new lives will start tomorrow."

~

"COME ON, Honey, wake up and play."

Slowly, my eyelids opened. The cold hit me firstly; the stale smell of mildew came next. Lifting my head from the pillow, I raised my hand to brush my hair out of my face, but the heavy weight around my wrist caught my attention. Blinking at the shackle, I opened my eyes wide. "What's happening?"

"There you are," a man standing beside the bed smiled at me. "I've been worried, I haven't heard from my brother Rupert in two weeks now. So, I decided, I'd drive out to the cabin and see if he was here. Instead, I find you chained to the bed in the basement. You're older than my brother usually likes them. He prefers pre-teens." The man touched my cheek, ants crawling under my skin from the contact. "You're the perfect age for me, and so pretty with those eyes open."

My brain was still fuzzy when the man pulled the blankets back on the bed and touched me between my legs. Screaming, I tried to kick my leg, but pain blossomed all along my limb when the shackle holding it restricted my sudden movement. "Now, I understand all the restraints," the man chuckled. "You're a feisty one. I like the wild ones, like taming them."

He went to a table and opened a box. Walking back towards me with a syringe in hand, he sat beside me on the bed. "This must be what my brother has been using on you." His eyes appraised my nakedness. "By the looks of those bruises, you're a fighter, and while I admire that, I also like the play time to end rather quickly."

"No, please, don't," I sobbed as he held my arm and injected the liquid into me.

"There we go. Now, let's play." Moving to the wall, he released a length of chain, and all the restraints loosened. "There you go. You can stand up and move around the room now." Stepping back, he started undressing.

Sure of his intent, I sat up, then, placing my feet on the floor, I held onto the bed head to pull myself to standing and stumbled towards the stairs. I was halfway there when the restraints jerked me back. When the man's hand grabbed my hip as he pressed himself behind me, tears trickled down my cheek.

Closing my eyes, I prayed to the goddess, and a purple glow encapsulated me. "Tynan." When I opened my eyes I was bleeding, but I was free, the chains acid etched and broken. A shard of glass still held in my hand, bloody and dripping, and on the floor was the body of a man, his neck gashed and bleeding. Dropping the weapon, I stumbled up the stairs, found the door, and walked randomly into the trees. Everything hurt, especially my feet, and back and my womb was cramping horribly.

Blue and red lights lit up the darkness surrounding me. "Miss, are you okay?"

How I got out or to the hospital, I couldn't remember. I blinked, and a nurse stood over me. "Honey, did you know you were pregnant?"

"Pregnant?" I tried to ask, but my mouth felt full of cotton wool.

"It's okay, sweetheart, we are going to take care of you." The memory of Tynan telling me I carried his child and the glamor he placed over me to protect it was suddenly vivid techno-color in my mind. The nurse lifted her face to other shadows around me. "She's high as a kite. I think whoever had her has been drugging her."

"We won't be able to give her anything for the pain."

"I doubt she needs it."

Everything blurred, and then period cramps brought me back to the room and the doctor and nurses. "Come on, honey, push."

Gritting my teeth, I curled up and pushed down as hard as I could as long as I could, over and over, every time the nurse squeezed my hand, I pushed, and then she smiled at me as the pain disappeared. "Well done, you can rest now."

"My baby?"

"We need to take him for tests. What is in your system might have affected him. Once he's checked over, we'll let you hold him."

A nurse walked into the room, blurry in features, big eyes wide as they recognized me, and then went to the baby. "She was pregnant?"

The nurse holding my baby handed it to her. "Take him to the nursery and check him over. He may have neonatal abstinence syndrome form whatever they've been drugging the girl with."

The new nurse took the baby in her arms, eyes full still, fear pulsing in her retina as she met my eyes. Through the blur, she shrunk, and for a moment, Margo stood there holding my son. "No! Don't let her take him," I screamed.

Pulse racing, the nurse became blurry again, and then she quickly turned and walked away, my son swaddled in her arms. "No, no, no, stop her!"

"What is she saying?" the nurse near me asked. "Shit, she's not even speaking English. We need to restrain her; she's bleeding and needs treatment."

My fear elevated, I needed to get my son back, and Margo was at the door. A sea of anxiety for the safety of my child filled the room drowning me in terror and rage for the woman who took my baby away, who took me away from the man I love. Then everything went black.

~

"Ah, here is tea," Mabon clapped his hands happily.

"Tynan, please," I begged the stone floor. "I love him."

The silence stretched through the room. "Don't be foolish, Messina," Mabon recovered first. "You are young. Soon you will realize he was just using you to gain your crown."

"No," I wheezed. "Tynan loves me."

"Such naivety. A hundred years from now, you will know better."

My anger boiled over, rose up around me like a tornado of pain. "The Dark Prince loves me!"

Sitting up, I was suddenly wide awake, heart pounding, and sweating from the memory of my pain. "He loves me." Peering around my stark white room, everything in here part of the molded furnishings to disable chaos. The only soft thing in the room was my mattress. "He loves me, he'll come for me."

Eyes catching on the painting on the wall, pulling me back to my present. Tynan, the first night I met him, standing tall and deadly as he gave his birthday speech. How long had it been? Was he still looking for me? Did he even try to find me? "He loves me, he'll come for me."

The movement of my fingers over raised flesh drew my attention to the scar on my wrist, a faded zigzag that was once a W. The doctors told me it was from a previous attempt to commit suicide, but I didn't believe them. Still, I'd stopped fighting them, and quit talking about Tynan as a real person. They told me the monsters in my paintings were my brain's way of coping with the trauma I suffered.

According to my psychiatrist, my sister admitted me to the institution when I attacked her thinking she was a demon. In my history, it said I'd been abducted and repeatedly raped and brutalized. There was no mention of my son, but I remembered he was born, and I know Margo took him away.

Margo. There was no memory of how I came to the facility; I just woke up here one day, my recollection of the Fae court all a coping mechanism to avoid dealing with the actual events that occurred.

Blinking back to my little hospital bedroom, I lifted the faded scar to my lips. "I'm still waiting for you to come and save me. Hurry up."

Closing my eyes, I let sleep fold me back into its arms. Always cold. I hadn't been warm since Tynan left my side that day. Remembering what it was like, made it worse. Now, I knew what it was to feel warm, safe, and loved, and have it taken away.

41

VIVID DREAMS

❖

"You have a visitor," Bradley, one of the nurses informed me. I didn't get excited. I'd stopped expecting it to be Tynan months ago. It was always the doctor or the mental health coordinator who sold my paintings for me. The white-haired goddess told me the pictures would take me home, but after months, I was still here, and the pain of not knowing what happened to my son had left me numb.

There was a murmur at the door behind me, but I kept my eyes on the painting. Goyle biting a Seelie's head off, blood spraying everywhere. "Rather morbid, Mess," his deep voice cut through the ambient noise of the recreation room.

Holding my breath, I kept my eyes on the painting in front of me. Was it truly him? "You took your time." Placing my paintbrush and palette down, my hands trembled with anxiety.

"I apologize for my tardiness," Tynan replied sincerely. Taking a breath, I looked over my shoulder. Tynan stood there. Quickly, I looked back at my painting, tears avalanching from my eyes. "Are you not happy to see me, Mess?"

"I'm terrified."

"I'm not going to hurt you, Mess."

Closing my eyes, forcing the tears to run faster, I shook my head. "That isn't what scares me."

"What does?"

"I've dreamed of this moment so vividly, so many times now, only to wake up and find it wasn't real. How do I know it's real?"

Moving closer behind me, Tynan wrapped his arms around me. They felt so real, so warm, just like I remembered, but that warmth didn't seep into me like it always had in reality. The comparison told me the answer; I broke down crying.

The room faded out, Tynan's warm embrace the last thing to leave me as I cried myself back to consciousness in my hospital room. Waiting for the sorrow to wane, another small piece of my hope burnt to ashes.

Was I wrong? Was none of it real and just my imagination? Perhaps what they told me happened was right, and I'd gone crazy as a result. Tracing the scar on my wrist, I shook my head and refused to admit they were right. It had happened, it hadn't been a dream.

A key in my door alerted me to someone entering. Drying my eyes, I sat up. If I acted normal, unaffected, they didn't drug me, so I tried to pretend I was staying in a hotel, and the nurses were the staff. I tried to push everything else out of my brain during daylight.

The door opened and Sandra, the psychiatrist I'd been appointed too, stepped in. "Morning, Mess. How are you feeling?"

"I'm craving a pizza," I responded blandly.

"Have you been crying?"

"I was thinking about Druce, wondering if he's started crawling yet."

Sandra's face fell in sympathy. She believed that I was stuck in a world of monsters, that I'd been raped and that there was a baby as a result of that rape. That isn't what I told them, but my story was even more unbelievable than the idea I thought monsters were real. "There is a policeman here to talk to you," Sandra explained gently. "Would you have a shower and talk to him?"

Confused by this change in routine, I studied her. Her hands were trembling a touch. What had happened to scare her? "Why?"

"Well, he's investigating the disappearance of a young woman, and he wants to see if you know anything about it."

"Why now? It's been a year. None of you has believed me this long."

"I'll let the policeman explain." Sandra walked back to the door where the nurse was waiting. "Let Janet know when you are ready."

Turning my attention to Janet, I felt my throat tighten. She was blurry, but I knew what that meant. Hope jumped high in my throat. Could it be? Finally, after all this time?

Moving steadily to the shower, I took my time washing. Dressing in a clean set of clothes, I knocked on the closed door. Opening the door, Janet smiled at me. "You look pretty today, Mess. You looked like a real disaster yesterday."

Peering at her, I tried to see who I was really talking too. "Who found me?"

The question made her smirk, and I caught a glimmer of chalk white skin, tattoos along her exposed arms, and lava red eyes. What gave her away was the steampunk outfit. Heart pounding in my chest, I covered my mouth to stop from screaming for joy.

"Brie?"

Janet stopped to consider me. "How did you know?"

In the time I'd been gone I forgot no one knew I could see through glamor. Only Tynan and Mabon. "Janet never had your fashion sense. She couldn't rock those scrubs the way you do."

The answer made Brie preen. "Come on, he'll never admit it, but he's jumping out of his skin to see you.

THE POLICE WERE real and nervous as I took the seat designated me. A female and male policeman wearing suits, not uniforms, sat watching me. They introduced themselves as detectives Jenkins and Collins while Brie shut and stood by the door.

"Miss Ui-Bayne-Ard?" Collins, the female greeted, her eyes full of concern.

"Just call me Mess, please."

"Mess, could you tell us about the circumstances that brought you here?"

"You won't believe me. I've been telling everyone here for months, and they just drug me up and lock me up."

"Try me," Collins soothed.

"I'm married to Tynan Wane. Twelve months ago, I was abducted. A lot of the year, I can't remember, but I know I escaped at one point when I went into labor. I gave birth to my husband's son, but then the woman found me, and she took my baby. I woke up here nearly six months ago, but no one believes me."

The male detective, Jenkins, placed photos of the room I gave birth in on the table, the staff lying dead. Covering my mouth, I resisted crying. Had I done that? My body was lying unconscious on the bed, did that mean it was someone else? Perhaps, Margo did that?

"We believe you, Mess. We've been looking for you as well." He placed photos of me from when the police who found me took evidence on the table. "Do you remember what happened at the hospital?"

Blinking away tears, I shook my head. "I'm sorry. They were all alive when the woman walked out with my baby. I was fighting them to try and stop her, but then everything went blank. The next thing I remember was being here."

Jenkins looked at a piece of paper. "The hospital ran a tox screen on your blood when you were brought into the emergency room. Someone had been giving you Midazolam. Do you know what that is?"

When I shook my head, he read from notes he'd written at the bottom of the page. "It's an anesthetic that is known for its amnesiac effect. The drug is usually used in date rape because it causes memory loss at the time it's being administered and for some time afterward. If your abductors were giving this to you while they had you, it accounts for your poor memory. There is also research going into the claims that it can cause worsening short-term memory. My understanding from your hospital records here is that you struggled to remember where you were for over a month every morning after you woke up." Jenkins lifted his gaze to Brie.

"That's right, yes." Brie agreed. "According to her file, Mess became increasingly distressed when she couldn't understand why she was here and why no one would believe who her husband was and call him."

The detectives looked at each other, the female sympathetic, the male grimacing. Removing the photos from the table, Jenkins continued with the questions. "Do you know who else was involved in your kidnapping?"

A sob caught in my throat. "My father."

The police looked at each other then back to me. "Mess, we believe you," Collins assured. My head flew up to see if her words were right. "Your husband, Tynan Wane, submitted a missing person report for you a year ago, but the police who received the report never followed up on it. They assumed he abused you and you ran away."

Collins licked her lips. "Your stepfather's body was found along with his friend. Witnesses tell us he ran into you at a nightclub where you revealed you were married to Tynan. We found evidence in your stepfather's apartment to show they planned your abduction, and an exact match for the ransom note they sent your husband was found."

My brow pinched as I tried to reason out my memories of what happened to Chris and this news. Tynan must have set that up, created a cover story for the humans. My eyes went to Brie in the corner and back to the police.

"We understand the woman who took your son was your husband's private chef?" Jenkins asked. I nodded. "We believe she was employed by your stepfather to lure you away from your bodyguard. However, once the ransom was paid, they tried to cut her out of the deal. Evidence suggests she killed her accomplices and took the money for herself."

"Mr. Wane tells us you were very close with Margo," Collins took over. "We believe she put you here where your story wouldn't be heard because she couldn't bring herself to kill you."

"She has my son," I whimpered.

"Unfortunately, no one knows where Margo is, or if she still has your son," Collins mourned. "The staff here have informed us of everything that has happened to you in their care, but the contact details Margo provided when she committed you were fake, and we haven't been able to locate her."

Tears streamed down my cheeks, anxiety for his well-being gnawing away my insides. Jenkins looked down at his notes, my tears more than he could handle. "You are going to be released immediately, and we will keep searching for Margo and your son."

"Is this real?" I asked between sobs. "I've dreamt this so many times. How do I know it's real and not another dream? I don't want to wake up again and find this wasn't real."

The police looked at me with pity. Jenkins stood up and looked at Brie. "Could we let Mr. Wane in?"

Watching through water-filled eyes as Brie opened a door, I wondered if I was about to wake up and find it all another lie. Just another torture of my psyche. His cane came through first, followed by his black suit, his black eyes, and short styled hair. Right behind him was Esha, glamorized, but it was Esha, and behind him, Pride in his human form.

Moving before I realized it, I jumped into Tynan's arms, wrapping my legs around his waist and holding on with pure relief and hope. My delusions never had the three of them in the same room, my brain's defense, so when it really happened, I would know.

"Ty, oh my god, Ty. I've missed you so much."

Wrapping me in his arms, Tynan held me tight. His heat suffused me, encapsulated me, a fire in my heart and belly ignited, warming me up throughout.

"Mess," Happiness filled me at my name on his lips. "My light in the darkness."

"My home and hearth. She took him," I whimpered. "I was too weak to protect him, and they held me down while she took him."

"Breathe," Tynan cooed, patting my hair and holding me tight. "Just breathe, Mess. It is all going to be alright. We'll find her. We know who we are looking for now."

Relaxing in his arms, all the emotions I'd been holding in hit me like a cannonball to the gut. Breaking down crying in his arms, I couldn't stop. Tynan held me, not admonishing me, just kept me tight against him.

"I've missed you too, Mess," Tynan whispered in my ear. "Everything is going to be alright, and we are going to be happy together. I swear it."

"I don't care," I told him, my tears finally abating. "I just need to be with you. I need our son in my arms, and goddess, Ty, I need you to fuck me so damn hard I can't walk for a week afterwards."

Smiling, Tynan took my face in his hands. "I love you so much, Mess," he laughed, then he kissed me, deep and slow and so full of everything we both felt for each other.

Melting into him, I soughed against his mouth, enjoying the pinch and pull of his hot lips on mine. My body tightened around his, and I forgot there were others present, that we were standing in the interview room of a psychiatric facility, of which I was still legally a patient.

"Um…" someone hesitated behind me as someone else coughed.

"Ty," Esha touched his shoulder. "We know you two have missed one another, but perhaps wait till you get home to show just how much you've missed each other."

Tynan pulled back from the kiss with a smile. "Let's get you released then."

Letting my feet drop to the ground, I turned around to see Collins blushing, and Jenkins looking mighty uncomfortable. "I want to go home."

42

DRAGNET

❖

Going home wasn't immediate. First, the police insisted Tynan take me to the police station and give a formal statement. No one questioned the fuzzy bits of my story; I'd been drugged for a half a year, locked in an institution where everyone told me I imagined my abduction, and god knows what else in-between. That seemed to be enough to let the holes in my story go.

We were still at the police station when Tynan's phone rang. "Excuse me," Tynan murmured as he stepped out of the interview room to take the call. When I struggled to let go of him, Esha came forward from the corner and placed his hands on my shoulders.

"Relax, Pride and I are still here," Esha soothed. Gripping his hand, I noticed for the first time ever, his touch didn't make my skin crawl. It still didn't warm me, but it wasn't uncomfortable.

Detective Collin's observed my struggle to watch Tynan leave with sympathy. "I think we have what we need, Mess. You can go home now. We will call if we discover any leads on your son's whereabouts."

Jenkin's eyes were on the door. "Or, if you were to remember anything else, or happen to find your son, we'd like to be kept informed." The phrasing left me puzzled, and I noticed Jenkin's eyes kept flicking between the door and Esha.

"Of course, Detective. Though, we will not wait to secure Mr. Tynan's son if we happen to locate him first."

"I didn't expect you would. You can leave when you are ready."

Standing the police moved towards the door. "What was that supposed to mean?" Collin's asked her partner quietly on the way out.

"Tynan Wane is known for his temper and the money to get anything he wants. There is a reason no one looked for his wife. They thought they were protecting her. Now that he knows who took his son, it'll be a race to see if our resources or the best Tynan's money can buy, find that woman first."

The door shut behind them and a moment later I was in the arms of Esha and Pride. They held me tight, my relief flooding out of me. "Mess," Esha used his finger to lift my chin, "Ty wants me to dig through your last year for clues, and he wants it now."

Flicking my eyes around me, I realized Pride stood hugging me in a way that blocked the camera from seeing Esha and me. "Can you do it without sex or bringing those memories back for me?"

Hesitating, Esha met Pride's eyes. "No to the first, which is why I need to get you down to the car. For your second question, you'll catch short bits of it, but for the most part, once I've retrieved what I need, you'll remember as much as you do now."

Inhaling deeply, I bit my lip. "Esha, you still feel wrong."

"Is there anything you wouldn't sacrifice to find your son?" Taking the time to consider his question, I answered honestly and shook my head. There is nothing I wouldn't do to bring my son home safely. "Good, because Tynan feels the same, which is the only reason this is being allowed. Let's get down the car."

Pride and Esha escorted me out. "Where's Tynan?" I panicked as they opened the door for the big black stretch car.

"He's organizing the Devils and Goblins in their hunt for Margo," Pride explained. "We won't leave till he is with us."

Sliding onto the side bench seat, I felt nervous and antsy. Yes, I wanted to find Druce, but I hadn't been with anyone that I could remember since Druce was born. Seating himself on the bench next to me, while Pride took up the back seat, Esha opened the minibar and took out a bottle of alcohol. Opening the lid, he handed it to me.

"I need you as relaxed and compliant as you can get, Mess. This isn't a one memory grab. I'm going in to do a dragnet of your last twelve months, so I'm going to need you willing, especially since Tynan isn't here to prevent your more potent powers decapitating me.

"Will it hurt?"

Esha's brow's lifted. "Not if I'm doing it right." The spark in his eyes told me we weren't talking about the memory collection anymore. When he winked, I shoved his shoulder. "If it helps, know that being with me now will help ease you back into being with your husband a little faster."

"Because of the way your spunk lubricates?"

"Yes." Pressing the bottle into my hand, Esha helped guide it to my lips. "Drink up, Mess. Let's find your son."

Opening my mouth, the liquid burnt down my throat, leaving an oak taste on my tongue. When I'd taken one too many mouthfuls, Esha eased the bottle out of my grasp and raised a brow at me. Already the inside of the car was disorientating. A memory of trying to cross a room while it was blurry and moving filtered through, but vanished almost immediately.

After putting the bottle away, Esha sat back and pulled me into his lap. The movement made me dizzy. "Are you okay, Mess?" I nodded. Lifting my face, Esha pressed his lips to mine. The heat of the alcohol ignited in my belly, and immediately, my satiability deployed. Closing my eyes, I let it sweep me away.

Heat and heavy breathing surrounded me, the distant sensation of skin soaked in sweat, of bodies sliding against each other. Through the crack in my eyelids, I saw Esha, naked, hovering above me, his eyes fully open as he moved his body back and forth, but his gaze unfocused. Glimpses of images like dreams kept stealing away my focus from the physical.

Margo all but carrying me down a concealed stairway, my brain addled and unable to form a coherent thought.

The forest outside a car window, a cabin in the woods, a man who leered at Margo and considered me with a sly grin.

Margo chasing me through the woods, tackling me and sticking me with a needle. *'I'm sorry, princess. It's too late to undo it. He'll kill me if he finds out, which means you can't go back either.'*

Another man pinning me down, my brain slowly boiling in my head. As I fought, I heard a mirror smash, then I picked up a shard and stabbed it in his direction repeatedly until he let me go.

The hospital where I cried, begging the nurse to find my son. *'I know, honey. The police are trying. Let me get you something to help you sleep.'* As she walked out, the innocent looking childlike creature came out of the shadows, the wide eyes observing me with interest before it lifted me from the bed in its small but strong arms, and carried me out of the room. Trying to call the nurse for help, but finding myself paralyzed in the child's hold.

Margo peering down at me, sweeping my hair back from my face. *'Is she okay?'*

'She'd be healthier without the poison you've been giving her, but that's none of my business. Where is the child?' Margo walked away and came back with an infant carrier.

'Druce?' Reaching for my son, but my body fell limp from the drugs Margo gave me.

'He'll be safe, Mess. Trust me.' Margo handed the carrier to the child demon. Without another word, he turned to walk away.

'No!' My body was immobile, but my spirit was fierce. I couldn't lose my son again.

'Mess, stop!' Margo screamed. She stared horrified as the demon fell lifeless to the floor. Panting, Margo turned on me. *'He was taking your son to his father. He would have been safe. What have you done? The Urisk is sacred to the goblins. Never to be harmed.'* Margo looked around as if she could undo the harm. Shaking her head, she picked Druce back up. *'You leave me no other choice. You need to go where you can cause no further harm, where they won't believe you, and where the Prince will never find you.'*

My soul fell into a pit of despair as a different sort of agony clutched my heart and crushed it. I was the reason Druce wasn't with Tynan.

"Mess," Esha called to me. Turning towards the door in my hospital room, Esha stood beside the painting of him and Tynan the first time I met them. "You can't linger here. You need to come home with us."

"It's my fault. I killed the demon child. Margo was sending us back to Tynan. I'm the reason it never happened." Shadows fell around the room, Esha eyed them warily.

"Margo was sending Druce to Tynan. She was never sending you back, Mess. By the time you'd escaped to give birth, she'd already found this place and contacted them about admitting you."

An ache filled my head as I tried to think. "How would you know that?"

"The dates in your file. Margo had already called the Sanitarium before you gave birth."

A baby cried down the hall, the piercing scream making me cringe. Esha looked over his shoulder surprised. "It's always crying, day and night," I told him. "If my dreams of Tynan don't wake me up, the baby does."

The center of Esha's brows pinched, his ruby eyes flaring. "Mess, there has never been a baby in the sanitarium."

"You just heard it!"

The shadows grew darker, the sun starting to set, darkness closing in. Esha's pupils dilated as he scanned the coming night. Turning his head to the baby crying, Esha's brow smoothed as he offered me his hand. "Okay, Mess. Why don't we go see why it's crying? Show me the way."

Unsure of why he wanted to go near that piercing cry, I moved closer to him and took his hand. With a gentle smile, Esha walked me out of my room and down the hall towards the baby. At the door where it cried the loudest Esha stopped and appraised me. "You need to open this door, Messina. It's locked to me."

My eyes were watering already, the crying lancing my eardrums, causing me extreme pain. "It hurts."

"Maybe the baby needs our help," Esha encouraged.

Struggling, the pain wanting to bury me in the floor beneath my feet, I reached forward and tugged on the door. It swung open. The crying baby sat with his mop of dark hair and turquoise eyes that were filled with tears. As soon as I stepped into the room, the crying stopped, the baby looking towards me with those beautiful Seelie eyes and reaching out for me.

Hesitating, I wasn't sure what to do. Unhappy, the baby reached for me again, but when I didn't pick it up, his eyes turned molten silver and pain erupted in my legs rendering them useless. Falling to the floor by the baby, he smiled at me, eyes clearing and fell towards me as I gasped for breath. "Esha?" I begged as the baby crawled onto my chest, pinning me down. "Esha, please, I don't want to be here."

Mesmerized, studying the child intently, Esha did nothing to help me as the baby nuzzled it's face into my neck and breathed deeply. "Mama," the baby giggled, and for a moment I relaxed. Then the baby's eyes turned blood red and fangs sprang from its gums as it lurched forward and sank its teeth in my neck.

"Esha!"

Waking suddenly, I lay there panting for several seconds. Vibrations purred through the car bench seat I sat on, my body still damp from exertion, and naked, but a blanket covered me. Lifting my eyes, Pride sat on the back seat, Esha sat opposite, fully dressed, but still tying his tie. A movement behind me made me turn to find Tynan sitting behind me, his location indicating he'd been patting my head on his lap while I dreamt.

Dreaming. What had I been dreaming? I'd been terrified of whatever it was, but now that I was awake, I couldn't remember what it was about. Did it matter? Scrambling forward, I climbed into Tynan's lap and his embrace, clinging to him like my security blanket. "Did you get anything helpful?"

"Esha was able to recover a lot of helpful information," Tynan soothed. His hand sweeping my drenched hair back from my face and holding me tight.

"It got scary towards the end." Tynan stopped breathing for a moment, his eyes lingering across the car. "Ty?"

Clearing his throat, Tynan dropped his eyes to mine. "We nearly lost you in your memories, Mess. It can happen, when the grief is too powerful, when someone gets lost in their trauma, it can be hard to bring them back out."

"Esha did though. I was terrified, and I can't remember why, but I woke up."

Tynan's jaw cracked. "Esha wasn't the one to pull you free. Our son, Druce, saved you. It appears you have remained connected over the months, and he's been feeding on you despite the distance between you."

Concentrating, I couldn't remember seeing him or feeding him. I didn't even get my milk in because I never put Druce to the breast. "I don't understand, I can't recollect seeing him."

Easing my head to his chest, Tynan kissed my crown. "All that matters is that we know he is alive, Mess, and we have an idea where." The back of the car fell silent as it moved down the road. Content just to be in Tynan's arms, I snuggled closer and breathed in his scent. "It's going to be okay, Mess. We will find our son, and I will take you home, and we will be the family we were meant to be."

Trusting Tynan, I relaxed in his arms. He wouldn't lie to me about finding Druce. If he were sure we'd be bringing our son home, I'd believe him and hold onto my hope. Tynan's grip tightened on me to the point of painful.

"My King, your wife has suffered enough without you adding to her hurt," Pride preached.

With great effort, Tynan relaxed his grasp. Lifting my face, I found the mercurial gates of hell peering down at me. "You're angry with me?"

"No, he's angry with what he's seeing done to you in your memories, Mess," Pride soothed. "Esha is sharing what he found valuable."

Having it pointed out, I noted that Tynan's gaze wasn't focused on me. Esha's attention was also vacant. Tynan's hands started forming fists again. "Ty," I whimpered.

Easing his grip, Tynan released me. "Go to Pride, Mess. Just in case I lose my temper." Scrambling across the car, I fell into Pride's embrace and hid my face against his chest.

"Shh, little one, it's a mark of how much he loves you that your pain causes him to lose control so easily," Pride murmured. "Here, get dressed, that way there is no time wasted when we arrive."

"Where?" Allowing Pride to help me redress, grateful he was wearing his human skin when he helped hook my bra closure, I tried peering out the window.

In answer, the car stopped moving. "Here, apparently." Pride hurriedly pulled my dress over my head and pushed me to his other side as the car door opened. Out of the darkness, black fur skeleton legs folded into the car and I felt my breath catch as Lucifer slid onto the seat next to Esha. Now, I knew why Pride moved me to the far side of him.

"My queen, Pride," Lucifer bowed his head. "It is good to see you alive, Queen Messina. We started to lose hope."

"As did I," I answered truthfully.

Bowing an acknowledgment, his eyes went to Tynan and Esha. "It must be a riveting conversation?"

"Esha is relaying important details of the Queen's disappearance."

"As I said, riveting." Lucifer inhaled deeply. "So was the means of garnering the queen's memories, no doubt." His beady eyes latched onto my neck. "Even a blood exchange? What the King won't sell to get his son and heir. He should be careful that his friend doesn't make a new prince himself."

Confused, my hand went to my neck and came away smeared with blood. Surprised, my eyes went wide. "It was not the Sluagh general who bit the queen. The young prince feeds on his mother using his telepathy," Pride explained.

Lucifer's bony brows jumped. "Ah, so the new prince already shows his powers like his father did. It is good he was able to bond with his mother; it is a pity he didn't reach out to his father, or he may have been found months ago."

"Babies favor the body from which they are rended."

"Right you are, Pride." Lucifer turned his gaze away. "I fear the soul is too damaged for saving."

"That is not your call to make."

"She is weak. The goddesses curse is the only reason she is still standing and coherent. If it is lifted, the memories that escape her will tear her apart in seconds."

Movement on the opposite side of the cabin brought everyone's attention to Tynan and his sword in his hand. Following the thin line of silver, the gleam identified the tip against Lucifer's throat. "Be careful about expressing your thoughts, Lucifer. I'd hate for you to lose your tongue."

"Of course, my King. Do you have a location?" Tynan focused his silver gaze on Lucifer and the Devil's eyes unfocused.

"The Devils have photographic memories. They remember every face or place they go. If Tynan shows him the place you were held and any of the Devils have seen it, Lucifer will lead us there," Pride murmured in my ear.

"How can he know what the others have seen?"

"Lucifer is the first true devil. All others were sired from him. He can access the memory of all his kin. Think of his family tree like one large database of information and Lucifer the monitor on which it can all be accessed." Pride fell into silence as Tynan blinked and put his sword away, leaving Lucifer dazed.

"Mess," Tynan called quietly. When his arm went out to the side, I almost dove across the seat to be in his embrace. "None of it was your fault. The young don't control their powers until they control their emotions. Margo knew that, and she gave you substances that forcibly stripped you of all control. The blame lies entirely with her for everything that happened from the moment she took you from the castle. Do not, for one second, think that any of us hold you responsible."

"She just wanted to try being human for a change. Goblins are the bottom of the pecking order in the Faerie mound. Margo wanted a chance at being just like everyone else," I empathized.

"She didn't understand, humans have a class structure too. I guess, no matter what species you are, it is natural for those with the power to hate and abuse those without it," Esha sighed.

"She doesn't deserve either of your sympathies," Tynan growled. "She knew the first day you tried to come home she had made a mistake. Had she sent you back then, none of this would have happened. Margo stole a year of your life, she took our son, stole months of our time with him, and she alone is responsible for the death of the Ursik."

"How very unfortunate for Margo," Lucifer chirped, revealing he was back in the present company. "I know where the cabin is. I will direct your driver." Saying no more, Lucifer stepped out of the car.

My eyes searched Tynan's in the dark. "I warn you now, Mess. You can't protect her. When we find her, focus on your son, let me deal with the traitor."

43

DARK PLACES

❖

The cabin was dark. No lights were on and the cold of the night permeated the limited clothing I wore. Noting how I shivered, Tynan wrapped his left arm around me, keeping his right hand free to use his cane if needed.

"Do you remember it?" When I shook my head, Tynan kissed my temple. "Don't be scared. No one is going to take you from me again."

"I'll search the grounds. I can smell death in our surrounds." Melding into the night, Lucifer vanished out of sight.

Pulling on a pair of leather gloves, Esha nodded once to Tynan before he and Pride strode forward to the cabin. "Be careful, there is the scar of bad majick on this place," Pride cautioned.

Peering over his shoulder, Esha's eyes met mine briefly before turning to Pride. "That might be our Queen's fear."

"Then it was old fear and rage, not her current state." Pride turned his head to regard Esha. "What happened here?"

"Margo, in her ignorance of human ways, brought our Queen to the lair of a pedophile."

"Did he...?"

"Not Mess, no. She was too old for his tastes, but his brother didn't care about age. Thankfully, he liked his victims conscious enough to fight him. In the end, it was his mistake."

At the door, Esha sniffed the air. "Don't touch anything with your bare hands. Margo was an excellent chef with very little majicks, but she was also a master alchemist. The door handle is tainted with poison, and she may have planted other traps too."

Looking disgusted, Pride put his hands behind his back. "After you then."

Watching anxiously as Esha and Pride disappeared inside, I cuddled Tynan harder. "They know how to hunt a goblin, Mess. Be easy. There is no threat to us here. I suspect Margo is long gone."

"Did Esha access all my memories?"

Tynan's fingers gripped where they held me a little tighter. "Yes. You tried to come home to me, Mess. Every day, you tried. The hardest part of watching what happened to you was how much you wanted to come home and the despair you felt at being denied."

"I will always try to come back to you, Ty. You're my home and hearth." His nose nuzzled behind my ear. "But I need to know. What happened to me here?"

Hot breath blew against my neck as Tynan exhaled dynamically. "Physically, very little. You tried to escape many times, but Margo always managed to catch you. As Esha just said, she is a master alchemist, and she booby-trapped the cabin so that if you got out, you wouldn't get far. There was a man who tried to harm you, but you fought back, and he lost, badly. Taking our son from you had a greater psychological impact than any of the physical hurts, Mess."

The door opened, and Pride stepped out, ensuring he didn't touch any of the door furnishings. Looking in our direction, he shook his head. Concerned we'd hit another dead end; I lifted my face to Tynan's to find he held that vacant stare. "What is it?"

"Esha is showing me what he's found," Tynan murmured distantly.

"Anything helpful?"

"Perhaps. There are tricks the humans have that Margo is

unaware of, and we are hoping to use that ignorance to our advantage." With a slow blink, Tynan turned his focus to me, his eyes drifting down my body. "You are cold."

"Not with you near."

"You may not feel it but ignoring your body temperature is not healthy for you." Nodding to his driver, Tynan guided me to the door being opened. "We can wait in the car for the others."

Sliding across the seat to make room for Tynan, I bit my lip nervously. I'd forgotten how hard it was to restrain myself from touching Tynan when we hadn't been physical for some time. Distracted with finding our son was only able to keep us occupied so much, and being alone together in the back of his car was more than my libido could ignore.

"Ty," I breathed his name as I turned to face him. "Do we have time?"

An eyebrow rising, Tynan lifted my hand to his lips. "It's not about time, Mess. You remember what is needed to be with me."

Straddling his thighs, I took Tynan's face in my hands. "Ty, I need you. I've lost so much, and I'm going insane worrying we'll not find Druce. I've been dreaming about you for a year. Prove to me this is real."

Staring up into my eyes, Tynan's eyes flickered silver, then bled out to red. "Mess, it won't just be sex. I'm hungry. I'll demand it all."

Pulling my dress over my head, I stood up enough to work my underwear down my thighs. "Take what you need, just be with me." Stradling his lap again, I lowered the fly on his pants finding him hard and yearning to sate his hunger.

Our mouths collided with force, tongues engaging in a swift battle of domination. Tynan won. He was always going to win. From the moment he'd found me, I'd been his. His shirt and jacket disappeared, our bare chests rubbing, pressing, heating with the contact. Tynan's hands smoothed up my back, gripping my hair as I lifted myself to take his vibrating curse within me. "Mess, we need to do the prework, your body needs to be more than ready..."

"Ty," Taking his hand, I placed it to my dripping core, "I am as ready as I am going to get. Esha did the prework. I need you inside me, now." His eyes studied me, concern filling them, nearly driving back the fire in them. "Please."

With a growl, Tynan lurched forward out of his seat, my back hitting the leather of the side-facing bench. Shoving his pants out of the way, Tynan niched himself in my opening stealing my breath as his tremors passed through the bundle of nerves that could bring me undone.

Capturing my mouth once more, he pushed his vibrating curse into my molten core. Discomfort bordering on horrific pain tore through me, making me grit my teeth and dig my nails into his back. Knowing I could take him was the only thing that stopped me from screaming for him to stop.

Waiting for me to relax, Tynan held himself above me. "Mess?"

"I'm okay. It's okay." Exhaling, I relaxed beneath him, and my body opened to accommodate his size.

Not looking convinced, Tynan rubbed his nose against mine. "I'll try and control the Sluagh in me as long as I can."

Kissing me, Tynan took his time to sink to his full depth, ensuring he was patient and gentle with my body. The first time we did this, it took us three attempts to bury him entirely, neither of us had the patience for that. When he finally filled me completely, Tynan closed his eyes and moaned long and guttural.

Peering down on me, Tynan panted with the agonizing restraint he was showing and the sheer pleasure of the moment. Lifting my trembling hand, I caressed his cheek, eyes filling with emotion as I met the red fired gaze of the monster that owned me.

"I love you. Thank you for finding me." Turning my head as I lifted my thighs to his waist, I offered Tynan everything he needed and released my satiability. Never one to deny his needs, Tynan took what I gave him. As his teeth buried in my neck and his thrusts drove me painfully to orgasm, I smiled in utter relief to be in his arms.

When Tynan finished, he bundled me up in his arms and lifted me back into his lap as he sat back. We kissed, the coppery taste of my blood still faintly in his mouth as the swish of his baby-making tentacles soothed the hurt of reuniting. It felt too good and unable to prevent it making up for lost time, my power of satiability took our mating to an entirely new level of ecstasy.

"Goddess, I've missed this," Tynan sighed as we came back to earth. "I've missed you." The rap of knuckles against the window reminded me that there were other more important matters to deal with tonight. "Give us a minute."

"We've given you thirty," Esha's teasing voice came through the glass. "Thought it would have only taken five considering how long it's been."

"If his cock were as small as yours, it probably would have. A monster must be gentle with those he cares about," Pride responded evenly.

"Well, thank god she wasn't riding your post, or we'd be waiting another hour."

"My sword is designed only to pierce the body of my own kind. No human or Sidhe would be masochistic enough to try it," Pride replied. "Let's give them space."

Watching each other, Tynan and I listened to Esha and Pride discuss who has tried Pride's assets as they moved away. Our lips turned up at the same time, then we both broke out in smiles.

"Thank the goddess it wasn't Pride's birthday I came home for that night."

With a teasing growl, Tynan threw me back on the chair. "Now they'll have to wait five minutes more."

WHEN WE WERE FINALLY DRESSED, Tynan opened the car door for the others. Esha, Pride, Lucifer, and a goblin I'd seen many times talking to Tynan, but never met crowded in around us. Pride taking his human form to fit more comfortably.

"Go!" Tynan instructed.

"I've got a list of the places called form here. Brie managed to get a forwarding address from the hospital for Margo's new employer. She's heading there now to try and get her new location," Esha reported.

"Hospital?"

"We knew where you were taken to give birth to Druce, we just didn't know Margo worked there until Esha rifled your memories. As soon as we did, I sent Brie to find our traitor or any clues to her location." Tynan checked his phone, pressed a few buttons, then turned it dark again as he looked to Lucifer and the car started moving.

"I found the remains of the man who owned the cabin," Lucifer lisped. "A goblin fed on the good parts before he was left for scavengers to forage. The other corpses I located were well buried and deceased at least a year. The majority of them prepubescent or early teens."

"The evil human's previous victims, no doubt," the goblin snarled. "Only humans would violate a child."

"There are some species of animals that occasionally exhibit the same sick behavior to their young," Pride debated. "All species have those who are sick in the head and their actions upon others deplorable. That does not make the entire species tainted by default."

"Either way, this predator met the bigger fish, and he will no longer prey on the helpless," Esha soothed.

"Did you mark their graves for the police to find?" Tynan queried, his phone screen lighting up with a message again, his eyes reflecting silver in the light as he started reading.

"Yes. The families should be able to know what became of their lost ones," Lucifer mellowed.

"Good. I know what it is like to be left hoping and wondering. I wouldn't want anyone to continue suffering like that if we could relieve it." Taking my hand, Tynan squeezed it in his without looking at me as if he was making sure I was still there. "Esha, give the police the address. Warn them it is booby-trapped with poisons and not to touch anything."

Retrieving his phone, Esha dialed and spoke quietly to whoever answered. Tynan's arm snaked around my shoulders, bringing me closer until the sides of our bodies pressed against each other, and he could kiss my head.

"Brie has a lead. We are heading there now. When we are close, the car will stop, and Garot will collect his Hoard to deal with the traitor."

"If you give me the address, I can scout ahead," Lucifer offered.

"She is ours to deal with," Garot argued. "Because of Margo, the Urisk is dead."

"Settle your short-overinflated head, Garot. I was merely offering to be the bird in the sky."

All eyes fell to Tynan. With a short nod, Tynan dropped his gaze to his phone and typed a message. Lucifer tapped the glass between the driver and the back, and the car pulled over. "If I see the traitor, I will follow from a distance and keep you up to date on her location."

"If she leaves the address, check for the child before you follow her." Giving his prince a nod of obedience, Lucifer stepped out, then the car started moving again.

"What if she doesn't have him?" I dared to worry. My stomach turned in on itself.

"Then I will personally question her until she reveals his location," Tynan assured. Everyone in the car shivered at Tynan's threat. Having seen him stand by while Esha questioned others, I could only imagine how much worse it was if the Prince decided to get his hands dirty.

"What if she killed it?" Garot thought into the silence.

My eyes opened a little wider, my breath leaving my body. Tynan flinched a little, and his right hand appeared lit with his power preventing my manifestation from rising around me. Pushing the thought aside, I stuffed my face into Tynan's chest, hoping his proximity could chase the darkness in me away.

"I believe the queen just answered that question, Garot. Hope for all our sake's that is not the case." Tynan pressed my face against him, the heat of his power still held there as he kissed the crown of my head. "She wouldn't be so stupid, Mess. Margo knows our son is her only bargaining chip, the only reason for which I would show leniency."

"You're not going to, are you?"

"Once I have our son, she will still have to pay for the death of their sacred Urisk. I cannot, nor will I, protect her from her debt to the Hoard."

"Will she suffer?"

"Terribly."

"That wasn't the reassurance I was looking for with that question."

Hot fingers gripped my scalp and pulled my head back, silver balls of fiery hell peered down at me. "She took you from me. Hurt you. Left you vulnerable to a predator. She took our son and was responsible for the murder of a sacred being. Then she left you to doubt your own sanity while everyone told you I was a figment of your imagination.

"Even now, even having had me inside you, your subconscious wavers in fear this is all a twisted and fucked up fantasy. What the Hoard will do to Margo is not near enough suffering that either of us has endured because of her selfishness."

The car came to a stop. Releasing his grip on me, Tynan pressed my face to his chest, his jacket growing damp beneath my tear-stained cheek. "Do not try to show her mercy, Mess. She will not receive it."

Cold air flooded the car for a moment, and then the thump of the car door cut it off. "Well, don't you two look cozy?"

Lifting my face, I spied Brie and Sauvignon dressed to kill. No, I mean that literally. If there were such a thing as steampunk hunting fashion, they'd nailed it. Their clothes were fierce and dangerous without counting the blades at their hips, and the smile of delight in their eyes was a little unsettling, and yet, homey. The car started moving again.

"What, haven't you missed us?" Brie challenged holding her arms open. Diving across the car, they embraced me like a lost lover.

"Damn straight you did. Don't you ever disappear like that again, you hear. The King wouldn't be able to bear it."

Ducking her face, Sauvignon sniffled but pretended there was nothing wrong with her eyes as she blinked back her emotions. "This car smells like sex. Now I'm horny."

Letting me move back to Tynan's arms, Brie patted her girlfriend's thigh a little higher than socially polite. "Once the hunt is done. Then, we can fuck in the traitor's blood."

To say Sauvignon's eyes lit up was an understatement. The inside of the car filled with a contagious buzz of bloodlust and hate, the very air I breathed becoming hot and stifling, encouraging my satiability to a new calling.

Shrinking in on myself, I held on to Tynan tightly. Never before had my power called for anything but lust. To feel it swelling in my flesh like liquid hate bloating my skin, yearning to tear flesh from bones and reach ecstasy as Margo screamed for mercy was terrifying. Was this me or a side effect of the drugs Margo gave me for a year?

My power pulsed, raging at the knowledge. Peering at my fingers, they looked normal but felt thicker, sharper, stronger, ready to destroy the one who harmed me. "Tynan, I feel wrong. My power is reacting and changing."

Taking my fingers, Tynan's hand of power lit up around my pale skin, the flesh of my hand almost translucent in his light, my bones sharp and black. "Victim to your emotions."

"Is that a bad thing?"

"Only for the traitor who earned your ire."

"I don't want to hurt anyone."

Lifting my hand to his lips, Tynan kissed my knuckle. "Then focus on your son in your arms, Mess. Leave the vengeance to those who can channel their emotions properly."

"Our son, Ty. Druce is our son."

The side of his lips quirked. Leaning closer, Tynan took the lobe of my ear in his teeth and bit it gently. "Once this is done, and you are crowned queen, I'm taking you to bed until another child of mine grows in your womb. I want a girl with a heart just like her mother next."

Eyes fluttering on the sensation of making another baby with Tynan, I felt my rage dilute, and passion strengthen. "There, Mess. Keep your mind right there. That's how you control your temper."

44

———

THE FINDING

❖

The illumination of Tynan's phone inside the dark car stung my eyes. Blinking rapidly where my head rested on his chest, I felt my eyes widen, my heart picking up its pace as I read the words on the screen. Behind my head, Tynan's heartbeat thudded, increasing its tempo as he read and reread the message before he replied. Sitting up, I turned to meet his eyes.

Black orbs shined out at me, the silver rage peeking out at me from the sides of his pupils. "Lucifer has eyes on Margo." The car collectively took a breath, silence enveloping us as we all waited for the rest. "There is a human woman in the house with Margo and a baby."

"Ooh, we get food too," Brie chirped.

"The human might be innocent." All eyes turned my way. "Human's employ strangers to babysit for them when they go to work. Margo may employ the woman to mind the baby when she is not home."

"But she is home," Sauvignon debated.

"She could be a live-in nanny. We can't hurt her. Not if she is innocent."

Silence. Tapping his phone screen again, Tynan sent another

message before he put it in his pocket. "Mess is right. The human may have no part in this. We need to play a game to catch our traitor without trapping an innocent. Pride, we are going to need your brother and his friends."

"That will not guarantee the human's safety," Pride warned.

"It will stop them when they are doing this in uniform."

"Not likely," Pride muttered as he took out his phone.

"You need to leave her somewhere safe for this," Esha advised.

Wondering who she was, I leaned forward to meet Esha's eyes. "Who?"

Tynan's shoulders tensed. "I won't be letting her out of my sight."

"She's unstable, and we risk everyone if we take her in. You know that. You saw her nearly lose it in the car with us."

"Oh!" My head hung low ashamed of my inability to control my powers.

Reaching into my lap, Tynan took my hand in his, warmth filling me, caressing along my bones, stretching to my heart, and filling me up. "Then I will trust the rest of you to do this right. Bring me back my son and the traitor who took my wife from me. We will wait in the Fae forest."

The car pulled over and unloaded leaving Tynan and I alone again before driving off. "I wouldn't harm my people."

"No, you wouldn't, not purposefully, but you have been through enough trauma. It is better to let the soldiers deal with this, and bring us the traitor for judgment. Like a true king and queen."

"Might I remind you it was a king's selfishness that set this all in play?"

"I am not that sort of king."

"Ty, you are one of the most selfish beings I've ever met, and in the court of the Unseelie, that's saying something. However, you care about your people, and you hold loyalty and respect above everything else. That is why you will be a great king, it's why I love you."

Tucking his arm around me, Tynan pulled me into his chest and kissed my head. "Rest now. It's been a long day and the night is proving to be just as long. I will wake you when there is news."

"You expect me to be able to sleep when all this is happening?" Remaining quiet, Tynan pressed my cheek to his chest, the steady beat of his heart thudding inside, his warmth surrounding me where he held me. Over a year without being warm, it was a heady thing to find it again. Closing my eyes, I focused on the steady rhythm of his life, and before I knew it, blackness stole me away to my first dream-less rest in too long.

"Mess, they're here."

Confused by the words that dragged me to consciousness, I snuggled further into the warmth surrounding me. Gentle hands eased me upright, forcing me to open my eyes and acknowledge the living. Tynan. Handsome as I remembered him, a smile filling his face. Blinking once, I waited for the memory to fade, but he stayed. "You found me," I breathed.

Cupping my face in his hand, Tynan's smile faded just a touch. "You don't remember yesterday?"

Pressure mounted in my forehead, memories surging forward in desperation. Images flashed behind my fluttering eyes, and I'm sure I looked like I was having a seizure. One vision took focus over any other. "Druce." Sitting up wide-eyed, I clung to Tynan now. "Did they find Druce?"

Exhaling in relief, Tynan took my hand in his. "They just arrived. Come with me." Opening the door, Tynan helped me out of the car and started walking me into the forest. Jeers of a mob reached my ears, my heart racing with thoughts of what waited ahead. Moving through thick scrub, we entered a large clearing filled with Goblins.

Around the edge, Sluagh stood guard, all dressed in their warrior best. Not far ahead, Esha and Pride were marching towards us, a tiny boy in Pride's arms, his fear showing on his face, tears staining his cheek as he cried *'No!'*

"Druce!" Pushing passed Tynan, I rushed forward. Hearing his name, my eyes in a smaller face turned towards me, my arms reaching for him automatically.

Catching sight of me, Druce started clapping, reaching for me too. "Maman." Taking him from Pride's arms, I cuddled my son for the first time. He looked human, his Sluagh markings having faded. Holding him, I told him it was all going to be okay, just like Tynan had assured me.

Turning, I found Tynan right behind me, his eyes a little full, and the softest I'd ever seen them. Taking a breath, hesitant to let Druce go, I pulled back to admire him. He was gorgeous like his father. "Druce, your daddy, wants to meet you too."

Moving him to see Tynan, I enjoyed watching Druce's eyes widen, his mouth open excitedly. He reached for his father and Tynan took him into his arms, and though he'll never admit it, I swear he was on the verge of tears meeting his son for the first time. "Why Druce?"

"It means courage. I knew we were both going to need it. We had to have the courage to keep hoping when it seemed there was nothing to hope for, the courage to believe you loved us enough to never stop looking for us, and the courage to live even when it seemed there was nothing worth living for."

Caressing my cheek, Tynan pulled me in to hug the both of us. Druce blew bubbles happily. "He has your eyes," Tynan praised.

"Wait till you see him not getting his own way. There is no denying he is your child." The humor of the moment died when I wondered how I knew that. "I don't remember seeing him before, but everything about him is so familiar like I've always known him. How is that possible?"

Stroking my neck, Tynan placed a kiss on my forehead. "Your connection was never severed. The hospital used steel not iron to cut the umbilical cord."

"This is a Sidhe thing, isn't it?"

Beaming happiness at me, Tynan touched his head to mine. "Yes, a Fae thing."

A commotion behind me caught our attention causing Tynan's head to snap up and his pupils to find pinpoint focus as silver bled through his irises. When Tynan's growl reverberated through his chest, Druce recoiled and clung to me. "I know, Daddy is scary when he's angry."

Turning to see what was happening, I felt my own anger rise. A burly police officer was dragging Margo through the woods. There was something about him that wasn't entirely human. There was no glamor, but the lack of emotion in his eyes reminded me of Pride the first time I'd met him.

"The big bad," I whispered to Druce. Peering at Pride who was watching everything unfold quietly, I saw a familiarity that couldn't be ignored. "Is he a relative of yours?" Lips twitching a touch, Pride gave a small nod of acknowledgment. My body started to feel swollen again. "Go to daddy. He won't hurt you."

Druce looked worried about going near his angry father, but as soon as I said the word daddy, Tynan calmed a little, his eyes checking me as he took the delicate being. "Mess?"

"I don't want to hurt him accidentally. Just hold him till I get control, please?"

"Talk to her, if that's what you need." Surprised by Tynan's suggestion, I watched Margo screaming for her captor to see reason as the Red Cap dragged her towards the hoard.

"Wait!" The forest quietened as I walked over to where the red cap was holding Margo. When she saw me, Margo stopped begging for mercy and started crying. She didn't apologize, didn't ask forgiveness, didn't tell me all the ways she was trying to save me. She just looked at me and cried.

"You didn't kill me, but what you did do was kill my soul. Day by day as they told me I was insane and Tynan was all in my imagination, that my love for him wasn't real, that I was too dangerous to be a mother to my son. All of it, bit by bit, killed me. A slow torturous death of the soul and mind. I am not that cruel. Your physical death will hurt, but it will not hold the agony of what you delivered to me."

"I just wanted-"

"I know what you wanted. You didn't need me to get a human life, Margo. All you had to do was leave." With nothing more to be said, I stepped back. Bowing his head to me, the red cap dragged Margo towards the hoard. Cries of the mob filled the night, and as Margo disappeared into the bodies of her kin, her screams reached the stars.

"You can't save someone from their mistakes, Mess. Don't pity her," Tynan hissed when I cringed.

"I still doubt this reality because of her."

Tynan pulled me close. "I'm sorry it took so long to find you, that you doubt I am real. I am, Mess. Pinch me, I will feel it. Scratch me, I will bleed."

"No, you won't."

Smiling, Tynan brushed my cheek. "I am here, Mess. I am real."

"The important part is that you came for us. That is all that matters."

"Are you ready to go home?"

Turning my focus to the little boy in his arms, I smiled at how much Druce looked like his dad.

When we returned to the car, it already had a car seat fitted. Bewildered by how that happened, I slid into the back seat of the vehicle, Tynan and I sitting either side of Druce in his baby seat.

Pride and Esha sat on the side bench seats, with Esha giving Pride a hard time about smiling at the baby. We stopped just before leaving the city where Trell joined us, bags from the baby store in hand. "There is more being delivered, but this should get us started."

"Did you leave anything in the store?" Esha teased.

"Yes. All the pink things."

"Am I the only one not moon-eyed for the baby?"

"My joy is in seeing our queen and prince returned to us, and in seeing the happiness both bring to our king," Pride answered evenly.

"Shush, both of you. It's the royal baby!" Trell gushed over all the outfits she purchased, pulling them out of the bag to show us on the drive home.

Two years ago, I'd never had thought I could be happy just to see these people again, to be held in Tynan's arms, to be willingly returning to the Unseelie court. Yet, for the last twelve months, it was all I longed for.

"Things will be different now. You are the queen of both courts. The faerie mound has united the Sidhe under your rule."

Meeting Tynan's eyes across the car, I felt a shiver of cold caress down my spine. "I don't feel like a queen."

Reaching over the car seat where Druce was now sleeping, Tynan gave my hand a gentle squeeze. "I will be right there beside you, Mess. As your consort, your husband, and your prince."

45

WISP WALK

❖

When we finally arrived home, I wouldn't let Druce out of my sight. I couldn't. There was a conscious acknowledgment that I was terrified I would wake up and it had all been another dream.

"Let me take him while you shower," Tynan offered as he came in the bedroom. He held out his arms for his son; guilt gnawed at me for even hesitating. "I will stand in the bathroom with him so you can see him every second."

"What about us?" I worried. "You don't want to..."

"Yes, I do." Touching my cheek gently, Tynan dropped a kiss to my forehead. "I don't want to rush it with you again. So, we will take you down to meet your subjects, and let them meet their new prince. Once done, we will put our son to bed, and then, I am going to work on our second child."

Smiling longingly, I flicked my eyes to Druce, worry clouding my happiness. "Where will he sleep?"

"By the time we get back a cot will be here," Tynan advised me as he walked to a spot we could both see from the bed. "I'm going to have it placed right here. Once you are comfortable for him to have his own room, he will have the room next door. If you gift me another child, they can share until one is old enough to take the room downstairs."

Smiling happily with his plan, I looked away and, once again, my heart dropped. "What happens now? How will we raise our son? Humans raised me, and they did it badly."

Moving to where I sat on the bed, Tynan got down on his knees before me. "Your mother raised you Seelie first, Mess. It will be no different for our children. You will raise them Sidhe, and I will raise them Sluagh. We will raise them to be good leaders for their people, to believe in unity for strength, to see past the differences in their people's appearances and judge them for their merits."

My eyes flashed up. "You'll make Druce run the gauntlet."

"Of course, but like you, Esha will train him, and we won't let him run until we know he is good enough to make it." Caressing Druce's mop of black hair, Tynan lifted his eyes to mine. Focused. Assured. "All parents worry, Mess. It is normal, no matter the species. We will raise him the best way we know how, and he will grow to be a man of whom his people can be proud."

Offering his arms, Tynan didn't try to take Druce from me. "May I hold our son while you shower?" With tears streaming down my face, I placed my sleeping son into his father's arms. Following me into the bathroom, Tynan smiled lasciviously as I undressed and showered.

"Damn duties to the people," Tynan grumbled to Druce. "I want your mother more than anything on earth." Smiling, I enjoyed the luxury of this moment of happiness.

Just after I turned off the taps and wrapped a towel around me, Tynan stiffened. "What is it?"

Shaking his head, Tynan handed Druce to me. "Business as usual. Get dressed. I'll be back shortly to present you."

Taking Druce, I watched Tynan stalk out, worry etching my soul. The last twelve months gave me a lot of trust issues, most of my sanity. Too many vivid dreams blurred the lines between reality and hope.

Placing Druce in the middle of the bed, pillows either side to stop him rolling, I turned my back to get dressed. Druce seemed so happy and content, and he appeared to be a sound sleeper, or maybe he was exhausted from all the excitement last night. It was strange, he was six months old, and I barely knew anything about him, but I felt as if we'd spent a lot of time together.

The sadness that owned me for the past twelve months overcame me. It took all my strength to stay standing and not crumple in a ball to cry my heart out. Druce needed me healthy and happy. One day, I would teach him that emotions weren't a weakness. But, not yet. Not when I still doubted.

Druce chuckling was sunlight breaking through the storm clouds around my heart. Wiping my tears, I let the smile he caused spread across my face. When I turned back around, my smiled vanished.

A woman of light and shadow sat on the bed, smiling down at Druce affectionately, playing with him. Her dress was silvery silk, her hair shiny and silver also, her smooth wrinkle free skin was alabaster, and when she looked up at me, her eyes were the deepest, coldest, black I'd ever see. Her eyes chilled me to my bone.

She was the woman who haunted me at the asylum, who burnt Nora's garden. Turning her eyes back to Druce, she moved the pillows so he could roll over. "I told you the paintings would save you," she spoke, but like always, her mouth didn't move. "Children grow so fast. You blink, then they are adults themselves. Going to war, becoming the savior of the Unseelie, and given titles no one ever thought the half-breed bastard deserved."

Tynan, she was talking about Tynan.

Shifting his legs under him, Druce crawled across the bed towards me. Tears of happiness ran down my face watching him. Stepping in, I picked him up. Giggling, Druce cuddled into me. "Are you Tynan's mother?"

"I am, in some respects. It was always Tynan's fate to lead the Fae into the modern world. Just as yours was to give them life again and give them a purpose."

"This was your plan all along?"

"Yes, two children of pleasure and sorrow, of light and dark. You were always meant for each other. You knew that when you were born because I gave you that awareness. When your mother sent you away, I needed to protect that awareness because children will say what they say. Now, it is time for you to be aware again."

"You offer me my memories?" I queried, unsure if I wanted them.

"I offer you your reason for being. Once, all Sidhe knew their purpose. They were gods of storm and rain, mischief and mayhem, goddesses of fertility and love. They lost their way, and they lost themselves. The earth needs my children to find their way again, to know their purpose." She stepped forward, closer than I was comfortable. "That begins with you, Messina. It all began with you."

Fear filled me. I knew whatever she was going to ask of me would not be easy. Lowering Druce to the ground, I gave him space to crawl around, allowing him to seek safety from the threat before us. "What would you have me do?"

When she smiled, light radiated out of her. "You are untainted which the Sidhe won't allow. You will be forced to walk the wisp before you claim your crown. That is where you will fulfill your purpose." She turned to leave.

"Wait!" I stepped forward to block her way. "Should I say goodbye before that happens?"

Her face softened in tenderness and regret. "Even for the immortal, life is always uncertain. You should always say goodbye; you should always tell those that matter you love them."

My watering eyes went to my son, playing happily on the floor. "But I just got them back."

"You know you can't rule; you are too damaged to be queen. At least, in this life. Tynan will be a good father, Messina. He won't let his sorrow win the war."

Lifting my watering eyes back to her, planning to beg for more time, I found she was gone. Raising my eyes to the ceiling, I allowed myself a moment to mourn my loss pre-emptively. After a few moments, I took a deep breath and accepted my fate. The lady was right; I was too damaged for this life.

Regaining my composure, I dropped to my hands and knees, then crawled across the floor to Druce. He clapped, proud of me. Kissing his nose, I enjoyed my time with him, playing and laughing, and taking every second I could to leave a memory of myself with him.

When Tynan opened the door, he found us having crawling races across the floor. "He crawls?"

"Just now."

"Why are you crying?"

Climbing to my feet, I looked past Tynan as I collected Druce up off the floor. "Pride, can you take him downstairs for a while? Some food would be good, though, I'm not sure what babies his age eat."

"Trell will know," Pride assured, taking Druce in his large hands and holding him over his head like he was flying. Druce's laughter rocked me to my core.

Shutting the door, Tynan watched me as I undressed. "Mess, what happened?"

"I don't want to wait to be with you again."

"Mess, your people..."

"Have already waited a year; they can wait for another hour or two." Looking torn, Tynan studied my eyes, searching for what I was hiding. When his face fell, so did his restraint. Throwing aside his cane, Tynan wrapped me in his arms and kissed me so passionately no crazy dream could replicate it.

Desperate to feel his warmth bare against my coldness, I half ripped his clothes from him. Laughing as he dropped me on the bed, Tynan looked at his torn and disheveled suit. Removing the rest, he joined me.

Placing my hands on either side of his face, I needed him to understand how desperately important this moment would be for both of us. My heart was breaking, but I needed him to know how much I loved him still, that if it were my choice, I would never leave his side ever again.

Meeting his eyes, I searched his intently, noting his pupils were dilating, his concern building into fear. Goddess, it wasn't something I ever thought to see in his eyes. Rubbing my nose against his, Tynan sipped the tears that spilled from my eyes. "I'll take what you give me."

Tynan soughed. His mouth closed over mine as he stroked the tip of his curse back and forth between my folds. Catching in my niche, Tynan steadily forced his way into my core. Gasping for breath, I arched as the inferno of need burned me up inside. Tynan and Druce were all that mattered to me, and if I wasn't coming back from the wisp walk, I was making sure I left my happiness here where it belonged. In the hearts and souls of my loved ones.

It seemed like Tynan understood that. His eyes were soft, caring, and already grieving me. "Mine for eternity, Mess. You promised."

Tears blurred my eyes as I caressed his face. "I will always be yours, for as long as the goddess grants me life. Even then, I will be yours in the afterlife. No one can take my soul from yours, Ty. The goddess made us for each other; we will always find one another again."

Asking no more of me, Tynan slowly pulled back, till only his head stayed vibrating within me. Then, with no more restraint left in him, he drove into me, pushing so deep he pierced my soul.

We both knew it was the last time, and that it had to matter. Putting everything we had into each other, we hoped with the hope of two people who understood the Goddess drew our fate, wishing with every fiber of our beings that she would change the design and keep us together.

The Goddess is never so easily swayed, and so we merged in the only way our bodies allowed us. Through sorrow and pleasure, we promised each other our tomorrows and screamed our oaths to the Goddess, defying her even in our defeat.

TWO HOURS LATER THAN EXPECTED, Tynan escorted Druce and me into the throne room. It was full of Unseelie, Seelie, Goblins, Red Caps, Sluagh, and even Lucifer had come in from the forest to attend.

Escorting me to the dais, Tynan turned me to face the room. "I present to the Fae, their queen, Messina Ui Bayne-Ard, and their prince, Druce Ó Wane-Ard."

Going to a knee, everyone as a collective swore allegiance and loyalty to me, their queen, and to Druce as their prince. Once the hall fell quiet, Tynan directed me to our seats, and we took the throne as king and queen.

As soon as we settled, a Seelie took a knee before us. "Queen Messina, I am Kyrenic, highest rank of the Seelie. I am aware you have just returned home today, but your people are aware that you have never followed custom and walked the wisp."

Eyes sparkling silver, Tynan leaned forward. "Not today, Kyrenic. It can wait for another day."

"How many times have you said that, King Tynan? Still, eighteen months have passed since even the Sluagh expected her to take the walk of fate. It is time."

Unswayed, Tynan sat back. "The walk is tainted. It is preposterous that we still insist on a tradition that has striped good Fae of their future out of spite."

"All must attend the wisp walk," Kyrenic insisted.

Glancing at me, his eyes silver orbs of rage, Tynan knew it must be, but he guessed already the cost. Holding myself together, I took a deep breath as I stood and nodded to Kyrenic.

Rising beside me, Tynan took my elbow. "Mess, you don't have to do this. Please, don't do this?"

"It is my reason for being. You know that. You've always known that because of the prophecy."

Druce watched the tears stream down my face, his eyes so like mine, looked worried as he reached out and stole my tears with his little hand. Kissing him goodbye, I closed my eyes causing my tears to fall faster. "Take care of your father, Druce. Make sure he stands in the sun regularly, and remind him every day I love him, and I will find him again one day."

"Mess, please? You are queen; you can refuse, or delay." Hearing Tynan beg was soul tearing, but it was a pain the last twelve months had already inflicted on me. Kissing him with all the passion of my heart, I left my tears staining his cheek. "I just got you back."

"Yours for eternity, Ty. My home and hearth."

Gritting his teeth, Tynan bowed his head. "My light in the darkness." Embracing me with all his strength, yet careful not to harm our son, Tynan kissed me deeply. As our lips parted, I moved Druce into Tynan's arms, kissed his head and turned away.

A path opened before me to a silver door on the opposite wall. Stepping down the stairs, I started towards it, Tynan one step behind. "What's happening," Esha murmured to Tynan behind me worriedly.

"The Goddess has chosen her fate."

"You knew, that's why you never let her take the walk of fate?"

"Yes, I knew. I understood the moment I knew who Mess was."

"She will be the one to take his coldness," Esha muttered astounded. "She will unveil the Unseelie darkness and show them light. She will unite what should never have broken."

"The daughter of the moon will teach him love," Tynan continued, "and the radiance of the sun. Her inner light will purify the tainted ones, and she will guide the Fae by starlight."

The doors opened; glorious blue light shined out into the throne room. Not bright enough to hurt one's eyes, but intense in its radiance to leave you in awe. Walking into the light, I shivered, the coldness making my breath come out in a fog. Each step brought clarity with it, an understanding this was my path all along. No longer fearing my fate, I checked over my shoulder.

My people watched on, confused by Tynan's reaction, and by mine. Standing at the threshold, acceptance glistening in Tynan's eyes, Druce cuddled into him watching me with his bottom lip quivering. After everything that happened to me in my life, the hardest was this right here.

"Eternity is a long time, Mess. Don't make me wait too long to hold you in my arms again."

"I will run into your arms and your warmth," I assured. Smiling through my tears, I turned into the cold blue light and took a step forward...

46

BELTANE

❖

Tynan marched to the throne room, Trell keeping step with him as they planned the next day of work. It was Beltane, the naming day of all Sidhe. As the oldest, Druce would come first. Mess should be here for this. She should be the one formally recognizing his name, and all the others. Like last year, it fell to him.

Halting outside the door, Tynan closed his eyes and took a deep breath. Thinking of Mess still caused pangs of loss. While the standard for a mated couple who lost their half, and like all before, he'd felt it the moment she gave her life up. A freeing feeling as she floated to her place of rest. While it was a relief to know Mess didn't suffer, the loss was a blade to his heart. That pain would haunt him forever more.

Scratching his chest, Tynan still felt the point of that blade jammed between his fifth and sixth rib. "Is something wrong?" A tilt of his head was all the answer Trell received. Trell lifted her eyes to the door and sighed. "It's been nine months. She died, or vaporized, or whatever she did. Accept it."

Dropping his hand, Tynan opened his eyes refusing to acknowledge Trell by sight. If she saw his eyes, she'd see it coming. "By midnight tonight, you will take a mate."

"What?" Trell stepped back, her eyes wide as she took him in entirely.

"Do I need to repeat myself?"

Trell's bottom lip quivered. "You, you, you need to explain yourself."

Still keeping his eyes on the door handle, Tynan kept his tone even. "I am your king. I don't need to justify my orders, just give them. You have until midnight tonight to mate. I suggest you choose wisely."

"Why? Why would you force this on me?"

Turning slowly, Tynan met her eyes. Trembling as those silver orbs streaked with blood fell on her, Trell broke into tears already knowing that she'd overstepped some invisible line by a mile.

"You will take a mate. I will wait long enough for the bond to settle, maybe even long enough for him to put a seed in your belly, then, in the room you use most, I will kill him."

With her mouth falling open, Trell dropped her eyes her breathing sharp and shallow. "My King, I'm sorry. You're right. I don't know what you suffer. Forgive my sharp tongue."

"No." Opening the door, Tynan marched into the throne room. Seeing his eyes, everyone got out of his way quick smart. The only person who stayed put was Esha, his arms full of a wiggling, frustrated Druce. Seeing his son was aspirin to a headache. Rage settling, Tynan's thoughts returned to the woman missing from this scene. "Let him down."

With relief, Esha put Druce on the bottom step and stepped back. Immediately, Druce charged towards his father, like a bull issuing a challenge. He was strong and determined and holding him back from anything he wanted was a lesson in controlled strength and patience. Esha already broached the subject of discipline, and while Tynan was lenient to a degree, he agreed with Esha that a prince should learn control earlier rather than later.

Picking the hurricane of a toddler up, Tynan swept him into his arms and cuddled him tight. "There's my boy." Wrapping his arms around Tynan's neck, Druce whispered his name to his father's ear, and then he followed that up with his mother's. "I miss her too." Rubbing his back, Tynan realized Druce was reacting to his emotions, feeding off his grief. "You're not the only one who needs to learn discipline. I'll try harder."

Reaching the dais, Tynan handed Druce back to Esha. "You have to go with Esha until you are named."

"He was fine until your fury came through the door," Esha muttered, wrestling Druce back onto his hip. "What did Trell do?"

"Later. I have duties." Taking the steps to the top, Tynan turned to face the crowd waiting while they all bowed, then he sat. His eyes locked with Trell at the bottom of the dais, she'd settled herself, but her bottom lip was still trembling. He could have lost control of his temper and hurt her physically, but Tynan preferred a punishment that fit the crime in most cases.

Once he settled, Tynan gave a nod to Trell. Legs shaky as she took the podium, Trell avoided meeting his eyes, or anyone else's. "Welcome all, on this fine Beltane, we gather to celebrate the creation of new life. All those who have received the Goddess's favor may present your child to the King for naming."

Esha stepped forward, Druce blowing bubbles as he babbled. "My king, I present your son, Druce Ó Wane-Ard."

"The only child of the eternal queen."

Every Fae in the room closed their right fist and kissed their first knuckle, even Druce. Mess gave her life to provide them with their path in life. Her sacrifice healed them when they didn't even know they needed saving.

"Welcome to the Fae, Druce Ó Wane-Ard. May you be as fearless as your father, and as beautiful as your mother - inside and out." Indicating the small throne to the side, Tynan gestured Esha set his son in his place before turning his eyes to the next in line.

Continuing to welcome the new babies for the next five brought before him without issue, Tynan was just easing into a comfortable rhythm when the last couple took the dais to meet him.

Last to kneel before him was the Captain of the Lunar guard and his Seelie wife. Tilting his head, Tynan noticed the similarities between this Seelie and Nora Ui Bayne-Ard. She must be a distant relative of King Titan or one of his bastards.

Lifting a bundle of blankets, Amp presented a newly born female with a mop of red hair and big turquoise eyes in a pale face. Tynan felt his breath catch as he looked at the child, her eyes mesmerizing him. "My king, I present my daughter, born only two weeks ago."

"What name have you chosen?" Tynan breathed, forcing his eyes to the red hair. While her eyes and pale skin were reminiscent of his wife, Messina had dark hair.

"I beg my King to allow me to name her for the beauty she resembles. We wish to name her Messina Ui Macha-Mór and call her Sina," Amp announced. Silence descended across the court.

Ready to decline and possibly rip Amp's head from his body, Tynan stood, only to be halted by Druce standing in front of him. Everyone held their breath as the prince went on tiptoes to try and see the baby. With his brows bunching, Amp obliged the small toddler and went to a knee so Druce could see her. Shocking everyone, Druce fawned over the baby, taking her hand and patting her red hair. "See-na," Druce struggled to pronounce.

"Aww, that's so cute!" Someone immediately within the crowd gushed. A few of the Sluagh groaned and rolled their eyes as they mouthed 'Seelie' at each other. It made Tynan's lips almost quirk in a grin.

Tracking his eyes back to Druce, Tynan lifted a brow as his son smiled at the little girl and dropped a kiss to her forehead. "Queen consort, one day."

How the hell a child who could barely say his name managed to get those words out confounded Tynan, but it made everyone around them laugh that the young prince had already chosen his future wife.

Lifting his son up, Tynan scrubbed his hair. "That may be so, but you're a bit young to take a wife. Go to Brie. It's your bedtime, and I need to get this party started, or we will still be standing here at dawn."

Setting Druce down, Tynan watched a happy Druce run to Brie and get swooped up in her arms. Sauvignon and Brie started blanketing the young prince in kisses until he went bright red and hid his face giggling. Returning his eyes to the couple before him, Tynan took a deep breath.

Stepping forward, Tynan put his arms out. "May I?" Hesitantly, Amp placed his daughter into his King's arms. "My wife, the eternal queen was a beautiful woman who held a tortured but brave soul."

Staring into those pale eyes, Tynan felt his heart tug towards this little Sidhe. "May you have your queen's beauty, and may you face your life with the bravery the queen faced hers. May you know the happiness and love that was denied her by the Goddess. Welcome to the Fae, Messina Ui Macha-Mór." Handing the delicate, fragile girl back to Amp, Tynan returned to the throne.

After Trell announced the end of the naming and that celebrations should begin, music and merriment broke out amongst the hall. "Trell, you should be first to dance the maypole."

Eyes wide, Trell gawped at Tynan while Esha raised both his brows. "But, my King, the maypole is for the debutants."

"The maypole is a representation of semen and virgin blood. You may not be a debutant, but you are looking for eternal love. Best you get looking." Peering after his long-time assistant, Tynan watched her swallow painfully and move off into the crowd.

"Should I ask?"

"Trell spoke out of turn. To teach her why her words were wrong she must now experience things herself." Rising to his feet, Tynan stepped beside Esha. "Make sure she mates by midnight. If she hasn't chosen someone by one minute too and marked him, you pick who will wed her."

"Do I get a clue?"

Considering the punishment, Tynan met Esha's eyes. "Not you. If she were smart, she'd choose someone she hated and could stand to lose."

Lips parting, Esha kept his eyes steady, despite their sharpened focus. "Oh."

"If I wake tomorrow and Trell is unwed, I'll pick your wife tomorrow." Not waiting for a response, Tynan left the dais returning to his suites and his son. The threat to Esha ensured he would not help his former lover.

Brie and Sauvignon were playing with the toddler on the floor, but as soon as Tynan entered the lounge, Druce stood up and clapped at his father. Then, he charged like a bull until Tynan caught him up in his arms and spun him around in the air.

47

INSIDE THE LIGHT

❖

"There's nothing to be scared of in the Wisp walk. The eternal queen cleansed it eighteen years ago, and now, it is safe to walk again. There is no chance of madness."

"Are you trying to convince yourself or me, Captain?"

Huffing, Amp realized his daughter was right; she wasn't scared in the least. "Why now. You could wait another year before anyone would expect this of you."

Her turquoise eyes smiled up at him like he was a senile old man. "You know why." As the words fell from her lips, two giant hands encompassed his daughter's waist.

"Sina, you ready?" Druce grinned as he placed a kiss on Sina's neck, right above her pulse. Amp stiffened. Fond as he was of Druce, and they were terrific friends, every time he touched Sina made Amp uncomfortable.

"Eww! Get your lips off me. I know where they were last night." Sina shoved Druce playfully.

"Jealous?"

"Of being the meat in a Prince and Tanish sandwich? Unlikely."

Chuckling, Tanish sidled up to Sina's side and whispered something in her ear making her smirk. Surveying the growing crowd,

Amp searched for the fourth mischief maker. Chenille was never far from Druce and Tanish, the three of them lovers since Chenille chose them both for her debutant into womanhood. That wasn't to say there weren't others for the three of them, but more often than not, they were a threesome.

Luckily, being good friends is as close as Sina was to all three. Amp's friendship with Druce enabled the inside knowledge that his daughter had a preference for more experienced lovers. Knowing Sina chose Esha as her debutant partner was hard to swallow, but to his relief, Sina's penchant for older and dangerous was limited to random occasions, and as yet, Sina avoided forming any long-term sexual attachments.

Still, the fact her friends were all taking the Wisp walk today in readiness to run the gauntlet, is why Sina stood ready to do the same, a year before her age would demand her to do so.

"You are already the youngest member of the lunar guard, isn't that enough achievement for this year?" The three teens fell silent. Damn it; he said it out loud.

Stepping away from her friends with gentle eyes, Sina brushed Amp's cheek. "Don't look so worried, Captain. You know that if it is not my time to learn my fate, the Wisp will not call me to walk. Be at ease that it is my fate to bloom early, or to leave here in tears."

That made Amp chuckle. "You never cry. Tanish cries more than you."

Puffing his chest out Tanish stood straight. "Hey! I'm merely in touch with my emotions, Captain. Some empathy wouldn't go astray on Sina's part."

"Her powers are why she has to stay cool, Nish, you know that." Everyone turned to see the Sluagh General had joined them. His ruby eyes all for Sina. "The king just arrived, and I thought I'd wish you all luck."

"He means he came to snog Sina before fate marries her to some Seelie lord."

"Really?" Sina tilted her head in an appraisal of Esha, her eyebrow quirking. "Just snog?"

Grinning ear to ear, Esha took Sina's hand and tugged her off towards the side of the hall. Reaching forward, Amp smacked Tanish. "You know better than to put ideas in her head."

"He's right, Sina takes everything anyone says to her as a dare," Chenille appeared behind them. "That's why she's running the gauntlet with us; you made such a big deal about doing it that she felt left out."

Tugging Chenille close to him, Druce nuzzled her blonde hair. "Esha trained her; she'll be fine."

Half-bred like most of the youth these days, Chenille still resembled her Seelie mother more than her Sluagh father. "Training, is that what they call it now?" Chenille pinched Druce's bicep making him snatch her up and molest her while she giggled and squealed.

"Children," Tynan stepped in beside Amp. "Are you ready?"

"Bring it on!" Tanish cheered. When his king just stared at him, Tanish checked himself. "Yes, sorry, my King. I keenly await the opening of the doors."

"Forgive him, father, his mother was full blooded Seelie," Druce teased, grabbing his friend's shoulder and squeezing in reassurance.

Smirking, Tynan turned his gaze to Amp. "I heard they dared your daughter to walk today?"

"Esha is just giving her a last-minute pep talk." Amp tried not to note the crease between his king's brows, acutely aware that Tynan did not miss the subtext.

Face clearing, Tynan took a breath. "I hear she successfully passed her lunar guard exams. You must be proud. Will she be one of the teams going to college with Druce?"

"No, I will only take experienced guards who blend. Esha chose two Sluagh guards to come with us that will fill out the two teams."

"Sina also has a severe case of human hate," Chenille jumped in; always keen to make her presence known to the King. "Like, she thinks they are evil incarnate and doesn't want anything to do with them. She's going to study her degree by distance."

"Really?" Tynan turned his attention back to Amp for confirmation.

"Ever since she was a baby, she's hated them. Taking her to the city was a nightmare. She physically attacked a human man who leered at her last year. It's inexplicable, but that's how she reacts on instinct. Even when pushed, Sina can't explain the feeling."

"Well, I doubt Esha will complain about her staying here instead." Tynan assessed the crowd. He avoided Amp's daughter since she matured purely because of how much she looked like Mess. If her hair were dark, Pride would need to restrain Tynan around her. With how much their mothers looked alike, he should have expected it, but it still took his breath away every time he saw her. Those turquoise orbs enticed him to do things to the girl, which up until last year, would get him beheaded.

Instead, Tynan tried to imagine Sina as a daughter. The first twelve years, the similarity between Druce and Sina made that easy. Once she started to blossom, however, and the closeness of her friendship with Druce increased, it became harder to keep his thoughts innocent. The fact his son adored Sina helped dissuade Tynan's interest. Still, it surprised him to find out that she and Druce weren't lovers.

"Trell, let's get started." Walking five steps forward the large silver doors opened, eerie blue light spilling out into the hall. Turning his back on the forest, Tynan did his duty. Messina should have been here to see her son become a man, and looking into the light tore at his soul. "Let all who seek their reason for being present themselves."

The hall quietened as those of age stepped forward, Druce leading the way. Patting his son on the shoulder as he passed, Tynan beamed his pride. "Do you think she's in there waiting for me?" Druce murmured, letting his friends pass by him.

Holding his breath for a moment, Tynan recognized his son feared to suffer his mother's fate. "Your Mother was born to teach me to love, so that I may love you. Her destiny was to give her people their reason for being again. She knew that from her birth, and she accepted it before she entered the Wisp forest. If you see her in there, it will be to guide you. Bring her home with you if you can, don't stay to be with her. Remember, you have a reason to be here, and it does not end in there."

Inhaling deeper, Druce focused forward. Hurried steps behind him stole Tynan's attention as flame red hair burst through the crowd and ran towards them, Esha grinning as he followed her through, stopping at the edge of the gathering.

Dropping his eyes to Esha's groin, Tynan lifted a brow. Peering down, Esha zipped up, giving Tynan a sly smile before his eyes returned to Sina. Goddess, Tynan shifted uncomfortably when his rattlesnake stirred seeing her all flushed as she stopped by his son.

"Come on, Prince Charming. I'll be right here beside you as your future captain of the lunar should be."

"You've been Lunar for a week. Don't get ahead of yourself, Sina." Smirking, Druce followed the ambitious redhead into the forest.

"This walk is pointless. I know where I'm heading," Sina teased. Watching her body language, Tynan noticed when Sina hesitated going forward. Looking down, she took Druce's hand. "I'm here for you; to protect you, and to be your friend."

Moving his gaze to the beauty next to him, Druce squeezed her hand. "I love you too." Together they stepped into the light.

THE FOREST WAS EERILY BEAUTIFUL. One by one, her friend's names were called, beckoning by the Wisp. When Druce stepped forward, his eyes keen on the forest, it took him a moment to remember they held hands. Looking back, he gave her a quick reassuring grin, and then he left her standing there alone as he chased a blue Wisp to his fate.

Sina was still waiting there minutes after the others vanished. Getting antsy, she fiddled with the blade on her hip. What if they didn't call her in to see her destiny?

"Do you fear your future, or that you will be left behind while your friends move ahead?"

Spying the movement to her side, Sina noted the woman of light pouring tea at a table that sat on a dais. "Who are you?"

Lips quirking, the woman purely poured a second cup of tea. "Sugar?"

"Not unless you want to see my best impression of a cat going psycho." When the woman quirked a brow and gestured to the empty seat, Sina sighed and went to join her.

Sitting at the table, she tried to get a good view of the woman, but the light emanating from her hid most of her features. White hair, silver dress, and ageless in her appearance was all Sina could determine. Still, she felt familiar; like a grandmother.

"Would it dishearten you to know you will never become Lunar Captain? Will you become disillusioned to learn that your father will hold that role for centuries still?"

Looking away, Sina wasn't sure how to answer. Her stomach fell out at that question. "If that is not my fate, I will have to accept it." Maybe just being the captain of Druce's guard will suffice.

"Would you? Would you accept fate as anything but a soldier? What if your fate is to be a wife, a mother, with only love and guidance to offer those around her?"

"That's not me. I trained hard to be one of my people. I'm happy to marry and have a child eventually, but for that to be my reason for being is insane. No one in the Fae has that fate."

"True for the Sluagh, but the Sidhe are not all warriors, are they not?"

Brows furrowing, Sina shook her head. "No. I want more. I am more. I can feel that I am meant for greater things. I am meant to protect the future ing; I've known that since I was a child. That's why I was sure I would become the lunar captain."

"Maybe you will protect your king from his bed. Bare his children, protect them with a mother's love?"

"Druce? Whoever he marries he will share with Tanish. I love Druce, but only as a friend, and Tanish is into some kinky shit. Nothing wrong with that, but it's not my thing."

The silver lady's lips tilted, then, she laughed. Bells rang through the forest as she rose to stand and gestured to the woods. "While unconvinced you are ready, to send you away with doubts would only make you more determined. You have ambition, Messina, and you are brave. I believe, you are what you should always have been and my debt to him paid. Go, seek your fate."

Turning her gaze, a Wisp of light bobbed above the ground. "Sina," the air breathed her name. Looking back at the lady, Sina found her gone.

Standing, Sina moved towards the light, it dashed into the forest, and she chased after it. Heart pounding, she raced through the eerie woods, hurdling fallen logs, winding her way through trees, running as Esha taught her for the gauntlet. "You'll take what I give you," a masculine voice whispered in her ear, nearly knocking her off balance. Shaking her head, Sina kept running.

Entering a glade, Sina was surprised when she jumped a rock wall, and a dark shadow of a man stood right in her path. Unable to avoid the collision, she closed her eyes and prayed it wouldn't hurt. Strong warm arms wrapped around her as he caught her and held her close. "You were born for me. Your body was designed for me."

Shit, was he naked? Sina could feel what he had to offer. Opening her eyes, Sina found herself surrounded in darkness, only the feel of his arms holding her, his warmth radiating through her, letting her know he still held her. Hot breath blew across her neck, his lips silk on her skin.

Damn, she was going to be nailed by a Wisp. No one warned her that happened in here. "You'll take what I give you."

"I'll take what you give me," Sina breathed, the heat of him curling into her body, stirring her lust as none had done before. Her skin started to glow in the darkness as discomfort that bordered on pain pulsed in her groin, mixing with the greatest pleasure ever to caress her senses. No, she wasn't having sex with a wisp, but the sensations were there.

"Who are you?" The masculine voice asked. Dark Smokey fingers penetrating the glow down her arm.

Breathless, Sina observed their conflicting presentations. "I'm light to your darkness."

Silky lips traced her jugular, sharp teeth pierced her skin causing Sina to moan and yank the dark body closer. "Do you understand?"

That she was having a hell of an encounter with a wisp? Yes. What her fate was...? "No."

Everything spun around her, then Sina was racing through the forest again, she jumped a wall and landed in the shadow's arms. "Who are you to me?"

"I'm your light in the darkness."

As his teeth eased from her neck, the shadow waited. "Do you understand?"

"That you're Sluagh, yes."

The world spun, and she was running again. Everything repeating over and over, all Sina's guesses resulting in her running into the dark and its hidden arms.

"Do you understand?" The shadow breathed again; numerous times had they repeated the sequence, all of them failing to get past this question.

Opening her eyes, Sina met the dark gaze, her mind reeling. "Yes."

"Why are you here?"

"To protect my people by loving the darkest of them."

The shadow released her, and the darkness eased, a gust of cold wind blowing it away, till Sina stood by herself in the eerie glow of the Wisp forest.

Exhausted and hungry, Sina followed the Wisp light back to the silver doors and stepped hesitantly back into the hall. It was dark and empty, just a small light glowing where a group of six huddled by the fireplace. "Hey."

Turning towards her voice, Amp was the first one to cross the distance and wrap his daughter in his arms. "Bless the Goddess. We've waited for five days. We worried we lost you."

Clinging to her father, Sina shook her head. "I'm stubborn. I didn't want to hear what they said."

"You're disappointed?" Amp's hands held her even tighter. Over his shoulder Druce, Tanish, Chenille, and Esha waited with her mother. Eyes filling with tears she gave in to the understanding her fate may be one of the men in the room, or it could be someone else. The thing that broke her was that her future was not what she would choose. She was not born to be a soldier.

Ghostly shadows of grey smoke raced across the room. Eyes wide, Esha stepped back. "Captain, her spirit power is escaping." The last thing Esha needed was for Sina to raise his victims around him. They'd fill the god damn hall and slaughter him before she could get control again.

Holding her tighter, Amp soothed his daughter. "Shh, you've gone five days with no food or sleep. It's just your emotions getting the best of you. Focus your thoughts, Sina. Bring your mind to me and my voice."

Closing her eyes, Sina focused her thoughts. She was still a lunar, a loved daughter, and Druce's friend. Nothing was lost. Running the gauntlet was weeks away, and depending who the darkness was, it may not change anything. Perhaps she could mate with a Sluagh and still be a lunar.

Her eyes flitted to Esha, and she wondered. No. She shouldn't hope. Keeping her mind open to whomever fate put before her was the best thing to do to avoid further disappointment. "I accept my fate." The ghosts of victims past faded into the floor.

A moment later, her mother was holding her too, her friends watching on with worry as her parents eased her towards the door to take her home. When her exhaustion nearly took her down, Amp lifted her in his arms and walked away.

"Has anyone ever taken that long before?" Druce asked. He'd thought he was the last taking two days.

Watching the beauty he adored be carried away, Esha shook his head. "The longest was three days, and he came back to win a war and take the throne. Your father was always ambitious."

"So is Sina," Druce reminded. "She's as powerful as me too."

Esha couldn't argue about Druce's assessment, but until now, she'd only ever desired to make her father proud. She was so sure of her path; maybe the wisps had to beat whatever her fate was into her; Goddess knows she was stubborn. Still, Esha's gut nagged him that his days of taking pleasure from her were over and that her fate would take her beyond what he could offer. "Which begs the question; should we be worried?"

EPILOGUE

A NEW CHANCE

❖

"Are you worried?" Esha's reflection was observing the forest over Tynan's shoulder.

Looking out his lounge room window at the dying light over the devil's forest, Tynan stood tall with a smile on his lips. "He is strong and as fast as his mother. He will make the light."

The King's confidence in his son's ability was also a compliment to the trainer, making Esha beam proudly. "We should make our way to the amphitheatre."

Inhaling, Tynan nodded and collected his cane. His eyes drifted to the painting above the fireplace, the one of Esha and Tynan that first day he met Messina when she was five. Tynan missed her like a craving, one that hadn't eased one day since she disappeared into the wisp forest, and purified the tainted paths.

Messina fulfilled her reason for being here. She abided by the Goddess's will and guided the Fae to their purpose. Everyone was in awe when their queen evaporated into blinding light. She was a supernova that saved them. No one knew whether to celebrate or mourn; no one but Tynan. He grieved for as long as it took to return to his throne; then he became the King solely.

Tonight, Druce would run the gauntlet, a man fully grown and ready to lead his people. Two days later, Druce would go off to college, studying business and finance so that he could join his father's business when he graduated.

Eighteen years passed quickly. The Fae found their way in the modern world, giving back to the earth, understanding, once again, their reason in this world. Before giving everything of herself for her people, Messina gave Tynan her heart. Treasuring it, Tynan scheduled regular time to stand in the sunlight to feel her warmth again.

Regretful, Tynan never told Mess his secret. All the time she claimed he was the only thing to make her warm; he'd never told her he was cold all his life, except when he was in a room with her.

Already, the amphitheatre was packed. More than the usual turnout was present because the prince was running tonight. Everyone wanted to see, if, like his parents, Druce was still standing when he emerged from the tree line.

"King Tynan," Captain Amp greeted. Tynan made him responsible for Druce's safety growing up; a smart way to ensure the lunar guard's loyalty.

"Amp, are you ready for college?" Amp would attend college with Druce, along with ten other lunar guards. The truth was, Druce and Amp were close. Tynan had no doubt Amp mourned Messina and gave his heart to the boy in honor of the woman he'd wanted. Esha was no different, always spoiling Druce, but being as hard on him in training as he had been on his mother.

Pride was already by the window watching. Out of all of them, Pride mourned Messina the most; openly anyway. His devotion to Druce was as intense as it was for the eternal queen. Formally, Messina was queen for ten minutes, but everyone knew she sacrificed her life and happiness for them. She was the queen of prophecy. Everyone believed it now, and no one dared speak poorly about her, not that there was anything to say.

"Are you worried for Druce?" Amp broke Tynan of his quiet remembrance. Messina would have been beside herself if she were here.

"No, are you?" Tynan observed his bouncing on the balls of his feet.

"For Druce? No, he can take care of himself," Amp rationalized. "However, Sina hasn't been herself since the Wisp walk. She's even more closed off than normal."

"Disappointed or the length of exposure to the wisp?" Tynan remembered the way Druce was coming home after Sina finally emerged; Esha looked like someone broke his favorite toy.

"A bit of both, I think. Sina tells me she accepts her fate, but I know how stubborn my daughter is, my King. If she is not happy with the wind blowing her west, she will generate a storm to blow her east."

"Sina has the power of storms?" Tynan's brows bunched as he tried to remember if Druce mentioned that. There was an incident which caused havoc with the girl when she was twelve, and a Sluagh hurt her, but that's all he could recall.

"Not quite, no. Sina..." Amp swallowed, unable to say it. "Sina reminds me a lot of our eternal queen in her looks and her power, but she doesn't have the sorrow in her eyes from the horrible childhood."

Lifting a brow, Tynan considered the captain, fascinated by his daughter's power. "What are her hands again?"

Licking his lips, Amp lowered his voice. "Blood and lust, like our eternal queen."

"Messina was blood and satiability. Lust is something different."

"As you say, my king."

Amp's easy acceptance made Tynan curious if the only difference was in the way Sina wielded her power as a component of sex, rather than a defense. "Her spirit power is chaotic if I remember correctly?"

"For the Sluagh especially. She wields the spirit of innocent victims. When she is focused, I've seen her utilize them with amazing capabilities, but when she is emotional, it can be disastrous for all near her."

"She lost control when she was twelve. I believe people were injured." Spirit wielding was one of the rare and dangerous powers, not dissimilar from Mess's manifestation. Again, Tynan wondered if the difference came down to the psychological state of the user.

"She maimed ten, and killed a Red Cap before Druce knocked Sina out to stop it all."

Brows lifted; Tynan felt his loins stir again. Goddess, he was talking about this girl losing control and killing people, and all he could think about was losing himself in her. Damn the consequences of her losing command of her power near him, as long as he got to hear he mewl for him first.

Gritting his teeth, Tynan focused. "I hope she has learned better control now."

"The Goddess save the devils if she hasn't." The fact Amp was smirking was Tynan's only reassurance.

The beacon lit up, and the windows slid open. "Our offspring are on their way," Tynan murmured to Amp.

"May the Goddess guide them through."

Tynan didn't join him. The Goddess took the love of his life from him. As such, Tynan hadn't offered her thanks or praise since that day and wouldn't till Mess was in his arms again. Instead, Tynan watched the tree line and waited while the first hour ticked by in the gauntlet.

"Someone is coming," the lookout shouted.

Everyone was suddenly watchful again. An hour and a half had passed since the beacon went up. Two figures emerged from the forest. Druce was walking comfortably, and beside him, leaning heavily on his shoulder was his best friend, Tanish. Covered in gashes and injuries that would need tending, Tanish dragged his wounded leg, Druce holding him upright.

"Another," the lookout called.

Everyone's attention went to the far wall. A girl, or young woman, wearing an outfit more comfortable on a Sluagh than

Sidhe, emerged from the forest. Walking tall, Sina carried a sword dripping blood by her side. She was striking. With her copper-gold hair, pale skin, and those turquoise eyes, there was no mistaking her.

"She made it still walking," Amp sighed with relief.

"That is quite the achievement," Tynan praised astounded.

"Yes."

"She obviously gets her abilities from her mother," Tynan teased, though, he knew if she made lunar, the girl had some lethal skills.

Amp shook his head. "Lilaise is stock standard Seelie. She prefers to use her tongue as a weapon and play politics, then get her hands bloodied. The psychological machinations Lilaise plays drives Sina crazy."

"Especially when Lilaise tries to match-make with Seelie lords," Esha teased, joining us. "Sina finds them all to be quite pretentious."

Amp almost growled. "Her mother should know by now that her daughter is very wild in her being. There is no taming that girl. I think it's the hair."

It made Tynan snicker. Amp would not have approved of his daughter dating a Seelie lord. "Do you object?"

Amp shook his head. "I learnt a long time ago not to try and force her hand. I didn't want her to run tonight, but after she walked the wisp, Sina told me it was her fate, that when she crossed the wall, she would have achieved her goal."

"What was her fate? She looked devastated leaving the wisp." Only a little too eager in the asking, Esha waited.

"Sina wouldn't say, only that crossing the wall would seal her future. I told her that waiting wouldn't change that, but Sina decided that it was best to get it out of the way."

Esha's eyes were pinpoints. Knowing that look, Tynan raised a brow at him. Esha lowered his voice so Amp couldn't hear. "I'm concerned. She was five days with the wisps and emotional coming out. I worry what fate could offend such an ambitious girl."

"Is it my health or the girls you worry for?" Tynan asked.

"Either way, I lose."

Inhaling, Tynan acknowledged the truth in that statement. "Do you love her?"

"Love? No. Lust? Very much so." The grin building on Esha's face as he gave Tynan a wink.

Shaking his head, Tynan smirked at Esha's cheek before he refocused his eyes on Druce and Tanish arriving at the wall. Moving forward, Tynan embraced Druce. "Well done. Your mother would be proud."

Pride was shining in his eyes, Druce hugged him back before Pride and Esha yanked him away for congratulations. Crushed in Pride's grasp, Druce smiled looking around. "Is Chenille back?"

"No, not yet. You are the first to cross."

Looking over his shoulder, Druce spotted Sina only a meter from the wall. "Sina, have you seen Chenille?"

Amp's daughter stopped. Closing her eyes, Sina concentrated, ghostly drifts of smoke rose from the ground and surged towards the forest. Enraptured by Sina using her soul power to aid her rather than attack, Tynan studied her intently. Esha was right to fear this girl's ambition. If she decided to challenge Tynan for the crown, he would have a hard time beating her.

After a moment, Sina lifted her head and cursed. Turning on her heel, she was running back across the open ground into the trees at speed. "Sina, wait," Druce called and went for the wall.

Grabbing him back, Tynan held Druce captive. "You have crossed the wall; you can't go back in to help," he snarled, his anger not with Druce, but with the one named for his heart, running back into the gauntlet. "Why did you ask her to go back?"

"I didn't."

"You know she wouldn't cross leaving any of you in there," Esha snapped. "By asking her, you dared her and time is already counting down."

Standing at the wall swearing, Amp glared at Druce before turning his eyes to Tynan. "Why didn't she just use the ghosts?"

"When a devil kills it eats its victim's soul. There is no ghost to avenge its death with them."

Druce wasn't bothered by this, but he could see Tynan was. "Sina is a good fighter. She was barely injured just now, but she is brave and fearless. She could have crossed the wall and left Chenille alone, but she didn't. She will save her friend or die trying. She has earned the name chosen for her."

Swallowing the venom he felt in his throat, Tynan turned his gaze to Amp who stood to his right, pale and anxious. "The wisp told Sina the moment she crossed the wall she would set her future. That means she will cross."

"As you say, my King." Stepping back, Amp focused his eyes on the trees hoping to the Goddess the King was right about these things."

Three more Sluagh dragged their way across the open field over the next thirty minutes, the beacon dimming with every ten-minute block. "There. Another!" The lookout shouted.

Barely visible because of the long grass, the blonde hair of a Seelie girl bobbed with the effort to crawl out of the forest. Movements inhibited; the girl was hardly able to keep going. Zeroing his focus in, Tynan recognized her, badly cut up and covered in her blood as she was. "It's Chenille. She's badly wounded."

"Goddess, where is Sina?" Druce worried.

Bursting from the trees, a Red Cap nearly stomped on Chenille. Stopping to assess her, he grabbed her arm and dragged her across the grass to the wall, dumping her just before it and stepping over. Racing forward, Druce yelled to encourage Chenille up to the wall. Memories of standing in that same spot as Messina pulled her self along with her spine severed made Tynan shiver.

"The fiery one saved her," the red cap announced to Druce. "Lucifer had her."

The beacon was all but out. "Damn it, Sina," Amp mourned.

"Another," the lookout called. "Or the same again."

The gathered watched as Sina waltzed out of the forest like she was on a Sunday walk, the sword at her side, dripping fresh blood. She was halfway across the clearing when Lucifer flew from the trees towards her. For Tynan, it was like watching history repeat itself.

Spinning around on a pinpoint, Sina swung her sword slicing at Lucifer's wing, causing him to drop to the ground to avoid losing the ability to fly. Turning back, Sina had the tip of her sword to Lucifer's throat before he could recover. The girl fought like she was merely an extension of her weapon.

"I want my rabbit!"

"Naughty, Lucy," Sina tsked. "You know the treatise makes the clearing a safe ground. Now, back you go to your Devils and leave me be."

"Argh, too much like her, you are," Lucifer snarled.

"Right down to the toxic blood. Since we can agree that taking me won't do you any good and your rabbit is safely over the wall, best you find another prey to eat. There were plenty to choose from who haven't crossed the line yet."

The beacon blinked and extinguished. Backing up quickly, Sina got clear of Lucifer and sprinted for the center of the window. "Come on, Chenille," Druce fumed, trying to get her to lift her arm to the top of the wall.

"Hurry up!" Amp called to his daughter.

"Lose the sword it's slowing you down," Esha advised as he moved to the wall to help Druce. Dropping her sword, Sina put everything into running. Goddess, she was fast. Watching her race for her life, Tynan couldn't believe the speed with which she moved, almost as swift as the spirits she sent into the forest before.

Shoving Druce out of the way, Esha pulled Chenille over the wall and dropped her on the ground unconscious. "Everyone move away now," Esha ordered, clearing the way for Sina to crash land.

Moving forward, Tynan focused on Sina, his body moving subconsciously to keep the determined girl in direct view. As the windows shuddered, only seconds from closing, Sina dove through the gap, rolled as she landed, and came straight back up to her feet in front of him. The momentum of her speed carried her forward and straight into Tynan's waiting arms.

Catching her somewhat awkwardly, Tynan held her against his chest. Breathing hard, Sina accepted his support to steady her.

After a few seconds, Sina cursed under her breath then started laughing.

Keeping her in his arms, Tynan enjoyed her warmth. Closing his eyes, he bowed his head, a smile slowly spreading on his lips. Finally!

Looking up, Sina was laughing, her eyes sparkling with adrenalin. Observing who held her, Sina seemed amazed. "King Tynan?"

"Messina," Tynan greeted, still holding her.

The girl swallowed, hesitation flashing. "I apologize, I didn't mean to fling myself into your arms."

"Didn't you?" He challenged. *'I will run into your arms and your warmth.'* Messina's last words to him were playing in his head.

A cheeky look fell across her face. "No, but I'm not objecting. I was freezing my arse off out there, and you are warm like a bonfire."

"Only for you." While everyone watched, Tynan lowered his face and kissed the panting girl. He expected her to pull away, embarrassed, but not this Messina. This one was raised in court, and she hadn't been assaulted and abused. This Messina was confident and secure. And yet, as she kissed him back, wrapping her hands around his neck, rubbing her heaving body against his, the eagerness in her was akin to the old Mess.

"The wisp said I would finish the gauntlet in the arms of my mate," Sina whispered against Tynan's lips, her eyes watching him, wary, but happy. "Are you sure you don't want to throw me at someone else, or the floor before I get the wrong idea?"

Enjoying her sense of humor, Tynan felt his entire being react to her offer. "I'm sure. You must know, I'm cursed. Are you sure you can hack me?"

"Oh, I'm damn sure. I've been waiting my entire life for you to find me," she whispered unapologetically.

Kissing her furiously, Tynan ignored everyone around them. Her body pressed tight to his was all that mattered. When his curse started throbbing eagerly, Tynan moaned, understanding he needed to get her alone and do all those things he'd been thinking every time he saw her for the last three years. "It's going to hurt," Tynan warned her.

Awareness she shouldn't have was shining in her aquamarine orbs. It cemented Tynan's theory of who this was in his arms more than anything else he'd seen. Her knowledge of her former self may not exist, but Tynan knew, and Sina knew she was his. That's all that mattered.

Rising to her toes, Sina sucked his lobe between her lips feeling his agony for her grow before she whispered in his ear. "I'll take what you give me."

The End

ABOUT THE AUTHOR

Ebony lives in Sydney, Australia, with her husband, daughter, and six cats. She loves to read fantasy, thrillers, and paranormal romance, spending most of her free time with her nose in a book or writing.

Having always possessed an over-active imagination she spent her younger years regaling friends with fantastic stories, holding her audience captive with the passion and suspense of her characters plights.

Now in adulthood she has numerous published works and shows no signs of stopping her imagination from spreading across as many pages as it can find.

If you'd like to follow Ebony or say hi you can find her here:

Website: http://ebonyolson.com/